Praise for Ch...

"With its lavish use of hi... ...ate story, and vividly detailed settings, Australian author Sawyer's American debut is a grand and glorious delight for fans of the classic love stories of Kathleen Woodiwiss and Rosemary Rogers."   —*Booklist*

"[Sawyer] infuses historical events with color, passion, and thrilling escapades. With impeccable detail and larger-than-life characters, this debut will be on historical fiction readers' must-have list."   —*Romantic Times*

"All the scenes in this marvelous epic tale are intense. A fabulous historical read . . . and one that I highly recommend."   —*Romance Reviews Today*

"Cheryl Sawyer's rich narrative and brilliant character-ization light up a neglected era in America's history. *Siren* is a beautifully researched novel with a powerful love story."   —RITA Award Winner Isolde Martyn

"Cheryl Sawyer's sensual and romantic historical epics will captivate readers. Sawyer creates lush tapestries woven with vivid images, rich prose, and historic authenticity."
              —National Bestselling Author Madeline Hunter

"A gloriously textured and crafted tale of history as well as a timeless, seductive love story."
    —*New York Times* Bestselling Author Bertrice Small

The Chase

Cheryl Sawyer

A SIGNET ECLIPSE BOOK

SIGNET ECLIPSE
Published by New American Library, a division of
Penguin Group (USA) Inc., 375 Hudson Street,
New York, New York 10014, USA
Penguin Group (Canada), 10 Alcorn Avenue, Toronto,
Ontario M4V 3B2, Canada (a division of Pearson Penguin Canada Inc.)
Penguin Books Ltd., 80 Strand, London WC2R 0RL, England
Penguin Ireland, 25 St. Stephen's Green, Dublin 2,
Ireland (a division of Penguin Books Ltd.)
Penguin Group (Australia), 250 Camberwell Road, Camberwell, Victoria 3124,
Australia (a division of Pearson Australia Group Pty. Ltd.)
Penguin Books India Pvt. Ltd., 11 Community Centre, Panchsheel Park,
New Delhi - 110 017, India
Penguin Group (NZ), cnr Airborne and Rosedale Roads, Albany,
Auckland 1310, New Zealand (a division of Pearson New Zealand Ltd.)
Penguin Books (South Africa) (Pty.) Ltd., 24 Sturdee Avenue,
Rosebank, Johannesburg 2196, South Africa

Penguin Books Ltd., Registered Offices:
80 Strand, London WC2R 0RL, England

First published by Signet Eclipse, an imprint of New American Library,
a division of Penguin Group (USA) Inc.

First Printing, June 2005
10 9 8 7 6 5 4 3 2 1

For David and Daniel,
with love

CHAPTER ONE

On the first day of March 1815, a short man wearing the green uniform of a French colonel of grenadiers came ashore on the Mediterranean coast within striking distance of Cannes. He was setting foot in France for the first time in ten months, and no ally was there to greet him, but he knew his path. The Emperor of Elba had escaped, and with nightmare rapidity loyalties across Europe were about to shift and crumble, while hundreds of thousands of private lives were about to be changed forever. He would begin with France: "I shall conquer this kingdom."

In the early afternoon of the same day, two gentlewomen were riding under the trees of Hyde Park, where the late-winter sun threw dappled light onto the crush of vehicles beneath and painted the parasols of the ladies on the Mayfair Walk with flecks of brilliance.

The bright-haired rider, wearing a toque with a single ostrich plume, rode a showy strawberry roan, but it was the dark horsewoman who caught the eye. Mounted on a hunter that was the midnight color of her own glossy hair, she had a dramatic beauty that drew glances, yet as she and her friend threaded their way amongst the carriages her face wore a remote expression, as though to warn onlookers away. This might be considered strange in a lady who had just returned from abroad and would presumably be eager to seek out her London acquaintances, but Lady Sophia Hamilton was driven more by her feelings than by convention. She always leaned first toward those closest to her, and the pleasure she felt in the ride through Hyde Park had everything to do with the reunion with her friend and nothing to do with the picture they made together. In fact, her secret wish was to not be noticed at all.

If Mary Ellwood had had her way, they would have paused to talk to people they knew. But Sophia preferred to keep on the move. She was at home in England, but not in London; high society made her feel friendless.

Catching up with her at the edge of the thoroughfare, Mary leaned over and said, "Don't look round, he's far too intent—but someone has been following your progress most avidly. Under the elm, on a big gray."

Sophia drew a breath in painful suspense. "Do I know him?" she asked, without altering her gaze.

"Let me give you a portrait. One face, tanned; two eyes, with thick lashes; smooth black hair. In short, as near to a Gypsy as he can look without losing the air of a gentleman."

Sophia felt a mixture of relief and shame. It was absurd to think of pursuit in this predictable milieu. "I don't know him."

"As you please," Mary said. They passed at a trot over a patch of grass to another less crowded alley. "What would you say instead," she continued, "to full red lips, a bibulous eye—two on his worst evenings—and the rosiest cheeks in England?"

Sophia raised her eyebrows and gave an appreciative chuckle. "I should begin with, 'Your Highness.'"

Mary laughed. "Ellwood and I are invited for tomorrow, after supper. We may safely present you. The party is not intimate enough for us to be an intrusion, nor large enough to mask the éclat of your entrance. You could not have chosen better."

Sophia said in her low, melodious voice, "Mary, I have not chosen. Tomorrow I go down to Clifton."

Her friend gave the rapid shake of the head that was her way of dismissing irrelevance. "Clifton has waited nineteen months for you; another few days will hardly signify." She looked at Sophia keenly. "You told me you wanted to meet the Prince Regent, for what purpose I can only guess, and I have just offered you an opening. Take it. Attend with us tomorrow evening. My own importance to him is nothing beside Ellwood's, and his is pitiful beside that of the close confidants; I may never be able to give you such a chance again."

"It is good of you, but you rank my powers rather too high."

Mary ignored the sardonic note. "Not at all. Prinny just now is in the most desperate straits for agreeable company, quite surrounded by the arid and the frivolous. Your every look, your every word, will be like a refreshing stream in the desert. In one evening you will captivate him. By the week's end he will love you. If you have a scheme, personal or political, you may broach it then."

Sophia gave her a smile that to another woman would have spelled disdain. "There would be no point in my wooing the favors of the Prince Regent."

Mary shook her head again. "This will be a seduction of no common kind. And I would far rather see you raising his spirits than *burying* yourself at Clifton." Then there was a stricken pause. "My dear, forgive me. How appallingly I choose my words."

Sophia's gaze remained steady, but Mary saw a darker shadow appear in her eyes, like the effect of a cloud passing swiftly over deep waters. Sophia did not reply.

They reached the end of the alley and turned to ride back toward Mayfair Walk. The horses wheeled gracefully, flourishing their tails. Glancing sideways, Mary noticed Sophia's supple, statuesque figure and her smooth skin, flawless despite the months she had just spent at sea.

"I understand how you feel. The memories. Dear Andrew. Your duties to the estate. You are forcing yourself to go back. Surely it would do no harm to take a little longer, prepare yourself? Stay with us another day or two at least, and allow London to see something of you before you go into retreat."

"You are very kind." The tone was even, but there was a warmth in Sophia's answering look that made Mary smile at once in triumph.

"You will find a vast deal to amuse you. I'm sure you will notice how the peace has brightened our existence— now that Bonaparte is in exile and America has been given the right-about-turn."

"Can we ever depend on the *French* desiring peace?"

Mary was taken aback but said lightly, "You recommend their being cast into outer darkness with their leader?"

Sophia turned, and the afternoon light caught the contour of her cheek like a pale reflection on creamy marble. Her eyes were half-hidden by her thick black lashes, so that Mary could not read their expression; but she did not miss the vibration in the voice.

"What do I think of the French? I hate them from my soul. They killed my husband."

None of the people in the ship of the line that slipped past Greenwich on the same afternoon would have posed any argument to the peace, for they were about to touch England after years of duty abroad—and every man of them, apart from a small contingent of the Chasseurs Britanniques, was coming home. As they drew level with the stately buildings of the hospital and queen's house on the north bank of the Thames, the order was given to stand to, and a longboat could be seen gliding across the river toward them, the oarsmen propelling it with the precision that spoke to the seamen of undemanding duties ashore and the bounteous city beyond.

"Seems you'll be turned on shore before us," the first mate remarked to one of the Chasseurs, who was standing by the rail. There was no resentment in the remark; it was a rough farewell to a soldier who had earned a certain admiration from the crew during their Atlantic crossing.

The Chasseur, his eyes fixed on the longboat, nodded but did not turn or reply, and after a second the mate moved off. The Frenchman was a mysterious mixture of a man; sometimes frank, engaging and ready to talk the night watch through, then the next morning silent and cold as a big gun before action. Yet the men had been drawn to him. Tall, with thick, amber-colored hair bleached into fairness by the summer sun of last year's campaign, he stood out, especially amongst the other Chasseurs. Yet the impact he had in a group owed less to his wide-shouldered figure than to something more essential about his physical presence; in a good mood, he was alert and ready to interact in any company, almost aggressively at ease in whatever surroundings. He noticed and greeted everyone each time he chanced upon a group belowdecks, a French habit that had an enlivening effect. True, at this moment he looked indisposed for chat, but when one of the midshipmen came to his side he turned at once to the boy, with the half smile he gave when he was preoccupied, so that one corner of his well-shaped mouth slanted downward, forming an expression that was ironic though not unkind.

The lad remarked shyly, "You'll not be wearing that uniform for much longer now, sir."

The man's smile gained a hint of self-mockery. He was far from entitled to the "sir," since he was a private, and during his time in the Chasseurs Britanniques had been punished, detained and even sentenced to a tour of duty in a British penal colony for his refusal to accept any other rank. The boy, however, was addressing him as he would any master-at-arms, because this was the unofficial role that Jacques Decernay always ended up fulfilling, wherever he found himself.

"It's falling off me like a snakeskin." Decernay looked down his nose at the red coatee with sky blue cuffs and frayed white lace that was pulling away in places from its stitching. The pantaloons were patched and discolored, and the wings of the worn coatee, though they still served to emphasize the straight line of the Chasseur's shoulders, were edged in a dirty gray instead of white. The only impeccable items were the pewter buttons on his breast—all complete, and as shiny as new shillings, though no one had ever noticed the soldier polishing them. Seeing the boy's eye follow his own rueful inspection, he gave a quick laugh and brought up one large hand to wrench the top button off the open neck of the jacket, then held it out.

"A souvenir, of a time never to be repeated, *Dieu merci.*"

The boy took it and blushed crimson. In his eyes was the wish to give something in exchange, but he was almost as destitute of personal possessions as the Chasseur himself. The other gripped the boy's shoulder with his long fingers, turning him shoreward and then letting go. "In return, you may describe Greenwich to me. What is the edifice with the domes?"

"The hospital. You haven't been here before?" The man beside him shrugged. "Nor London?"

"No."

The boy quickly named the other buildings. Meanwhile the longboat had almost reached the ship; just as the ladder was let down, the midshipman plucked up courage to say, "Why come all the way here? Why not Lymington, with the rest?"

"*Mon brave,* London is just a little nearer to France."

The boy got no more out of him, for the order came for the Chasseurs to present arms before the captain of marines.

Neither the ship's officers on the quarterdeck nor the sailors before the mast failed to register the uniqueness of the sight as the Chasseurs Britanniques formed a line in front of the corps of marines drawn up in the waist of the ship. For they were the last of their kind: four soldiers of a regiment that had been mainly recruited in Portugal, had served with Wellington's army in Spain, been shipped to other posts after victory in the Peninsula, then employed—with mixed results—as marines against the Americans, and had finally disgraced itself at Hampton, Virginia, the year before. The Chasseurs had been disbanded, some officers and men being paid off at Halifax in Nova Scotia, the rest at the Hampshire port of Lymington; now only these four men remained, still clad in their own regimentals, though officially they belonged to the corps of marines who had accompanied them to England.

Discharge awaited them the day after they stepped ashore, yet there was pride in the precision with which they presented arms for the last time. Their uniforms were shabby, but their shining weapons spoke of dedicated attention during the weeks of drill and practice at sea. The wood of the rifles gleamed in the weak sunshine, and so did the black, brass-tipped scabbards of the bayonet swords, which reached to below the knee. Contrary to their shipboard custom, the Chasseurs wore their shakos at the regulation angle, and a gentle shore breeze ruffled the green plume fixed at the center of each above the gilt plate in the shape of a bugle horn.

The inspection over, the soldiers shouldered their arms and gave a farewell salute, which was acknowledged by the captain of marines and, more distantly, by the ship's commander. Then they were detailed to depart. Jacques Decernay was the last to lower himself over the side into the waiting boat, and before his head dipped below the gunwale of the man-of-war he threw a glance around the vessel. Suddenly a grin spread across his tanned face, and there was a warmth and a rakish sort of mischief in it that drew every one of the watchers. There was a spontaneous outburst of voices; sailors shouted their farewells, and the marines nearest the Chasseur wished him luck. Then, without a word, he backed down out of sight.

All the way across to the quay, Jacques had a haunting wish that he had followed the instinct to load his rifle. Which was absurd, for England was not a country in which instinct would be of the slightest use to him. He was also aware of his silent companions. He could feel in his sinews how everything was about to change, how they were about to lose one another, not because of British orders this time, but because they were to be given their freedom—which they had no idea what to do with, and which would force them apart. Already, as the dripping oars moved beside them, sleek and rhythmical, each man was planning a subtle betrayal.

There was a welcoming party on the quay, more marines. He would have preferred fellow soldiers, light infantry. Absurd again—he and the lads had no fellow soldiers.

They set foot on a flight of shallow stone stairs, with the lobsterbacks in a double rank not far from the top— smart looking, well fed, holding rifles with fixed bayonets. Striding upward two steps at a time, Jacques slipped the strap of his own rifle over his shoulder. His gear was in his knapsack, so both hands were free. For nothing, he told himself, but it did not stop a shiver of wariness that made the hairs on the back of his neck stir under his collar as he paused with the others at the top of the stairs.

The quay was wide, the buildings that lined it imposing, with long stone avenues between. There were other figures in the middle distance, all in naval uniform, including a commander standing under a portico to the far left, whom he recognized, with a darting inward shock.

As Jacques approached, he gave the marines a frank stare, but their wooden expressions did not change. He had forgotten; on such occasions English curiosity was a covert affair, almost shameful. Perhaps they thought they knew enough about him in advance. He felt disoriented.

The marines' officer said something, and Jacques saluted with the others while quickly scanning the environs. The nearest person was a groom leading a chestnut horse slowly away down the quay. A beauty and, by her fine shape, a filly. Slim, dainty legs that spoke of swiftness and dexterity, though she was out of condition, her head hanging low as she walked. Her floating tail shimmered gold in the afternoon light.

He turned back to the officer, who had just read out three names from the list in his hand. Jacques' companions stood a few yards away at the head of the column, flanked by a couple of lieutenants. The marines were at attention, rifles resting on their shoulders, topped by a frieze of bayonets. As his name was called, Jacques hitched his right shoulder so his own rifle hung straight at his back. Then stiffened.

"Jacques Decernay. I arrest you in the name of Our Sovereign Majesty King George the Third. You will be conveyed to barracks and held there in custody until court-martial."

"*Quoi?*" His own roar engulfed the officer's voice, which was high, though firm enough. He felt hot blood rise to his forehead and had to struggle to summon his English. "On what charge?"

"Desertion."

In two strides he had him by the throat. "Liar. You say my name, I am here. Who is this man who deserts? Not me!"

The captain went pink, the list fluttered from his hand, the line of bayonets behind him rippled. "I have my orders. I advise you to come quietly."

Jacques, snarling, just managed to prevent himself from further violence, and stepped back suddenly so that the captain staggered. The weapons moved with precision, forming a semicircle of bright spokes with Jacques' chest at the fulcrum.

The captain swore. "Hold your fire! Dickson, Malahide, arrest him."

Jacques swung his rifle forward, gripped the barrel. There was no time to debate this with himself—instinct would have to serve after all. He beat down on an angle to smash three weapons away, then hooked the butt up and across to connect with the jaw of the man on the outside. He took two quick steps back, his eye on the rest of them, his right hand on the hilt of his sword bayonet and his empty rifle now balanced in his left hand.

He risked a swift glance behind. The filly flicked her

tail, still tantalizingly close. His sword bayonet flew from the scabbard.

They were all shouting now, including the lads, though he could not see them or the captain for scarlet coats.

A thrust from the nearest bayonet, which he parried with his blade, slipping out of range. If he ran they would shoot him down; he must get nearer to his one chance of a way out, cover himself as he went. He diverted two of their points at once, the concussions jarring his wrist, then beat down a third with a flash and a whine of steel. And a jab to the man's throat with the rifle butt, which they seemed to have forgotten.

He slid back three yards, four, in a hail of light from the blades, his hobnailed boots rasping sparks from the paving, the sound of his own breath whistling in his ears. He would have sworn at them, but rage choked him like a band across his throat.

A bayonet sliced through the strap at one shoulder and the knapsack swung round to encumber his sword arm; fending off a thrust with the rifle barrel he whipped the knapsack free and then flung it in the face of an attacker who was trying to circle to his rear. He could feel them on the other side, which necessitated a windmill spin with both weapons that held them off once, twice, then allowed him a lightning dart through the smallest of gaps.

His shoulder was on fire from the stab, but his sword arm was intact. He parried once more, dropping to one knee and using both weapons like a crucifix, then twisting to disarm. Not quite fast enough—two marines outflanked him, shouting, and he heard the officer's voice again, higher still with panic.

"One more move and we fire! Men, take aim!"

Dead end. In the sudden, thick silence he lowered his hands. He looked at the ground, cursing, seeing meanwhile out of the corners of his eyes the arc of avid faces, the silver spikes of the rifles.

He laid his weapons on the cold stone. A parting of old friends.

He raised his head, seeking the marine captain's youthful face. But there was an observer, beyond the scarlet coats, a tall man in naval uniform. Commodore Metcalfe, the father of the woman Jacques had come to England to seek.

The commodore had a hooked nose and eyes of a piercing, Arctic blue, and he surveyed the scene before him with austere surprise. The last time they had seen each other had been in New South Wales, on the other side of the world, and he could never have expected to find the Frenchman in England, much less at bay before marines.

"Decernay! I'm sorry to see this."

Jacques sat back on his haunches, tore the shako from his head, and smashed it to the ground beside him.

The commodore turned to the captain of marines. "What is going on?"

"This man is under arrest, sir. For desertion. He will also face charges for resisting arrest."

Jacques closed his eyes. Resistance. What other choice was there; what else had he done for so long now, but resist? He opened his eyes again and encountered the alert gaze of the commodore. On a shuddering wave of hostility he said, "What do you know of this?"

"Nothing. But rest assured, I intend to find out."

CHAPTER TWO

Cannes, the Bay of Angels, 1 March

The sand dunes stifle noises. You'd never guess there were a thousand men here unless you paced it like Bonaparte did an hour ago in the dusk, up and down the hummocks, round the campfires. When he went by, the voices softened like waves at ebb tide.

My name is Bertrand. I swore an oath and now I must fulfill it, for Bonaparte has flown from Elba. He's no eagle yet mind you, more of a bantam cock. The little emperor freed from his henyard island. Trying tiny wings.

He's got no cavalry. No artillery. And with the horses we have . . .

Give him the right company, though, and we might see a difference. Until then, until he's really on the move again, do I have to do anything?

Even on that night years ago when we all swore to kill him, I couldn't really believe it would ever come down to me. I remember the dark attic in Paris and the ten men gathered, and I knew not a soul except for Ménin, my good friend who brought me there.

But none of us had any doubts about the justice of it. French, English, Prussian—we were united by a hatred that just about gave off smoke. When we decided to do the thing alone, in turns, and we drew straws to establish the order, the big man next to me cursed and smashed his fist onto the table when he drew the longest straw and knew he would be the last man in line.

The gentleman opposite threw him a level look and said, "Are you that keen to turn murderer? Bonaparte's a human creature, after all."

The other one said nothing, but Ménin alongside of me burst out, "He's not human. Mark me, when the bullet goes in he'll fall like a statue, without a drop of blood."

Seven of those men are gone now, swallowed into the shadows as though they'd never been. And I didn't even know their names. Except Ménin, who was the seventh. The plan was simple: each man, when it came to his turn, had to set the day of the assassination. And he'd send a strip of paper with nothing on it but the date and the sign, to the next man. So the next man would know, if the date went by, and Bonaparte lived, that the one before him had been caught in the act and killed.

It was Ménin who handed the task on to me. I was in Austria then, and he in France. When the date went by, and the tyrant still lived, I knew what I had to do. I went to Paris to tend Bonaparte's horses—with the finest recommendation a horse master ever had, though I say it myself—and all at once the emperor abdicated and I found myself on a ship to Elba.

We'd drawn the line at assassinating Bonaparte in exile. So I served him for ten months with death in my soul. But now he's in France, and it's time.

All I know is the ninth man's name and direction. All I have to do is decide when to act and send the note. God help me, though, I can't decide. Is there ever a right time to wring the neck of a bantam cock? How can you know when he's about to work another miracle and turn hawk?

The next morning, Sophia was at the stables at Greenwich with Harry, to see how Scheherazade was getting on. The filly received them with a haughty air that thinly disguised her resentment at being housed in another strange place. Harry by contrast was ecstatic; wherever he found Scheherazade was home.

The navy man detailed to look after the filly had fallen in love with her and understood Harry's enslavement. He and the four-year-old exchanged serious conversation on feed and exercise, while Sophia stood in front of the filly's head, cradling the hard cheekbones in both hands, observing how the huge brown eyes melted. Sophia had brought her all the way from New South Wales—once she had seen her race, she had not been able to leave her behind, despite the long voyage back.

"Mama, Sherazade's hooves are all soft."

"That's all right, darling. She doesn't have to walk home yet."

Harry came to stand close beside her, his bright head as glossy as the straw. "Can I go with her?"

"No. We'll get there first. She's going to wait for Mitchell to come up from Clifton."

He looked up, and Scheherazade swung her head out of Sophia's grasp and downward, to bring the two pairs of brown eyes level.

"She doesn't know Mitchell. I don't know Mitchell."

She heard the groom's voice behind them. "I'll make sure they get acquainted, young man." She was grateful, knowing the gruff reassurance was meant for her as well. He seemed a kind man and had the right touch with horses. She was reminded of another, whose power over horses and whose secret power over her lived in her memory so vividly that she felt guilty at the tremor it caused her.

Harry reached up and softly patted the white star on the filly's forehead. Scheherazade blinked at him, then gave him a quick nudge in the chest that sent him backward into the straw. Sophia exclaimed as he landed with a thump on his bottom, but after a second of pure shock he gave a gurgling laugh. "Sherazade bumped me!" He scrambled to his feet. "You naughty little horse." He approached her again, eyes shining, and positioned himself, feet apart and stomach puffed out, in exactly the spot he had occupied before.

The filly swung her head away playfully and then

snapped it back. Sophia was about to speak, but heard footsteps and went to the open doorway.

When her father appeared, Harry abandoned his pose at once and ran over to him, throwing his arms around his knees. "Grampa, Sherazade bumped me."

"Did she, by Jove?" Her father stroked Harry's head, but his eyes were on hers. There was anxiety in them, which made the blue gaze look watery.

"What is it? What have they said?"

He reached out and put a warm hand on the tip of her shoulder. "Don't be alarmed. You are speaking to a rear admiral."

"Oh, Papa." She embraced him, so that Harry had to wriggle free. The little boy looked up at them both for a second, then trotted back to stand before Scheherazade.

Sophia said, "I knew it. That's wonderful. And? Will they station you near home?"

"Watch!" cried Harry.

Her father shook his head slightly, glancing toward Harry. "Let me talk to you outside." He said to the groom, "You'll be good enough to keep an eye on him for a minute or two."

"Pleasure, Commodore Metcalfe."

"Grampa," Harry said loudly, "Sherazade is going to *bump* me. Like this." He threw himself backward, landing in a pile of hay that the groom had thoughtfully forked into place after the first episode. Harry did not laugh until he saw his grandfather smile. Then he picked himself up, pink cheeked and studded with straws.

"Stay and look after Scheherazade, darling. We'll be back in a moment," Sophia said firmly, turning away.

There was a wooden bench in the yard, which her father brushed at with a glove before she sat down. Then he placed himself beside her with one arm along the back, facing her with a stern expression intended to give her courage. Which of course made her instantly nervous. She so wanted to go down to Clifton, to her old peaceful life, but she needed her father there too, otherwise something else that had occurred in Sydney Town would continue to prey on her. "Where are they going to put you? Somewhere miles away, so we'll hardly see you?"

"My dear, they have given me one last active duty." Before she could protest he said, "In charge of a convoy to Lisbon. It is not a posting—it's a return trip, escorting a member of the Portuguese royal family. The board was very decent about it, not to mention flattering. Only a commander for the job and so forth."

"Lisbon! And I was fearing *London*. Couldn't you have refused?"

"I protested as strongly as I deemed proper. It would ill become me to serve for forty years and then balk at doing my duty the moment I was promoted rear admiral."

"It ill becomes *them*—" She broke off. She knew just how far his arguments would have gone, her father being steadfast in everything but his own defense. During her lifetime, her mother had been able to resist this tendency by judicious nagging. But Sophia had never learned to nag him—they were too close.

"It's not fair."

"Not entirely, no." His eyes were uncertain again. "Of course, if you have serious reservations I shall insist on staying."

She took a breath, went to his rescue. "Don't worry about us. We'll be all right. Once I'm at Clifton."

"I must confess, it floored me at first. But I've been thinking it over. I was lucky enough to have my daughter and grandson with me every day for a year and a half, around the other side of the world and back. There are not many navy commanders who can boast that. This mission will take a fraction of that time; you'll scarcely notice I'm gone. And afterwards, I'll be back in the bosom of my family for good. I have their word on that."

As his voice grew more cheerful, she withdrew her gaze and looked at her hands clasped in her lap. For nearly two years her father had been sustaining her, comforting her in her grief. Yet it was not grief that disturbed her now; it was doubt about herself, about her own deepest feelings. Something had happened to her in New South Wales that made her avid to be home—as though only family life could protect her from the new, challenging experience that haunted her. But it would worry her father if she showed distress. Anger was safer.

"They have no right. They as good as promised to retire you before, and instead they sent you to New South Wales. And now, when you've been back in the country *four days* . . . They must have scores of commanders breaking their necks for something to do now that the war's over."

"Possibly that's why they've chosen me," he said dryly. "My ambition's more than satisfied—I'm not likely to start a skirmish somewhere in order to attract attention to myself." Then his voice changed and he put his fingers tenderly over hers. "But say the word, and the only duty I undertake to discharge is the one to you."

"How long before you go?"

"Ten days."

She gave him a fond smile. "The sooner you leave, the sooner you'll be home."

It was not by chance that the Prince Regent chose to wear scarlet that evening; other features of his life might fall victim to hazard occasionally, but his dress never. There were two motives behind the choice of his favorite uniform, each to do with color.

The meal would be in the Gothic dining room, where the somber paneling would set off his gold epaulets and braid, while answering the rich scarlet of his coat with the traces of dark crimson and russet that lay deep in the grain of the splendid timbers. He would at once stand out against the setting—no one could fail to note his breadth of shoulder—and marvelously complement it, seated before his guests as the modern exemplar of a warrior tradition that stretched back to the giants who sacked Rome, the steel-clad horsemen who smashed in the gates of Jerusalem, the generals and statesmen who had crushed Bonaparte and who were now meting out

Europe's fate in Vienna. And it would be quite natural to wear a saber.

To follow the meal, he had chosen the Rose Satin drawing room, where the clash between his brilliant uniform and the blushing walls and draperies would at first shock the eye. But it would lend just the excitement that he relished himself in the bright, intricate glazes of Chinese porcelain or the contrasting hues of Imperial fabrics.

He was just considering the hang of the saber when he was reminded that Colonel Coole had been waiting above an hour.

He frowned. "Show him to the study."

When it came to his hair he was tempted toward a military style, but it would have taken a deal of time and some sacrifice of length. He contented himself with a lingering look at his profile in the hand glass; the chin, he rather thought, spoke of decision.

Frowning again, with the awkward idea that the colonel too might be in uniform, he made for the study. Then came the recollection that Coole was no longer in the army—in fact his ostensible return to civilian life was part of the scheme.

The scheme was a discreet but thorough overview of Britain's secret agents in the aftermath of war. It was not the kind of procedure that would normally have come anywhere near the prince, but there were issues of security that might touch the royal person. Apparently there was some doubt surrounding the disappearance of certain officers in the field, a speculation as to whether the enemy might have known more than they should. If that was the case, the source of the information had yet to be uncovered. If it was within the present ranks of the service, it must be rooted out, and in peacetime there were opportunities to do so. No section of high-ranking officers could be held immune from investigation.

When it was first suggested to the prince that there should be an undercover check on his own military staff in London and Brighton, he was inclined to take it as a personal affront. But the more they told him about the reasons for it, the more alarmed and fascinated he became. He had stipulated that he should get a look at the man charged with the task, though he was rather vague about what was to be done if he did not fancy him; he had after all been recommended by Sir Henry Hardinge, and Sir Henry was the Duke of Wellington's head of espionage.

Before entering the room the prince realized that, though he had insisted on seeing Coole, he had no notion what they were to talk about. Mentioning the scheme itself was unnecessary and perhaps unwise. All he really wanted was to see if the man looked likely.

He was, as it turned out, a pattern of elegance. His deep bow and his opening words were as impeccable as the tailoring of his evening clothes. They spoke of the colonel's recent return from India while the prince studied him. No taller than himself but with an enviable length of leg and a taut body that showed not an ounce of unwanted flesh. Black Irish good looks. Smooth hair brushed back off the brow emphasized the clarity of wide, light green eyes, bordered by lashes as thick as a woman's. Yet his was a wholly masculine beauty, softened only by a certain animal grace that recalled the colonel's reputation as a swordsman.

The prince did not sit; it would have destroyed the impression he gave of a general handing out his depositions.

"We are somewhat hard on you, Colonel. You have already made your contribution to the safety of the realm, and here we are demanding additional service that may never be acknowledged."

"It is nonetheless willingly rendered, Your Highness." This was said without ostentation in a cultured voice.

"There is no need to dwell on the importance of what you are undertaking." A subtle smile. "Or put it into words at all."

The handsome mouth curved for the first time. "It is a delicate matter, to be sure. But manageable, please God."

There was the faintest, rather appealing burr on the T's and D's.

The prince said sincerely, "I wanted the opportunity to convey my appreciation to you at this juncture, because it's quite impossible to risk any contact in the future." No sense in giving him ideas.

The colonel registered the point but took it well, with just a slight compression of the lips and no reply. The prince felt obliged to continue.

"Have you settled yet? Taken a house in London?"

"I have. But I shall be in the country for a short while. I've an estate in Sussex that I've not seen since I was a boy. It came to me not long ago, through the death of a relative."

"Sussex in the spring—charming." He said crisply, (hoping for the tone of a general farewelling one of his trusted commanders), "We are relying on you, Colonel. And we have every confidence."

"I shall endeavor to vindicate it, Your Highness."

The prince drew himself up, rather expecting the man to salute, but he did not move. Should he salute himself? The colonel at least would know.

There might have been a flash of amusement in the green eyes, but the colonel hid it by making a bow of exactly the proper depth.

The prince said, "I wish you an agreeable visit to Sussex. If I had my wish I would stay in Brighton oftener than I do, but at present, with affairs as they stand in London just now"—he gestured resignedly—"I cannot be spared."

He watched Coole as he was ushered out, marking how his walk, for all its grace, belonged unmistakably to the fit, trained military officer. He considered rehearsing just such a gait for his entrance into the drawing room later on, but fortunately caught sight of himself in the glass above the desk.

He chuckled and grinned back at his own rosy reflection. There was such a thing as overdoing it.

Jacques paced the cell, his stockinged feet making no sound on the stone flags. He could hear a great deal of what went on nearby in the barracks and none of it was encouraging. The comfortable murmur of a couple of officers taking a last pipe in the dark courtyard, the banging of doors, purposeful footsteps up and down stairs as the men carried out the final duties of the evening and prepared for tattoo, lights out. He was alone, like a fox in a trap. No one here knew him, let alone gave him a thought.

At least he knew why he had been arrested; the marine officer had informed him of that, with relish, while his shoulder wound was being dressed. They were punctilious about keeping him alive and fit for court-martial and were allowing him time to put together his defense—three days, which meant they would try him on Saturday.

He stopped in the middle of the cell, and looked up through the little barred window in search of a star in the clear sky. So far he had not asked to contact anyone. It was impossible to gauge what to do until they said a bit more to him, gave him some sort of clue. He could fire off a letter—but whom could he trust to deliver it? It might only foul things up further if it were intercepted.

The pain in his shoulder licked along the collarbone, flickered at the base of his throat. He remembered hearing about the summary execution of twenty Chasseurs after Badajoz, and about the veterans who turned away from the sight to vomit and weep. Someone intended to make his own execution less public but no less shameful. Someone was making a scapegoat of him. But who?

Mary Ellwood was delighted with the evening at Carlton House, particularly for Sophia, whose attendance Ellwood had arranged with gratifying ease.

Their entrance was every bit as dramatic as a scene at Drury Lane—better, for the single member of the audience at which it was directed was just then standing opposite the door, conversing with no one.

Mary did not hear their party announced; she was too busy observing Prinny. His round face—a trifle flushed in the warm room—went quite still as he caught sight of

Sophia. Then the plump, shiny lips pursed, and he drew himself up to stand more squarely in his outrageous uniform.

He gave Ellwood a receptive look; they advanced and the presentation was made. Sophia sank into a graceful curtsy. He quizzed her about never having received her at Saint James's—he would unfailingly have remembered such a "vision"; she mentioned her secluded life in the country, her early marriage, the rarity of visits to London. He bent toward her at first, as though her voice were too low, but in response to his kind questions it soon gained the thrilling quality that Mary so loved herself, which made it beautifully audible to her host and nearby listeners.

General conversation was renewed, and for a while Mary was distracted by the other guests. Sheridan was amongst them—sadly drunk, and by the smell of his breath he had *started* the evening with brandy, a habit that his association with the prince was unlikely to cure him of. He was amusing, however. There was a very elegant and urbane French couple there, émigrés who had close relations with Louis XVIII; they exchanged wondering glances with each other at Sherry's demeanor.

Later, during the dispensing of coffee, she was able to observe the prince. He and Sophia were together again, on a sofa near the center of the room, a signal honor for a new guest. They were talking of Sophia's time in New South Wales, but Mary could tell he was not really listening; he was simply looking at her. A rewarding pastime, for man or woman, though Mary was often rather irritated by her husband's favorite comment that her friend was "an English rose." It was true, however. Sophia's skin, miraculously unblemished by the antipodean sun or her passage home through the tropics, was so fine that it was as translucent as the pearls she wore around her neck. The prince's scrutiny raised the faintest blush in her face, which set off the natural red of her full lips, the great dark eyes and the long sweep of her eyebrows.

Sophia meanwhile was relieved to be speaking to just

one person, even if he was the most august being in the land. She had been brought up to act irreproachably in company, and she did so—it was just that she disliked being in a crowd. She so often found conversations superficial or insincere (even when Mary insisted they were sophisticated and clever!) and just as often found that she had nothing to add to them. She knew she was considered too reserved, but somehow there was nothing she could do about that. Only when she spoke to just one other person did she manage to express what she really felt or thought. It would never turn her into a grand society hostess, but it did cause her to value true friendship, perhaps more than most women. And it had made her marriage very precious to her, for her husband was the closest friend she had ever had.

Tonight she was here to talk to the prince about the influence he might bring to bear on peace in Europe. She was not sure that he had ever heard a woman's view on the subject, but if he was to do so, now was the time, and for some reason she thought he just might listen to her. In her mind it had become a duty, linked to the memory of Andrew. She must find an opening and will herself to speak.

The prince was saying, "You are very brave about living on the other side of the globe, but you must surely have missed the comforts of home?"

She gathered her courage. "To be honest, Your Highness, home held few joys for me at the time. I think I mentioned, I had just lost my husband." He looked blank at this, and she continued with quiet emphasis. "Sir Andrew Hamilton. Of the Tenth Hussars. Your Highness's own."

The prince's expression became animated at once. "Of course. Matter of fact I heard his name only recently— If I could just recall—" Then he broke off. With a sudden frown he went on. "Missing in action in France, of course. Bad business. Terrible for you, yes, yes." Sophia flinched, and he sent her a look of such tenderness that she almost expected him to stretch out and take her hand. "If it is any consolation, my poor Lady Hamilton, he is not forgotten by those who hold the safety of England nearest their hearts."

She nodded but without smiling; she had to force herself to remain calm. Her head was buzzing. *France?* "He did not fall in France. It was in Spain. At the Battle of San Sebastian. He had just been given a command in the Ninth Regiment."

"But surely—" Then consternation crossed the prince's face and he said hurriedly, "I see. Of course. Pray forgive me."

He struggled for another topic, but she was too swift. "Your Highness, you are aware that I was never able— His body was never found. I do not know how he died. If you can recommend anyone who could give me information about my husband, I should be most grateful."

He looked at her in alarm. "My dear Lady Hamilton, if I gave the impression of knowing anything more than yourself, then pray forgive me. I spoke without thinking. I spoke as I *felt,* about a struggle that has demanded the ultimate sacrifice of so many brave gentlemen." He continued. "You have a son, I think you said?"

"Harry. He is four years old." *France?*

The Prince shook his head solemnly. "Old enough to feel pride in such a father."

"Old enough for me to pray that *he* will never have to face such a choice."

The prince looked at her in surprise. "You would not wish him to serve his country?"

"On the contrary. But I pray that he never has to do it with a sword in his hand."

This man, and Andrew's superiors, wherever they were, obviously knew much, much more than she had ever been told about her husband's death. She was stunned and appalled. The army had demanded the ultimate sacrifice of her husband, and now they coolly imagined that she would one day deliver her son to war . . . and by the most dreadful irony she had come here tonight to talk of peace!

The prince leaned back against the corner of the sofa

and smiled complacently down at the military sash that stretched across his chest and ample belly. "Amen to that, dear lady. We must trust our peace to the Duke of Wellington. Victory at Vienna is what we look forward to, what?"

Sophia waited until he raised his eyes. "What kind of victory do you really think we shall see?"

The prince, oblivious to her meaning, smiled again and addressed Mary's husband, who was standing a few paces off. "Ellwood, we are being charmingly quizzed about the state of affairs in Vienna. We can only go to the oracle—how do your Foreign Office fellows rate the Duke of Wellington's chances of negotiating the peace to our best advantage?"

Ellwood replied, "The desired outcome, Your Highness, must be lasting peace in Europe. It is perhaps too early to say how the other powers will manage the claims of Prussia. Prince Metternich is a force to be reckoned with."

"And Talleyrand, now," the prince laughed. "Who could have imagined Wellington would so soon be at combat with another upstart Frenchman?" Sophia noticed that the French count and countess exchanged a glance with each other on overhearing this. But the prince was concentrating on her instead. "I would give a great deal to soothe your anxieties, dear Lady Hamilton. When next we meet, let us hope the news from Congress is just precisely as you could wish."

She had been deflected, as so often happened when others joined in a debate. And she was in no state to carry on the argument. There would perhaps be another opportunity, when she felt less devastated. "Indeed. I look forward to our speaking of this again, Your Highness."

Mary, who was still observing them, thought he was flattered—more so than Sophia seemed to notice. When they had taken their leave and were driving home, Mary congratulated her on the start of her campaign. "You have very deftly opened up the field for maneuver, but without alarming him."

Augustus Ellwood gave them an inquiring look, and Mary waited to see how much Sophia would reveal. She gave no reply, however, and did not renew the topic as they drove home. Mary accepted her silence, trying hard meanwhile not to let it make her uneasy.

CHAPTER THREE

Sophia had to wait two days before she could see her father again. He was the only one she could ask about Andrew. She had a private pact with herself never to seek advice from Ellwood, for that might bring them closer together and so disconcert Mary, who adored her husband. Sophia had seen friendships destroyed over less, even between women who had neither of them cared overmuch for the man in question.

She wanted to see her father alone, and at last she was lucky; on the afternoon when he called, Mary was with her children at Astley's Equestrian Theatre and Harry had gone with them.

Her father sat near a window in the gold drawing room, where the sunlight slanted in from Bedford Square and lit up his thick mane of white hair. He was in uniform, having just been at the Admiralty.

She approached and took a chair on the other side of a low, gilded table. "I was presented to the prince the other evening."

"So I heard. Congratulations."

"He spoke to me of Andrew. He told me that he died in France." Being prepared, she was able to watch her father's eyes much more attentively than she had watched the prince's. "Have you ever heard that said?"

He shrank back in his seat.

"You may tell me, Papa. I would rather know. *Now,* I would rather know. Has anyone ever mentioned such a thing to you?"

The answer was hesitant. "Not in so many words, no."

"But it is possible?" She took a breath. "That he was never at San Sebastian, that he was somewhere in France instead? Did they lie to me, cover up how he died?" When he did not answer, she rose to her feet. "I have a right to be told. Great God, if he was not killed in the battle, then how do I know he is not still living?"

"No!" The exclamation was rough and his voice took a moment to soften. "No one has tried to deceive you on that score. We must accept that he is gone. He may have died at San Sebastian, and if he did not, I honestly cannot tell you where. I have never inquired. I am certain the army acted in the proper manner."

She stopped by his side and looked out at the square. It was bright and busy; there was a small knot of people outside the lord chancellor's house across the other side. She kept her voice level.

"At the time of the Battle of San Sebastian no British troops had broken through into France. If a British captain died beyond the Pyrenees, he could only have been a spy, a prisoner or . . . a traitor. Andrew. Which was he?"

He reached out and caught her hand. "Come. You have no need to ask."

"He never said." It came out as a whisper.

"He could not."

"He *could* have, to *me*."

"No, it would have added to your burden. He told me, he would never forget your face when he first appeared before you in uniform. Sit down, my dear."

She did so, bereft of words, and he continued.

"You must know, he did not confide in me either. But there are certain things I can deduce. Think of it from the army's side. There were qualities in Andrew that fitted him for espionage. He was a natural linguist. He had a quick, active intelligence, which almost everyone he met tended to underestimate at first."

"But—"

"But no, he did not have the cast of mind or the moral view that would have made him volunteer as a spy. Did he, however, have the courage and sense of duty that would have made him say yes if a secret mission were proposed to him? I think we have to agree, he had."

"And that is enough for you? Enough to condone the fact that the army exploited him, and abandoned him, and then lied to his wife and child? Well, it is not enough for me. I shall find out what happened to him, what they did to him, and throw it in their teeth."

He said nothing. For a moment, this made her even angrier. But it was not anger that twisted her hands together in her lap or drew a film over her sight that distorted everything in the room, including her father's startled face. In the first months of bereavement she had played over and over in her mind the scene of Andrew's death. She believed she had conjured up all conceivable horrors, but now the unimaginable resurged, with new power. British officers in civilian clothes captured behind enemy lines were shot instantly as spies—if they were lucky. If they fell into the wrong hands, however, they would be tortured for information. For days, weeks, months. Until they were broken.

Her husband had been used as a pawn by his own country. Thank God *she* had never used or betrayed him in his lifetime. And she would not betray him now that he was gone.

Into her breathless silence her father said, "I would do anything to make this easier for you. If I had the slightest influence in that regard I would employ it, but I can tell you, tackling the army over this issue would get me nowhere. Let alone yourself."

She took a shuddering breath and looked down at her hands. "Of course. I realize that." It had come to her, all at once, that she was about to go down to Clifton. There, if anywhere, among Andrew's papers and effects—the very things she dreaded to see again—the clues were certain to lie.

As sometimes happened, he read her mind, though

with a subtle difference of interpretation. "I did hope that the time had come for you and Harry to return home and find some peace at last."

"Yes, Papa. Do not concern yourself about us."

He shifted in the chair. "As a matter of fact, I came here to tell you an item of news. About an old acquaintance in Sydney Cove. Scarcely *good* news, though, I'm afraid." He gave her a shrewd look. "Best left unsaid, perhaps."

She accepted the transparent change of subject. "No, do tell. Has Governor Macquarie been ousted by another rum rebellion? Have his infantry officers bankrupted themselves at their own racetrack?"

He shook his head. "You will recall a French soldier by the name of Jacques Decernay."

The name took her by the throat, and she stared at him without moving. At last, when he did not continue, she forced out one word. "Dead?"

He shrugged. "As good as." He leaned forward, elbows on his knees. "You recall the first time you met him? In the forest, not far from the South Head Road?"

"I could scarcely forget!"

"Yes, well. You told me Decernay was moving *up* the hill when he came upon you, and shortly afterwards the lieutenant ordered him back to the road works, correct?"

She was overcome by a violent impression: two deep gray eyes, a shock of fair hair, the sun behind his head glinting on eucalypt leaves overarched by an intense blue sky. "Yes."

"But you remember, late the same day, it was discovered that three of the Chasseurs on road detail had disappeared into the forest. Never to be seen again. Not the first or the last of the convicts or their like to try their chances in the wilderness—and pay the price." He shook his head again. "Well, not so, apparently. It seems they escaped in quite the other direction—took a boat out from the very cove where you were headed that day and intercepted a Norwegian vessel sailing out of Port Jackson. They were taken onboard without the slightest hitch, which shows it was all planned, down to the last detail." He lifted his head and gave her a compassionate look. "When Decernay put himself in your way at the top of the hill, his comrades were in the very act of sneaking out from the beach below. His action prevented you from seeing them and giving their game away."

"I don't understand. How can you know this?"

"I got the full story today. A month or so ago, it appears two of them showed up at Bristol. Why on earth they didn't scuttle back to France like the other man, I cannot imagine. They thought they had gotten away scot-free, I suppose. But they reckoned without the army. They were identified, arrested, court-martialed for desertion, and shot. But not before they talked a great deal about Private Jacques Decernay. They said he planned the whole affair, paid the Norwegian captain in advance for their passage, though they couldn't explain where he had obtained the funds—and he had every intention of going with them. But he was held up, so they took off without him."

She thought back instantly to the last time she had glimpsed Decernay. "But he never deserted. He was with the seventy-third Foot. He left with them last year, in April, on the *Wyndham*."

"True. Subsequently he served with the Chasseurs on the east coast of America. But four days ago he sailed into Greenwich. The army was waiting for him, of course; they had been waiting for weeks. The moment he set foot onshore he was charged—with desertion, and with resisting arrest. The court-martial is tomorrow. As things stand, he must receive sentence of execution."

She realized he had risen and was standing by her chair. He put his warm fingers on her shoulder. "Stay where you are, my dear. I shall see myself out. You might do something, if you will; have a think about what happened that afternoon and ask yourself, what was Decernay about when you came upon him? In particular, in which direction was he moving? Up the hill—or down?" She looked at him. "It may not make the slightest difference to anything. But a man's life is at stake, and I feel it incumbent on me to at least ask you the question. Have a think. After church tomorrow, give me your unvarnished opinion."

Jacques almost stumbled from weariness as he came into the dark-paneled room where they were to hold the court-martial. He had had no sleep the night before because he had spent it thinking. There was one man who by the nature of his work might be in a position to hear of this fix and quash the court-martial. The trouble was that Jacques had not seen the man in years; he did not know whether he was in London, and there was no way of guessing whether he would intervene. His best move was still to see how the proceedings opened.

He scrutinized the three adjudicators. Lieutenant-Colonel Osborne was unknown to him by name or reputation; he was unimpeachably turned out, had everything disposed before him on the shiny tabletop, and returned the stare with a quick, level glance that was as near neutral as it could be, given the aura of confidence that radiated from his firm, aristocratic features. He was flanked by Major Trusk, a heavy-cavalry officer, who had a ruddy complexion and looked as though he would rather be out riding a stout cob strong enough to carry his corpulent frame. He seemed faintly uneasy. Major Gore-Wilson glanced away and leaned back in his chair the moment Jacques entered. He did not look up, but his face expressed the deepest contempt. Jacques had heard of both the majors: Trusk was fiery but respected by his officers, while Gore-Wilson was one of the hardest taskmasters in the infantry.

The first formalities over, the charges were read out. Conspiracy to desert. Aiding and abetting deserters, manifest intention to join them on 25 February 1814, prevented only by the vigilance of commanding officer, Lieutenant Jones of the 73rd Foot, then stationed at Port Jackson. (Jones was in India, but a deposition had been obtained from one of his fellow officers, since repatriated.) Additional charges: resisting arrest on 1 March 1815 at

Greenwich, use of arms against the officer and men making the arrest.

"Plain admission of guilt. Not much to discuss, is there?" Gore-Wilson said with a sneer.

The lieutenant-colonel, without looking at the major, called upon another officer to read out Jacques' record.

Considering how little assistance the prisoner had given him with it, the man did well. Watching the faces before him, Jacques could not help feeling a certain pride in the account. There were interesting facts there, if you managed to seize the thread that held them all together.

The lieutenant-colonel, tapping the documents into shape with his fingertips, chose an oblique line of questioning.

"While in the service of France, you were an officer in an elite corps, the cuirassiers. Can you tell us why you have remained a private ever since you signed on with the British army?"

"I did not seek promotion, sir."

"You *refused* promotion, several times," Major Gore-Wilson said sharply. "I have the dates here. You were not only put in solitary confinement for it, repeatedly—you were sent on punishment duty to Botany Bay!" He tapped another sheet of paper. "We'll have the truth, here and now. What reason do you allege for deserting your own army in Spain, and joining ours?"

"There are two, sir. After the Battle of Vitoria I was a prisoner of war, with no hope of release except into the British forces." He saw Osborne's frown and Gore-Wilson's grimace of abhorrence. "And I had come to believe that Napoléon Bonaparte did not deserve the trust and devotion of his army or of the French people."

Major Trusk spoke for the first time. "So you turned coat and gave your own boys what for, because you had a grudge against Boney?"

"Yes."

"Come now, you joined up to get out of prison and then snatch what chances you could." It was Gore-

Wilson, his voice cold. "Joined the pack of mongrels who were all itching to slip over to the French lines. We had standing orders from the Duke of Wellington— never entrust 'em with the outposts. More cogent orders were never given."

Osborne let the statement hang in the air for a moment and then resumed. "What would you say, Private Decernay, to the imputation that you were less than serious about fighting against your countrymen?"

"I would cite my record, sir. San Sebastian. Roncesvalles. Sorauren—"

"San Sebastian!" Gore-Wilson said. "Damned poor showing the Chasseurs made there!"

"Ah," Trusk interrupted with a faint air of apology, "except for Private Decernay. We just heard the record. He was in the force that reached the Cask Redoubt. After that they were entrusted to bring up ladders while a storming party made a breach in the ramparts. Having done so the Chasseurs threw them down and fled, leaving a Corporal Mason and the forlorn hope to erect them as best they might—"

"In an impossible situation," Jacques cut in.

Osborne raised his eyebrows, but after a second took up the account without rebuke. "You alone remained. You helped set up the ladders and attempted the assault with the forlorn hope. All were beaten back, most were lost. But we just heard Mason's commendation of your conduct. A very close-run thing, and next to a miracle either of you survived. He volunteered to lead a second assault the next day, with no better result."

"Fine show of courage," Trusk remarked thoughtfully. "Odd—I'd have expected Mason to have received promotion. Yet he seems to have been overlooked."

"Perhaps his commanding officer knew more about him than we do," Gore-Wilson said dryly. "And about Private Decernay."

Osborne sat forward. "To business, then. How do you explain your actions on the twenty-fifth of February last year, on South Head Road above Sydney Cove?"

Jacques observed the three faces, none of which displayed the faintest nuance of encouragement. "I was attached to a platoon supervising a roadworking party. They were convicts—about twenty men, in chains."

"The three Chasseurs who deserted, they were all in your own platoon?" Trusk asked.

"Indeed, sir. At some time—I do not know the hour—I asked permission to go into the forest to relieve myself."

Osborne gave a grim smile. "And you went off one hundred yards or more to do so? Rather unusual delicacy in a trooper, what?"

"It was very hot. There was a spring just below the brow of the hill. I wished to drink."

"And where were your three friends at the time?" Trusk persisted. Jacques, studying the high-colored face, could see nothing but dogged curiosity. If he had an ally at the table, it was not Trusk. And it was certainly not Gore-Wilson. With a hollow feeling in his gut, he fixed his gaze on Osborne.

"I have no idea." He took a deep breath, which was audible in the heavy silence. "As I came out of the bushes a horse and rider appeared. The horse was startled and I calmed it. The lady was alarmed at first, but I spoke to her." All of a sudden he was back in the sultry glade with the two frightened creatures before him. He could see their flashing eyes, hear the woman gasp, smell the pungent eucalypt leaves crushed beneath the horse's trampling feet. Her pale face loomed above him as he put his hand on the horse's neck and felt the vibration under his palm, the jolt as his eyes locked with hers.

"Private Decernay." Osborne's crisp voice penetrated again. "It is reported that you insisted Lady Hamilton ride no farther. Why?"

He responded with plausible fluency. "The slope below was very steep. In that part of Sydney Cove the sandstone is precarious; it crumbles very easily. It was dangerous to take the horse down. I explained this to Lady Hamilton. Then Lieutenant Jones came up. He ordered me back to the road and I obeyed."

"And there's the end of the story?" Gore-Wilson cut in. "Oh, no, not by a long shot. We have the evidence of Privates Courcelle and Servoux, both of whom swore on oath that you planned the escape, arranged their passage, and had the boat placed in position. I put it to you, you were about to slip down to the beach and join them when Lieutenant Jones prevented you. A pity he was not vigilant enough to notice your friends' absence from the forward party until half an hour later—but we're not here to examine *him*. Do you deny, on oath, that you were deserting?"

The words came smoothly. "I do."

Gore-Wilson snorted. Trusk looked away.

Osborne's gaze hardened. "Your two compatriots have since been taken into custody and brought to trial. They confessed to desertion on the date in question—"

"Not much option," Trusk murmured.

"—and were executed. But not before they implicated you. You say you knew nothing about it. In that case, why did they swear you did?"

"They were hoping for mercy, sir. They tried to put the blame on me." He could not help a wry smile. "After all, what had they to lose? I was far away. They were pleading for their lives."

"They paid the price, just the same—and they did not withdraw the accusation. It's your word against theirs, Private Decernay. What justification can you give us for believing you?"

The bitterness was suddenly so great he could taste it. He drew himself up, compressed his lips in a grimace until he trusted himself to speak, then growled, "I have already mentioned my record. I stand by my actions."

He had silenced them for a moment. Gore-Wilson was the first to recover. "And what are we to make of those actions?" He held up one hand and counted the fingers off with the index finger of the other. "You desert your army for ours—which proves you can turn coat at least once. Why not twice? You refuse promotion, thus ensuring you stay in our forces but without taking any responsibility for attacks against your own. You remain with the British army, unsuspected and unchallenged, and meanwhile you have the chance to observe it in operation in three important theaters—the Peninsula, Botany Bay, and the United States."

"What?" Trusk said. "You're not implying . . ."

Osborne gave a first sign of impatience. "We are not court-martialing this man for espionage, Major."

"Perhaps we should be," Gore-Wilson said with a shrug. "To conclude. You take part in the most disgraceful episode of the American campaign—the pillage and rapine at the town of Hampton, Virginia, for which your whole regiment is condemned and disbanded. Peace having been declared with France you do *not* arrange a return to your native land—where no one, after all, is likely to do anything but spit on you—no, you decide to come to England instead. Explain *that* action to us, if you please." He tapped the last finger smartly and lowered both hands.

The fever that was building as an aftermath to Jacques' injury had not yet made his limbs tremble, but he could feel it as a humming deep in his chest, a faint buzzing in his ears. He had been concentrating, however, and watching Osborne's cold face as he listened. If there was any outside influence bearing on this case, it had not made Osborne favorable toward him. So nothing he said actually mattered.

He gave the slightest shrug. "I was curious about this country for which I have fought. A foolish curiosity, perhaps."

The long-nosed, well-bred face in front of him hardened further. "Do you have anything more to say about the very grave charges brought against you?"

They were expecting him to beg. He said with revulsion, "No."

The three officers sat back as one. Osborne said coolly, "Private Decernay, you are dismissed. You will be brought before us on Monday morning, to hear the verdict of this court."

CHAPTER FOUR

Barème, 3 March

You can't help wondering what Bonaparte's old guard is up to right now, the ones who are supposed to be keeping King Louis under their wing. Masséna might have caught us, from Marseilles, if he'd gotten off his ass. And Maréchal Ney—what's he doing, just lying back and waiting for us to turn up? He'll be expecting us by now, because of the semaphore, the new message system they've got, with signal shutters moving on every peak from here to Paris. One of the boys said to me with a laugh, "Look, Bertrand, news travels quicker than we do." But by God nothing else does. I'm too tired to figure out how many horses and mules we've whipped and goaded and cajoled up these passes and then had to leave broken-down by the wayside. But the bastard'll force his way through, and then I can watch as they cut him down before Grenoble. That's one stone wall he'll never get past.

Sophia told Harry a horse story when she tucked him into bed that night, about a chestnut mare who came safely to a green field after incredible adventures and had foals that ran swift as the wind, and always the very swiftest on the home stretch. She knew from his satisfied smile that after she left the bedchamber he would conjure up a dream about Scheherazade dancing down to Clifton.

She spent the next hour in her room, but it was impossible to think. She fiddled about, perching on the edge of the bed, staring blankly at the curtained windows, then getting up and going to rearrange the items on the desktop near the door.

The event that her father had asked her to reconsider could not be analyzed. Only relived with a vividness that always caught her by surprise.

The revelation that came upon her that day outside Sydney Town, far away on the other side of the world, had torn away barriers, and she could put nothing up again in their place.

Mrs. Macquarie, the governor's wife, had made the horse available, a big hack that Sophia had ridden before. She would have loved to go out alone, as she used to do at home on the Sussex downs, but an escort was indispensable here, so she was accompanied by Lieutenant Jones of Governor Macquarie's regiment. Instead of galloping free, tasting the sense of risk and adventure that she could never indulge in except on horseback, she put the hack to a sedate trot alongside the lieutenant and they went up the rutted streets of the settlement and onto the eastern ridge where a new, wider road was being constructed by convict laborers.

She was already familiar with the route, so she recognized the giant red gum tree at the fork, the strip of open ground that led to a track she had not yet explored. She had been told that it ran to a lookout point at the far end from which one could see the vast, beautiful harbor spread out below. Lieutenant Jones left her to make the short detour while he rode ahead to the work party. There could be no danger here, no watchers in the woods—the road makers and the soldiers supervising them were too close by. The invisible cordon around the area was as secure as the fetters around the convicts' ankles. She was riding through redcoat country.

Above her, silver gum trees reached up like suppliants to the cobalt midsummer sky, insects shrilling in their high crowns. The hack flicked its ears back and forth, stepping gingerly, wary of snakes and big lizards in the knee-high undergrowth. It should have picked up the presence of the man behind the dense foliage at the turn of the track, but it did not.

Suddenly he was there. A tall, broad figure, with feet firmly planted, arms outstretched, palms open, he blocked off the track like a gate slamming in her way— yet without a sound, for at that very instant all the insects on the ridge stopped singing. As the silence crashed down she took in an impression of his face: a lock of thick, sun-bleached hair over his forehead, deep-set gray eyes smoldering in shadow.

Then the horse shuddered under her and flung its head sideways with a whinny that was like a strangled scream. It reared and plunged into deep leaves to the left of the path, hooves trampling the ground.

She managed to stay on, gripping the pommel of the sidesaddle so hard that she bruised the inside of her knee. She lost one rein as she grabbed for the horse's mane.

The man growled something that might have been a curse, then stepped forward, despite the animal's dangerous panic, and spoke to it very low. Sophia righted herself but could feel the massive body beneath her tense and gather, ready to rear again.

The soldier put his hand over the top of the horse's neck, directly behind the ears. Four heavy thumps resounded through the glade as the creature brought its hooves one by one to the ground and kept them there. The big head stopped tossing, and the body stilled. Sophia could feel the sides of the neck quiver under her fingers, but the horse remained immobile, poised on the edge of violence but momentarily subdued by the man's voice and touch.

The soldier stroked one hand down the horse's nose, talking in French, soft words that she could not catch. Once his hand was on the bridle he met her gaze again.

If he had spoken to her at once, she might have been able to cope, to ignore his eyes, to mask her own response. But he looked startled, as though she had taken him unawares instead of the other way around. His eyes were wide now, and a lighter gray than they had seemed at first, the color of rain clouds just beginning to gather. He gave her a look that was somewhere between politeness and impudence: naked, frank and demanding in a manner she could not define. But she could feel it, as though he had laid a hand on her in the tender, authoritative way that he had touched the horse.

It was a sensation of pleasure so acute that it shocked her, and her voice shook as she said, "How dare you!"

"Excuse me." His open gaze did not change.

"What, pray, do you think you're doing?"

There was the faintest access of color across his cheekbones. Was he embarrassed? To mask her own confusion she leaned quickly forward and scooped up the dangling rein, her hand coming so near his that he gave an involuntary movement. The hack shook its head and stamped its forelegs uneasily.

"Excuse me," he said again. His voice had a caressing timbre that seemed too gentle for his big frame, and he spoke with a slight French accent. She realized he was one of the Chasseurs and by rights should be up by the roadway, on duty. But she could not dismiss him; she had no authority to do so. And could not summon the will.

He said, "You must not continue in this direction. The ground is unstable—rain has washed away the side of the path and it's not safe to go near the edge. This horse is not bred for the terrain—you are risking an accident."

"An accident? You very nearly caused one!"

"Forgive me." He let go of the bridle and stepped nearer, running his hand smoothly down the side of the horse's neck. "*Tiens, mon brave, ça va mieux?*" Then he looked up at her as though she had already granted the forgiveness he asked for so confidently. "I heard you approaching, but I did not realize you were close. I was too hasty. But you are a superb rider, and there is no harm done. After all."

There was a smile in his eyes now, a warm, complicit

smile that seemed about to spread to his expressive
mouth. His fingers were tangled in the horse's mane,
inches away from hers, and he was standing too close
for courtesy. He looked at her as though he knew her
but had been longing to know her better, as though this
were the most fortunate of circumstances, a meeting in
the woods between new friends. Friends who might so
very easily become something more to each other. That
was what the glint in his eyes said, and the half smile
that now touched his full lips and the tilt of his head as
he looked up at her. He was letting her see into him
with a bold candor that she could not resist, despite all
her will and training. She simply looked back without
protest.

She had never been so shaken, so thrilled, by a man's
sheer presence. She had never been in this kind of delicious danger, where one look was like a touch, one word
an intimate caress. It was as though all her life she had
been a stranger to herself, and it had taken this stranger
to break down the barriers to her own desire.

He frightened her. But it was not his glorious, inviting
smile or the closeness of his strong body that caused this
panic in her; it was the depth of her own reaction.

Then Lieutenant Jones rode into the glade, and she
recognized that the sound of hooves had been approaching for some time. She glanced back toward the
lieutenant and tapped a rein against her horse's neck to
send it smoothly out to the side, farther still off the
track.

The soldier remained looking at her, unmoving, as she
brought the horse to a halt and faced the two men. She
was trembling inside. She could hardly meet the lieutenant's gaze, as though he might discover her shameful
secret if he looked at her too hard.

He said, "Lady Hamilton, are you all right?"

"Yes, thank you."

"I thought I heard a cry." When she did not reply,
Jones said impatiently, "Decernay. What are you hanging about here for? Report back to duty, at the double."

The soldier saluted—not to the lieutenant but to her. His face was solemn now, the eyes opaque as gunmetal.

It was absurd: he wanted to stay. And, even more absurdly, she needed him to. Her body rebelled at his going, while her mind struggled to encompass what was happening, to understand who she had become in this extraordinary encounter.

She had a ridiculous impulse to say some word of farewell, but it was too late; he turned and sprang away, and seconds later he disappeared through the trees.

Lieutenant Jones said, "Would you like me to accompany you to the point, your ladyship?"

"Thank you, no." She put the hack in motion. Her heart was pounding, but her voice obeyed her. "I'll return to the road. It's safer. I find my mount is not very sure-footed over this ground."

As they rode back up to the crest, he said, "Private Decernay was not making a nuisance of himself, I hope?"

"Not at all. He warned me about the track."

At the top, they put their horses to a trot. She tried to concentrate on their progress, on her surroundings. To quell the tumult inside.

The road, built by the infantry only a couple of years before, had neither paving nor gravel, but it had been cleared of outcrops and stumps and the holes filled in with broken pieces of the sandstone that formed the bedrock of the ridge. The surface was firm if not very level, a shallow layer of sandy soil. It was compacted by the traffic of carts, horses and people on foot who went as far as the lighthouse at South Head, eager for news of incoming ships, or for recreation, in a colony where choices were limited and the fresh sea breezes along the ridge could be counted as a blessing.

Then suddenly they rounded a bend and overtook Private Decernay jogging along by the shallow ditch at the side. He had a vigorous action, and his boots thudded purposefully, the sound accompanied by the rattle of a short sword in a scabbard that jolted against his thigh.

Lieutenant Jones took no notice of him, but Sophia looked down irresistibly. As the Chasseur ran, his bright hair and his high, well-defined cheekbones caught the sunlight. He had the hard, rugged strength of a common foot soldier, but his features—the generous brows, the straight nose and chiseled lips—suggested a character formed for other pursuits, another kind of life. The range of expression in his face and his beautifully modulated voice had astonished and compelled her, and in their sudden meeting he had revealed emotions that no other man had ever offered her so freely. Just now, his face was as alive and intense as a beacon, and through that one incandescent glance she took in the knowledge that he wanted her. And knew that she wanted him.

She passed on.

When she got back to the house in town it was late afternoon. She checked on Harry; Nurse said he was still having his nap. She went to her chamber, closed the door, stripped down to her shift and lay on the white satin counterpane of the smooth bed, waiting for the cool of the evening, while the heat flicked around her like a rough, silent tongue.

Simply looking at Decernay, inhabiting the same space as he did for a few snatched moments, had aroused her in a way she had never known before—except in the dark, in the bedchamber, safe in the arms of the husband who loved her.

This was lust. This was betrayal. If she had ever thought herself capable of such intensity of feeling she might have guarded against it, but it was as unfamiliar as being struck by lightning, swept away in a flood. Even now, when the man's remembered presence overtook her senses and filled her imagination, she felt a throb of sweetness. And loss. For he was forbidden to her.

Decernay was a Chasseur, a captured soldier who had turned coat to join the lowest ranks of the English army. He was French, of the race that killed Andrew. He was her enemy.

*   *   *

Sebastian Coole met Admiral Metcalfe early that evening in a coffeehouse near the Admiralty. He would not have to spend too much time with him; the place was private enough for their discussion and there was no need to bring documents—a short exchange of correspondence between their agents had settled affairs to the satisfaction of both. Or so he sincerely hoped.

The older man had gotten there first and was occupying a booth in a corner where Sebastian could just see him through the smoke. He rose, a spare, well-turned-out, impressive figure, and they exchanged formal greetings. With quiet ceremony Sebastian was invited to sit, and his host remained standing until he had called over an attendant to offer him a tray of cigars. The man cut it for him, and lit it, and Sebastian took a couple of deep puffs to encourage it, then disposed himself comfortably on the bench while Metcalfe ordered coffee.

As they conversed, Sebastian recognized the dignified bearing from long ago, when he was a guest at the Sussex property and he had first met the then Captain Metcalfe and his wife from the neighboring Clifton estate. Even as a schoolboy, it had opened Sebastian's eyes to witness a man without hereditary means behave with as much aristocratic ease as the lady whose fortune he had married into. Sebastian's cousins, the Hamiltons, might just as rightly have provided him with a model for gentlemanly British manners, but they were all too markedly individual to serve as examples, and moreover did not intimidate him, even though he was the impoverished relative to whom they extended hospitality. No, it was the Metcalfes who had awed him—the self-sufficient, urbane, irreproachable Metcalfes of Clifton. He had met the husband and wife once more in London, when he was fourteen, and their manners had struck him again— they could talk to a field hand with as much attentiveness as they would to a friend on Bond Street, and would no doubt stroll into St. James's as though it were as jolly and commonplace as the public ballroom in the local town.

It was the Metcalfes who had pointed him the way to much of what he had sought, and in large measure achieved, in the intervening years.

During ten minutes or so of polite questioning on both sides, he caught up on the admiral's service for the navy and the admiral heard about his own for the army.

He leaned forward, nudging away an empty coffee cup. "As chance would have it, neither of us ever fought face-to-face against Bonaparte. Do you regret that, Admiral?"

"Not the way a young man like yourself might. Chance dictated that I was with Nelson in the West Indies, however." A slow smile. "As his commander."

The hum of voices around them surged in to fill the thoughtful pause.

Then Sebastian said in quiet tones, "We have gone over every aspect of my assumption of Birlingdean. All except the one that causes me the most anxiety: the emotion that Lady Hamilton will feel on finding me installed in her late husband's home."

"My dear sir," the admiral replied, "you underestimate my daughter if you imagine her resentful of the plain legal facts. Harry is the heir—whilst you, as sole adult male of the family, are the trustee until his majority. If Sophia did not possess Clifton, she might well have thought of taking up residence at Birlingdean herself, which I grant might have been awkward. But she does have Clifton, which descended to her entire from her mother's side."

It was a rebuff, even if unintentional. Sebastian had just expressed regret at being viewed as a usurper, but he was forgiven in advance, for the Metcalfes had already arranged their lives with complete indifference as to how he intended to conduct his.

In the distant past, this superior attitude might have made him cringe; as it was, he felt grateful to have the matter smoothed over. "We shall soon be neighbors, then. I look forward to meeting Lady Hamilton again."

The admiral raised his silver eyebrows. "It has been how many years?"

"I was nine years old when I was last at Birlingdean."

There might have been something in his face that caught Metcalfe's attention—at any rate he gave Sebastian a somewhat keener glance and then said gruffly, "It's decent of you, by Jove, to think of my daughter's feelings in that regard. I can't pretend to say it won't be a strange homecoming for her. I wish I could go down with her and Harry, but I sail next week."

"I shall be glad to show her every attention. Will she consent to be my guest at Birlingdean, for instance?"

"Possibly, possibly. As a matter of fact, there may well be things of Sir Andrew's—personal, trivial items, of interest to her and the boy—that she will wish to retrieve. Provided you see your way clear, of course."

Sebastian had an amusing vision of old toys from the dusty attics of Birlingdean being carted across the downland to Clifton. "By all means."

Then the older man's expression changed. He leaned forward and said, "May I ask you a favor? If you were not an army man it would not occur to me—but your record is such that my daughter may decide to turn to you for advice." The blue eyes looked transparent and uncertain. "She has taken it into her head that there is some mystery about Sir Andrew's death at the Battle of San Sebastian. I think I have persuaded her not to tackle the army directly on the subject. But I suspect she thinks the answer may lie at Birlingdean or Clifton, in his papers, or whatever. When she finds that it does not, she may turn elsewhere for information." Then he shook his head, embarrassed. "No, I don't feel I should burden you with this."

Sebastian said gently, "You would like me to set her mind at rest, as far as I am able?"

Metcalfe sat back. "I'm obliged to you. You must know, compared with the welfare of my daughter and Harry, everything pales into insignificance for me."

When Metcalfe had gone, Sebastian took up a newspaper and stayed on to finish the cigar. He needed to relax.

It was odd, the tension that he had felt before this interview—caused not so much by present circumstances, but by his memories of Birlingdean.

He had made just the one visit, yet it had gone deep, perhaps simply because it was unique. Everyone had been kind, in their own way, to the Irish cousin who for some reason was not going home for the summer holidays. But the weeks had seemed long to him.

He was pleased with himself at first, because his stammer, which he had just managed to overcome at boarding school, did not recur in these new, trying circumstances. Andrew Hamilton, a year older than himself and an adored only child, was great friends with Sophia Metcalfe. Sebastian envied their ease and their intimacy, but the two of them did not exclude him. He was admitted to their games, and if they exchanged long-suffering glances over his unwillingness to manhandle family property in their own insouciant way, he could understand why.

The adults were not quite so tolerant. He remembered one painful incident in the great hall at Birlingdean when Captain Metcalfe had come to call and to fetch his daughter home. Sebastian, waylaid in flight up the grand staircase, was submitted to a lofty interrogation about his parents, his studies and his general views on holidaying in Sussex. His stammer reasserted itself, and Captain Metcalfe reacted to his agonized silence by insisting on a reply. It was Andrew who rescued him by saying that Cousin Sebastian was needed to teach him something about the forging of weapons in Ireland in Cromwell's time.

"You'll not get much out of me on that!" he dared to whisper to Andrew as they raced up to the first floor.

"Do we ever?" Andrew countered, and then dissolved into giggles, so doubled over he could scarcely make it upstairs. Sebastian had laughed too.

But nothing could put off the inner misery. He wrote letters home to County Antrim, which went unanswered. Then in the August heat he succumbed to what the family physician called summer sickness. Andrew's mother,

Lady Miranda Hamilton, an invalid herself, took care to see he was well looked after.

The longer he stayed indoors, the more of a disappointment he felt he must be. One morning when he was convalescing, and breakfast had been served his room, tears kept him in bed. Unluckily, it was at this time that Andrew paid him a visit, so his only recourse was to pretend to be still asleep—a pathetic ruse, considering his devastated breakfast tray was in full view.

Andrew lingered for some time in the doorway, then tiptoed out.

Later on, Sebastian heard him talking to Sophia, below his window, on the terraced lawn. The day was calm with no breeze, but they could not have been expected to realize that their childish voices would rise in the clear morning air and float through his open casement.

"Where's Sebastian?"

The boy held his breath, waiting to hear how much Andrew would reveal.

The tone was not unkind. "He's brooding." A hesitation. "Mama says he's homesick."

"Then why," Sophia remarked with admirable logic, "doesn't he go home?"

"There seems to be a hitch. His family was very hot for him to spend the whole summer here."

"Don't his mama and papa want him?"

Even at this long remove of time, he could hear with poignant clarity the shock and sympathy in her voice.

It was said that she had grown up a beauty. He had no trouble believing it. The trouble he did have, which seethed through his veins despite the relaxed atmosphere of the coffeehouse and the effects of the luxurious cigar, was of a disturbing kind. He had tried hard to prepare himself for his reunion with Lady Sophia Hamilton of Clifton and Birlingdean—but he had no idea whether it would lead to pleasure or pain.

On Monday morning, when Jacques was marched into the room to hear the verdict of the court-martial, the three adjudicators looked no less grim than they had on the Saturday.

Osborne's voice as he summed up was cool. "Private Decernay, we have given your case careful consideration. We have heard a wealth of evidence regarding the crimes with which you are charged. The very least of these, that of laying hands on a superior officer, is enough to earn you a very severe penalty. You have not denied—you cannot deny—what you did at Greenwich on the first of March. Unfortunately for your case, those acts against His Majesty's Army give us strong reason to believe that your behavior at Sydney Cove in February of last year had the same treasonous intent. You have denied any conspiracy to desert—but you have offered us only your unsupported word against a damning amount of evidence to the contrary." Then, with a certain gruffness in his tone and a look almost of anger: "Do not imagine that my fellow officers and I feel any satisfaction in bringing in this verdict. You were given an opportunity to prove to the army that it has not been harboring a poltroon and a traitor in its ranks for the past two years. When you are challenged, you are very ready with your weapons, it seems—but when it comes to plain talk you scarcely come out with a word in your own defense."

Trusk broke in, with equal roughness. "Come, man, you surely realize the gravity of your position?"

Gore-Wilson said impatiently, "He is wasting our time."

Osborne, who had been watching Jacques' face with a mixture of exasperation and puzzlement, said abruptly, "You have a final chance to explain yourself to this court, Private Decernay." Over an inarticulate sound of protest from Gore-Wilson he continued. "Make no mistake, this *is* your final chance."

There was a pause. Jacques made an effort, but it was unreal and impossible to think about his own death; instead he had a vision of his brother that was so immediate it blotted out for a moment the dark walls of the room and the expectant faces of the men confronting him.

His brother could not speak, but as he lay on the cold ground, with his head supported on Jacques' thigh, he looked up with an eloquence that Jacques understood. *I am dying. But as I would have wished it, on a battlefield, in your arms.*

He could only wrench his mind away and focus his thoughts by seeking the inimical gaze of Major Gore-Wilson. Thus, when he began, he directed the speech at him.

"I have already told this court why I joined the Chasseurs Britanniques. Since then I have served the regiment to the best of my ability. It has been called a mongrel regiment—if that phrase means a mixture of men and of principles, then it could not be more accurate. Nearly all our officers were émigrés, from families who came to England last century, because of the Revolution. They were nobly born, trained to lead; I can swear to you, gentlemen, that when I fought under those commanders I saw a loyalty to king and country that was deeper, more enduring, than that of the bravest Englishman in the field. Because they were fighting, and would not cease to fight, to rescue our country from the usurper."

He shifted his gaze to Trusk. "Alongside our émigré leaders were republicans; men who had fought for liberty in France, who helped to set up constitutional government. These men believed in just and equal laws and they were ready to sacrifice their lives to French independence. They fought for their country's liberty, but they could not prevent it from being overthrown from within by the emperor. They continued to serve, they stayed loyal to France, only to find themselves in the vanguard of the greatest despot of our time. You know the mighty deeds of the Grande Armée; those who rode with Bonaparte left death and devastation behind them across Europe. And meanwhile at home, in France, younger and still younger citizens were being fed into the deadly machine of empire."

He caught Osborne's eye. The lieutenant colonel's puzzlement had turned into frank surprise. Jacques could not help a sarcastic smile. "And the rest of the Chasseurs? To be sure, there were soldiers of fortune in our ranks, miscreants, outcasts, men brought low by accident or poverty or injustice. Mongrels, yes; men with nothing to lose. But there is one factor that bound us all together and gave us strength. For many years, gentlemen, the Chasseurs were the only free French soldiers on earth. Our country was in thrall to Bonaparte. We chose to serve with you because we wanted what you did—his ultimate destruction."

When he stopped, the stillness was intense; they could not believe that this was all he had to say. It was Trusk who broke the silence.

"Then am I to take it, man, that you never had any intention of quitting the Chasseurs?"

"Correct."

Osborne said, "What about the three deserters from Port Jackson? Did you aid and abet them?"

Mentally, he crossed his fingers. "No."

Gore-Wilson rallied. "Lies—in this pass, what else can he come up with? As for trying to make that pack of hell-bent rabble sound like blessed crusaders . . ."

Osborne overrode him: "Why did you draw weapons on the officer and men sent to arrest you?"

"I lost my temper."

"You knew your time was up!"

"Major," Osborne said with ice in his voice, "we are not here to browbeat the prisoner but to give him our verdict." He had kept his eye on Jacques. "You are pale, man. You may be seated if you wish."

"Thank you, I prefer to stand." He braced himself. He was *in extremis*. Now was the time to decide which of his secrets he should reveal. But which, if any, would be believed?

Suddenly there was a brisk, loud knock at the door. Everyone started and looked toward it; then it opened and an ensign marched rapidly down the side of the room, stopped at the end of the table and saluted.

"Lieutenant-Colonel Osborne, sir, I have a dispatch

from Colonel Morton. I was to pass on his opinion, sir, that it may have a bearing on the case."

Osborne held out his hand. "Thank you, Ensign Parker. Dismissed."

The soldier handed over two folded sheets of paper, saluted and left. Osborne opened the papers, ran his eye over the top one, glanced at the second and then laid them on the table and looked up.

"This is a letter from Admiral Metcalfe of the Blues." Catching Jacques' eye he said sharply, "Bring a chair for the prisoner." Then, as the room subsided into quiet again, he said, "It contains new evidence, addressed to Colonel Morton, which the court must hear. I shall read it in full."

Sir, I understand that under your jurisdiction a court-martial is presently being held in which Private Decernay of the Chasseurs Britanniques is charged with conspiracy to desert whilst serving a punishment duty at Botany Bay last year. I do not know the evidence against Private Decernay, but it occurs to me that at such a remove of distance and time, reliable witnesses both for and against the prisoner may be lacking; and if I possess any information bearing on the case, it is my duty, as a member of His Majesty's armed forces, to make it available to the court-martial.

Let me preface that information with a remark about Private Decernay. I am not well acquainted with him, but what I saw while I was at Port Jackson suggested he was held in respect and affection by the military and civilians alike. I regret that I had no personal dealings with him and thus cannot furnish a character reference.

My daughter, Lady Hamilton, did however meet Private Decernay just once, on the very occasion which, I believe, forms the focus of your inquiry. The following is a summary of what occurred, recorded by myself from her own testimony.

On that day, Lady Hamilton was promenading on

horseback along South Head Road with an escort, Lieutenant Bevan Jones. She turned off the road alone to ride a short distance toward a cove which offers a view over Port Jackson. Before she reached the end of the track, Private Decernay appeared abruptly before her. This caused the horse to shy, but he brought it under control, apologized courteously, then advised her not to ride farther. When she questioned this advice, he warned her that the track was unstable and that the horse risked slipping on the descent.

Lieutenant Jones then rode up, ordered Private Decernay back to the road and accompanied Lady Hamilton on the remainder of her ride.

My daughter neither saw nor heard any other soldiers in the vicinity, and she states that Private Decernay was alone when she met him. He was hidden by trees as she approached, but it was her distinct impression that he was proceeding toward her, that is, up the hill toward the road. At no stage did she feel there was more than one motive behind what Private Decernay said or did. On the contrary, he was uniquely preoccupied with her safety.

Lady Hamilton attests this to be an accurate account and attaches her signature to my document. Considering that she was the only witness apart from Lieutenant Jones to the incident in question, it seemed to me that in the interests of military justice I had a duty to lay it before you.

Written this fifth day of March 1815.
J. Metcalfe, Rear Admiral

For a few moments after his voice had died away, Osborne sat staring into Jacques' eyes without moving. Then he rose and said, "We must discuss this, gentlemen. The court will adjourn for ten minutes. The prisoner will remain seated."

They took the papers with them, including the letter with her signature on the second page. He had an absurd wish to snatch it away from them and examine it. Waiting in the feverish silence, he tried to imagine her handwriting. As a girl she would have been instructed to adopt a style that was flowing, even and elegant; and he could see her as an earnest child, copying out lines, the pen held at the right angle in her tapering fingers. But there would be more to read in her hand now. If he could see it, perhaps he could begin to understand why the letter had been written, what consequences she had hoped for.

In the meantime, she remained what she had been to him since the day they met—the most seductive mystery.

CHAPTER FIVE

Mary would have preferred not to go to the ball at the Piggott-Staceys' that night, but Sophia persuaded her into it. Ellwood was going straight there from the House, where the Corn Bill was in the committee stage. And, as Sophia ironically reminded Mary, phase two of Prinny's seduction was due. Most important, the admiral would also be joining them, which meant Sophia had a secret, dire reason to attend: she expected and dreaded to hear news of Private Decernay.

The evening was to be a splendid affair, the result of weeks of frantic politicking on the part of the Piggott-Staceys, who were almost beside themselves at the prospect of playing host to the Prince Regent.

"I still don't like it," Mary said as they rattled across town toward Curzon Street. "Anything could happen. The streets are full of people who've sprung from heaven knows where, intent on the most horrible mischief."

"I should imagine if they were going to riot, it would be outside the House," Sophia said.

"How can you talk so, when my own husband is inside it!"

"All I mean is—they're likely to make the most noise where they want to make the biggest impression. And they've petitions to present. It's said they have hundreds of thousands of names."

"You really aren't the least bit nervous, are you?" Mary said with some exasperation. She pushed at the top of the window with her gloved hand. "I wish this would shut properly. Do you know, ruffians tried to set alight to Lord Gorley's carriage with burning straw—they hurled it through the window in broad daylight, when he was going down the Mall if you please. I wonder if we should close the curtain?"

"No, it is better if we are visible. No one could be fool enough to think that roasting two gentlewomen alive would be the slightest hindrance to the passage of the Corn Bill."

Mary shuddered. "Anyone would think you were *enjoying* this!"

"Come, Curzon Street will be ablaze with lights and full of alert coachmen and grooms to ward off troublemakers. And I'm sure the targets are elsewhere. The city has ordered in more troops; Ellwood has all the protection you could desire, depend upon it." She tried to smile. The danger in the streets meant nothing to her; today Decernay had met his punishment, and she could concentrate on little else. "If the prince sees you with those saucer eyes he is much more likely to pay court to you than me—he loves to be gallant."

Mary shook her head and gave a little laugh. "He will be in such a pother himself he will hardly notice either of us. In fact, I shall be surprised if he has the courage to put his nose outside Carlton House."

Sophia raised her eyebrows. "He is not at risk, surely?"

Mary looked tragic. "My dear, you have been far from us too long. You cannot conceive how heartily he is detested. His politics have been the despair of our own circles, and as for the rest, it is his extravagance that most offends. He tries for dignity and decision—the country calls him proud and selfish. He seeks to be amiable—he is condemned for being lax, profligate, a satrap wallowing in his own splendor, what you will."

Sophia murmured, "And I am trying to make him act as the arbiter of peace in Europe. He is wiser than me then; he must feel there is little respect to be gained out of that."

"I don't deny you have a challenge ahead." After a quick glance out at the chilly, empty street, Mary at last leaned into the comfortable cushions at her back. "He has always had *la nostalgie du militaire,* poor dear, despite never having served a day in his life. I wonder if he will wear that monstrous uniform again tonight?"

The Prince Regent instead wore evening dress without decorations, and was smuggled to Curzon Street in a plain carriage with armed equerries up behind. The event had so far been a tremendous success, and the entrance of His Royal Highness was calculated to heighten it further. Sophia watched from the other end of the ballroom as the crowd swirled and eddied around the prince and the three friends who had attended him to the house, quite engulfing the eager Piggott-Staceys. Then he danced with the eldest daughter of the house, though Sophia could not help noticing that he often looked her way.

It all made a magnificent picture. The hostess had decorated the long room in the spirit of the spring that was in reality still to come. There were great swags of green silk above the uncurtained windows on the street side and over identical bays on the other, all linked by garlands of flowers that an hour or two before had looked deliciously fresh—thus justifying, Sophia trusted, the fortune the hostess must have spent on obtaining them. The bays and the intervals between the windows opposite were filled with delicate trellising of woven, painted canes, with bouquets and ribbons attached to the supports, so that ladies who took advantage of the low ottomans within were sitting in floral bowers.

From end to end of the room, looped between the chandeliers, ran a massive festoon of ivy, from which the occasional leaf, crisped by the lights, drifted down and lay like a little curled hand amidst the dancers' shoes. Many of the flowers too had wilted, but the hothouse bulbs had held up, and fragile tendrils of nectar from the daffodils could be detected in corners amongst great sensuous wafts of perfume thrown out by narcissus and freesia.

As the prince moved down the room after the dance, he made no pretense of aiming for anyone but Sophia. She was unprotected, having walked away from the ladies she had been talking to and lingered by the musicians, alone for the moment, between dances. She did not enjoy crowds one whit, but if the prince was going to pay her attention she would be surrounded by a curious one very soon. Trying to observe him calmly as he edged from group to group, she could see something boyish in him—despite the cheeks bulging over his high collar and the corpulence—that must always have been part of his charm.

He arrived before her with a little knot of others, but spoke only to her. He asked her how the evening had gone so far and she praised the musicians, since they were just a few paces away and between pieces at the time. He ran a connoisseur's eye over the ballroom and made a kind remark about the arrangements, though there was a comical expression on his full lips as he struggled over an adequate phrase with regard to the flowers.

She saved him by saying, "Mrs. Piggott-Stacey is too cautious to open windows onto the street, so the air is rather close for the bouquets. I'm afraid you have arrived in the blowsy part of the proceedings, Your Highness."

"Only to find you fresh as a new-picked rose," he said with a smile, then looked at her with his head tilted to one side. "You have been dancing, however, we are sure."

"I have." She continued, rather too fast for politeness. "Though I do not waltz."

"Then we hope to have the honor of the quadrille, unless we are far too late, and your card is filled?" She would have spoken, but he continued. "Why do you not waltz?"

"I have never learned. I had not the opportunity before I went overseas, and somehow Botany Bay did not seem the place to take lessons."

He beamed. "You will find it a delectable exercise when you do. And it will afford us a fine prospect to look forward to—seeing you waltz at the Pavilion. We may be taking up residence in Brighton for a while. It would give us great pleasure to receive you and your friends one evening."

She could see that the people around her were variously impressed, envious and piqued at this, but despite his rather orotund delivery he was not making a show of his favor to her; in fact, as the musicians struck up again and he dipped his head in formal invitation, there was even a kind of timidity in his voice. "You have not said; may we have the honor of leading you to the floor, Lady Hamilton?"

Since this was exactly what she had courted and feared, she managed to accept, though her voice was inaudible.

Their slow parade, which took the full length of the ballroom, was daunting. Nervousness alone kept her erect and forced each foot to glide forward in step with the prince's majestic progress. There was a haze around her vision that blocked out the rows of watching faces on each side, and all she could really see was the Piggott-Staceys, near the double arch of the entrance to the room—the hosts and their three daughters standing in a tight group with identical expressions on all their faces as they inwardly debated whether they approved of the prince's second choice of partner.

Then, at the very instant that she and the prince took their places at the head of the row of couples, another guest was announced, the crowd of guests near the entrance parted, and the hosts were obliged to turn and greet a tall figure who made his dignified way up to them.

Out of the corner of her eye, Sophia saw that the gentleman was her father. A tremor seized her: what would he tell her?

The music struck up and the dancers made their bows. She looked across, trying to read on her father's face the dreadful news—for it could only *be* dreadful—that he was bringing about Decernay.

Meanwhile, at least there was a mournful pleasure in knowing that her father would take such images with him on the lonely voyage to Lisbon. He would remember seeing her hand in the prince's as they took the first stately steps, His Highness's smile as he enjoyed the dance while keeping his eye constantly upon her, the shimmer of soft colors as the ladies crossed and recrossed the squares, circling and then tripping away from the sober black-and-white figures of the men.

She might have mixed feelings, but she knew her father's emotion would be simple pride. In his love and admiration for her, it had always seemed natural to him that she must shine in society. When she was very young, his way of coping with her reserve in front of strangers was to pretend not to notice it. Once she married, Andrew had been a second ally in almost every situation, but still, where her husband had looked forward to social engagements, she wished she could avoid them. Now, in her widowhood, she had felt her father growing anxious about her. Tonight's triumph, if it achieved nothing else, must sweep those anxieties away.

"You have a beautiful smile, Lady Hamilton, but we have never seen such an intriguing one on your lips before. May we exercise a privilege and demand to know the thoughts behind it?"

She replied at once. "My father has just arrived, Your Highness, and I was thinking what surprise and pleasure it must give him to see his shy daughter so honored."

With a quick glance he picked out the admiral, who was looking their way. "Shy? We never met a lady more serene."

"I am delighted to hear you say so. My disguise is complete?"

"Absolutely." His eyes flashed as he laughed at her, and to her confusion her neck grew hot and she could feel a blush radiating up to her cheekbones.

Noticing, he laughed even more, with bright mischief in his glance. "Rest assured, your secret is safe with us."

"Oh dear." She could not help smiling. The flush had reached her eyes, but she continued. "I was the most exasperating contradiction of a child. With my parents and friends, I was extremely free with my opinions. I loved to speak the truth far oftener than others wanted to hear it, and altogether I was an out-and-out rattle-pate—but put me before an unknown person and all I could do was gaze at the floor. It will appall you to hear that as a grown woman I have hardly changed. I can talk with freedom only when I am among those closest to me."

He beamed. "Madame, that is the most touching thing you could have said. Now we know to which enchanted group of people we belong."

The dancers around them were agog, paying heed as avidly as the movements of the set would allow, but Sophia went on. "*I* am honored that you listen to me. As it happens, there is something I should dearly like to discuss with you, if only I were bold enough."

At this point the dance separated them for a while, leaving Sophia free to observe, on the prince's heated face, the powerful effects of her last statement, which had not come out in quite the way she intended.

As soon as they were together again, the prince replied before she could form a word. "Henceforth we have a pact, my dear Lady Hamilton: when you are with us, reserve is no part of your nature. You may confide in us. Completely."

"Your Highness is very good."

She was in a dilemma. It was impossible to speak her mind whilst dancing a quadrille. On the other hand, if she remained silent until the set was over, or talked of something trivial, the prince would imagine her coquettish.

She thought quickly. "It would take some time to canvass my ideas. And after this piece Your Highness will be much occupied. Perhaps later in the evening—"

"Madame," he cut in, "would you object if we withdrew now?" He followed with a proper excuse: "It would give us great pleasure if you would present your father to us."

She murmured a hasty agreement, and they stepped gracefully out of the set. The musicians faltered on seeing this, but the prince threw them a glance and with a little motion of his hand requested them to play on. She noted that he had led her to the opposite side of the ballroom from where the admiral stood.

"Dear lady," he said softly, standing close enough to her to discourage other people from approaching, "what is this important matter you wish to mention?"

She took a deep breath to steady her voice. "Your Highness will recall a conversation concerning my late husband?"

He started, and the expectation in his eyes dimmed. "Certainly."

"Do you remember, I said that I hoped my son would never be faced with the choice imposed on Sir Andrew?"

"Indeed." Now there was caution in his eyes.

"Your Highness, my husband served England, not because he was a man of war, but because he felt called by duty. He was killed in that service, though all he ever wanted was to live in peace with us at home. I would do anything to save my son from such a fate. Do you think my feelings unnatural?"

He was listening now. "By no means."

"Do you believe that there are men and women like me, all over England, who blessed the day that the war ended?"

"No one could argue with you on that count."

"We must rejoice that we have won the war. But I fear we need even greater strength and vigilance to win the peace."

He gave a protective smile. "You are nervous; that is natural. But allow us to reassure you. If you are concerned about the unrest of the last few days, take heart, the situation is under control."

"Your Highness, I do not mean what is happening in

London. I am talking about what England is doing on the Continent."

There was a shade less indulgence in his expression, but he continued. "There we must exercise our power with justice and discretion. The government has absolute faith in the Duke of Wellington."

"But he does not act alone. Lord Castlereagh dictated all the terms before he came home from Vienna. And the duke—do you deem that his *first principle* would be to prevent England's plunging into another conflict?"

"My dear madame," he said smoothly, "sustaining the peace is just what every party to the Congress is aiming for."

She could see that under the charm he was unhappy with the turn of the conversation. Politics and diplomacy were hotly discussed in the saloons of London, certain ladies often taking part more keenly than the men, but it was neither male nor female practice to debate such issues with the Prince Regent, even when he brought them up himself. If he began to feel cornered, he would not listen to her. On the other hand, if she resorted to flirting with him, he might lap up every word—but she had never flirted with a man in her life, and now seemed a terribly dangerous moment to start.

"Your Highness, they are carving up Europe. Peace for the instant means satisfying the appetites of the strongest. *Lasting* peace cannot be achieved unless England looks beyond greed."

His only reply was a thoughtful nod, while he looked over her shoulder for help.

She said, "Have you thought about what you might bring to Vienna? With the exception of Talleyrand, all the statesmen are warriors. Whatever they decide, it will lead one day to another war. But you are not a warrior."

He pouted a little.

She had said the wrong thing.

All at once he brightened again, and turning her head she saw her father approaching. "My dear Madame," the prince said, "will you have the kindness to make your father known to us?"

He was avoiding the subject. She felt a disappointment that she could not hide, and he saw it; but he shot her a winning smile, with the hint of boyish mischief she had seen in his face before. She played a last card.

"I shall be delighted. If you promise me one favor in return—that we may speak of this again."

She read consent in his sparkling look. Then he turned and took a step toward the admiral.

She was rather nervous with introductions, but the encounter passed off well. She had the satisfaction of hearing her father give easy, sensible answers to the Prince Regent's courteous questions about his recent service and of feeling that if their little family group was just now the focus of everyone in the room, they were at least carrying it off with aplomb.

The quadrille had ceased, another dance would soon begin, and it was time for the prince to rejoin the press of people around them. He said a few closing words to the admiral, then bowed meaningfully to Sophia.

"We shall remember every word you have said, dear lady—as long as you promise not to forget our invitation."

She curtsied and found herself blushing again, which made him chuckle as he moved away.

She at once put a hand on her father's arm. "Decernay. What has happened?"

"They came to a verdict this morning."

His voice was so severe she felt her cheeks go cold. She faltered, "Our letter was useless?"

He caught her look. "My dear, he is not condemned to death. And that is possibly thanks to the letter. I do not know. But the sentence was—" He glanced around him. "Do you think this the place to talk of such things?"

"Tell me."

"Three hundred lashes, then dismissal. This afternoon."

It was as though she had been struck herself. She gasped and put a hand to her face, and her stomach clenched. "How could a man survive such savagery?"

"That was the penalty, I'm afraid. Whether he received the full number was no doubt discretionary." He gave her a moment, then said, "Let us join Lady Ellwood. I see her looking our way."

She crossed the room on his arm, her mind shuddering at the terrible image of Decernay being bent to such punishment. Even if he had not defied his tormenters—and she had a swift, instinctive dread that he would have done so—the glow of strength and energy that belonged around him would have seemed like defiance in itself. She could not avoid imagining what brutality would have been exercised to break him.

She was scarcely listening, but her father continued. "You have the knowledge of having done right and of seeing some mercy shown to a stranger in consequence. You have not mentioned this matter to your friend?"

"No!"

"Quite right."

They were approaching others. She must try to appear normal, but let no one expect her to speak.

Mary, having left the floor, was standing alone within one of the bowers. After greeting the admiral, she said, "Have you seen my husband tonight, sir?"

"No, are you expecting him?"

"He should be here by now. The House cannot have gone this long. What was happening in the streets as you came?"

"I'm afraid there was some disturbance." He said this so calmly that it did not alarm Mary, but Sophia, her mind full of horrors, challenged him at once.

"Where, in Westminster?"

The music struck up again and he kept his voice low so that no one else could hear. "I do not know all the facts. But my cab was held up in the traffic and the news passed down the line that a mob is heading for the chief justice's house."

Sophia caught Mary's eye and felt another cold fear strike at her heart. "What if it is Lord Eldon next?"

"The chancellor has iron railings before the doors."

Mary had gone pale. "But there is nothing to stop them crossing the square to us—our house is much less protected. What if they seek Ell*wood*?"

"I understand your husband opposes the bill," the admiral said.

"And you expect that to mean anything to a bloodthirsty rabble? Oh, if only Ellwood were here! Where *is* he?"

Sophia had a sudden vision of the chancellor's house in flames, an angry crowd seething in Bedford Square, battering on the doors of the grand houses, throwing bricks against windows behind which little children slept or huddled, terrified and in mortal danger.

She put a hand on her father's arm. "I must go to Harry."

"Do not *think* of it," cried Mary. "We shall wait for Ellwood; he will know what is happening. He will know what to do. It is insane to go rushing off without him. We are just as likely to strike some frightful disaster ourselves."

Sophia snapped back, "I do not require your carriage, Mary. We will find another, or take a cab—Papa, say you will go with me."

"Calm yourself, my dear. Of course I will; but taking a cab is by no means wise."

"I am staying," Mary said in anguished tones. "And you should too. But if you think I am not frantic about our little ones—" And she burst into tears.

Everyone by now was observing them with interest, and the dancers nearby were falling out of step.

"Dear God," Sophia cried. "I must go!"

She turned, lunged away, and was brought to an abrupt halt—she had practically thrown herself on the breast of the Prince Regent, who had left the dance in haste. He took her by the upper arm to steady her and regarded her with startled eyes.

"My dear Lady Hamilton! Whence comes this distress?"

She was panting with impatience. "Your Highness, I

am leaving. My son—I must go to him. Papa—you will escort me." She put a hand out to her father, who had joined them.

Though perturbed, his voice was firm. "A cab is out of the question."

The prince clasped her fingers and addressed himself to the admiral. "You apprehend some danger on the way?"

When the admiral nodded, the prince turned a tender and admiring gaze on Sophia. Frustrated and wild to be gone, she felt her eyes fill with tears. "I must leave at once."

"And so you shall," he said. "Our carriage is yours." He said to the admiral, "The equerries are armed. They will be at your command." Still with Sophia's hand in his, eyes shining with the promptness of his own action, he drew her toward the doors, then beckoned a footman forward and sent him scurrying off with instructions.

The host and hostess approached, Mary rejoined them and the prince himself explained the matter to the little group of listeners while Sophia quickly prepared to leave.

With her father at her side, she stepped toward the prince and looked her gratitude. "You have not let me thank you. How very, very kind."

"Do not thank me, dear lady. Go in safety. If only I could escort you myself, but I cannot take the risk of drawing peril your way if I am recognized." He raised her hand, kissed it and said with emotion, "Never have I so much regretted who I am."

"Do not say so. Tonight you are my friend."

She shed no tears in the carriage, but neither did she speak, the tension was too great. All along the streets she felt death prowling like a wolf, teeth bared to fasten on its random victims. She had felt like this often since Andrew had died. It was like a nightmare, where she was frozen into immobility and forced to watch others carried off into a cold darkness where she could not follow.

Her father, with the instinctive understanding she blessed him for, made soothing remarks now and then as they rattled along, and did not expect a reply. He drew the window curtains but frequently pulled them aside a little to look into the street.

At one point they heard shouts, and a stone rattled against the carriage door, startling her out of her paralysis.

Her father closed the curtain and said, "There are plenty of people about, but they don't look like business as yet. We're moving too fast for them."

She said, *"I won't lose Harry."*

He nodded, as though they were discussing everyday affairs. "I think you should take him down to Clifton as soon as possible; the country will do you both the world of good. Colonel Coole is in residence at Birlingdean by now, so you'll have a congenial neighbor."

"Sebastian Coole!" She stared at him. "You're making this up. To distract me."

"Nonsense. We expected it to happen. I saw the man himself the other day, and you'll be setting eyes on him as soon as may be."

Her hands twisted in her lap. "Is it a visit, or is he taking up residence?"

"The latter, I think. He craves the life of a country gentleman. The fruits of the peace, to enjoy while he can."

He caught her keen look and turned away slightly, pulling back the curtain again.

She said quickly, "What do you mean, while he can?"

He murmured, "A figure of speech, my dear."

"No. Tell me. Amongst all the dreadful things we have heard tonight, is there worse to come? From Vienna? What have you learned at the admiralty?"

He faced her, the sea blue of his eyes shifting in the unsteady light of the little oil lamp above the door. He took a breath like an inward sigh. "It will soon be common knowledge. Perhaps it is best you hear it first from me. My dear—" He hesitated so long she thought he would not continue. Finally he said rapidly, "Bonaparte has escaped from Elba. Word has reached Paris that he is marching north from the Mediterranean with a growing army. English people are fleeing Paris in droves. Military intelligence has given us the news—I charge you to mention it to no one."

"It's not possible."

"My dear daughter, the British Navy has the best intelligence system in the world, bar none."

She said desperately, "I mean, he cannot be at large again." She gripped the edge of the padded seat as the carriage rocked over the uneven cobbles of a crossing. Her mind raced ahead. "They will recall Wellington from Austria."

"I imagine so."

"The Congress of Vienna will collapse." Her father did not reply. She heard herself say, above the din of the carriage wheels, "Chaos is come again."

CHAPTER SIX

As they neared Bedford Square there were more and more people in the streets. Sophia had no need to pull aside the curtain; she could hear them, the scuffle and thud of feet, cries that echoed back from the facades of the buildings on each side, insults flung at the speeding carriage and answered with a roar from the coachman or the two equerries up behind.

As they rounded a corner she heard a shout. "Cromwell!" It was taken up by many voices. She thought she heard a woman's amongst them.

"Cromwell?"

"Possibly some local leader elected for the day." Her father caught her sardonic reaction. "No, a natural catch cry in the circumstances. I could not say this before Lady Ellwood—there is an immense crowd surrounding the Commons, too great for the city constables to keep back. But troops have been called in, and when last I heard the lobby and approaches were still clear."

"Ellwood!"

"So far the members have been subjected only to threats and shouting. But it must be impossible to hear each other inside, so he is sure to join her soon. I could see no sense in adding to her distress."

"You should have told her. If *I* had known, I would never have gone to the ball tonight. And what will hap-

pen to the other guests? Have they no right to know
what awaits them when they leave Curzon Street?"

"I had a word in our host's ear before we left."

"A conspiracy of men." But her father did not hear
because of the noise outside.

The pounding of feet, and what sounded like the clash
of metal on stone, rose to a crescendo as they neared
the entrance to the square.

Her father leaned toward her and shouted, "I have
instructed the coachman that if there is a crowd inside
we shall pass on and find a way into the house from the
lanes. Never fear, I will not take you amongst the mob."

But they had no choice. The scores of running feet
were hastened by fear. The sound of metal on the road
was that of hooves, for behind the crowd drummed a
troop of Horse Guards.

In another instant the horsemen were upon them, jostling past the carriage so that it rocked and flung them
about. They heard a shout of "Halt, let us pass!" and
the prince's coachman yelling at his frightened horses.
Saber and stirrup scored along the panels as the vehicle
lurched to a stop, just inside the square, and the guards
clattered past.

Her father pulled the curtain back, shot his window
down and risked looking out. Then he shouted to the
coachman, "The third house to the right," and pulled
his head in quickly. "The guards are sweeping the place,
taking all before them. Now's our chance. The servants
will have barricaded the coach yard, so we'll have to
dash in from the street. When they open the door, prepare to run up the steps. Are you ready?"

She nodded.

The instant the carriage came to a crashing halt, one
of the equerries leaped to the pavement, his rifle at the
ready, and ran up the steps crabwise, with one eye on
the square, covering himself as he went, then pounded
on the door. He yelled something that Sophia could not
catch because of the din behind her, but she hoped
Mary's majordomo could hear it; the servants must have

had sense enough to post someone behind the door for the return of the master and mistress.

Sure enough, the big door opened a crack, there was a short altercation and then the equerry beckoned from the top of the steps.

"All clear," the admiral said, then got quickly down, drew his sword and held out the other hand to assist Sophia.

She kicked her shoes off before jumping out, and once she was on the cold paving she pulled her gown up to her knees. As they ran, the noise behind them swelled, but there was no one near enough to attempt any mischief.

A moment later they were inside, and the door was slammed shut. A servant shot the bolts and seconds later they heard the thump of the equerry's boots in retreat, a roar from the coachman and a rumble as the carriage plunged away.

An hour had gone by, and Bedford Square had descended into eerie quiet. From a window of the drawing room on the first floor of the Ellwoods' mansion, a great deal of the damage could still be detected, despite the fact that the sky was low and overcast, every lamp in the vicinity had been shattered, and there was no illumination from the casements around the square, since all the householders had ordered lights out.

The chancellor's house opposite had suffered the worst, but no one would venture out to put things right until dawn. Iron railings lay twisted in fantastic shapes on the pavement. Every window on the lower floor front had been broken, and most of those on the second. Furniture tossed from upper casements lay smashed below; costly items from mantelpiece and sideboard lay in fragments, and there were drawers from desks and commodes, rifled by the looters, then flung out to the seething crowd.

One pile of broken possessions was blacker than the rest; the remains of a small bonfire that the guards had managed to beat out with wet swathes of torn-down curtains. Another few minutes, and the same kind of fire might have been lit indoors.

If anyone had been injured in the raid during the chancellor's absence, they were being cared for unassisted within, for after the rioters had fled before the Horse Guards, no one had issued through the barricaded doors, and not a soul had been seen entering again.

A fine rain began to fall as Sophia watched from the window. She had persuaded her father to go to bed and ordered the same for most of the servants—a groom with a musket at the attic windows, and the cook stationed in the kitchen with a cudgel on the table and an eye on the scullery door seemed enough to keep vigil. The majordomo, Lawrence, was dozing in the vestibule, awaiting the Ellwoods' return.

Harry and Mary's two children had slept throughout the crisis. Sophia had gone at once to check on her son and found him in deep slumber, his breathing scarcely lifting the counterpane. She had lowered herself very gently onto the end of his bed and sat watching him for a while, the flood of anxiety gradually draining away. He had been like this as a baby—able to sleep through the loudest disturbances. On their long journeys at sea he was the same. When it came time for his nap she would pick him up, take him below and prepare him for bed, and as she lowered him into the cot he would keep his smooth, plump arms around her neck until the moment his head touched the pillow, then pat her cheeks with his hands and smile at her as he let her tuck them under the coverlet. If it was she who laid him down, the wildest storm could not wake him. She used to creep softly into the cabin when the wind howled over the ship and find him sleeping with a serenity that calmed her too.

She looked out the window into the rain, thinking irresistibly of an utterly different place, another time.

She had seen Private Jacques Decernay on only three more occasions after their first encounter, for nothing in the life of each made it likely or appropriate that they would meet. Once she had been shopping at an importer's, and he had come into sight at the bottom of the main street, marching a group of convicts up the slope. She stayed in the shadows behind the shop window, transfixed, watching the scene as though it were taking place on a brightly lit stage. A scene that she wanted never to end, as long as he was at the center of it.

The convicts looked sullen when he first put them in order, but even at a distance she caught the forcefulness and humor of what he said, to them and to the idlers on the street, and by the time they came abreast of the shop some of the men were laughing. He was too, and she began to see what it was about him that attracted her physically. It was his male energy, untrammeled, generous and unselfconsciousness—offered as a gift, and with such carelessness that he was already making her jealous. She wished for those eyes, so full of zest and laughter, to rest on her alone. She wanted those hands to take hers and bring her to his side. She wanted to walk up the street with him, free, full of life, complete.

And instead she stood still in the shadows, yearning for him to glimpse her, while having no idea at all how she would act if he did. But he was preoccupied with his duty, and passed by unaware. She felt sick and bereft. And guilty.

The second time, she was walking in Farm Cove with her father, having been invited to inspect the gardens that the soldiers were trying to establish. Decernay suddenly appeared from one of the sheds, a spade over his shoulder, out of uniform and wearing an open-necked shirt and canvas trousers. He must have been off duty and had come to borrow tools from the gardeners.

He stopped when he saw her, as though she had put her hands on his chest to bring him to a halt, and the impact on him was so strong he could not summon a smile or a greeting. He just stood there, partly in her way, waiting for her to make another move—to speak, and recognize his longing and his misery, or pass on. This was all as clear to her as if he had spoken it. Yet her father noticed nothing untoward. In his courteous way he slowed his steps and nodded at Decernay, giving him time to step aside.

Sophia, only inches away, could not help looking up into his eyes. Passion blazed in his, unveiled and challenging.

Her own reaction took her by the throat and she could not speak.

He moved back, her father took her elbow, said, "Thank you, my good man," and they parted.

When they were out of earshot, the commodore said, "That was the fellow who rendered you a service on South Head Road, was it not?"

"Yes, Papa."

"You might have offered him a word, my dear. He may be rough, but he has his pride. They tell me he commands respect among the troops."

And then came the afternoon when the Chasseurs Britanniques were leaving Sydney Cove. It had been a hot day, the sun striking sparks from the mica in the sandstone paving of the quayside and ricocheting off the choppy waters of the harbor. The ornamental trees around the Macquaries' house, where she was a guest for a few days, were utterly still in the oppressive heat, and the short ride down to the Cove was punishing, though Sophia wore a riding hat with a wide, sweeping brim, held on by black gauze to keep off persistent flies.

She was accompanying Mrs. Macquarie and the governor to the troops' final parade; the 73rd Foot, of which he was commander in New South Wales, had been posted to India.

She knew the contingent of Chasseurs Britanniques were going with them, on the first leg of their voyage to the American War. It should have been hard to pick them out in the packed square of redcoats, since all that distinguished them from a distance were the green plumes on their shakos, but she saw Decernay at once, in the column nearest the edge of the wharf. Under the intense light, the shiny peak of his shako threw a black shadow across his eyes, but she could feel his intent gaze as certainly as if they were face-to-face once more. Down at the quay, Sophia was invited under an awning and onto the dais from which Lachlan Macquarie would farewell his soldiers, but she remained on horseback, in the sidelines, not intending to linger if the ceremony dragged on too long. Nonetheless, she stayed through the military music and noise and the speeches, while the sky began to darken overhead with a swiftness that never failed to astonish her, even in this land of extremes.

Great drops of rain were hissing onto the dusty paving by the time the soldiers were ordered onboard. When it was the turn of the Chasseurs Britanniques, she could see Decernay march up the gangway, then twist around. He was jostled by the man behind, but he remained absolutely still for a moment, facing her way. The last ray of sunlight turned the hair at his collar to gold and lit up one tanned cheek and the pale blue of his shoulder. Then he was gone, and the downpour began, rippling like a curtain.

Lightning cracked as she rode up the hill. The track became instantly muddy and then turned into a small torrent, while the rain pounding on the bushes to one side made them dance as though a wild breeze had taken them, and thunder crashed across town and harbor.

When she got back, she went to see Harry before going to her room to be helped out of her drenched clothing. He was blissfully asleep, one arm flung out from under the thin sheet. She stood and gazed at him for a while, until she caught sight of herself in the glass over the dresser. She looked dark and brooding in contrast to his bright little form—bedraggled and solitary, hovering over him like some black-feathered bird. She glided away.

Huddled now in Mary's house, looking down at the deserted square, made her feel cold, and she pulled her shawl more tightly over her and wriggled her toes in her silk indoor slippers. She heard the sound of feet on the stairs, recognized the majordomo's tread, and turned as he appeared in the open doorway, holding a candlestick.

"Excuse me, Lady Hamilton, I've just had word from the kitchen. There's a trooper come in from the back lane, sent on detail. He asked if he could have speech with you, milady."

She rose eagerly. "Of course." She took her own candle and followed him down. This might be a last attention from the prince. Or a message from Ellwood. Or the Horse Guards had sent soldiers back for a final round of Bedford Square.

Then she reached the turn of the stairway and saw who stood in the hall below.

Decernay.

For a terrible moment it was like seeing a ghost, as though he had stepped through the barred doors of the dark and bolted house to haunt her. Then he tossed his wet hair out of his face with a flick of his head and met her gaze, and the shock hit her. She took three faltering steps downward and remembered the sentence he had received.

Lawrence reached the foot of the staircase and looked at her inquiringly. She stopped a few stairs above, one hand on the banister, her eyes still fixed on Decernay, her heart racing. He was in uniform—it was sodden and worn, he had no headgear, weapons or kit, but he was still recognizably a Chasseur.

His hair, darkened by the rain, emphasized the extreme pallor of his skin. By the light of the candles she and the majordomo held and a shaded lantern placed on the floor on the other side of the hall, his tall form seemed to tremble, but his gaze remained steady, his eyes under the drawn brows gleaming like river stones.

She shivered, and broke the silence. "How can you be here?"

"I walked." He said it softly, with a lopsided smile.

"Dear God in heaven." She took four steps and raised her voice. "Lawrence, put the lantern in the reception room, if you please." She looked across at Decernay, terrified by the immensity of this moment, desperate not to fail him, as though he were someone to whom she had been linked for a long, uncountable time. She gestured for him to follow her. "This way, monsieur."

He obeyed in silence, with the heavy tread of exhaustion. As he passed by her into the little room and Lawrence emerged, she said to the majordomo, "Can you bring some brandy?"

Decernay stopped in the middle of the floor and turned. His intent look belied his quiet remark: "Thank you, but do not trouble. I cannot stay long."

She waved the majordomo away and entered, the candle wavering in her hand. She put the candlestick on a narrow table just inside the doorway and moved away from it so that the light showed him in all his solidity, sculpting the strong planes of his face, the athletic frame within the travel-worn uniform.

Questions she could not ask surged into her mind. *What have they done to you? Beaten you half to death, then flung you off? How can you still wear those clothes?* She must speak. She heard herself say, "Why are you here?"

He gathered himself, as though about to stand to attention. "Madame, you must allow me to express my gratitude."

"What for?"

His mouth twisted into the sardonic half smile. "What else but the letter? You saved my life." Then he shook his hair off his brow, and with an effort managed to straighten his back. He stood looking down at her with a kind of wild surprise that made her wonder whether he really knew where he was, what he had been doing for the last pain-filled hours. He said again, in a tone of wonder, "You saved my life."

It was like a hand on naked flesh, as though he had reached out and touched her at last. She had never felt so close to him, but it was still not close enough. She had an urgent impulse to draw even nearer, to read him—not with her eyes, but her hands. If she put her fingers to his temple, she could feel whether the beads of moisture there were raindrops or the dew of high fever and exertion. If she laid her palms gently on either side of his

neck she would know whether the stains across the back
and shoulders of his jacket were printed there by rainwa-
ter alone, or by blood when it welled up under the lash.

He shivered, as though she had touched him. He said,
"Who wrote the letter, you or Admiral Metcalfe?"

It startled her. Of course, he might see the letter as a
symbol, a commitment. A claim. She flinched and looked
away, formed words quickly without thinking. "My father and I were concerned that justice should be done."

She did not retreat, but she could not look at him.
His voice was no more than a murmur. "Please thank
the admiral also."

She said automatically, "He is abovestairs." And at
once it hit her that she should have called her father
down, instead of receiving a common soldier alone in an
ill-lit room after midnight. A rough, disgraced enemy
soldier, besides—a renegade Frenchman.

He made an odd sound between his teeth, and she
looked up quickly into his face. His half-open lips had
gone white and his eyelids were fluttering closed; he was
about to faint.

"Sit down at once!" She grabbed an upper arm with
both hers and prepared to take his weight. He staggered,
subsided against her, and she held on, powerless to stop
him collapsing at the last, but able to prevent his back
from connecting with the edge of the chair behind him.

He was half-sitting, crumpled sideways, one elbow on
the floor, with his head lolling over his shoulder. She
sank down beside him, moved his hand so that his forehead rested on one wrist. She had touched his jacket as
he slipped through her hands, and when she took them
away they were sticky with blood.

"Oh heaven. How terrible." Then she cried out for
Lawrence, and when he appeared in the doorway she
sent him away for water and brandy.

Decernay was coming round. With one leg crooked
before him and the other outstretched, he put his palms
on the floor and tried to raise his upper body.

"How can I help you?" She dreaded that he would
subside again. She leaped up, got the candle and brought

it nearer, placing it on a low table next to him. She put one hand to the thick hair that hung over his eyes and pushed it back with her fingers, the other hand cupping the side of his face. The blood was returning to his lips and his cheek felt warm. Even at this, his most vulnerable point, there was a strength in his features that gave him a stern beauty she had seen at once on their first meeting and had yearned to come close to again during all the long intervening months. Now that she was touching him at last, she could hardly resist tracing the generous line of his brows and the smooth curve of his high-bridged nose. She wanted to caress the heavy eyes, brush his half-open lips with hers.

Lawrence returned with a decanter of water, a glass and a bottle of brandy. He paused, fascinated, in the doorway. Sophia's hands drifted away from Decernay and she sat back on her heels.

She beckoned. "Put those here if you please, Lawrence. And tell me, who is Lady Mary's physician?"

With a suppressed groan, Decernay sat up straighter. "No need. I must leave."

"How can you?" she cried.

"It is not far. I was on my way. But I had to see you first."

She looked up at Lawrence's avid face. "I shall call if I need you."

As the majordomo withdrew out of sight, Decernay reached out, poured some brandy into the glass and brought it to his lips. He drank, shuddered, then took another gulp and closed his eyes. He opened them again, straight onto hers.

"In a moment I will . . . *débarrasser* . . . disembarrass your floor."

She shrank back a little, feeling suddenly helpless and torn. "Please. You must not move before you are able."

His gaze darkened. "But you want me to go. It is my pleasure to oblige you. Then you will be safe. Papa is upstairs."

It felt like mockery. She shrank back and her lips trembled as she said, "I tried to help you."

He did not reply. He put the glass on the table, gathered his long legs under him and with the aid of the chair pushed himself up onto his feet. She rose and moved away, recapturing the shawl that had caught at her elbows and wrapping it across her chest.

His eyes were half-closed, but his look was penetrating. "This is the first time I have seen you out of mourning."

She started. "We have met but twice, monsieur."

"No, I saw you often in Sydney Town. Whenever I could catch a glimpse of you. And you came to watch me sail away."

"Really!" She sounded indignant.

He said, "What does *really* mean? I beg you to talk to me. Say what you mean."

He could have no idea how such words and looks offended her delicacy. Or perhaps he did, and the offense was intentional. Perhaps he resented having received mercy at the hands of an Englishwoman who was above him in breeding and station. Yet she had cast herself down on the floor to minister to him. She was absurdly hurt and confused. And at the same time she understood his resentment—for all she wanted was to press her body to his and wrap her arms around him, and he knew she would not.

He looked at her with a kind of fierce compassion and made her a bow, as meticulously as if he were a guest departing the house after supper. His manner and voice had a refinement that was eerie in the circumstances. "Lady Hamilton, you have no idea how much I would like to confide in you about the event that brought us together. But the story is not mine alone. If I can find the man who—" Then suddenly he put one fist to his forehead. "No. I came to thank you. Now I must leave."

Baffled, she said at once, "Where can you go? To the barracks?"

He lowered his hand. "Madame, I am no longer a soldier."

"Then why do you wear that uniform?"

"It is all I have. But tomorrow I put it off forever. I

will never fight again, for your country or mine." He walked out of the room.

The majordomo was hovering in the hall. As they approached him, Sophia said, "Would you open the door and see that the way is clear?"

While Lawrence pulled back the bolts, Sophia looked sideways at Decernay, with the insane impulse to say, *I spent the day in terror for you.* Instead she took up his last comment. "In one respect you have reaped an advantage, monsieur. You cannot be called back into service against Napoleon Bonaparte."

The door stood open before him, but his head turned and his eyes bored into hers. *"Quoi?"*

"Bonaparte has escaped from Elba." Too late, she remembered the promise to her father. She could only plunge on. "He is heading for Paris, with an army."

He went white with such cruel rapidity she thought he would faint again. He put a hand against the doorpost and hissed, *"Non."*

She had never seen such fear. It was as though she had him at knifepoint. She drew closer and put a hand on his free arm. "Remember, you have been discharged. They cannot make you fight now."

He rounded on her, his eyes haggard. "Is that what you think of me? *Si vous saviez.*" He pulled himself away and strode down the steps. Before he walked off, he turned and gave her a last look, his chin thrust out and his eyes burning. *"Comme je vous plains."*

If you only knew. How I pity you.

CHAPTER SEVEN

Grenoble, 8 March

It's the first time I've been warm for days; we're surrounded by fires and food, and the town is dizzy with
drink and ambition. First time you can imagine spring;
when we marched through the snow here today one of the
boys swore he'd seen swallows darting over the column.
Tonight they'll be snug like us in sheltered niches, the
blue skies of tomorrow filling their tiny heads. Bonaparte
claims he'll be in Paris in time to see the violets bloom.
He has spring fever too.

Eight hundred men came out to stop us at Laffrey, led
by General Jean-Gabriel Marchand, who once received
the Grand Eagle of the Legion of Honor from the little
bastard himself. And all they did was beg us to withdraw!
So he took his golden chance, yet again. "Soldiers of the
5th Infantry Regiment, I am your emperor. If there is any
man among you who wishes to kill his emperor, here I
am," and he bared his chest. Sore temptation, but I didn't
have the right line of fire. Then there was a great shout
and they broke ranks and flung themselves at him, press-
ing their lips to his coat, his boots, his sword.

I've gotten the picture now. Took me a while, but I
have it clear. There's no one fit to stand in his way between here and Lyons. And when he gets there, you can't

*see the king's brother putting up much of a fight. If they
break ranks under Marchand they'll give the Comte d'Ar-
tois the finger before we even come in sight.*

*So I'll have to choose my moment before Lyons. I've
sent the message, addressed to Monsieur Robert in Paris,
with a courier I can trust who's going north, along with
a flock of dispatch riders. By the time the gentleman gets
it, I'll have done the deed. The date: day after tomorrow.
The means: foul. I have no illusions. And no mercy. It's
time to pluck the eagle out of the sky.*

Word that Napoleon was on his way to Paris reached
Vienna late on Wednesday 8 March and Prince
Metternich was the first to receive it. He had just enjoyed a festive evening that included some inventive parlor games, and he was preparing to sleep off the mild
stimulation it had afforded. The news was like a scouring
dose of salts.

Thereafter, the powers at the Congress summoned an
energy for action that they had not shown in months,
preparing to name Bonaparte an outlaw and prohibit
intercourse between him and the countries of Europe.
Any government that he might form was to be condemned as contrary to the law of nations. Now allies in
a common cause, they came to further decisions with
novel swiftness: Bonaparte was to be destroyed, and the
commander charged with his destruction was the Duke
of Wellington, who was expected to return to England.

He was preceded by hordes of English refugees, who
had resumed visiting Paris since peace had been
achieved the year before, to pursue the pleasure, entertainment and fashion that it traditionally supplied to the
refined members of the British ruling class. Now they
fled in droves, packing in haste and heading for the coast
through relentless rain that turned the highroads into
quagmires.

A week or so later they were still straggling in through
the ports of southern England. If they stopped over at
the better inns of Hastings, Eastbourne or Newhaven
before going on to London, they exchanged commisera-

tion and news amongst themselves but brought few details to pass on to anyone else. All they could report was that Louis XVIII had so far remained at the Tuileries, and Marshal Ney had marched south to intercept his former emperor, with the public promise that he would bring him back in an iron cage.

Sebastian Coole gathered this kind of news on visits to Newhaven, but superior information was in fact to be had nearer home at the army barracks at Exceat. He had struck up an easy acquaintance with the commander and his officers, and it was pleasant to ride west along the edge of Friston Forest on a raw day and be invited to dine in the mess, in their agreeable company.

The place was only a few years old, built on the land of Viscount Gage to furnish one of the army's training grounds during the war against Napoleon, and it still supplied soldiers to garrison the Martello towers along the south coast. In the present crisis, the officers felt an added sense of their own importance, and red coats had surged back into fashion.

"Decent set of chaps in the Bengal Light Cavalry?" Major Hooper asked him one afternoon, as they lingered by the fire in the guard room.

"Highly experienced."

Hooper's hazel eyes lit up. "Skirmishers, eh?" He was a neatly built, busy man, who sat well forward in his chair, as though ready to leap out of it at a moment's notice to perform some urgent task. "You don't miss the action?"

Sebastian shrugged and lounged back on the wooden settle he occupied on the other side of the hearth. "These days I get quite enough at home."

"Not thinking of going back into active service, then?"

"I'd need to be damned sure there was good cause."

"Cause! Bonaparte's waltzed into Lyons without shedding a drop of blood. King Louis can't rally any support, even from his own family. No one even looks like stopping Boney; they're going down before him like ninepins and every town he's touched flies the tricolor. Wait until he gets to Paris—then we'll see cause enough and to spare."

"I'm happy to wait," Sebastian said. "I came down to Birlingdean for a bit of quiet, but I've never been so occupied in all my days. Farms, coverts and grounds—there's a deal to be put in train. Would you believe there's scarcely a pheasant to be seen about the estate? Now, there are the things I miss about India—the shooting, the hunting and the horses. What I'd give for a string of the fine, nimble ponies we had in the northern hills."

"Nothing else you miss?" the major said jovially. "What of the women, eh?"

Sebastian gave him a measuring glance and suddenly wondered whether Hooper had heard anything. He said suavely, "Despite the climate, English beauty is as refreshing to see there as anywhere. And it's in stunning contrast to the people. To see an elegant Englishwoman side by side with a beautiful Indian woman is an extraordinary picture."

The major grinned. "Then I take it you pledged allegiance to both?"

Sebastian rose. "I shall do that for one person only." He gave the major time to look confused. "The lady who consents to become Mrs. Coole."

When he rode away, he paused to look down on the barracks, and well beyond them at the shadowed Cuckmere River and the bridge, before turning his hunter along the high ground toward home. There was no way of knowing whether the officers could possibly have caught the whispers from Bombay. It ought not to matter to him one way or the other, but it did, because of Delia.

He allowed himself to think about her for a while as the hunter ambled along in the pale afternoon sun.

Delia Goulding, the beautiful wife of his general, openly admired and secretly coveted by all the officers, and accepting their worship without flirtation or disdain. Before he met her, he heard one of the other colonels say, "She is the most complete little Venus." And he promised himself at once that he would never fall so abjectly under any woman's spell.

The devil of it was that she fell under his. Or so she gave him to understand, when he had known her just a month. They were in a group playing croquet on the dreadful stretch of parched lawn by the club, and he was advising her on how to retrieve an errant ball without too much disadvantage to her game. They were at a distance and standing with their backs to the others, so he suggested several ploys, all contrary to the rules and all rather silly, and they dissolved into hilarity.

She looked up at him with moist eyes and exclaimed, "Oh, it is *so good* to laugh!"

In that moment he saw how young and vulnerable she was. He felt the nearness of her slender, pliant body and pitied her for being yoked to a humorless automaton twice her age, whose vigor resided solely in his bristling sideburns. He told himself she needed a friend and vowed to amuse her.

It was easy; he was always part of the group and she did not distinguish him overtly. There was no dalliance, just an understanding that both wanted to deepen. He never realized he was in danger because there were no consequences to threaten him—just a sweetness added to his life that he was completely unprepared for. His first love, years before in Dublin, had been fraught and painful, and he could not remember it without wincing with a curious kind of anger. By contrast, the progress of his attachment to Delia had been disarmingly smooth.

Then, somehow, the desire to be close to her became harder and harder to disguise as companionship. And when she began to arrange secret meetings, with a dexterity that took his breath away, he had neither the will nor the power to refuse.

He told himself he should seek another posting. He had no right to risk her reputation, to injure her husband or allow her to violate her marriage—but knowing all this did not give him the strength to break it off. Instead he took precautions that were as elaborate as those she contrived herself. He made sure it was rumored that he kept an Indian paramour in a house on the outskirts of the city. He volunteered for every mission that would take him out of town—it was torture to part from Delia, but the reunion when he came back was all the more passionate.

He knew it had to end before it led to her ruin and his, but he could not manage it alone. In a sense, the most thrilling period of his life was also the most frightening—because he was faced with something intimate and profound that was quite beyond his control. From then on, he believed that any man who discounted the power of women was an idiot.

Finally, the army made the decision for him. He learned that General Goulding's whole division was being transferred north, and the news came at a time when a number of career choices were being offered to him. After a short, agonizing battle with himself, he made the commitment to leave also—for England.

He remembered the moment in the club where the British residents gathered to farewell the officers; he tore the words out as the others looked on, some of them perhaps guessing what they cost him. He fixed his eyes on her, fearing what her reaction would be, because he had not warned her, or had more than a few snatched words with her since her husband's announcement. He remembered her look of wounded surprise, her white face, the way she pressed her lips together as though he had struck her. He still did not know whose suffering had been the greater when they parted—hers or his. Reason told him to hope she had already banished him from her thoughts. As for himself, neither his journey nor his return to England had taught him to forget.

When he broached the green curve of upland above Birlingdean, he pulled out his watch. The sun had not touched the horizon, but it was later than he had thought; he had still to get used to the progress of the seasons here. He did not adjust his pace, however, since after all there was nothing to hurry home for.

Birlingdean, a vast, rambling, two-storied Tudor house

in intricately patterned red brick, was sheltered at the head of a valley. A spring just below the house fed the ornamental lake, then flowed through the grounds, meandered along the bottom and lost itself in marshy land a few miles farther on, well before it could reach the sea at distant and invisible Birling Gap. On the other side of the valley, perched on higher ground with views of rolling pasture and the ocean, was Clifton, the old home of the Metcalfe family.

Sebastian gave it all a sweeping look as he reached the brow from which both the great houses could be seen. The sun behind him threw his own long shadow across the track he was on, which joined a wider road ahead that dipped down the slope about a quarter of a mile from Birlingdean and continued to the floor of the valley. The past week of steady rain had turned the bottoms into mud, but on the chalk heights the water drained away quickly, leaving the white paths and highways powdery and dry.

The part of the road that sloped past Birlingdean was so steep it was known as the Chute, and the weight of a carriage pushed so relentlessly downward that the horses before it were always driven at a steady walk. Once they got past the grand gates of the Birlingdean drive, however, the angle of the descent eased, and equipages tended to put on speed so that they careered across the ford at the bottom with a dramatic crashing of hooves and flurry of water.

In the still evening air he could hear the progress of a vehicle and four horses below, and when he reached the road and looked down he could see it through a gap in the trees as it began its swift run to the stream. It was a private carriage of modest size, but it looked overloaded; he could make out two figures up beside the coachman—a woman and a child.

It was at about this time that Lady Hamilton was expected to go by on her way to Clifton. But surely she would not ride outside the carriage? Here was an eventuality he could not have foreseen.

Neat and well sprung, the vehicle swayed as it rounded

the curve approaching the ford. Suddenly the horses faltered and then ran ragged, the front of the vehicle plunged downward before giving a great bounce in the air, the back slewed round as it reached the bank of the stream and then the whole equipage collapsed to one side, hitting the stones on an angle and plunging with its screaming horses and helpless occupants straight over the edge into the deep water on the downstream side of the ford.

Without a second's hesitation, Sebastian put spurs to his hunter and took the Chute at a gallop, racing headlong to the disaster below.

Sophia could not open her eyes. She could hear a pounding, like hooves, and beneath that the rushing of a torrent that had wrenched something from her arms and borne it away. Her hands were empty, for she could feel mud under her palms, soft and slimy. Perhaps she had sunk deep down to the bottom and was already drowned, and what pressed on her mouth and eyes was the heavy, cold course of a river.

She could not breathe; her chest had collapsed under the same massive pressure.

At the same time, while she struggled against the paralysis, she heard other sounds—a confusion of voices in the distance, and nearby the thud of feet on grass, the jingle of spurs, the scrape of boots over rocks.

Her name was called out. "It's Lady Hamilton, sir."

And another man spoke from directly above her. "*This is she?*" The shocked pause seemed very long. Then he was beside her and she felt fingers on her neck. "A pulse. Come!" he called. "We must get her out of the water."

At some distance there was a squelching and slithering of boots along the bank. Meanwhile she felt an arm slide behind her neck and shoulders and a hand smooth the hair back from her face. "Mother of God," he whispered. "Look at her."

Released by the slight movement, her lungs were at last able to expand properly, and she shivered and took a breath. Her eyes opened and she looked up into a handsome face hovering over hers that betrayed, in that unguarded moment, all the anxious tenderness a lover might have shown.

Then she came to herself, and gasped, and brought one hand up to catch at his arm. "Harry."

Her coachman loomed into view on the other side and the gentleman looked up. "Take her around the knees, carefully, man, and we'll get her to the bank."

She took a deeper breath. "Harry," she said again, and frantic tears flooded her eyes.

They began to move her. The hands under her shoulders were strong and adept and his voice was curt. "The boy?"

"On the bank, sir."

"Fetch him," said the voice of authority.

As the coachman disappeared, the gentleman snatched off his greatcoat, laid it on the grass and lifted her onto it, then doubled the wings over her body, trapping her limbs. She tried to move, but he knelt beside her and caught her hands through the thick flannel of the coat, locking them down with his fingers. "Lie still until you are warm. You were winded; you must breathe deep. Then tell me—are you in pain? Are you hurt anywhere?"

"Where is my son?"

"In a moment."

"What has happened to him?"

"You were all thrown from the perch when the carriage went over. You and the man went into shallow water, your son was swept downstream. But he fetched up against bushes and made his way out. And here he is."

Harry was deposited on the grass beside her—soaked to the skin, his hair plastered to his scalp, his brown eyes wide and staring like those of a little hunted animal. As soon as she turned to him, he opened his mouth in a high, desperate wail. She sat up at once, against the gentleman's cautionary hand on her shoulder. Opening the coat, she swept Harry in, wrapped him against her and poured tears and kisses on the top of his head.

He could not stop howling, but, as she felt hastily all over his body, he seemed to have no fractures or grazes.

"Excuse me just a few seconds." The gentleman rose to his feet and went to assist the coachman, who was cutting two of the stricken horses away from the wreckage in midstream. The other two had been trampled beneath them and had drowned with the frightful rapidity of their kind. One body remained submerged, but the other, once released from the trailing harness and the weight of its fellows, shifted downstream with the current until it rolled against a sandy embankment and came to rest with its legs in the air.

Holding Harry tightly, weeping into his hair, Sophia kept his face turned away from the scene as the two men helped the other horses up the bank. The coachman took off his waistcoat, wrung it out, and rubbed down their backs and chests, trying to curse and pummel them out of their terror.

Harry stopped crying and buried his face in her shoulder. The gentleman returned to her side.

"My gamekeeper was by and saw the accident. I sent him at once to the house. He should be here any moment with the gig. Allow me to drive you both to Birlingdean, and the men will follow with the horses. As for this"—he jerked his head toward the stream—"it can all wait until morning. It will be dark soon."

"Birlingdean?" She looked up at him, her mind beginning to assert itself. "I was on my way to Clifton."

"You cannot possibly go on now. Permit me to offer you shelter for the night."

"You are Cousin Sebastian."

"At your service, Lady Hamilton." He dropped neatly onto his heels, slipped his hand into a pocket of the greatcoat where it trailed on the grass, and handed her a square of white, spotless silk. Then he watched in silence as she wiped the mud and tears from her face. Through her fingers she saw his eyelids flicker, then open into a lingering glance that still held, in the depths of his green eyes, a hint of the wonder that had been in his voice when he first saw her.

Sophia rather expected Harry to be frightened in the vast, lonely house, but the next morning he slipped out of her bed where she had brought him in the small hours, unlocked the door and padded downstairs wrapped in a rug. Before she was awake he had found the kitchen, where his clothes were hanging warm and dry before the fire, and the cook had buttoned him into them and given him breakfast.

He informed her of all this as she sat before a glass pinning up her hair. He looked refreshed, his eyes bright. "Cousin Sebastian said I can poke about a bit. But not outside."

"That's very considerate of him." She looked at him sideways. "But don't go running off without me. It's easy to get lost in Birlingdean if you don't know it."

"But *you* do, Mama?"

"Yes."

"Show me, then."

When they went out into the corridor, she hesitated. It would be polite to go down, greet her host and join him in the breakfast room. But she had no desire for breakfast, and she felt a strange awkwardness about facing Sebastian Coole. The night before, he had driven her to the house and then put his servants at her disposal so that she and Harry could get out of their wet clothes, have hot baths and change into dry garments—those she wore being in fact old spare ones of her own, which had lain in storage for years and were somewhat musty in consequence. There had been little time or inclination for talk between them, and once the bedrooms were ready she was too exhausted to do anything but retire, though she made sure Harry took some supper. It was nothing like the meeting she had planned: a polite invitation for Colonel Coole to call at Clifton, a chance for her to see what she thought of the man who now lived in Andrew's house, slept in his room and presided over the park and the farms that had been the care and pride of his life.

She took Harry's hand. "I'll tell you what; I'll show you just one spot." She walked along the corridor to a set of back stairs. "Up there is the old nursery. And there's a big room next to it where your papa and I used to play games when we were little."

Harry pulled ahead, let go of her hand and pounded up the wooden stairs. "What games? Are there toys?"

"All sorts," she said, against the noise that rang down the stairwell. It seemed a long time since her son's voice had woken the echoes of Birlingdean.

Harry had found the room and was already clambering up on the rocking horse when she paused on the threshold. The place had been a haunt on wet days, a refuge at the end of cold afternoons where she and Andrew could balance toasting forks before the fire and think up the next morning's excursions. Where later they had read or written letters together, and talked of the future that was to bring them a miraculous continuation of the happiness they already shared. A place for the exchange of secrets and vows.

She stood in the middle of the room while Harry rummaged about, answering his comments on each new find at random. Here among the boxes and chairs and screens, she and Andrew had devised treasure hunts. They had hidden notes—slipped under the cover of a book, tucked into the hatband of a sailor doll, poked through the window of a miniature wooden coach drawn by hand-carved horses.

And then it came to her. Nineteen months before, when Andrew's death had been confirmed and she could bring herself to settle his affairs, she and the steward had searched out and gone through all the papers relating to the family estate. Most of them had been locked away in drawers and coffers in the study and library; some had been in legal safekeeping. She believed she had read every document Andrew would have wished her to see. But that was before she learned that he might have been a spy for England.

She closed her eyes, asked herself a disturbing question. Andrew had concealed that particular truth from her while he was alive, but, knowing the danger that he might be killed, could he have left her an explanation, a farewell, a kind of apology for the only secret he had ever kept from her? If so, surely he would not have wanted it to be amongst his official papers, the first ones she would see in the freshness of her grief. No, the letter would be here, in their private place, where she would find it eventually, at a time when any perils it described would be past. When it would be far safer, a little less painful, for her to discover it.

It was poignant, fingering the dusty, abandoned toys. The dolls had all but crumbled away and only their porcelain faces retained the tender colors of the past. The carousel music box jangled when she lifted it to look underneath, as though begging her to turn the stiff little key and wind it up. She was glad Harry did not ask her to; he was busy pushing the coach across the carpet.

He looked up, however, when she crouched down in front of the fireplace. "What are you doing?"

"There used to be a loose brick. No one noticed it except your papa and I. They all fit so well, you see?"

"Oooh." He came over. "Is it this one?" And with the pressure of his chubby fingers, she saw it move a little.

"Yes!" Together they pried it free, and she nearly dropped it on the hearth.

There was no letter. But something was there, resting against a cavity in the brick behind. It was a key. Not a door key, and perhaps not even the key to a desk or chest, for it was no larger than that of the music box.

Harry took it out. It glowed on his palm—it was brass, kept untarnished in the airless space behind the brick.

"Can I have it, Mama? What is it for?"

Shaken for a moment, she could not answer. She maneuvered the brick back into place. Harry slipped the key into his pocket, and she looked up and past him.

Sebastian Coole stood in the doorway.

She rose quickly.

He was very still. Standing half in shadow, with his

smooth black hair framing the tanned face and dark-ringed eyes, he looked watchful, even menacing.

She stammered out, "Good morning."

Then he stepped into the room and smiled. "Good day, Lady Hamilton. I wondered where I should find you. I hope you are fully recovered?"

"Thank you, we are both very much better."

"I am delighted to hear it. Will you join me for breakfast?" He stepped to one side and gestured toward the door. As she went past him he gave Harry a swift, speculative glance. There was no way of telling whether he had seen Harry take the key, or whether he was annoyed if he had. She did not feel obliged to raise it with him.

Jacques lay on his front in the rumpled bed, listening. It was his first opportunity to gauge the sounds in the household and form some idea of the lives of the family friends who had taken him in. The de Villiers, of an old Normandy line like his parents, had lived in London since 1793 and had no intention of going back to France, but they had kept up contacts across the Channel. He had never meant to make use of them while he was in England, but he had had no choice. Once he got to their door, he could go no farther.

Since then the days had melted one into the other, and there were times when he had no idea where he was. They brought a physician to him, but the strangers around his bed all seemed equally his enemies, and he pushed their hands away when they tried to give him liquids, which were all he managed to keep down.

The half-conscious stupor that followed each fever wiped away all memory of what he might have said or done to his long-suffering hosts and their servants.

He could recall only one visit with clarity. Virginie, the youngest of the family, had come to his bedside late at night with a candle in her hand, while one of the upper maids was snoring in a big chair by the fire. When she glided into his room, the dim, wavering flame lit her like an apparition.

"What is it?" he said in French.

She looked nervous but determined. "You cried out. I heard you from my room."

"I'm sorry." His cheek was buried in the damp pillow, but he tried to raise his hand to clear his eyes.

She sank down beside the bed, put the candle on the little table and wrung out a cloth that was lying in a bowl of water. Then she lightly pressed the coolness onto his skin.

"You must rest and get well. They say you are past the worst fever. Don't be afraid. We are looking after you."

Her voice was gentle, and her face by the light of the candle glowed with youthful conviction.

She took his free hand. "You're so hot." She wound the wet cloth around his wrist and kept his fingers in hers.

The pain came in waves, as always. When this one ebbed, he sought her gaze again and his mouth twisted. He could no longer see her clearly, but he felt the touch of her cheek on the back of his hand.

"You must not be lonely. When you are better, we will help you to get home." He murmured his thanks as she glided from the room.

Now that his strength was beginning to return, he must reorganize his affairs and leave. But not for home. There were too many failures to admit to, and a promise unfulfilled. And, most imperious of all, there was a woman to whom he was linked in more ways than she guessed, whom he could not leave behind him.

All his life, Jacques had followed an impulsive, restless spirit that made him plunge into action for the thrill of it, for the sake of the change and adventure to come. Even his older brother René, who loved and understood him, said once, "Don't you ever stop and think? Are you ever going to be serious about anything?"

Jacques had laughed, then said, "Everything I do, I choose. With the greatest anticipation. With my eyes open."

"And what do you get out of it all?"

"Life—to the hilt."

He had been right, but in the wrong way, for he had discovered again and again what chance could throw in his path. All his brave choices, taken in the heat of each encounter, had brought the cold consequences of guilt and remorse.

Then he met Sophia Hamilton. Until that day, he had believed there was no escape from a past full of wrong turnings, or from a future dominated by one dark, fell purpose. But his first confrontation with her had illuminated all his crowded, burdensome thoughts and all his confused desires as if with a clean, penetrating light.

His world had been made new again. From that moment, he lived with the idea of her in his consciousness and the sound of her voice in his blood. This, at last, was what René had meant. This was serious. He could never let her go.

Sebastian admired the way Sophia Hamilton dealt with the aftermath of the accident. She was calm and efficient, quite different from the wounded creature he had folded in his arms the day before.

He sat in the morning room with her while she interviewed the coachman. Sebastian had ridden down to the ford himself an hour earlier, and she turned to him once or twice as the man summed up.

The coach seemed past repair. The remains, squashed as flat as a cigar box, were still in midstream, but the man had waded in to take a good look. If she and the boy had been traveling inside, instead of with the coachman—a treat that Harry had begged for at the top of the Chute—there was no doubt they would have been crushed and drowned like the two unlucky horses.

The cause of the accident lay in the road itself, where no one had noticed the havoc wrought by recent heavy rains. It was explained to Lady Hamilton that runoff from the hillside must have taken a new course and scoured a channel into the stony surface, just before the ford, that was as deep as a ditch. In the dusk, the coach-

man had failed to see it. The horses had cleverly negotiated the gap, but when the front of the coach plunged
into it, the impact was enough to sheer off one wheel.

Lady Hamilton refrained from looking at Sebastian
when that detail was mentioned, and he was grateful. He
had been down in the country only a few days longer than
she, he had a host of other responsibilities, and he could
scarcely have been expected to get around to looking at
the road; but he was partially liable for its upkeep, along
with Clifton. It was not a high road, so its maintenance
fell on the district—which of course meant the landowners,
who bought the stone for mending and paid the laborers.

He debated with himself for a second and decided not
to tell her that he had in fact paid some road menders
to attend to the surface only the day before yesterday.
It might sound self-defensive to her ears.

He had three men down there now, making it passable
before her other vehicle went by, carrying her maid and
a couple of other servants with all her effects from
London.

A message had been sent to Clifton the night before,
warning the household of her late arrival and ordering
the curricle for midday.

"A curricle?" Sebastian said.

"Indeed. It will be here, Combe, without fail?"

"I can vouch for that, milady. It's in better shape than
your coach will ever be, more's the pity. Speaking of
which, are we to haul the wreckage home, or dispose of
it some'ow?"

"Have three men bring the Shires down with a dray
this afternoon."

Combe stood in the middle of the room, turning his
hat round and round in his big hands by its brim.
Throughout, he had borne up under the disaster as
though it were a personal tragedy. Lady Hamilton gave
him an understanding look. Her voice was low and hesitant as she said, "And the horses, Combe?"

"The two dead 'uns are buried, milady." A dejected
pause, "The others will be fit to walk home tomorrow."

"I'll see they're well cared for," Sebastian said.

She gave him a grateful look, then nodded to the coachman as he withdrew. "Thank you. And take heart—we are all very fortunate to be alive."

"Milady," he said with feeling, bowed and went out.

Sebastian raised one eyebrow. "A *curricle*?"

"It is the only thing on wheels that I have left, apart from the farm carts. It has not been driven for years, but Combe is an expert. It will cheer him up to drive me home in it. And amuse Harry."

"For a moment I thought you were going to take the reins yourself."

"I don't think so. Though I've often wondered how it might go on a hunt. Queen Anne used to drive after the hounds in something similar, up hill and down dale, forty or fifty miles in a day."

He smiled. "I remember better than that. You said you would never hunt."

"Oh," she said. "You recall the day, then?"

"Perfectly." The three children had been on an expedition into Friston Forest, dodging amongst the trees in some game, when they came across a fox in a trap. They all saw it at once: the mangled body, the orange fur darkened with blood, the dull eyes, too exhausted even to express fear as they crept forward. And there was worse: someone had cut off the brush as a trophy, while the fox was still alive, in its last agony.

Sebastian had shuddered and turned away. Sophia had cried out, then shed tears. Andrew had stepped forward and sprung the trap. As he lifted the animal's body from the jaws it went limp and died in his hands.

Sebastian said, holding her gaze, "Will you despise me if I tell you that I intend to hunt with the local meet while I am here?"

She looked at him gravely. "I must be forgiving to any gentleman who asks me such a question. There are few to whom it would even occur."

"I took your son to see the puppies in my kennels this morning. Do you mind?"

She gave a little laugh. "All you risk there is his undying devotion."

He saw with interest a faint blush on her cheeks as she said the words. It gave him the courage to say, "May I know, Lady Hamilton, whether you have told your son in what relation he and I stand to Birlingdean?"

Her eyes widened. "You mean, does he know he is the heir? No. I shall not discuss it with him, and I would prefer others not to either. I do not believe in young children debating such things."

"As you wish. Since you are so firm on the matter."

She gave him a look of apology. "I had a sad example before my eyes once. I was fifteen, staying with relations in Kent, on a beautiful estate, well worth coveting. I was in the park with the children, three little girls, and their cousin from France was with them; his name was Nicolas. I shall never forget him standing on the top of a mound where the girls were playing, and looking about him and saying, 'When your father dies all this will be mine. I'm a boy and I'll inherit. You're girls, so you don't count.'" She shook her head.

"And did he?"

"No." Her lips twitched. "The countess had a son the very next year." After a pause, she said, "I cannot wish any child to grow up with such attitudes."

"Nor be the mother who would allow him to," he said gently.

She looked at him with a smile; it was the first she had granted him. "But you observe that I spoil him, nonetheless."

It was a test. "I think . . ." He tried to be tactful. "I think you find him a most agreeable companion."

Her smile broadened and she said on a whimsical sigh, "How pleasurable it is sometimes, just to be understood."

CHAPTER EIGHT

After midnight, 20 March

My name is Robert. Eight days ago I received a message I have long dreaded to see, from a man whose face I have difficulty recalling. But his name is clear enough in my mind, though he dared not add it to the note. Bertrand. Who is now dead.

What must I do?

Nothing, for now, except wait for Bonaparte to reach Paris. Meanwhile the king has fled. The review of the Royal Household Guard in the Champ de Mars was a blind, with only two ministers being in the know. Others have left with him, given the inducement of one hundred thousand francs each, cash in hand.

When I got the message from Grenoble on the twelfth it was a shock. Then when Bonaparte was reported to be on the move again, and I knew Bertrand must have paid the price at Lyons, it chilled me to the bone. I thought I'd been spared this task—but here it is, after all. Eight men have gone before me and it's my turn.

Napoleon is well past Auxerre, Ney has joined him and deserters from the king's army are tramping the roads to meet him on the way. Today is the fourth birthday of Napoleon's son, the little King of Rome—how many more portents do we need? Though it seems doubtful whether

*the empress will bring the child to Paris to greet his Papa;
I mentioned it today to Joseph Fouché, Duke of Otranto,
and got nothing but a cynical smile.*

*The situation of Napoleon's former ministers and ad-
ministrators is extremely delicate. Watching people realign
themselves when he arrives will be a fine study. For myself, I intend no preparations. Sufficient unto the day—a
policy that has always worked superlatively for Fouché,
the jackal.*

*I have nothing prepared. If the man before me has
failed, despite the opportunities that the long march must
have afforded, how am I to succeed in a city imbued with
fear, ambition, mistrust and patriotisms of so many hues
that there could never be space for them all on the
same flag?*

*I burned the paper the second after I unfolded it, and
singed my fingers. No plan sprang to mind. All I can
think is: he is coming.*

Sophia was riding Scheherazade over the Downs on a
glorious day. It was the first time she had been able
to take the filly on an outing, and the exercise was badly
needed. The beautiful chestnut had made it down to
Clifton much earlier than she, walking in easy stages and
glutted with feed at every stop. Settling down with her
new handlers and spending day after day in the stables
had made the filly thoroughly bored, so she was frisky
when ridden out of the yard, and responded with eager-
ness to Sophia's touch.

Sophia rode toward the sea, across farmland of close-
cropped turf that was the color of emeralds. A southerly
breeze carrying the tang of salt stirred her senses, and
for a while she gave herself over to the enjoyment of
the ride.

She was glad to be home amongst her own familiar
scenes, and that surprised her. She had expected the return to be troubled and sad, but somehow the violence
of the accident below Birlingdean, her bizarre arrival,
had swept her misgivings aside. She had imagined there
would be some pain in introducing Harry to the home

that he had been too young to miss, and which he had shared with the father he could scarcely remember. Andrew had understood her love of Clifton and had known what a wrench it would be if he took her away from it directly after their marriage—so, in one of the many sacrifices he made for the good of others, he had taken up residence with her there, and managed Birlingdean from across the valley. Sophia deeply wanted Harry to feel as safe and sheltered in Clifton as she did. Fortunately, he adored it at once.

With some advice from a Newhaven coach maker, it was concluded that her carriage could be repaired after all. A shaft and one axle needed replacement, but the rest could be reconstructed. The coach maker had shaken his head about the broken axle; no matter what the impact might have been, he reckoned it should not have snapped. He promised a much sturdier chassis for the renovated carriage, which he would put together at his premises in town. Meanwhile he had let her have another vehicle on hire.

She saw no one on the ride, apart from a couple of shepherds far off with their flocks. There were no farmhouses on the great green expanse that faced the sea; her tenant farmers all had dwellings in the shelter of the valley below Clifton. Some ran bullocks but most had sheep, which were held in folds so that they grazed the grassland by stages to within a safe margin of the tall white cliffs that formed the edge of their world. By now she had seen and spoken to all the tenants and to the manager of the home farm, in company with her steward. A quick survey of the countryside had shown her that there was much to be done before the spring advanced too far. But she would attend to all that another day.

She brought the filly to a halt, a hundred yards or so from the clifftop. On a more experienced horse she would not have hesitated to take the bridle path at the edge, from which a rider could look along the undulating margin of the land toward the slope that led to the tiny village of Birling Gap. But it was too soon for Scheherazade, who stood with her ears pricked toward the ocean, tossing her head and sniffing the salt-laden breeze. Sophia had rather expected the filly to dislike the smell of the sea, after being shipped halfway around the world from New South Wales, but the quivering, lithe body beneath her seemed to respond to the place as she did herself. Poised on their green platform, before the great crescent of blue sea under the wide, cloud-flecked sky, both were seized by exhilaration.

The next move was irresistible. This was Sophia's favorite place for a gallop—a smooth expanse of resilient turf on which her family had trained horses for three generations. True to family discipline, she trotted the distance twice to observe the ground. Finding no rabbit holes or small obstacles on the way, she wheeled the filly at the farthest limit, then gave her her head.

Scheherazade gathered herself up and took the chance like the thoroughbred she was. It was as though the long, stifling voyage belowdecks and the transition to Sussex had never occurred. She picked up her heels and darted across the sward with the same speed and grace that had caught Sophia's eye on the raw dirt racetrack outside Sydney Town the year before.

It was like flying. Sophia wanted never to stop.

But the end of the stretch was approaching, and another rider abruptly appeared, dead in front of them, surging up into view from the direction of Birling Gap on a big gray horse.

The sudden apparition was startling, and the rhythm of Scheherazade's stride altered at once. If Sophia had not been such a practiced rider she might have been unseated, but with a struggle she managed to keep in control. The jolt was such that she felt angry with the other rider, unreasonably—after all, it was not as though he had done it on purpose!—but she composed herself and the filly, and by the time they reached the lone rider they had slowed to a trot.

Sophia said, a little breathless, "Good day to you, Colonel." Scheherazade gave a snort and eyed the sleek gray hunter as she came to a prancing halt.

"Good heavens." Sebastian Coole swept off his high hat. "Lady Hamilton. You fill me with awe." But he looked slightly disapproving, and after a glance at the empty landscape behind her he could not help asking, "You have no groom with you?"

She shook her head apologetically, then chided herself. Another gentleman might have felt *he* should make an apology! But perhaps he was not aware that he had nearly spooked Scheherazade. Her reply sounded cold. "I always ride alone."

"At such breakneck speed?"

"That depends." She turned so that the horses could walk on side by side, in the direction of Clifton. During the small silence that followed she willed herself not to explain. But she had phrased her answer badly—it required a sequel.

Finally she said, "I was trying out Scheherazade's paces. I brought her here from New South Wales, and we have not decided what to do with her yet. We may race her. If not, she will become a broodmare, the finest we have."

"We?" He looked amused now, and the smooth Irish voice had a teasing lilt to it.

She stole a further glance at him. He rode the tall hunter with confidence, his taut body erect, and he had a firm hand on the reins. There was a kind of easy completeness about him that bespoke the country gentleman of means. Yet the perfect portrait hinted at a more vulnerable man beneath the surface. When the sun caught his eyes the green irises went quite pale, as though he had been momentarily taken off guard. And his well-defined mouth, with the ideal bow on the upper lip, sloped down on each side when in repose, as though his private thoughts were less than happy. It reminded her of the time they had met, when he spent most of one summer at Birlingdean.

She said, "I don't know how much you remember of Clifton and my family." She paused, but he did not reply. "My mother's father, Grandfather Sinclair, kept a stud and stables and trained racehorses. It was more than a pastime for him; it was a life's work, and he had many successes. My mother took an interest when the property passed to her, and my father renewed the license in his own name; but Mama was never robust, and Papa was away a lot, so our activities dwindled."

He was very attentive, and did not interrupt. She caught his sidelong glance under the thick, shielding lashes, and knew that he had already guessed what was to come.

For the first time it struck her what an agreeable listener he might be. She smiled at him as she went on. "I grew up amongst experts who had served my grandfather, and they encouraged my passion for everything to do with horses and racing. I confess to you that I would as soon spend an afternoon in the exercise yard as in the most elegant shops on Bond Street. In short, sir, jockeys still race Metcalfe horses at Newmarket and Epsom Downs, and though they do so under a man's name, they wear a woman's colors."

"Ah. Now I understand your admiration for good Queen Anne. She kept a fine stables herself, did she not?"

"And built the lovely palace at Newmarket." She quizzed him: "You are not shocked by my riding alone?"

"No. Concerned. What would become of you if you took a fall? Accidents can happen—as we well know!"

"It is far too dear a habit for me to give up. Besides, I enjoy the privacy, the time to myself."

"Is that my cue to be gone?" he asked.

She felt embarrassed. "By no means."

He smiled. "Excellent. Because I was headed for Clifton, to pay you a call."

It would be his first visit. As they rode on, she felt grateful that he had put it off for so long. He had waited until after the other calls were over—from the few families she saw in the district, the rector of the parish, the yeoman farmers who came to welcome her home. The news of where she had spent the first night of her return would have gone the rounds of local society the very next morning, and though it had been quite unavoidable, and far from improper in view of her marital status and her relation to Colonel Coole, she still had not fancied promoting the idea that this was to be the pattern of her behavior. It was one thing for him to offer her shelter in an emergency; it would have been quite another if he had made his kind inquiries after her in person rather than by messenger over the next few days. She would much prefer not to have it put about that the widow and the cousin of Sir Andrew Hamilton had scarcely spent an hour apart since her arrival.

"Are you settled in yet?" he asked as they turned inland along the well-worn white track that led toward Clifton.

"More or less. But there are so many things that I thought we had about the place, yet are nowhere to be found. I am going to Brighton soon to stay with friends, and I shall make some purchases."

"Are you? So am I. The regent's own regiment, the Tenth Hussars, are giving a party on the thirtieth." He hesitated a split second before asking nonchalantly, "Is there any chance you might attend?"

She regarded his profile. "That will depend on my friends. I usually fit in with their schemes when I stay."

Mary Ellwood loved Brighton. It was fashionable to stare somewhat if one announced a visit there, as though there were something faintly ridiculous about the place, but it was precisely the oddities and the gaudiness of it that charmed her. The ever-changing crowd, which gave the impression there were no permanent Brighton residents, only visitors. The surprise of seeing a friend strolling along the esplanade, when one had thought her soberly ensconced in Holland Place. The vast military encampments outside town, with their endless, grandiose parades and field days. Sea bathing in the summer months, from the machines tucked into the shelter of the ocean wall. And Prinny's curious Pavilion, which at first sight always drew from her a fond smile.

This evening, she and Ellwood were invited to a ball

at the Montagues', where Sophia Hamilton was staying.
Mary had dressed for it with great care, as the Montagues had one of the most elegant homes in Brighton
and never ruined the effect of their beautiful interiors
with a clutter of guests—there were to be twenty couples
tonight, in a ballroom large enough to give everyone the
chance to look like a precious jewel in a very expensive setting.

"I hope they'll have cards," her husband said as they
relaxed in the sitting room of their lodgings.

"They'll have everything you could wish. Superlative
music, and they are renowned for their suppers. Honoria
Montague is to perform afterwards on the harp. And
have no fear as to the guests, there is a stimulating assortment—apart from the usual, there are three French
people from London, a Viennese gentleman lately from
Paris and a Swiss lady who claims to be an intimate of
Madame de Staël."

"Thank Lucifer for the cards," he murmured.

"And dear Sophia, of course. We have a great deal
to catch up on." She thought for a moment. "I wonder
if—" then paused for so long that Ellwood began to
look at her impatiently. Her husband's neat figure, thin
face and acute hazel eyes spoke his quickness and intelligence in a way that tended to put people on their mettle,
and he never scrupled to turn them on her if she aroused
his curiosity.

"Well?"

"I don't know whether I can ask her about something
so odd. But it irks me that she said not a word to me
at the time. It's too secretive by half."

"For pity's sake, Mary, be specific."

"You recall the dreadful night of the riots, when we
got home so late. Well, it appears that Sophia received
a caller that night, long after midnight. No one said a
word to *me*; I only pried this out of Lawrence yesterday
when he referred to it by mistake."

"Who was it?"

"A soldier."

"A Guards officer, come to give the all clear?"

She shook her head. "A common soldier of the lowest rank. Lawrence said he looked for all the world as though he'd just crawled out of a roughhouse and was about to bleed to death on our floor. Sophia called for brandy, spent upward of a quarter of an hour with him alone, and then he took off into the night."

"His name?" he said sharply.

"He gave none. Lawrence knows no more than what I just told you. Oh—except he was French."

Ellwood got out of his chair and began to pace across the floor, his hands clasped loosely behind him over the black tails of his evening coat. Finally he said, "If it was he, she's sillier than I would ever have dreamed."

Mary bristled at this attack, but he was not looking at her. "Be specific, Augustus, if you please."

"I only hope for her sake it wasn't Jacques Decernay." He stopped and faced her. "Late of the Chasseurs Britanniques, court-martialed a couple of weeks ago for attempting to desert. Intelligence has been onto him for some time." He hesitated a second, then went on. "I'm going to tell you this, for the sake of our friend. But you cannot reveal the details to her, or to anyone else. Agreed?"

Mary nodded. It was rare for Ellwood to confide such things to her, but on the occasions when he did, she remained solidly discreet. He knew it, and he trusted her—it was one of the bonds she valued most between herself and her clever husband.

He began to pace again. "Intelligence went so far as putting a man on the court-martial panel to ensure the death penalty."

"Why?"

"It seems pretty well certain that Decernay was a spy for Napoleon in New South Wales, and no doubt elsewhere."

"*What?* What possible interest could New South Wales have for the French?"

He said dryly, "There have been spies there since the moment the colony was set up." He saw her disbelief and went on. "Have you considered why it's there at all? Convict settlement is the least of it; the place is of the utmost strategic importance. Port Jackson gives us a secure base from which to monitor French activity in the Pacific, and it provides a back door to India. If Admiral Metcalfe were here he would tell you the same; in fact, he and I have discussed this very issue. Baudin's expedition, for instance, a decade or so ago. While the French ships were in harbor it became known in Sydney Town that two of the so-called botanists were spies—they were swarming all over the place, sketching more than flora and fauna, I'll be bound. Governor King lavished attention on them for weeks without the slightest suspicion, and he only twigged to the problem when they left for Van Diemen's land. Panic—he was convinced they were about to set up a base there, so he sent some cockleshell of a boat after them with a few officers onboard."

He smiled at her grimly. "What followed was a frantic farce. They caught up with them in a godforsaken bay where the French had a camp set up onshore—collecting specimens, they said. Our lot were so poorly fitted out they had to ask Baudin for provisions. He handed them across like a gentleman and then they asked for gunpowder. He obliged, and next morning there was our gallant band onshore, hitching the British colors up to a tree and firing a salute to claim the territory—with French gunpowder."

"Oh dear. I've never heard about that. What happened then? And how do we know?"

"Baudin wrote a stiff letter to Governor King, which the officers took away with them. Baudin was on the home run, so he agreed to ferry dispatches from them to us—I hope the poor devil enjoyed the funny side of *that* before he perished. He never made it back, but our secret dispatches did."

Mary said slowly, "Espionage is still going on?"

"Undoubtedly. Hence the urgency to nail Decernay; and the army had the evidence to do it. But there was an intervention that no one could have predicted. Admiral Metcalfe got to hear of the court-martial quite by chance after he landed at Greenwich. I wish he had mentioned it to me, but he and Lady Hamilton kept silent about the whole thing."

"Sophia!"

He nodded. "Apparently she met Private Decernay on the very day he was trying to desert. She and the admiral were both convinced he was blameless, and wrote an independent letter to the panel, which was read out in court. The panel adjourned, and the man in the know did his best to make sure execution would be handed down, but he could not prevail against the lieutenant-colonel in charge. Decernay got three hundred lashes and dishonorable discharge."

Mary shuddered. "How awful."

"Indeed—because it wasn't enough. Normally you can more or less guarantee such a drubbing will kill the man anyway, but the moment they stripped him down, they could see he was of another caliber. They gave up at a hundred; it was a waste of effort. Then he was thrown out into the street."

"And you think he made his way to our door, and asked for Sophia? Good heavens, what on earth made him think she would receive him?"

"I have no idea. But according to you, she did."

Their eyes locked.

She said, "I don't like any of it. But I would lay my life there is nothing whatsoever between him and Sophia."

"That's as may be." He withstood her angry glance and said deliberately, "You cannot be as frank with her as I have just been with you. But there must be no further communication between her and this fellow Decernay. Not a meeting, not a message, nothing. For her own safety, she must act as though he never existed."

Sophia had no particular intimates amongst the Montagues; rather, she was a friend of the whole family. She was a few years older than the eldest daughter, Honoria, who admired Sophia's experience of the world. Honoria was just "out," and the ball was in her honor; the two younger sisters, Elizabeth and Pauline, were envious, but nothing could spoil their enjoyment of dancing, their favorite form of amusement.

There was a great deal of to-ing and fro-ing among the bedchambers while the young ladies were dressing and having their hair arranged. The girls exclaimed over Sophia's new gown of silvery Chinese silk and the jeweled clasp with pale ostrich feathers in her hair. When she hesitated over her necklaces, they talked her into a fine collar of rubies.

She felt a curious detachment about the evening. For a while now she had ceased to suffer the deep pang of regret that used to come with the idea of attending an event without Andrew, the mournful wish that she could keep to her room and avoid company. Instead she prepared for it mechanically, without anticipation, as though her softer feelings were frozen, never to be revived.

In point of fact, she reminded herself, as she stepped down the staircase to the first floor, Andrew had not been overfond of dancing. He did not have that slight touch of exhibitionism that animates the best dancers, and was just as happy standing on the sidelines talking and watching his wife take part. Before supper, however, he would always claim her, coming to her side with an invitation in his eyes and leading her onto the floor with scarcely a word spoken between them. He showed the same pattern of behavior even in their most intimate moments together—considerate and attentive. If he had ever felt a driving, importunate desire for her, he had had the self-control never to become demanding. He always took her wishes into account, and it was this tenderness that she had responded to. She had been physically happy with Andrew, without ever learning what it was to feel raw sexual need for a man. Above all, it was his companionship that she missed.

Lady Beatrice and Sir Walter Montague, who were still welcoming guests, smiled at her over the shoulders of some newcomers as she glided by, and Elizabeth and Pauline, who were standing with a couple of young subalterns in dress uniform, looked over at her eagerly.

There was a change in the conversation as she walked

in alone, caused by a collective intake of breath that she could feel rather than hear. It surprised her, for she had not intended to make an entrance. She looked about for the Ellwoods, but they had not yet arrived, so when Honoria glanced up and smiled from the other end of the ballroom she went over to join her.

Set at regular intervals within the single row of chairs along each side of the room were tall candelabra, with thirty candles blazing in each. Standing in front of one of these with Honoria, Sophia was surrounded by a dazzling halo that was quite hurtful to the eyes, so she turned to face the crowd.

There was a cheerful mixture of young people, with local officers in regimentals. There were some more mature guests amongst them; not far off she could hear the Viennese gentleman conversing in lisping French with an elegant couple she remembered from the prince's reception at Carlton House. Farther off, a stout lady in swathes of purple satin and amber beads the size of chestnuts was haranguing a pretty youth on the subject of music, ancient and modern.

The players, ensconced nearby behind a looped velvet rope, began a stately piece that formed a counterpoint to the hubbub of voices.

A gentleman stepped away from the Montagues and entered alone, his figure dominating that end of the room. With one raking glance around the company he found Sophia, and the impact of his look forced from her a wordless exclamation. She knew him: the deep-set gray eyes that flashed at her from under dark brows; the tawny hair, shorter than when she had last seen it and fashionably cut, but still with the untamed look about it that went with his vigorous presence.

She knew him, yet it was impossible that he could be crossing the Montagues' splendid ballroom toward her. There was nothing out of place in his appearance—she had a fleeting impression of a white cravat, an evening coat in dark blue superfine cloth, black breeches and hose—but it was as though she were looking through the clothes, to the lithe strength of the body beneath.

Meanwhile as he strode toward her he was holding her gaze, catching the charged message in it down the length of the room.

It was a double shock—seeing him, and finding herself unable to conceal her reaction.

When he got to her she was trembling.

CHAPTER NINE

Decernay made Sophia a faultless bow and she managed to curtsy correctly.

"Lady Hamilton. You are surprised."

"That is not the word."

"I hope I find you well?"

She stared at him. "And you, monsieur?" She struggled against the image of him half fainting under her hands, the sensation of his skin touching hers, her fear for his life. "Are you quite recovered?"

The lopsided smile made its appearance, and he did not reply. There was amusement in it, as though he had known in advance she would not burst out with the questions that really mattered—*What happened to you after that dreadful night? What on earth are you doing here?*

She tore her gaze away from him and saw that Honoria was looking up at him with unrestrained curiosity. The introduction must be made, before the situation became altogether bizarre.

"You are perhaps not acquainted with the first daughter of the house. Miss Honoria Montague, may I present Monsieur Jacques Decernay."

Into the silence that followed the bow and the courteous "How do you do" from each side, Honoria said, "You are most welcome, monsieur. Are you new to Brighton?"

"Yes."

"Do you stay long?"

"A few days. I came down with Monsieur and Madame de Villiers." He nodded toward the French couple who stood not far away.

"The marquis!" exclaimed Honoria. "He is a great friend of my father. That is, they belong to the same club in town. It is a wonder we have not had the honor of meeting you before."

"I arrived in the country just recently."

His voice was soft and sensitively modulated, in unsettling contrast to his big frame. It was just like their other meetings—she was acutely aware of him, the way he spoke, the way he stood, the way he looked at her. Sophia knew he was examining her and making every word a test—he was willing her to break into the conversation. *Who are you?*

It was not the condemned Private Decernay who stood before her; the soldier's rank had been sloughed off with his tattered uniform. His new guise fitted him like a glove, as though he had been wearing perfectly tailored clothes and moving amongst people like the marquis all his life. Yet that image too must be false. She glanced at him under the guard of her lashes and recognized his direct, searching look from their first encounters. He was waiting for her to make a move, to say something—but she had absolutely no idea whom she would be addressing.

She forced her voice to function. "Do you spend long in Brighton, monsieur?" Honoria looked at her in surprise and a glint came into Decernay's eyes at the inane repetition of the inquiry. She hurried on. "That is, are you here for any particular purpose?"

"Yes. To see you."

Honoria's eyes grew even wider as she looked from one to the other.

Sophia's heart began pounding. "Do you think," she began angrily, then subdued her voice, "that our slight acquaintance justifies such a declaration?"

His tone was mild. "All I know is that I found the invitation for tonight irresistible." He turned to Honoria and said with a pleasant smile, "You see, mademoiselle, Lady Hamilton and I have already met, more than once."

Honoria stared at him, far out of her depth but fascinated, avid to hear the confession he seemed about to make.

Sophia could not bear him to discuss their secrets with a third party. She said rapidly, with an uncertain smile at Honoria, "Yes, twice in New South Wales and once in London. Monsieur Decernay was lately in His Majesty's armed forces. We know each other a little through my father."

She saw his shoulders stiffen, and he looked down his nose at her with an expression she could interpret with devastating ease. Reproach, tinged with contempt.

Honoria's voice was quick and admiring in reply. "You have fought for England? In which corps, monsieur?"

"The Chasseurs Britanniques."

Honoria obviously neither knew the name nor cared about it. Her cheeks were pink from finding herself in the midst of a mysterious contretemps between this gentleman and her friend, but she was not obliged to share Sophia's hostility.

He gave her a charming smile that included Sophia. "Will you permit me to make my friends known to you?" He had bowed and walked away toward the French couple before either could reply.

Honoria turned at once to Sophia, her eyes gleaming, and said in an unsteady whisper, "Do tell me, who . . . who *is* he?"

"I know practically nothing about him," Sophia said. "And I have no idea why he insists on introducing his friends; I have seen them once before, though we have not spoken, and you must have greeted them at the door, I imagine?"

Honoria shook her head. "I was speaking to Uncle

Philip when they arrived. He is to stand up with me to
begin the ball, you know. I should vastly prefer someone
else, but since Papa . . ."

Her voice trailed away as Decernay returned.

Sophia joined in the exchanges while she took in the
older couple. They were trim, smooth skinned and exquisitely turned out, so it was hard to assess their age,
which might be anywhere between fifty and sixty. The
marquis was a few inches taller than his wife but built
on the same neat scale, with a thin, clever face. The
marquise stood close to her husband, resting a hand on
his sleeve in a way that suggested a close rapport. Sophia, looking into her eyes, could see no knowledge of
what Decernay had just seemed on the point of confess-
ing to Honoria.

"You live in the region, I collect?" the marquise said.

"Yes." Sophia felt an odd caution about saying the
name of her house or its location while Decernay was
watching her so intently. "I am Sussex born and bred."

"Ah!" The marquise took up her fond tone. "I used
to feel the same about Normandy. In fact," she said with
an ironical little shrug, "I still do. De Villiers and I
planned a visit there in June, but who knows now
whether that would be a wise thing to do?"

The music ceased at that moment, and the chattering
groups were silenced by the deep voice of Sir Walter,
speaking a welcome and calling on his guests to join his
daughter and his brother in the set for the first dance.

Sophia, looking over toward the door, saw that Mary
and Augustus Ellwood had at last arrived. There was no
chance for more than a nod and a smile in their direction, however, for at that moment Philip Montague was
advancing across the floor to claim Honoria as his partner, and other couples, including the de Villiers, were
beginning to move toward the center of the room as the
musicians tuned up again behind them.

"Madame," said a compelling voice, "may I have the
honor of this dance?" Sophia looked up. He said
quickly, "You will not refuse me?"

She shook her head and lowered her eyes.

He gave a little sigh. Then she felt his fingertips on her upper arms. She had a gauze stole over her shoulders, which he removed, drawing the gossamer fabric away and letting it drift over the back of a chair. She had a reticule looped over one wrist and as she stood there, immobile, he relieved her of that too. She felt the lightest touch through her glove as he slipped the silk ribbon free.

Then he was beside her, taking her hand.

They walked onto the floor in the formal, unhurried glide, the regulation arm's length apart, her gloved fingers resting in his bare ones. She had never had such a sensation before; it was as though his one hand enveloped her entire body. There was a warmth in it that felt like ardor, a strength that felt like a passionate claim. For the time that it took to cross the ballroom, she forgot that they were strangers; instead there was a whole language of understanding within their clasped hands.

They reached the set and took their places. Sophia did not know the people around them, which was just as well as she had no desire to communicate with them. To speak, even to the man opposite, would break the spell. All her senses were heightened, so that when the music began it floated into her with the air she breathed. The brilliantly lit room unfolded like a stage set, in which the dancers provided a colorful backdrop for the one figure that held her gaze.

He danced with grace and deftness and she had time now to observe how well the evening clothes became him. They had the understated elegance that belonged to the best English taste, with just one individual touch—an unusual pin buried in his cravat, an onyx horseshoe with the curve uppermost, surrounded by diamonds.

She was silent in suspense. At any moment the extraordinary link between this man's body and her own would snap, the thrill of his touch when their hands met across the set would be gone. The physical magnetism he exerted was overwhelming, but it must surely be denied to her when the dance was done.

He chose to speak, however, when they were standing still, toward the end of the set. His words, though they could be heard quite clearly by the people on each side, sounded more like a caress than a question.

"Do you waltz, Lady Hamilton?"

She met his eyes at last. In the gray depths there was a glint of amusement, like sunlight on wintry waves. She shook her head.

"What a pity," he said. "You dance divinely."

She was not going to tell him she thought waltzing improper—he would only laugh. So she said nothing for a while, holding his gaze, and realized that her desire for him was as imperative as it had been on the hot day when they met, as deep as it had been when he came to her after midnight during the riots. In another second, he would be able to see through her and know how much she wanted him.

The only disguise was conversation. "Lady Beatrice does not permit the waltz. The girls are very fond of reels, as you will soon discover."

"And what are you fond of, Lady Hamilton?"

Confused, she said at random, "I have no special favorites."

They began to move again, and as he passed close to her he murmured, "You never tell me what you are really thinking. Why is that?"

Embarrassed, she said, "Debate in the midst of a quadrille is not an English custom."

His eyes widened. "So you would argue with me, if politeness did not forbid it? Madame, I am French—you may contradict me, chastise me, tease me. I shall receive every word with delight."

She executed a turn away from him and felt her cheeks go warm with dismay. What was he expecting—a flow of badinage for the benefit of the couples around them? Did he imagine that she would be willing to *flirt* with him, in the light, ingenious fashion he must be used to? It was a shaming thought.

She must not seek to know more about his identity—

as he said, he was French. One of the race who killed her husband.

When she faced him again he must have seen the caution in her eyes, for the spark of humor in his instantly went out. Controlling her voice, she said, "Very well. You once said to me: 'If you only knew.' To what were you referring?"

He compressed his lips. "I am afraid I do not recall."

So much for candor—she had him in retreat already. It was safe to ask the next question, since it would leave the bystanders as baffled as they had been by the first, but it was harder to pronounce. She said, too low for anyone else to hear, "You also said you pitied me. Why?"

A second later, the lines of gentlemen and ladies neatly reformed, there was a final flourish from the orchestra, the couples bowed to each other and the dance was over.

As before, he reached over and took her hand. As before, they crossed the room without a word. He led her to a spot by the wall where no one was within hearing distance and remained before her, shielding her from the room. The rich candlelight caught his face, delineating the straight nose, the dark arches of his eyebrows, the bright nimbus of hair.

"I expressed myself abominably just now." He frowned at her, marshaling his thoughts. "I mean that I want us to be able to speak to each other freely. Life is so short. Why waste it? I cannot say anything but the truth to you—grant me the same."

He still held her fingers. It was all she could do not to close her other hand over his, to pull him nearer. Such behavior was quite impossible—it was not guilt that prevented her from giving in to it, but the realization that he had just avoided answering both her questions. Slowly she extracted her hand from his, lowered her eyes and took a little step back. It was like cutting a thread in a finely woven tapestry, unraveling a rich, enchanted scene.

"I should like you to tell me why you pitied me."

He hissed something under his breath. Then after the briefest pause he said, "I was thinking of your situation. It is tragic that you lost your husband—"

He broke off when she looked up. He was in retreat again. She said, "You meant more than that."

She saw a rapid debate take place behind his eyes. Finally he said, "*Bien.* I was sorry that this war made you suffer, when God knows there was already suffering enough in the field. I was sorry that there were no obsequies for your husband, that you could not even identify the spot where he fell. That is hard."

She bit her lip. "How could you know that?"

He said very low, "From the day I met you, I asked about you, all over Sydney Town."

She shook her head. "No. I never discussed this with anyone—and nor did my father, because I asked him not to. These are *private* matters! This is *my life* you intrude upon!"

He gave her a beseeching look. "No, listen to me. You did speak to someone—the Prince Regent, remember? The Marquis and the Marquise de Villiers were at the prince's house one night and heard what you said to him. When I learned this, I made them tell me everything about you, how you looked and spoke, the smallest details. That is how I know."

With these words, she took one more step away. Her voice was level and cold. "You came to Bedford Square direct from prison. *That* information the marquis must have given to you afterwards. You say you value frankness—if this is your idea of it, monsieur, I cannot share it."

As she turned he said something—but she did not hear the words, for standing before her was Augustus Ellwood, a friendly smile and a look of expectation on his face. Ignoring Decernay, he bowed and said, "Lady Hamilton, may I partner you in the Boulangeries? I had not the pleasure of dancing with you in Curzon Street— I beg you will not deny me now."

She returned his smile. "Thank you."

He held out his arm, she put her hand on his wrist, hoping he could not feel her shaking, and they glided out onto the floor. He led her toward the farthest set and she did not look back.

Before they took their places, Ellwood said quietly, "I trust I intruded? Mary sent me, to interrupt what looked to us like a very determined pursuit. Was I wrong?"

"I am obliged to you."

"I thought so."

He took up his position and waited for the cover of the music before saying, "We made some inquiries of our hosts. You know the gentleman is an intimate of the de Villiers?"

"Yes."

"I found that astonishing, considering his rank in the Chasseurs. But not so amazing, it seems, considering his lineage. He is the scion of an old Normandy family. I have not the slightest regret about having rescued you from his clutches, Lady Hamilton, but believe it or not, he holds the title of Vicomte de Cernay."

CHAPTER TEN

❦

She was avoiding him with perfect ease. She was never without a partner, and between dances she took care to be on the opposite side of the room. Jacques entertained himself by dancing with all three Montague daughters in turn, drawing them into conversation and inwardly comparing their charms with her remote, glowing beauty.

When he tired of that he withdrew into the card room and played whist. He and the marquis won heavily against the partnership of one of the officers and Sir Walter Montague, who vowed to take his revenge on them both at the tables of White's in the next month. The officer seemed unaware of the recent ignominious discharge of one Private Decernay, so the word had not gotten about town yet. Jacques knew in his bones that Lady Hamilton would not broadcast it, and if it did leak out, he hoped by then to be well-known to the army in Brighton. No one who met him in those circles would care to challenge him to his face with the story.

He thought of claiming her again just before supper, but there was a tedious ritual to it all that would probably have gotten in the way of this maneuver. The Montagues were old-fashioned, as he discovered when he entered the supper room with Miss Pauline Montague on his arm and saw that men and women were being placed on opposite sides of each table.

He had an array of pretty faces before him but paid heed to only one, which never turned in his direction. She was seated at the next table beside the marquise, too far off for him to hear what either was saying, but close enough for him to watch every move and expression and guess the nuances of feeling. She often tried to shade her reactions with her thick black lashes, but her lustrous eyes would catch the light sometimes and sent a flash of meaning straight into his consciousness.

At the thought of the way she had said, "These are *private* matters!" he gritted his teeth. The only passion she had willingly shown him so far was anger. It had been a foolish move to mention her husband; she had tripped him up before the breath was out of his mouth. And bringing the de Villiers into it had made them sound like his personal spies. He would give a great deal to know what the marquise was saying to her right now, as Silvie de Villiers might consider it an act of friendship to speak highly of him—but any attempt in that line could have a contrary effect.

Much later the girls got what they wanted and all the young people joined in some spirited reels. Lady Hamilton was coaxed into the first, but spent the second on the sidelines talking to the fetching, vivacious wife of the sly gentleman who had cut him out of the Boulangeries. Sophia Hamilton avoided glancing toward his side of the room, and her face was grave. She was aloof, in a still, contained way that went with her statuesque beauty, but he saw much more—a slight drawing down of the full lower lip, a veiled disappointment in the eyes, an uncertain color that came and went across her high, smooth cheekbones.

He knew the name of the ill-disposed couple by now— they were the Ellwoods of Bedford Square, who had not been home on the night of his invasion. The Honorable Augustus Ellwood was a Whig Member of Parliament and had a high post in the Foreign Office, all of which

Jacques knew through the inquiries he had made before seeking her out on the night of his release. He had not thought Ellwood himself important until now, but the man's interruption earlier had been colored by more than normal English rudeness. He merited research. As did the wife, who was just now gathering her things to go. Before leaving, Lady Ellwood threw him a look across the room, and he built the clearest message into his stare: *Yes, madame, you may count on my outstaying you.*

As she turned away he saw a hint of something that intrigued him. It was fear.

Sophia lingered until after Pauline and Elizabeth had been persuaded to retire and there were only a few guests left, one party finishing a rubber at the card tables, the rest in the supper room taking coffee. She lingered for Honoria's sake, and for her own. She knew Decernay would approach her at the last, and she had been obsessed with the idea all evening. There were questions to ask.

She thought Honoria might make herself part of the conversation, for one effect of her first ball was an absolute fascination with the Frenchman who had come straight to her side at the beginning and danced two sets with her since. But she was doing her duty at the coffee table, where one of the junior officers claimed her attention. Decernay accepted his cup from Honoria with a smile and a few pleasant words, then made his way to the corner where Sophia sat alone.

"May I join you?" Once again the voice was like a soft caress.

"If you wish."

She was on a small sofa, holding saucer and cup in one hand, with her gloves, stole and reticule on the velvet seat beside her. He chose a matching chair that faced the room, so that their voices could not be heard by anyone else and her face, turned to his, would be safe from the scrutiny of others.

It was delicate and discreet of him—which was perplexing, because his manner was so often one of challenging frankness. In a second, he reverted to character. "You are angry with me, for knowing so much about you in so little time. Forgive me, but you are too beautiful for any man not to want to learn everything about you at once. And it is not such a little time, because I first met you more than twelve months ago." There was no possible answer to this, and fortunately he did not seem to expect one. He went on. "Ever since then, I have been on the other side of the ocean. If I have said anything that shocks you, put it down to my impatience to see you again."

She lowered her eyes. There was a long pause. Then he said, "Won't you tell me, just this once, what you are thinking?"

She looked up in amazement. After a speech like that? He could scarcely have chosen anything more likely to silence her! For a split second, she wished she were like the adroit Frenchwomen he must be used to, who could receive such compliments wittily, with their heads clear and their hearts untouched; who could look into those eyes and prevent them from reaching out and grappling her soul.

She bent to put her cup down on a little table beside her. "Whatever you believe you know about me, monsieur, I know very little about you. Did you intend ever to enlighten me?"

Another man might have been chilled by her tone, but he gave her a level look and leaned back in the chair, crossing his long legs and taking a sip of coffee while he stared thoughtfully at her over the rim.

"The Marquise de Villiers told you nothing?"

He was assuming she had asked about him! But of course she had. She said coolly, "Apparently you are the Vicomte de Cernay. You—"

"Correction: I was. My father renounced the family titles in 1792, on republican principles."

She looked at him in surprise. "And you?" He held her gaze and she continued slowly. "You are a republican? Not a royalist, after all?"

He just said, "What else have you been told?"

"You joined the French army under Napoleon Bonaparte. You fought in Austria and Prussia and in the Russian campaign." He gave her a sharp glance there, which she could not read. She continued. "Then you served in the Peninsula, where you were wounded and captured some time in 1813. After that, you became a Chasseur. One of the battles in which you served was San Sebastian. I know no more. Perhaps you will elaborate."

He bowed. "You have been admirably informed."

"But there are some points you could explain." She snatched a breath, holding his gaze. "My husband was also at the Battle of San Sebastian. Did you know that?"

He bowed again.

"Did you ever meet him?"

"The Ninth Regiment attacked from a different part of the foreshore. They were two miles away from us. I could not have encountered your husband at San Sebastian." His keen eyes caught her reaction and he continued emphatically. "No, Lady Hamilton, I cannot tell you how he lost his life. And if you will take my advice . . ." He paused as though regretting what he had said, then pushed on. "You will not allow it to torment you." He leaned right over toward her, planting the coffee cup on the floor and putting one hand on the velvet seat by her gloves. "Do not seek what you can never find. Such obsession is one of the worst legacies of death. Believe me, we cannot go back and mend what was ripped away from us; we can only go on."

It was the voice of pure feeling. She could not resent him for presuming to give her advice, because the vibration in his tone spoke of similar suffering.

"You have lost someone very dear to you."

"Yes."

She said softly, "And do you follow your own counsel?"

"*Touché.*" He gave a short, bitter laugh. "No. I do not forget or forgive." He shook his head and the thick hair fell back over his brow. "Not ever."

"Then I shall do as I wish."

"You don't understand. Mine is an affair of men."

"So is mine, but if it takes a woman to unravel it, so be it. There is a Colonel Belton stationed in Brighton—he was my husband's commanding officer at San Sebastian. I cannot think that he will deny me a hearing."

He looked startled. "You plan to meet him?"

"I plan, monsieur, to do exactly as I think fit."

"*Don't*—" he began. Then he looked up beyond her, gave a grimace of irritation and sat back.

Surprised and annoyed, Sophia looked at him in silence, before becoming aware that two people were approaching across the carpet behind her. She turned to see Sir Walter and Honoria.

They halted and Sir Walter said heartily, "I have finally prevailed upon my daughter to retire. She is bidding our guests good night."

Decernay rose at once. "Then it is time I left." He smiled at them both, no doubt to compensate for the grimace, supposing they had seen it, and looked down kindly on Honoria. "What a splendid evening you afforded us. Thank you. If I had not been able to come, I would have regretted it all my life."

As Sophia rose too, it struck her that all at once he sounded very French—*Eef I 'ad not been able to come, I would 'ave rrregrrretted eet*—but also totally sincere. She saw the effect on Honoria, and to hide both the girl's disarray and her own, she leaned forward and kissed her cheek. "It was a wonderful ball. Happy?"

Honoria returned the embrace, her eyes shining.

Sir Walter was turning away, but Decernay said something more to Honoria. Sophia moved back to the sofa to pick up her things, no longer listening. In a few moments he would be gone.

Then he was beside her, and as her hands touched the gloves and reticule his fingers brushed past them, scooping up the stole. They both straightened at the same moment and Sophia registered that Sir Walter and Honoria had paused a few paces away and were waiting so that they could all walk out into the hall together.

Sophia looked down, avoiding the observant eyes, and

folded her gloves across one palm as Decernay arranged the stole over her shoulders. As usual he stood too close, yet she wished it were closer. The gesture was possessive, yet it did not evoke the resentment she had felt only minutes before when he was trying to tell her how to conduct her life. When the film of gauze had settled across her back, he caught the tips of her shoulders in a brief, firm clasp and gave a little squeeze, as though to say, "There!" It was familiar—far too familiar—but instead of shrinking from it she was seized by a rush of intoxication that left her unable to move. She longed simply to stay in the space he had created around her, to breathe the same warm air.

He began to move away and she managed to step forward and follow the others across the room, down a wide corridor and out into the hall at the head of the stairs, Decernay silently accompanying her.

In the hall, Lady Montague was saying good night to the stragglers from the card room. When the little group had bowed to one another and the footman began to precede the guests down the staircase out of sight, Sophia realized that Jacques Decernay would be the very last guest to leave. It did not stop her from wishing she could delay him, to say and to ask all the things that were now locked inside her head, frozen into place by the formal farewells.

He stood on the top stair with his eyes fixed on her, and still she had not been able to say a word; it was as though a steel bar lay across the base of her throat, forbidding breath and speech. His gaze probing hers, he gave a fleeting smile and bowed to her.

"Good night, Lady Hamilton. *A bientôt.*" Then he turned and went lightly down the stairs, almost at a run.

Soon. He had said soon.

CHAPTER ELEVEN

Paris

If I am a fool, then I am in perfect company, for no one knows how to act from one day to the next. The very surroundings change before our eyes. The first afternoon when we were all waiting for Bonaparte at the Tuileries was a pattern of everything since. The ladies were lamenting the fact that the throne room was still carpeted in the royal blue and the fleur de lis, and then someone got a toe under one of the squares and kicked the corner back—to expose the next layer down, which had Bonaparte's bee design all over it. Next thing everyone had set to, women included, in all their magnificent finery, ripping the Bourbon work to shreds and rediscovering the buried imperial carpet. He was pleased, when he arrived, with that and the reception. And he flew into action at once: decreeing the exile or arrest of all the powerful royalists—like Talleyrand, La Rochefoucauld, Montésquiou—and seizing their lands and wealth; unstopping the presses; declaring, "I am a product of the Revolution."

And he's managed to form a government even though he's had to draw on men whom he's disappointed, abused, hated or sacked in the past. Caulaincourt, who's accepted the Foreign Office after pleading for an army command instead. Davout, the greatest general he has left, if he can but see it. Carnot, who once denounced him as consul and as emperor, and is now helping to fashion the new "Liberal Empire."

Paris, the capital of chameleons. Benjamin Constant—he of the supremely ironic name—blasted the new regime in the Journal de Paris *and went about like a martyr in consequence ("I would rather perish than fall into his hands!"). Next thing he's summoned before Bonaparte at the Tuileries and commanded to draft a new constitution. Joy, wonder. "What an amazing man he is!"*

No one except Constant believes a constitution means more than a paper kite to Bonaparte, who is convinced the people want "the emperor's famous firm hand." And like it or not they'll feel it.

The night after the arrival, before Fouché was named Minister of Police, he and old Cambacérès were discussing the situation, maneuvering around each other like battle-scarred dogs from rival packs, sniffing out weaknesses. I sat there in a corner of Fouché's study, looking quietly attentive but without putting a word to paper. There's a panel in the wall somewhere in that room, through which Fouché slipped to safety on the day the king's men came to arrest him on the nineteenth. A lot's changed since then, though you wouldn't have thought so, watching the devil's smooth face and listening to that whining voice.

Cambacérès was pointing out the inconveniences, one being that in Bonaparte's system of ideas there seems to be no distinction between "justice" and "national safety."

Fouché said with a bored air, "He hasn't changed. He's as much of a despot—and just as insane—as he ever was."

Cambacérès looked at him warily. "No one knows where they stand. My secretary here has been expecting the police to knock on his door any moment." When Fouché failed to react, the old man continued. "But he's prepared to sit it out. He gives Bonaparte fifteen days; in fact we have a bet on it."

Fouché turned toward me and his little mouth gave a

*tight smile, his lazy-lidded eyes squeezed into narrow
lines at the corners. "What are your odds, Robert?"*

*I said, "If he's out by then, it's one hundred and fifty
francs to me. If he stays in power, for every day he lasts
after that I'll hand over ten francs."*

The thin lips parted. "You're on. Make it a hundred."

Sebastian was enjoying his third visit to the encampment. With the expectation of war filling every mind,
it was a lively place, and if there were any distempered,
scheming or traitorous elements in this huge collection
of men he did not think it would be long before the
signs appeared to him. The Peninsular veterans knew
him as a retired officer whose record was gained in
India, so could not consider him as a rival for glory.
From those within the prince's own regiment, he met
with a nice readiness to be comradely and confiding. He
had paved the way with a long chat with the commander,
the only one who knew of his mission, in which he
warned that there might be a little whispering in corners
on his part, to "draw the poltroons out," should there
be any. His being Irish would assist credibility—though
he came from an old Protestant family, might he not
have been subverted to the rebel cause, through some
sharp grudge against the English, or against the army
itself?

In the midst of that very conversation he was careful
to imply, without releasing any facts, that he had once
or twice fulfilled the role of agent provocateur in India.
The commander's curiosity was piqued, but Sebastian
left it at that. It put him in a strong position. The Prince
Regent, the prince's advisers and now army command
in Brighton trusted him. He allowed himself a sly grin
of satisfaction.

It was a fine day and there was even a little warmth
in the sunshine as he strolled along between neat rows
of tents toward the exercise yard of the Tenth Hussars,
accompanied by Major Hooper, who was over visiting
from Exceat, and a lieutenant of dragoons called Paine.

He had voiced an idle wish to see some of the regiment in training, and Paine led them toward a copse of trees near some sheds, which he said housed stores and equipment, with a bit of bare ground beyond for sword practice. They could hear the clang of metal and the thud and scuffle of feet as they approached. Then a burst of shouting, followed unexpectedly by laughter.

There was a crowd there, all soldiers except for a couple of workmen who had been whitewashing a wall, but had stopped, riveted, to take in the fight. When Sebastian first got a glimpse of the men in the ring he took it for a duel in earnest, and a dangerous one at that. The face that was turned toward him, that of a stocky, dark-haired young dragoon with a grim expression and bared white teeth, looked like that of someone battling for his life.

They were at it with sabers that flashed wickedly in the sun, and it took Sebastian a moment to notice that the points and edges of the blades were filed blunt. This would still not make it exactly comfortable to take a sweep from one, a fact that seemed uppermost in the youngster's mind as his saber disengaged with a grating whine and he sidestepped to come back into the circle on a new angle. The bystanders on the opposite side scattered away from the other man as he whirled under his own momentum and spun back into the fray, with a mirthless grin and a toss of his fair head.

As the big man smashed the other back across the circle, Sebastian took a good look at him over the shoulders of the soldiers in the first row. He was not in uniform, but he wore standard leather padding across chest and arms like his opponent. He had long legs built on the same strong lines as his upper body, but he had the knack of keeping his center of gravity low, which meant the weight slipped fluidly from one foot to the other, under the command of a prescient brain that sensed each of the other's moves a split second before it was made. His alertness was frightening. He scarcely seemed to blink, and the gray eyes were wide open in a stare that took in all the other's lightning maneuvers.

A few feet away from Sebastian, the dragoon used his muscular right arm to stop a powerful slash toward his chest, and riposted. The crowd gave a concerted sigh, the blades clashed raggedly and then their devilish din began again. The big man put up a creditable defense, but without taking advantage of a few strokes that to Sebastian's observant eye looked like openings for sharper retaliation, and he could have sworn that the odd flash in the all-seeing eyes was laughter.

He remembered his own master-at-arms saying to him long ago, "When it comes down to it, you need only one cut to kill. The rest is a game." He was watching a consummate player.

Now at the end of the arena, where the storage sheds threw a dark shadow across the ground, the tall man did something insane—he disengaged completely for a full second, whipped his blade into a pan of whitewash that was standing at the feet of the two workmen and waggled it in the air before the infuriated dragoon, a huge grin splitting his tanned face. The soldiers in front of Sebastian chuckled as white drops spun from the tip of the blade. Then there was another shout as the sabers connected again, ringing like a blacksmith's hammer.

From this angle, Sebastian could see the dragoon's padded leather jerkin, and for the first time he noticed the marks on it, one at each side of the chest. On the left was a white cross drawn by saber point with two flicks of the wrist. On the right, a single diagonal line had been executed with the same precision. Everyone was now waiting with unconcealed delight for the finishing touch.

The dragoon fought like a demon to wipe out the ignominy of the joke and strip the other man's blade clean before it could complete the second cross. There was no sign yet that he had been able to touch his opponent, but by this stage of the fight he needed to devote his strength to defense. He did well. In the gray eyes that glittered behind the other's whirling blade, Sebastian could see a kind of hilarious approval.

Meanwhile the workmen at the far end were laughing.

"For Christ's sake, sir, never let it dry out!" On encouragement from the bystanders they pushed the pan of whitewash farther out into the arena with a pole, shouting advice to the big man as they did so.

The dragoon, seeing his chance, threw all his energy into a resounding counterattack, forcing his opponent back toward the object that had just been poked within a yard of his heels. There was a shout of warning and amusement, and the big man took a huge step back and crumpled. The dragoon lunged, was caught off-balance and went down on one knee. Then his saber was sent spinning out of his hand. The shock was so great he lurched forward and ended on both hands and knees, staring into the untouched pan of whitewash, as pure and level as a dish of new milk.

The victor executed the feint, the classic movement to disarm and the spring to his feet with such speed that the crowd were stunned to see him standing only a foot away, his saber tip balanced lightly on the ground, his chest rising and falling rapidly under the cuirass of leather.

Then he laughed, dropped his blade on the ground and bent down to put his hand flat in the pan of whitewash and offer it, dripping, to the dragoon. After a second's bemused hesitation the man accepted it and was hauled to his feet. To another roar of laughter he was embraced. Then the two men stood face-to-face, both daubed with patches of white, both panting, until the dragoon turned away with a shake of the head and a rueful grin, and picked up his saber from the dust.

With an arm flung across the dragoon's shoulders the tall man marched him around the ring to accept the bystanders' cheers, and only then did he stoop to retrieve his own weapon.

"Did you have a wager on that?" Sebastian asked quietly of the man in front of him.

The soldier turned in surprise. "No. It always happens too quick with him. Besides, it's all in jest, like. You never know what he'll do next."

Sebastian watched as the duelists walked into the shade and began to take off their gear. "Who is he?"

"The Frenchy? Name of Jacques Decernay." Through Sebastian's intense surprise, he continued. "It seems if he was back home he'd be a viscount. But he fought for us—he was a Chasseur until just lately."

"Until he was drummed out," Sebastian said in crisp, audible tones. Hooper and Paine, on each side, looked at him quickly.

The soldier shrugged, and it was Paine who took him up. "True, sir, and he was given a right royal flogging."

Seeing the Frenchman swing the leather jerkin onto the ground, Sebastian could not help imagining, with a shudder, what the man's back must look like under the thick cambric shirt. "Drummed out," he repeated with emphasis, "for conspiracy to desert."

Paine nodded helpfully. "Indeed. A friend of mine gave me the story straight. I'd have liked to see it, though normally a drubbing turns my stomach. They were all set to bind him to the frame, but he broke free and jumped the man with the whip. It looked like he was out to kill him, but no, he dealt him one clean blow so he fetched his length. And then before anyone could move, the Frenchy stepped forward and helped him up, just like today, and he said, 'Now do your duty. I forgive you.'"

Sebastian's lip curled. "Honor among thieves, eh?"

"Well, now," Paine said slowly, "you wouldn't find anybody here too keen to call that particular gentleman a thief. Or anything else of a like color."

"Nonetheless," Sebastian persisted, "considering his nationality and his record, isn't it damned . . . singular . . . for him to be granted the freedom of this camp? On the eve of war, and he thrown out of this very army but a few weeks ago?"

"You've a point," Hooper said, and turned to Paine. "Do the commanders know he has these bouts with the lads?"

"Everyone does. The Peninsular veterans, officers or

men, won't hear a word against him. They say his record
stands from Roncesvalles, Sorauren and San Sebastian
and that's enough for them. Colonel Belton knows him
and he was giving us chapter and verse of his exploits
the other day. As for being on the eve of war—if Decernay could pass on his gift with the weapons to more of
the boys in this camp, we'd fare a sight brisker when we
face up to Boney."

Sebastian changed the subject. "Who's the fellow
helping him off with the gear?"

"The master-at-arms," Paine said. "Name of Silcock.
They're two of a kind—you'll not see their like anywhere."

"How do they go when they're matched?"

He watched as Decernay rolled down his sleeves and
began to sling on his coat. The Frenchman caught sight
of Paine and gave him a friendly nod, the observant gaze
taking in Sebastian as well.

Paine shook his head. "It's never happened. The
Frenchy won't go a serious round with anyone. It's all
play to him. Sharp enough, but still play."

Sebastian gave a kind of muffled snort, at which
Hooper turned and said slyly, "What, you know someone fit to take him on? Maybe wipe the smile off his
face for a bout?"

Decernay said something to Silcock, cuffed him lightly
on the upper arm, and turned to walk across the circle.

Sebastian shrugged. "Given the right time and place,
who knows?"

Both Hooper and Paine looked at him with eager
speculation.

Oddly enough, as the Chasseur came toward them,
the reaction Sebastian felt had little to do with the surroundings or the event they had just witnessed. It was
connected with something more basic—and no doubt
more base—such as the cockpit. He wondered if Decernay felt it too, that raw male challenge, that blind disre-
gard for the consequences. The other man's long limbs,
the heavy tread, the forward thrust of his square shoulders made him look like a monolith, worth toppling. The

hard steel of Sebastian's own will leaped out to meet him, and as the other came near he could feel in the air around them something like a collision of two fronts, the other incandescent, his own as chilly as ice, with electricity flickering between like subtle lightning.

The man stopped a yard away and greeted Paine with a smile.

Paine said, "That was fine work, monsieur—a pity we missed the opening. Will you be back tomorrow?"

"No, but how about sharing an ale the day after, at the Rainbow?" He registered Paine's answering nod and was about to move on.

Paine said, with a quick gesture, "Colonel Coole, Major Hooper, may I introduce Monsieur Jacques Decernay."

The big man paused, bowed, and as his head came up his glance played over Hooper's face and then met Sebastian's. It was a stare of frank assessment that irritated Sebastian, though he was confident of revealing nothing.

Then a smile lit up the tanned face. "Colonel Coole. I met a friend of yours once in an Irish regiment. Macready. He was skillful with a sword, but he put you far above him in technique. Do you still keep in practice?"

"I do. But not as a public show."

The Frenchman jerked his head back as though Sebastian had clipped him under the chin, then laughed—a full-bodied, appreciative laugh that gave a glint to his narrowed eyes. He strode forward, laid a hand briefly on Paine's shoulder and moved on. "Farewell, *mon brave*." Then, as he passed Sebastian, he said with a grin, "One day, given the right place, who knows?"

CHAPTER TWELVE

Sophia was riding in the sunshine, with Harry up in front of her on Scheherazade. It was preferable to helping him tidy his toys, which he always protested against.

From the playroom windows that morning they had looked out across the green expanse that rolled down to the cliff edge, though today the sea was not visible, wiped away by a thick bank of fog that came right to the clifftop.

Harry had stood on the window seat beside her. "Will the fog get Clifton, Mama?"

"No, only if there's a sou'wester, from the sea. And there's no wind today."

He had jumped down from the seat and looked around the neat room, dissatisfied. "Now I can't find anything!"

She said, "You haven't put the flags up on the castle."

"There's no soldiers." He stumped to the door.

Sophia felt a pang, looking at the wooden castle pushed into one corner of the room. It had been Andrew's most splendid plaything, which as a child she had always felt privileged to be allowed to touch. Beautifully proportioned and painted, with medieval turrets and a keep, crenellated courtyards, broad ramps and spiral staircases, it could be disassembled to make two opposing fortresses if necessary, each flying a gaudy collection

of flags. All the model engineering functioned: the port-
cullises could be raised and lowered, the sturdy gates
could be barred, the chains in the dungeon gave a satisfying rattle and you could set bronze ordnance up in the
field and menace the sentries on the battlements with a
hail of marbles.

The protagonists in her day had been lead soldiers,
clothed with dazzling precision in British and French
uniforms of the 1790s. Andrew and his friends had paraded them along the carpet below the walls or shot
them off the highest fortifications. But all those soldiers
and miniature cannon, if they still existed, must be now
buried in a chest at Birlingdean, and she had no intention of letting Harry know about them. Similarly, he had
no toy pistols or lances, and had never asked for any.
He sometimes wanted Mitchell, the horse master, to tell
him war stories from the Peninsula days, but Mitchell
had orders not to.

"Mitchell might carve you some animals to keep in
the castle, if we ask him nicely."

Harry had paused in the doorway, given her a quizzi-
cal look, then said as though conferring a great favor,
"You can ask him. If you want to."

Now he was leaning contentedly against her, perched
on a cushion on the pommel within her grasp, one arm
around her waist, while Scheherazade stepped sensitively
over the bright turf, conscious of her small extra burden.

"Mama, is Sherazade going to be a racehorse?"

"Mitchell and I haven't decided. But we both think
she may be just be a little too delicate. So perhaps we'll
let her have foals."

He twisted to look up at her, then thought better of
what he was about to say and wriggled back into position
again. He had been going to ask if the first foal could be
his. She hugged him proudly; he was the least acquisitive
person she had ever known. In that, he was like Andrew.
She herself was filled at that moment with a possessive-
ness as fierce as a flame.

They were riding east, toward Birling Gap. The fog
cloaking the clifftop on their right was dense and still,

like a curtain, and they played a game where they imagined that there was no sea out there, but another land, with its own people and buildings and animals. What would you find, if you parted the curtain and stepped through? Meanwhile, with an inward shiver at what was really there, she kept Scheherazade well inland.

This was her home territory, the place that meant freedom. To outsiders, she knew that she had always appeared conventional and cautious, a woman whose life was shaped by the expectations of others. Even Mary misunderstood Sophia's love of Sussex, her preference for months filled not with London balls and routs but with peaceful contact with neighbors in which everyone had the time and opportunity to talk of the enduring concerns—family, friends, the rich round of the seasons. And no one, including Andrew, had ever fully fathomed the deep impulses that kept her loyal to this green place where she had grown up, where all her first dreams had come into being—sprung from the earth itself, never to be cut down. Only here could she feel free and completely herself. She knew she was lucky, because she had been able to make all her choices near home. In that sense, her marriage to Andrew, which had been exactly what her little rural society had predicted all along, was the most natural thing in the world to her as well. Never in her life had she disappointed anyone—Lady Sophia Hamilton fitted in every way the picture of feminine rustic gentility. She had never had to step outside the bounds of the familiar and the predictable in order to be happy. So lately, when she had wondered what it would be like to defy everyone she knew in order to follow a secret desire, she had felt torn. She knew instinctively that she had the courage to pursue what her heart wanted—because that was how she was made, even if no one else recognized it. But she also knew she could never betray those she held dear.

As she rode across the downland with Harry, Sophia did not notice that a gray mass was closing in around them, for she was captivated by her surroundings. There was gorse growing in this trackless area, ranged alongside them to make an informal pathway. Its spring flowers gave off a scent of warm nectar, and bees were busy among the thorns. Farther up the gentle slope were copses of trees and much farther off she spied the roofs of Joliffe Court, the local manor house, tucked into a fold of ground. Behind again were the foothills and then the Downs on the horizon. But one minute she and Harry were basking in the sun, taking in the scenery, and next a curl of mist snaked across in front of them.

She looked to her right; apart from a fast-fading strip only a few yards wide, there was nothing but fog. Close up it was white rather than gray, but nonetheless opaque. Yet there had been no breath of wind to stir it—the impetus must be coming from far out to sea.

A chill went through her, and Harry said excitedly, "Mama, look!"

"Yes, darling." She wheeled Scheherazade to the left, feeling the filly's anxiety. "We'll go this way now, so we don't get damp."

It was impossible to turn back in the direction they had come; there the bank was advancing toward them in a sweeping curve. And on the other side, from the direction of Birling Gap, there was a rampart of spindrift rolling up from the ocean. The wind was not the usual southwesterly, it must be almost due south. Which meant they were advancing, now at a trot, along a colonnade of fog that threatened to collapse upon them.

All Harry said was, "We're ra-cing!" the syllables chopped by the jolting pace. "Can we go faster?"

"No, my love. I don't want Scheherazade to put her foot in a hole." She had made a promise to herself never to ride at more than a trot with Harry up.

She slowed when she knew it was hopeless. It would have been more pleasant to stop in some shelter instead of on the bare plateau, but when the visibility finally gave out they were far from trees or banks or hedges, and all they could see around were a few stunted gorse bushes, spectral in the mist.

Through the last drifting window in the damp air, she had glimpsed some way ahead a copse of trees that looked familiar, and she held the filly pointed in that direction.

Harry snuggled closer. "Are we going to wait here? Shall we play the game?"

She thought of the three-day fogs that rolled in from the Channel in the worst part of the year. "We might get very, very wet if we do that." She bent and did up the top button of his coat. "Lean over and hold onto Scheherazade's mane. I'm going to jump down." She slid out from around him and then to the ground. "I want you to wriggle back onto the saddle and hold the pommel." She caught the cushion as it fell. "Let me tuck this under your arms. Now, hold tight with both hands."

"I'm riding, all by myself!" Harry was thrilled.

Scheherazade's neck quivered under Sophia's fingers and the filly rolled her eyes to each side and tapped one hoof—she was deeply nervous too. It would not be wise to lead her on a long rein, in case she shied. Sophia smoothed a hand down over her soft nose and then, gathering the reins just below her mouth, stepped forward, scanning the ground. The filly, reassured now that they were not going to come up against any gorse, which she hated, consented to move.

With every step through the fog, Sophia's tension grew. She could not speak to Harry, because she had to remain alert to their surroundings. She had to force herself to take each step onto the little apron of visible ground at her feet, fighting the fear that she was about to lead horse and rider straight down over a bank into a lime pit or a chalk quarry. She had to remind herself that when she set out into the featureless whiteness, there had been nothing directly ahead but a clear slope.

She smiled up at Harry. "Don't speak to me, darling, I'm listening for what's ahead."

She had intended to keep going uphill, but the land was deceptive. At one point she found herself picking her way down instead, along a chalk path already covered with a treacherous sheen of moisture. When she reached the bottom of the depression the bare ground ceased; there was no path leading out, just a sheep track cutting across her way, which she could not follow because she knew that nine out of ten of the livestock trails ran parallel to the cliffs. She stepped across it and led the filly up onto close-cropped turf.

Ten, twenty yards on, she stopped again. She had lost her sense of direction, for the land had ceased to slope. Which way was she heading now, to the cliffs or away? And then she heard it—the sound of hooves, slithering on bare ground, coming to a heavy stop. Back behind her, in the hollow she had left a few minutes before.

She froze. To other ears, it might have sounded like a bullock blundering through the fog. But she knew it to be a horse, weightier than Scheherazade, therefore bigger. With someone on its back.

She looked at Harry. His face was pale in the diffused light, and tiny drops glistened all over his lustrous hair, but he smiled at her reassuringly.

She turned and walked into the mist again, her hand clenched hard on the filly's reins, her eyes straining ahead. She could call out, she could hail whoever was there—but why had the rider not done so? Why was he following and why had he stopped when she did?

A shape loomed ahead and she stifled a gasp. A furze bush. Farther on, a patch of heather. Their progress crackled in her ears; her hems, sodden now from the grass, flapped at her ankles, the filly's leathers creaked and her hooves squeaked on the wet turf. There was no hope of detecting the sound of a following horse.

Shivering, she turned, reached up and patted Harry's knee. She put her fingers to her lips, waited for his obedient nod, then took a fleeting glance behind them. Nothing presented itself except white haze, but suddenly, a little closer than before, she caught the scrape of a boot in the stirrup, the snort of a horse blowing through its nostrils. Once again, the rider had halted.

There was just a chance, if the three of them remained completely still, that the pursuer would start moving again, cast about for them in the mist and ride by without finding them. But she could not rely on a nervous filly and a small boy to remain silent for such a game of blindman's buff. Whether there was a cliff ahead or not, she must move faster.

As she did so, her throat contracting at every sound, the alternatives flashed through her mind: gypsy, horse thief, highwayman, smuggler. The last would surely be seeking to avoid her. Smuggling was a thriving trade on the south coast, and those who engaged in it relished fog if a landing was due. But the other three . . . If the rider had seen her before the mist engulfed her—a lone woman on a fine horse, with only a child as protection . . .

A dense shape rose up in her path, arms out, and she bit back a cry. The filly threw up her head, nearly tearing the reins from her hand. Then Sophia reached up and placed a hand on her neck and whispered to her, "It's just a tree. Come."

A few more paces, and they were in a copse. The mist had not penetrated it fully, there was little undergrowth, and through the wreaths of vapor she could make out where the trees grew most densely—hornbeam and oak distorted by the winds from the ocean. She was facing down the length of the copse, and if it was the one she had identified earlier, she could summon an image of what was beyond.

Beneath her feet was a carpet of leaves and moss, spongy with damp. There was only one thing to do. She reached up and pressed Harry's fingers firmly around the pommel, whispering, "Hold on tight. I'm going to mount."

She put her foot in the stirrup and swung up, and as she did so, above the rustle of her skirts and the swish of leaves as Scheherazade shifted her weight, she heard it again—the sound of hooves, faster, out to the left.

Then they were off, the filly springing forward under the floating, ghostly branches, Sophia bending low with one arm clutching her son, the other extended over the flying mane. They were running blind, with no idea of what obstacles might lie in the way; and deaf, for as twigs whipped by and Scheherazade's hooves thrummed on the ground, Sophia could not guess where the other rider might be—behind, on the margins of the wood, or swinging round in an arc to cut them off.

Then all at once they were out of the trees and on bare ground, small stones and fragments of chalk spattering up from the filly's hooves. The fog was stifling. Sophia could feel the horse's fear surging up with the sweat that ran on the dark, plunging neck. The ground sloped; she prayed it was for the right reason. The fog here was parting, dissipating—in its long glide in from the sea it covered the high ground, but had not yet filled the hollows.

There was gravel now, spitting under Scheherazade's hooves, and when two stone sentinels leaped up ahead Sophia was ready for them. She guided the filly between, they shot through the gateway like an arrow, and the world changed. She slowed the filly to a canter, which took them farther down a gentle slope into clearer air. They were in an avenue of pleached limes, with shadowy ornamental gardens on each side that she knew almost as well as those of Birlingdean, since they had been modeled on those of the older house.

She took a sighing breath and slowed the filly to a trot. She kissed the top of Harry's head. "See what we find when the curtain opens? This place is called Joliffe Court. Soon you'll see a fountain with a dolphin. Here it is!" She could not prevent her voice from shaking. "Over there is the carriageway to the stables. But if we go straight ahead there's a sweep that takes us to the front steps. We're going to knock on the door and see if Mr. Joliffe is at home."

"He won't chase us, Mama, will he?" Harry said in a small voice.

"No, sweetheart."

But they did not get there. On a path to the right, from the direction of the stables, a man appeared through the swirling mist, a bulky figure, striding purposefully, and before they could distinguish face or feature a voice called, "Who goes there?"

Her hands tightened on the reins and the filly came to a trembling halt. The man advanced, came into view.

He was booted, with a shotgun over one arm, and he wore a long greatcoat with capes. Beneath the curled brim of his tall hat she could see fair hair darkened by the fog, and a wide gray stare. The man with the gun was Jacques Decernay.

CHAPTER THIRTEEN

Harry was trying not to cry. Mama was frightened, his ride on Sherazade had gone all wrong, and now there was a giant.

The giant swept off his tall hat and ran up to them in his big heavy boots, and Harry shrank back.

"What's wrong? What is it?" Mama did not answer and the giant went on. "I could hear you coming. At the gallop, in fog like this—what were you doing? And with a child."

The eyes fixed on Harry were not so fierce close up. Without the hat he looked more like a man, though he had a funny way of talking. He said "ear" like Mitchell, not "hear" like Mama. His voice was nice and soft. "I wager you've done enough riding for one day. Now, let's have you."

There was no time for Mama to argue or for Harry to wriggle away; he was seized and lifted down and hooked to the man by one strong arm, with the hat cupped over his knees. It was not too bad because the man was looking at Mama instead of him. Harry held himself very straight but put one hand on the man's shoulder, just to see how it felt. It was rough and warm.

Mama cried out, "How dare you! You're frightening him!"

"No, *you* are. Tell me, in the name of God, what is

happening? Let me help you." When she still did not answer, the man gave an angry sound through his teeth and nose, very like a horse, which suddenly made Harry want to laugh.

The man saw and gave him a crooked grin. "But first we'll take you indoors. Rogers!"

It was a huge roar, right next to Harry's ear, but it just made him hold on tighter, as the man started to stride off toward the steps at the end of the sweep. A groom came running from the stables. Sherazade stepped daintily along behind them, watching Harry in a questioning way; he could tell she was curious about the man.

Now Mama looked angry.

When they reached the steps, the man stopped, the long gun swinging from one hand, and said to Rogers, "Assist Lady Hamilton to dismount, if you please." Then he said to Harry, as Mama dropped neatly to the ground, "What is your filly called?"

"Sherazade."

"Rogers will take her to the stables. She'll be well looked after." The man nodded to Rogers, who began to lead her away, and stood watching for a moment, and then his head went back and his eyes opened wide and he said a couple of strange words that Harry did not understand, and then: "I know that filly! I saw her in Greenwich. And she's yours?" He looked at Mama as though he had just seen the most astonishing and wonderful thing in the world. Harry was pleased: he liked people to like Sherazade.

Then the man bowed his head to Mama and said, "Will you do me the honor of coming inside?"

"This is absurd," Mama snapped. "What are you doing here? Where is Mr. Joliffe?"

"In Florence." He was at the door now, and he rested the gun by a pillar and gave the door one great bang with the side of his fist. It opened at once, the man picked up the gun again and nodded to Mama. She walked by, holding her back all stiff, which meant she didn't want to go in. But Harry did, because he always liked new houses.

A servant went ahead of them and led them into a large room with tall windows. The man lowered Harry carefully with one arm, not letting go of his gun or his hat, then dropped down on his heels in front of him.

"And what's your name?"

"Harry."

" 'Arry?" The man gave a lopsided grimace.

"What's yours?"

"Jacques."

Just one name. Not Mister anything. He must be the gamekeeper, or the head groom.

"What kind of gun is it?" Harry said.

"A shotgun. It's not loaded. You can touch it."

"Oh no, he cannot!" There was a swish of skirts and Mama came up and stood right beside him, but he already had his hand around the cool, smooth barrels.

The man looked up, and his voice changed. "*Tell me* what frightened you."

"We were being followed. By someone on horseback. I couldn't see them, but they were there. Whenever I stopped, so did they."

"What *exactly* did you hear?"

"Hooves, like this." Harry stamped on the floor.

The man nodded. "You would make a good scout. And?" He looked up at Mama again.

She said, "Someone on horseback, that's all."

"You didn't call out?"

"Would you have?"

The man gave a little laugh. He looked down at the shotgun, thinking.

"How do you fire it?" Harry asked.

The big hand with the long fingers took the middle of the gun in a firm grasp. The thumb hooked over the curled piece of metal that was sticking up. "You cock it. First one barrel. Like this." The thumb came back with a click. "Then—"

The words burst out of Harry. "I heard it!" The man's

eyes flicked up. "That. I heard that. When we were in the fog!"

"*Jésu*." Harry knew that word; it was a wicked one.

The man sprang to his feet. He said quickly to Mama, "Wait here. I'm sending the men out. If there is someone prowling about, I want him." And he turned and walked out of the room.

Sophia was by the window, with no intention of taking a seat, though pressed to do so by the housekeeper of Joliffe Court, Mrs. Lillywhite. She was infuriated at being told so peremptorily to wait, and she was certainly not going to do it sitting down. Harry meanwhile was hoeing through the refreshments Mrs. Lillywhite had had brought in, ensconced near the fire that had been lit in case their clothes needed airing.

"I fancy the fog is about to lift, milady."

She turned from the window. "The sooner the better. I want to be on my way."

"But the danger—" At Sophia's look, Mrs. Lillywhite thought better of her protest.

Sophia said calmly, "If there were any ne'er-do-wells in the vicinity, I imagine they are long gone by now, with every groom and gardener beating about the place." After a short struggle with herself she gave in to curiosity. "I am surprised not to find Mr. Joliffe at home. He is abroad?"

"Yes, milady, in Italy. Monsieur Decernay has taken the lease for six months."

"Good heavens. Why?"

Mrs. Lillywhite patted her gray hair into place and assumed a look of tactful discretion. "Mr. Joliffe found himself in circumstances where . . . he decided to live abroad for a while, milady. He has taken a villa outside Florence for the summer. We were naturally rather anxious about the new tenant, but I'm grateful to say Monsieur Decernay has kept everyone on. Without exception. I do believe Joliffe Court will be in fine train when Mr. Joliffe returns."

It was frustrating. She wanted to know why on earth

Decernay was here, but the housekeeper had misunderstood the question.

"Mrs. Lillywhite," Harry said solemnly. The housekeeper looked at him as he got up from his chair. "Have you got a billiard room?"

"Why, yes."

"Can I look?"

The housekeeper glanced at Sophia and she gave a nod and a smile at Harry. He was tall for his age, and had gotten to the height where he could see over the edge of a billiard table to the smooth green baize of the surface. Even when it was empty, when the cues were hung up and no one was playing, he was somehow fascinated by the hushed atmosphere of a billiard room, which he entered with an almost reverent air. He would do no harm, for everything associated with the game was a sacred object to him. As he and the housekeeper walked out together, she could see that he would be asking for further exploration once the billiard room had worked its ineffable magic.

She had been expecting to see Jacques Decernay striding down the sweep when he returned, but he entered from the back of the house and walked into the room behind her. She turned as he tossed his hat onto a table by the door and shrugged the greatcoat off his shoulders. She was just silently rejoicing that he no longer had the shotgun, when he reached into the pocket of the coat and laid a pistol next to his hat, before flinging the garment across a chair back.

"I should be obliged if you would conceal that firearm, monsieur."

He thrust his chin out at her and his eyes narrowed. Then he gave an ironic snort and, lifting the hat, clapped it down over the pistol, then advanced to stand in front of the fire.

"We found no one. He must have made off at great speed. If you had told me at once what was going on, we might have had a chance."

"You saw nothing at all?"

"In the copse they found a cushion, made out of a

saddle blanket. Yours? It's in the stables. That is a beautiful filly. Did you bring her all the way from New South Wales?"

"Yes." She managed to say in a tolerably pleasant manner, "I must thank you for taking all this trouble on my account. I'm afraid I have very much disrupted your day."

He looked at her in astonishment. "Disrupted . . ." Then he said, "Won't you take a seat?"

He was hovering by the sofa now, but of course he could not sit down while she remained standing, so she chose a chair not too close to the fire. If she glanced sideways, she could keep an eye on the weather; the sun was beginning to break through the grayness.

"Why did you leave Brighton so soon?"

She was startled and took no trouble to conceal it. In the coolest of tones she said, "I never outstay my welcome at the Montagues'."

Quite apart from the fact that his question had been insufferably personal, he had no justification for asking it, since in the three days following the ball she had not seen or heard of him—not a call, not a visiting card, nothing.

"You did not attend the officers' party."

As though he had expected her to seek him out! And how was she supposed to know he had been going to it?

"There was no point," she said in the same tone, then watched his face carefully as she continued. "The person I wished to see was not attending: Colonel Belton. When I made inquiries I discovered he was very recently given a new posting in Ireland. He left Brighton before I could contact him."

He fell into the trap immediately. "Good."

It was too much. She rose to her feet. "I can do without your suggestions as to how I conduct my affairs." She walked to the window again.

"Can you?" He got up too, came to stand beside her. "Wasn't it essential that you found shelter today? And you did find it—with me."

"Coincidence." She refused to look at him. In Brighton, after the ball, she had told herself that she could not let him chase after her. And here she was in his very house!

"Really? Why do you think I have leased this place, so close to yours?"

She did turn to face him then. "I hope you are not going to say that it was in pursuit of my company, Monsieur Decernay. If I resent your dictating my every move, I'm sure you realize you are likely to be even less welcome at two miles' distance."

She had never in her life used sarcasm in such a way, but having him near made her act unlike herself. She expected him to recoil, but at each word his eyes lit up further, his expression became more open. "You are forgetting what I owe to you. It is like you to forget it— it is like your generosity. But put yourself in my place for a moment. How could I leave England with such a debt behind me? And then again, how could I repay you? You do not lack friends, family or comfort. What could I offer you that you do not already have?"

He paused. As he spoke she felt an inward jolt that she strove hard to conceal; there was one gap in her life, one terrible gap, that was more important to her than anyone could ever guess. She knew now, far too late, that having a man in her life was as necessary to her as breathing. In her own eyes, she had everything—and nothing. For the only living man she desired was the one beside her. She drove her hands together, kept her gaze fixed on the sunlit garden and willed him to continue.

At last he said, "All I could offer were my services. Anything you wish done, however humble, it will be my pleasure to perform."

She forced herself to meet his eye. "I can assure you the sacrifice is unnecessary."

"It is no sacrifice."

She tried to ignore the look that went with this statement. She also tried to quell the response it evoked inside her. She said rather thinly, "On the contrary. Mr. Joliffe is very fond of this house: he could only have been persuaded to let it at an exorbitant sum. You have been put to huge expense to remain here—and also prevented from going home to France."

Her mention of France was intended to remind him of how he stood in relation to herself and her family—in the enemy camp. But it had no such effect. There was a light in his eyes that she thrilled to see, despite herself. For it showed that as far as he was concerned his chase after her had only just begun. "The expense is nothing. What are banks for? The affair was easily settled. As for going back—" He stopped. She wondered if he had been on the brink of saying the word "home," and then at the last second had refused to pronounce it. "As for France, it can wait."

"What about your parents?" She saw him flinch slightly at that. The Marquise de Villiers had told her that his mother and father were living; they had been spared the worst horrors that befell aristocrats during the Revolution and still inhabited the ancestral château in Normandy.

He said evenly, "We are in regular correspondence."

Regular! In the last three years he had been in Russia, Spain, southern France, New South Wales and America. After a slight pause she said, with the kind of irony that she used only with intimates like her father and Mary, "But of course. What is the post for?"

In the hall she could hear Harry's voice, speaking in the confidential tone he used as soon as he felt comfortable with someone. She looked over her shoulder as he came into the room, leading the housekeeper gently by the hand.

"Mama, Mrs. Lillywhite has a harp. She let me touch it. Are you going to play a tune? Mrs. Lillywhite says you may."

"That's very kind," Sophia said smoothly. She did not miss the glance of quiet amusement that the housekeeper exchanged with Decernay—they had a relationship of mutual respect already, yet he could not have been in possession of the house for more than a few days, or she herself would have heard about it. In a neighborhood like hers, it was astonishing that she had not been told of Joliffe's plans well before he vacated Joliffe Court. Reading between Mrs. Lillywhite's careful replies, Sophia could only conclude Joliffe must have been considerably in debt, was forced to let Joliffe Court to improve his circumstances and was too embarrassed to breathe a word before he left.

She realized all three were gazing at her. "However, I'm afraid we must go. There is a great deal to do at home. I must thank you for looking after us so well." This was said to the room at large; she felt wary of meeting Decernay's gaze while under the watchful eyes of Mrs. Lillywhite.

"Are you fit to ride?" he said.

"Thank you, yes."

"Mrs. Lillywhite, arrange for the filly to be saddled and brought round, if you please. With Mezrour."

Sophia looked at him sideways. "Who?"

"I shall accompany you."

"I am quite capable—"

"I shall accompany you. Excuse me."

He left the room, Mrs. Lillywhite bobbed respectfully and withdrew too, and afterwards Sophia could hear his agreeable, decisive voice as he gave directions in another part of the house.

She picked up Harry's coat from the chair back closest to the fire. "Time to go."

"There is Clifton." She pointed ahead as they topped a long rise and home came into view—slate roofs above an apron of spreading cedars, tall chimneys atop the two wings that reached out toward the ocean.

"I know." He glanced away toward the clifftop. "You could see the fog coming in when you left the house. Why ride out in such weather?"

"How did you know?" she said quickly. On both counts: How did he know Clifton; how did he know when she had left that morning? Had he been spying on her? The idea gave her an extraordinary frisson—half shameful gratification and half fear.

"A few days are long enough to learn this country. It

is fine land." He was looking around him as he spoke, instead of observing her, so for once she could study him.

He rode with a magisterial, instinctive ease that was all the more impressive because Mezrour was a big, powerful stallion that Sophia had instantly recognized as a handful. With characteristic insouciance Decernay had offered to take Harry up before him on the ride home, and at her incredulous refusal he had laughed. By contrast, she could tell that Harry, oddly enough, had been disappointed.

He possessed the classic suppleness that her grandfather had taught her to recognize, which depended less on the action of the hands than on the balance of weight, the pressure of the legs, so that she could hear, in the stallion's heavy tread, its grudging acceptance of the man's discipline.

Then, over the thud of the hooves, she said, "What were you doing this morning, when Harry and I rode up?" He gave her a quick glance. "Why did you have the gun?"

"I was cleaning it."

"Had you been riding?" Something in his gaze, a kind of challenge, made her catch her breath before she went on, "That is, you were dressed for the outdoors."

"No. I took a walk, down to the home farm."

Silence. He made no further comment, and she had nothing more to ask. She had no sure grounds for posing the questions; it was just that the sound of the pursuer in the fog was still stark enough in her memory to be terrifying and deep enough for her to know it would haunt her for a long time to come. With a feeling of desolation, she knew that what she had really wanted, when Decernay first came striding out to meet her, was to throw herself into his arms and feel them close safely around her. Which was worse than folly.

She looked at the boots he had worn that morning on the supposed walk down the lane and across the fields to the Joliffe home farm. The high polish on them was spotless. He had abandoned the vast greatcoat and was wearing a hacking jacket of traditional British cut, yet as usual his air was as un-English as anything she could imagine. Nor did he look typically French—one explanation was that he was a true Norman, so amongst his ancestors there must have been Vikings, of the hordes who marauded down the coast of the low countries and France centuries before William the Conqueror landed at Hastings. A predator, with a predator's physique.

He said, "What must you do this afternoon, that takes you home so urgently?"

She replied without thinking, "There are instructions to be given for tomorrow's dinner." He looked across at her and she felt a silly moment of confusion. Then she went on. "When I arrived back in the district, everyone was very kind with their visits of welcome, and then I made endless rounds of return calls. I have decided to thank them all with one big occasion. I have never given a supper or a ball on my own, but a dinner in the middle of a spring afternoon I think I can manage. And I shall not be frightened if they all come, for then they will be able to amuse each other instead of my having to try to entertain them." She stopped, aware that she had been running on witlessly.

He said nothing, looking ahead at Clifton as they turned into the short, statue-lined avenue fronting the seaward facade. His silence was only too eloquent.

At last she heard herself say, "Of course, if you are so inclined . . . if you are able to attend, do please make one of the number. I should consider it . . . ah"—she searched wildly for a phrase—"a neighborly gesture."

"Thank you," he said quietly. She had no hope of reading his expression, therefore no clue as to whether he would in fact turn up. She chastised herself: as if she needed one! He went on, looking up at the building. "Clifton is very exposed to wind and weather. Birling-dean is much more sheltered."

"I can see the sea from my window!" Harry said.

"And can you see the ships sailing to Newhaven?" Decernay asked.

"Yes, there's lots. Some of them come from France," Harry replied.

Sophia said, "Have you called at Birlingdean? Do you know Colonel Coole?"

"I have met him twice," he said. "Briefly—we have hardly spoken."

"He will be here tomorrow."

"And you will be surrounded." He said this sotto voce and she was not obliged to reply, for at that moment they were approaching the steps leading up to the double doors in the central portion of the house. A groom came forward from an archway in the hedge to their right, and the doors were flung open at the same moment by the majordomo. Her household would all be concerned by her disappearance in the fog; as she had come up the terraces she had seen the gardener abandon his work in the rose beds and go scurrying off to let everyone know that she was home.

She could feel Decernay watching her as they brought the horses to a halt. He was perhaps curious to see whether she would allow her servants to make any kind of fuss about her absence, or he was waiting to see whether she would invite him in.

The groom lifted Harry down and she dismounted herself. Decernay did the same, and Harry suddenly looked up and issued an invitation of his own. "Do you want to come upstairs and look out my window?"

"Another day, perhaps."

"Are you coming tomorrow?"

"I should like to, thank you."

"Oh good." Harry said cheerfully to the groom, "I can *ride* now. I want to ride Sherazade to the stables."

Sophia caught the groom's eye. "At a walk only, mind."

The man nodded and took the filly's reins, and Decernay suddenly bent, scooped Harry up again and settled him astride the sidesaddle. "Hold on tight, but remember, try to keep your back straight."

She and Decernay stood and watched him go, proudly erect, under the arch of greenery that led to the stables. Behind her, the majordomo had moved back from the top of the steps and into the house. Decernay's big hunter shifted its hooves on the gravel, flicking its ears back and forth and looking wistfully after Scheherazade.

Decernay said, *"C'est un brave garçon."*

"Yes." Then she added wryly, "He does not take his courage from me!"

"But I perceive that he takes a great deal from you. For instance, he has very deep emotions."

The words slipped in under all the barriers that lay between them, like the touch of silk over her skin, like warmth from the sun, quickening her blood. She said, "You hardly know him."

"But I begin to know you. It is not hard to see that he is devoted to you. Soul and body."

It was like the other times, when his closeness deprived her of an answer, robbed her of thought. He had moved nearer, the fingers of one hand hooked through the hunter's reins, the other by his side. It was a relaxed pose, yet the gaze that rested on her held another message.

She said in a muffled voice, "I must go." It was an absurd thing for any woman to say when she was standing on her own ground farewelling someone else.

Her hand was taken in a quick, firm grip. "Before you do, there is something I must say to you."

She froze, in shock and pleasure.

He waited for her to raise her eyes, and when she could not, he continued in a deep, earnest tone. "Never be afraid of me."

He raised her hand, and as he pressed his lips to it she knew he heard her intake of breath and felt her shiver.

But she stood quite still as he mounted smoothly, tipped his hat to her and put the big stallion to a canter along the avenue that led out from the gardens toward the sunny farmland and the sea.

CHAPTER FOURTEEN

Paris

Civil war threatens in several parts of the country. Bonaparte's new empire is under threat from Brittany to the Vendée; Bordeaux and Provence will be next, and he'll end up having to replace the administration in every town. All he has done so far, however, is raise the rate of conscription even higher so he can send extra troops out to the garrisons. Everything is sacrificed to the war effort, including the fleet, which he's virtually scuttled: "As long as this crisis lasts, it really doesn't matter whether we have a navy or not."

His greatest concern is money, since he found only fifty million in the coffers, a twentieth of what he had available back in 1812. He's selling off state property and forests, he's revived the war tax, extorted contributions from colleges and polytechnics, gotten promises of about two hundred million in loans to the government from the finance sector—all to provide three hundred thousand muskets and as many men.

I was speaking to Fouché yesterday and couldn't help asking where the police prefect of Paris had come up with the startling contribution of twenty thousand francs.

All I got, however, was a subtle smile. Then he said, "The only way the emperor seems to understand loyalty,

Robert, is through the tangible. Otherwise he's tortured with doubt about what's going on inside people's heads. You heard about the scene on the seventh, when we were debating the constitution? He suddenly turned on us all, totally lost control, told us we were plotting to finish him off. He was screaming. I thought he was going to have a fit. He rammed a knife into the table right in front of me."

"Good Lord," I said, my brain spinning. I had heard, of course, but nothing quite as vivid, and I wondered why Fouché was being so generous with the details. *"What did you do?"*

"Calmed him down. Took note. Continued to wait."

"For what?" I said, my skin suddenly crawling with anticipation.

"Until he has bankrupted the country and dragooned half of France into the worst trained and most pitifully equipped army in its history. Until it is quite clear he intends to throw them against the combined might of Austria, Prussia, Russia and Britain, and watch another generation smashed into the soil of our frontiers to slake his thirst for blood and glory."

Breathless, I had to pause a moment before I could speak. Finally I said, watching Fouché's eyes, under their drooping lids, *"He plans a massive review next month: the 'Champ de Mai.' It will cement his whole war project in place and send the most brutal message to the hostile powers. In your opinion, would it be in the national interest for him to hold the review? Or might it not be fortuitous if . . . unforeseen circumstances . . . were to prevent him?"*

He replied at once, in his rather whining voice. *"I believe I am a little like Bonaparte, in one respect. I see desires and wishes and deliberations as fluid, evanescent, untrustworthy nothings at the best of times, though of course as police minister I must deal with such nothings every day. I confess to you, my dear Robert, a growing nostalgia for the tangible. I sense that we may have more to say to each other. As soon as the picture becomes clearer."*

Sophia had talked very airily to Decernay when she spoke about the dinner, but she was filled with nervousness. She dreaded having to welcome and entertain twenty or so people; at one moment she was worried that she had made the party too large, then next she feared that she had offended some self-important neighbors by leaving them out. She had ordered all the right arrangements, but had a hollow feeling they would produce quite the wrong results. The seating at table, for instance: precedence demanded that she place Viscount Gage on her right and the wife of the commander from Exceat on her left—but Gage and the commander had been at a stand-off ever since the viscount sent a stiff letter to London protesting against the barracks on his land and the consequent disturbance to hunting and agriculture, in that order.

An hour before the first guests were due, she was pacing up and down the saloon when the majordomo brought her a note from Birlingdean. She unfolded it and read the message written in Cousin Sebastian's firm, angular hand.

Dear Lady Hamilton,

I have taken the liberty of sending around something for young Harry, so that while his mama is preoccupied with her fortunate guests, he will have something to amuse him. I found the box at Birlingdean and realized at once who has most right to it and who will derive most pleasure from what it contains. It precedes me by half an hour at most; I shall wait upon you early, in case I can be of any further service. With sincere esteem, Sebastian Coole.

"Where is this box?" she said to the majordomo.

"At the side entrance, milady."

"Have it taken up to Master Harry's playroom, if you please." She went up herself, to check on him for the last time before the house was invaded. She could not help feeling bad about making him stay upstairs while the meal was served, but no one expected to glimpse children at such an occasion. His nursemaid was to bring him down, however, not long before the guests departed, because unlike herself he was indefatigably curious about new people.

He was at the window, kneeling on the cushioned seat and looking down onto the sweep. "There's no one coming," he said over his shoulder.

"No, not yet. Hop down, darling, and see what Cousin Sebastian has sent over for you." The groom put an oak chest in the center of the room, bowed and withdrew. It had been dusted off, but the wood was dull and there was rust on the two metal clips that held down the lid. With an odd sense of foreboding, she knelt down and helped Harry open it up.

It was full of lead soldiers. Layer upon layer of them, lying in ranks like enameled jewelry on soft pieces of felt in alternating red and blue. Harry gasped, then began to lift them out in rapt silence. Infantrymen with puffed-out chests crossed by white diagonal lace. Hussars with tall, bagged shakos. Bowlegged cavalrymen and lancers, each with one hand raised, into which could be fitted the shiny weapons that Harry found at the bottom of the box, stored in a drawstring velvet bag, amongst the horses and the wagons and the bronze cannon.

She rose and stepped away, her hands pressed together, not trusting herself to speak. She watched Harry's intent, blissful face, and recognized that it was too late, in fact, to say anything at all. This was not Cousin Sebastian's fault—she had never told him how hard she tried to keep the horror of war away from her son. She could spurn the offering of her husband's old playthings, but it was at the risk of offending Cousin Sebastian and wounding Harry, for he would never understand if she snatched such treasures away.

His eyes were shining as he looked up at her. "They can be in the castle!" Then he turned back and delved again, coming out with a long, flat tin that rattled as he placed it on the floor. He tried to lift the lid, failed, then said, "Look! It's got a keyhole. Mama, it's the box for my key!" He leaped up and ran to the desk where he kept his special odds and ends. Amongst the assortment of pebbles, shells and feathers was the key that he and

Sophia had found behind the fireplace at Birlingdean. They had combed Clifton to find a piece of furniture that it fitted, but without success, much to Harry's disappointment. Now he came running over with it in his hand.

Sophia said, "Wait, I remember this box." She knelt beside him. "All these toys used to be your papa's. The hole's too small for our key, sweetheart. I remember now, this lid always stuck. But if you put your fingernails under the edge—" With a grating sound, the top came off, and Harry dropped the key on the rug and forgot about it, for the container was full of minuscule rainbows trapped in tiny glass marbles.

She stayed on the floor with him for a while, showing him how the cavalrymen could be fitted onto the horses, carefully straightening a few figures that had been crushed by the weight of others in the box, resisting the unexpected urge to demonstrate what the marbles were for. The spring mechanism for the miniature artillery was simple; you rolled a marble down the barrel so it rested against the spring, pulled the spring back with a fingertip around the catch and locked it in place, then aimed. The charge was released by flicking the catch off while holding the cannon steady to the floor. She wondered if he would discover it by himself, and hoped he would not.

Finally she rose, smoothed her gown and said, "I must go down now. Your dinner's coming up from the kitchen when we have ours. You can eat it at the desk with Maud. All right?"

"Yes, Mama." But he hardly heard her, he was too engrossed.

When Sebastian arrived he was told that Lady Hamilton was abovestairs but would soon be coming down to receive him. Instead of taking him up to the saloon, the majordomo showed him into a reception room off the vestibule—she must intend welcoming her guests the moment they came through the door, which he took to be a country custom.

He was surprised to find someone there; a youngish man of medium height in a buff coat, who started, gave him a quick glance and then retreated toward the farthest corner. He did not allow Sebastian to get a good look at his face, so the only feature visible was his thin crop of sandy hair. He was clearly not a guest, or he would have made himself known, but Sebastian gave him a "Good day" nonetheless.

He received no reply beyond a convulsive nod, then the man turned away again. There was an alcove a couple of paces farther on, and the fellow ducked into it, murmuring as he went, "Excuse me, exquisite miniatures . . ." and began looking fixedly at the walls within. Sebastian could only conclude he must be some kind of valuer or art purveyor, though it was a mystery why he should be admitted on a day when Sophia Hamilton had guests.

Then he heard her low, beautiful voice in the vestibule and went out to meet her. The usual thing happened with him: her loveliness flooded into his consciousness with the effect of strong intoxication. His gaze lingered on the full, red mouth, the pale skin set off by the lustrous eyes and the glossy black hair, swept back today with a simplicity that looked Grecian, almost severe. If she but knew, the nervousness that she had so touchingly confessed to him only added dignity to her natural grace. She was a prize to be coveted and conquered, and seeing her walk toward him he was reminded of having just that urge to possess her when he saw her by chance riding in Hyde Park, not long after he arrived back in London—without having the slightest suspicion, in that amazing moment, of who she was.

She smiled at him as they greeted each other. "How remiss of me not to be here when you arrived. Especially since I want to thank you for the toys. Harry is delighted."

"Don't mention it. After all, they're of no use to me!"

"Just the same, it was very thoughtful. And I appreciate your coming early. I shall greet people here—when the first ones arrive, will you be so good as to accompany them upstairs, when Ford takes them to the saloon? I am a poor hostess. I never know quite where to be and I am always terrified of leaving people to languish."

"No one who knows you could possibly find anything wanting."

He had forgotten how easy it was to make her blush and how quickly her emotion came and went; it was a subtle coloring in her fine skin, noticeable only if one stood close to her.

She spoke, to disguise the slight disarray. "You have been in the country long enough to be acquainted with most of my guests, I think?"

"I imagine so. There is one I am curious about, however: does Viscount Gage attend today?"

"Yes."

"That will be interesting. He has a mighty fierce reputation amongst my military friends."

Her eyes grew wide. "*Has* he? Whatever for?"

"He's a stiff-necked, crusty individual by all accounts, rails against the Exceat barracks being on his land but refuses to discuss the issue face-to-face. I was warned he's something of a recluse, but just the same I rode up to pay a call at Firle Place the other day. Well, I was refused—they told me the viscount was not at home. I begin to guess that most of the time he's at home to no one. He must be a right old conservative, a stickler for pride of place."

Her surprise changed to sparkling amusement. "Really? But do come with me; Ford tells me another guest has arrived just before you. He is in the reception room, and he will never emerge unless we go in and hunt him out. You must allow me to introduce you."

He followed her, intrigued: the sandy-haired young man skulking in the alcove must have been invited after all.

When they entered the room together the fellow started again like a frightened rabbit, but came forward and bowed, looking a little shamefaced at having been run to ground.

"L-lady Hamilton. I trust you are well?"

"Perfectly, thank you, and so pleased you could come. May I present the Honorable Sebastian Coole? Colonel Coole—Sir Henry, Viscount Gage of Firle."

He managed a smooth bow, keeping an eye on her sidelong. She was enjoying this, the minx! She returned the look with a teasing smile unnoticed by Gage, whose murmur in reply was too muffled for him to make out.

Voices were heard again in the vestibule, and they all left the room together. Several people had arrived at once and, standing by her side as she received them, Sebastian had the rather amusing impression of playing the host of Clifton. Gage meanwhile, still with a glazed look on his face, lingered awkwardly in the background. There was a little bustle of general conversation for a while; then Ford, the majordomo, poised himself to escort the party up to the saloon. As they began mounting the stairs, with Gage darting in front as though he were hoping to find another alcove to hide in, Sophia put one hand on Sebastian's arm and he hung back.

She said in a half whisper, "Thank you for being so obliging. And do forgive my laughing—it's just that Sir Henry is the only person I've ever met who is actually more nervous in a crowd than I am. I couldn't wait to see your face!"

The doors across the other side of the hall were thrown wide again at that point, and over her shoulder Sebastian could see the Frenchman, Decernay, looming on the threshold. The disagreeable sensation this produced was more than countered by the picture that he himself made with their hostess, and he relished their pose as they stood alone, he leaning lightly on the newel-post, she with her hand on his arm.

He gave her a smile of fond complicity. "I can't wait to see Gage's face when I tackle him about Exceat. But fear not, I'll treat him with kid gloves while he is under your roof." She smiled and stepped back, and he turned and went up the stairs.

He devoted himself courteously to the ladies when he got to the saloon, which he knew would stimulate their secret interrogatory about how well he was getting along with the mistress of Clifton. They had not missed his proprietary stance beside her as they were all welcomed to the mansion. Their husbands of course had not noticed a damned thing, being too preoccupied by their stunning hostess and the prospect of her presiding over what everyone knew would be a superlative meal. They would soon be privy to the speculations, however.

He took a certain malicious pleasure in bringing the most attractive of the younger ladies into conversation with Gage, and watching the latter grow even more tongue-tied.

When everything seemed to be humming along nicely, and before Decernay appeared, he requested a quick visit to Master Harry. The majordomo, impressed by his condescension, took him up to the next floor and along to the playroom at the front of the west wing, a magnificent room with two huge mullioned bay windows looking out toward the ocean. For such an overindulged child, Harry was surprisingly polite, rising at once to his feet and taking the trouble to say thank you for the gift.

"I didn't come to be thanked," Sebastian said, perching on one of the window seats and stretching his legs out before him. "I just wanted to see how the troops have settled in."

Harry was standing amongst the columns lined up in front of the toy castle that Sebastian recalled from his long-ago childhood visit to Birlingdean. Wooden flagpoles with hand-painted bunting were stuck into sockets along the crenellations and on top of the keep. He could remember Sophia as a girl, earnestly stringing up the flags while he and Andrew disposed their armies. She must have done the same with Harry, on her knees amongst the toys, the bright and dark heads bent together. It was odd to feel so jealous of a little boy.

Harry held out a figure. "Mama says the blue ones are the French and the red ones are English. Do you know what's this green one?"

Sebastian took it and burnished it with his thumb. "He's a Chasseur."

"Oh. French," Harry said, taking it from his fingers

and stumping round to the other side of the drawn-up armies.

"No, he's one of ours. Let me see what you've got here." He squatted down and viewed the ranks. "You've done well. But these cuirassiers—see the shiny breast-plates?—they belong with the French. And you've got some good old British artillerymen mixed up with your Frogs over there."

Harry giggled, and they began sorting the figures. Then Sebastian lifted a gun carriage and found a key on the rug beneath. He picked it up, held it on his palm. A quiver of excitement made him want to close his hand over it—could it be the very one that the child had had on the morning he surprised the two in the storeroom at Birlingdean?

"What's this?" he said.

"That's my special key," Harry said, busy with the French foot soldiers.

"Did you find this at Birlingdean?"

Harry looked up. "Mama found it," he said with an innocence that aroused Sebastian's grudging admiration.

"And what's it for?"

"Don't know. We tried, but it doesn't open things."

But you didn't try at Birlingdean. He had not invited her back yet, to spare her any awkwardness. But she showed no comparable delicacy with him, for she had blithely walked out of his home with this key in her possession and had not deigned to share the discovery with him. Amongst all the things she concealed from people—her thoughts, her emotions, her desires, her plans—what secrets might this key unlock?

It had been found in his house; it was intended to open something there. His fingers were curling over it when Harry reached across and took it. "I better put it away. Mama will be sad if I lose it." And he slipped it into his pocket.

Sebastian gritted his teeth. He'd have to do something, or this would be round *three* to the infant in his own secret vendetta.

At that moment the nursemaid stepped into the room,

and bobbed a curtsy when she saw Sebastian. He cursed under his breath: he had never known a child so dotingly cosseted and guarded.

Then he rose briskly to his feet, chiding himself. Mother of God, there could be nothing more ridiculous than being caught trying to wrest a trifle from a child. With a quick word of farewell to Harry, he left the room.

It was Harry who found the treasure trove, only half an hour later. His first great discovery was what you could do with the marbles, which gave Maud, his nurse-maid, a bit of a shock, and he had to promise to stop by dinnertime. He stopped before then, though, because he hit one of the horses and made a dent and he felt sorry for it. After that he built two castles, one with the big courtyard and the other with the keep and a whole pile of other pieces that you fitted together like a jigsaw. The armies fought, and the British took a huge amount of prisoners. Harry sorted out the best-looking French soldiers and made them officers, and decided to lock them inside the keep.

The keep had only a painted door, and none of the slits in the side was big enough to push a soldier through, but still he was sure there must be a way to get inside. So he had a better look, and found he could tilt back the pointy roof. Under that there was a circle of wood, with a square trapdoor in it, made of brass. And in the trapdoor was a keyhole.

Harry was so thrilled he called Maud to come and look. "See! There's a door, and guess what, I bet you can open it and drop the soldiers into the dungeon!"

She tried the trapdoor with her fingernails. "How?"

Breathless, Harry reached into his pocket for the key. Maud watched, fascinated now, as he fitted it in and turned it. When he pulled back on it, the trapdoor opened with a satisfying little squeak.

"It opens!" Harry said and peered in. His head snapped back and he cried out, "There's something in there!"

"Goodness. Let me," said Maud.

But he was much too quick for her. In went his hand, and out came a little paper package, closed with a seal. He put it on the floor, yelled, "There's another one!" and dipped in once more.

There were two folded pieces of paper, with writing on the outside. Maud bent over, picked them up gingerly and stood there examining them, mouthing words.

"What do they say? Who are they for?"

"This one says, 'To my dearest wife.' And this one, 'For my son.'"

To Harry, it was terrifying and wonderful at once, like the first time he and Mama sailed in a ship. He looked up at Maud's solemn face. His voice came out in a whisper.

"For me?"

CHAPTER FIFTEEN

It was the kind of dinner she would have thoroughly enjoyed if it had been hosted by somebody else. It was dominated by the unpredictable, though the food and wine were served without mishap. At different parts of the table there seemed to be a play of personalities to bring conversation to life, and nowhere was this more obvious than in the center, where Sophia had positioned Jacques Decernay.

Truth to tell, if she had succumbed to temptation she would have placed him nearer to the head of the table, but she was afraid that if she did, she would find it hard to concentrate on her other guests—and this could not fail to be noticed. Instead, he was close enough for her to observe him, but too far away for her to monitor what he said, which meant that she spent the whole meal in agony in case he said something embarrassing. The livelier his section of the board grew, the greater the suspense.

It had started the moment he walked into the house. An elderly couple, Mr. and Mrs. Addington, had arrived at the same time with their son and daughter, so when Decernay strode into the vestibule to greet Sophia they were only a few paces away.

He bowed, raised her hand to his lips and then said,

"Lady Hamilton. This is a great honor. I must ask: I hope you have suffered no ill effects from yesterday?"

She looked at him in consternation. She had no intention of letting anyone know about the incident in the fog and her headlong flight to Joliffe Court. What good would it do the neighbors to hear about it? And could he imagine her making a drama of it at the dinner table? He must have seen her fright, for even before the words were out of her mouth his eyes twinkled with amusement.

She said with the utmost meaning, "I am perfectly well, thank you."

"Splendid." He released her hand and straightened, casting a rapid glance around the vestibule that took in the approaching group. He wriggled his shoulders under his coat and his smile turned to one of satisfaction. The gesture, the smile, were familiar to her, and she was beginning to realize what they meant—a complete sensual engagement with the here and now. A second later he captured her gaze again and said, "Thank you for asking me here. It gives me the chance to prove what I promised you yesterday."

"And what was that?" she said helplessly.

"You need never be afraid of me."

On the contrary—for he was just then exposing her to a battery of curious faces, as the Addingtons pressed in to receive their welcome. She muddled through that, while he stood at her side and beamed at them. She was about to introduce him, when it turned out that they had already spoken when they all alighted in the avenue—something about coaches or horses. She had no need to explain that he had taken Joliffe Court; they already knew.

More guests arrived, and Decernay accompanied the Addingtons upstairs. As he moved away, she had to fight the urge to reach out to take his hand and keep him by her. All the time she was speaking to the others, she followed his voice until it faded into the rooms above, and even after the words were indistinguishable she could feel the vigor of it, the directness, the edge of humor. She could never be sure what he would say next—but still she yearned to hear it.

When everyone had arrived and she ascended to the saloon, she found the crowd had dissolved into groups, with no one standing alone or unattended. Sir Henry Gage, who normally had a tendency to drift into corners, was in conversation with Decernay and, as Sophia paused not far away to talk to a merchant and his wife from Cliffe, she had the chance to observe the two men. Gage was more animated than usual; he had been drawn out on the subject of fishing, which was almost as near to his heart as hunting. Decernay was well aware of her, as a lightning glance had shown, but he was giving the viscount his polite concentration. She was struck by the contrast between Sir Henry's pale, freckled complexion and Decernay's healthy color; no one could have guessed that only weeks before he had been beaten to within an inch of his life. She felt an inward shiver, and to banish it she drank in the image of how he looked now—the straight back, the easy stance of his strong frame. He wore a dark blue coat over a silk waistcoat in the same shade, and the breeches were calfskin, molded to the leg in cavalry fashion that went with the high Hessian boots, which today had a fine sheen of dust over the polish. He did not look out of place, and though he was French, no one seemed to see him in the light of an enemy except herself. Even she, at this moment, could not feel that Andrew would have resented his presence at Clifton. Decernay was a soldier, and at the Battle of San Sebastian he had fought for England.

He did not try to approach her again in the saloon, but moved from group to group, discovering conversations and prompting new ones. By contrast, Cousin Sebastian remained near her, as though ready to spring to her aid at any moment. She had the idea at one stage of bringing him and Decernay together, since they were a little acquainted, but when she suggested it he threw a sarcastic look across the room to where Decernay was standing with Sir Henry and the Addingtons, and said, "He seems to be making himself sufficiently at home already."

She was surprised, but let it pass. Later, when dinner was announced, Cousin Sebastian helped to encourage the couples to move in due order to the dining room, where of course he was placed at a high position at table.

Sophia was occupied by those closest to her, but she could not help stealing glances at Decernay, who began a fluent conversation with Miss Millicent Addington, seated opposite him. Sophia had thought that by placing him at some distance she would perhaps be able to read him unobtrusively, to get to know him better. It was impossible; his face was never in repose. She had to catch and interpret every expression at speed, without the advantage that Millicent had, of looking straight into the flashing gray eyes.

Everything at her own end of the table went swimmingly at first. Sir Henry, on her right, seemed oblivious that the lady seated on Sophia's left was the wife of the commander at Exceat, and they were well into a discussion about traces of the ancient South Downs Way before he realized who the absent husband was.

"We think of getting up an exploring party to Firle Beacon in June; should you advise it, Sir Henry, or would it be impossible on a day's outing from Exceat?"

"A party of ladies? The peak itself is not attainable by carriage. I think the ascent from the road would be too fatiguing—my mother attempted it once and managed no more than fifty yards." He caught Sophia's eye at this point and embarrassment crossed his face, for he was addressing not a feeble dowager but a young, energetic woman clearly intent on summer outings.

The lady was not offended, however, and said lightly, "Oh, my husband and the officers may go scrambling to the summit if they will; the rest of us are content with a picnic on the slopes. All I need to be quite sure of beforehand is that the barracks staff can pack a tolerable luncheon."

"You *reside* at the barracks," he said quickly. Then, "Ah. I see. Silly of me—I heard the name but did not make the connection."

A mixture of emotions crossed his face while the young lady, who had not been forewarned of the viscount's dislike of being landlord to the military, regarded him with curiosity.

Sophia would have liked to find a way to turn the conversation, but one effect of seeing diffident people in trouble was that she became paralyzed herself; so she was grateful when Sebastian Coole leaned forward and spoke to the young wife.

"Your scheme sounds delightful, but a great deal is bound to happen in the next month or so. Your husband will have his hands full with recruits."

"Indeed we must *hope* he will," said Mrs. Addington, and when the commander's wife looked up with protest in her eyes she continued. "Unless the south coast is to be left entirely undefended."

"There is no fear of that," Coole said. "Anyone who has visited Exceat or Hailsham Barracks must come away with a strong impression of our preparedness." This earned a grateful look from the commander's wife, but Gerald Addington, the son, was not satisfied.

"And what if Bonaparte decides to mount an invasion? What sort of resistance could we muster? A few recruits with a month's training would look very green about the gills then, I think."

Decernay, who had been following the exchange with an ironic look on his face, said, "He will not."

Everyone was taken aback. Gerald Addington recovered first. "And, pray, how can you be so sure, *monsieur*?"

There was just enough emphasis on the last word to rouse a spark in Decernay's eye, and to everyone's astonishment he laughed. "Because he wrote to me last week and told me so!" Then his voice subsided. "No, but consider. He had a much better opportunity in the past and he let it slip by. Now he must recruit at an even greater rate than England. For he needs not one army but many, to prepare for battles on three sides—on land."

Miss Millicent Addington, already fascinated by him, was about to pose a question. But she was forestalled by Coole's suave voice.

"You don't see France as a comfortable place to be at the moment?"

Decernay did not answer at once. He held Coole's gaze, as though assessing any barbs concealed in the question. Then he said gravely, "I am not sure if I can answer to your satisfaction. How do I compare Joliffe Court to a little property on the Vire? Difficult. As for what is happening in France, I cannot tell you who are the more uncomfortable—Bonaparte's enemies, or his friends."

"And which are you?"

"I have been in the British Army for the last two years. That speaks for itself."

The exchange held the top half of the table captive, and heads were turning from lower down, not so much because of what was being said but because of the tension between the two men. Alarmed, Sophia scrutinized Coole's profile: why this antagonism toward a man he scarcely knew? But, of course, no Frenchman except for a painstakingly self-advertised royalist could escape some acrimony in English circles at present.

She made her voice carry, but kept it calm. "With this talk of invasion, I think we are forgetting one gentleman—the Duke of Wellington. If he apprehended a strike against England, he would surely not be in Brussels as we speak."

Miss Millicent Addington threw her a glance of admiration, which made Sophia suspect that she approved of the attempt to turn attention away from Decernay. Wondering whether Millicent guessed her motive as well, she felt a faint warmth spread along her cheekbones.

"Lady Hamilton, how reassuring. But you are so brave. I declare, if the enemy were at the gates you would look as serene as you do now."

"On the contrary. I have always been rather timid."

Mr. Addington protested. "My dear Lady Hamilton, a gentlewoman who has sailed around the Horn to Terra Incognita and back has no hope of imposing upon us in that way—timid indeed! Not to mention your prowess on horseback. Tell me, are you reviving the stables now you are home?"

"Yes. We have a filly that I should like to run at Epsom Downs."

Decernay turned and asked the first question he had addressed to her during the meal. "Sherazade?"

She could not help smiling, for his voice glided over the *h* just as Harry's did. "Yes."

"She is fine and delicate. Is it wise?"

She raised her eyebrows. "We shall soon find out. This first race will be a trial—of her strength, and our training."

"Who rides her?" He was engrossed, as though the rest were not listening; but precisely because of this, they were hanging on every word.

"We have not decided."

"There is a boy at Joliffe Court who may suit. He has a great sensibility with horses."

Mr. Addington said with amusement, "I would recommend you take this advice very seriously, Lady Hamilton. The Vicomte de Cernay is an expert on horses."

She could not imagine how Mr. Addington had formed this view after an hour's acquaintance, so she had nothing to say. Decernay spoke instead.

" 'Monsieur' will do for me, Mr. Addington. I claim no title. Sir Henry is the only viscount at this table."

Mr. Addington said with some surprise, "As you wish. I merely . . . You were announced as such."

"Uniquely through the generosity of Lady Hamilton." He smiled at Millicent Addington as he continued. "She seeks to protect me in English high society."

Miss Millicent could not have given him a more indulgent smile if he had called *her* a princess. Meanwhile Sophia felt all the danger of his conversation. *Protect* him! The fact that this was exactly what she was doing only made matters worse.

Sebastian Coole intervened again, with a question for Mr. Addington. "You're ready to admit another expert in our midst—you, the greatest judge of horseflesh south of Friston Forest?"

There was a private joke here, no doubt to do with some hunt they had both taken part in. Addington did not rise to the bait, however, but took the question at face value.

"To be sure. When we arrived today the near leader was cutting up in a frightful way, the coachman could barely rein him in. *Monsieur* Decernay pulled up alongside and sprang down to attend to our trouble. He and the coachman adjusted the harness and I'm convinced that when the beast is between the shafts and ready to pull out again he will be as right as a trivet. Set me at a fence on a good goer and I'll chart you his finest reactions down to the last half inch, but a horse in harness is a mystery to me. We're grateful for the advice, monsieur, believe you me. Just to see you handle your own team was a treat in itself."

Sophia cringed inwardly at the tone of Addington's delivery, but it was so sly that she wondered whether Decernay would pick it up. Amongst the compliments there was a subtle condemnation of everything about Decernay that was foreign. Helping a coachman attend to a gentleman's equipage was beneath another gentleman's dignity. On the other hand, you could claim that driving a coach and four oneself had a panache that set one above such considerations. No wonder Decernay's boots were covered in dust! No wonder he looked as though he belonged to the outdoors even while he sat at her table.

He grinned. "I was glad to be of help."

"Why did you drive yourself?" Gage said. "Has Joliffe no coachman?"

"I am teaching the horses better practices. I took them out early this morning and found they had gotten into bad habits. We had a very amusing run along the covered ways. They must be very muddy in bad weather?"

"Disastrous," Gerald Addington said. "No doubt you've heard the story of the man who found a hat in a Sussex road."

Decernay shook his head.

Miss Millicent exclaimed, "Oh no, Gerald, really."

Gerald continued with a teasing smile. "He stopped to pick it up and saw there was a head under it. When he addressed the head he found it belonged to a farmer who had become stuck in the mud. No sooner had he pulled the man out than he discovered the fellow had been on horseback. The horse, when they got down to him, turned out to be eating hay from the back of a cart."

Everyone laughed at this old joke, Decernay more indulgently than the rest. Then Sebastian Coole turned to Sophia and said, "That reminds me. Do you have your carriage back, safe and sound?"

She shook her head. "Not yet. They assure me they are taking great care with the repairs. I shall see it again in the fullness of time—you know 'Sussex folk will not be druv.'"

"Where was the accident?" said Mrs. Addington.

Sophia looked at her; she was sure the whole neighborhood had been privy to it from the day it occurred. Except Decernay, who was staring at her.

"At the ford below Birlingdean. We came down the Chute too fast and overturned into the water."

She had decided not to mention Sebastian Coole's rescue, but he did it for her. "Fortunately I was on hand, so I went to Lady Hamilton's aid."

Decernay's keen gray gaze shifted to Coole. There was a core of antagonism in it, like an ember amongst ashes. She had seen the same flicker when he first entered the house and found her talking confidentially to Coole at the foot of the stairs.

She was rigid with apprehension. If the two men did take it into their heads to be unpleasant to each other at her table, there was nothing she could do about it—

she was hopeless at smoothing over that sort of thing. Fortunately the puddings arrived, a very traditional collection—flummery, baked apples from her stores, and three flavors of calves' foot gelatin—and the guests began exclaiming over the palette of spring colors: cowslip yellow, leaf green and primrose, quivering in scalloped white porcelain dishes.

She watched Decernay as he was given a serving of each; was he used to this kind of fare in the family château on the "little property" by the Vire River? He looked up and caught her gaze and for a second it was as though a shaft of pure sunlight lit up the board, dazzling her. She had a sudden, intense yearning to be alone with him, and it was so strong she sat quite still, oblivious to the conversation around her. When Sir Henry claimed her attention she felt such resentment she was sure it must have been visible on her face; it was a dreadful thing to do to a shy man, and she tried hard to make up for it while the meal drew to a close.

Before the music and the coffee, Harry was brought down. As he did the rounds of the drawing room, talkative and engaging, she watched his bright, open face with pride. When he made his way to her he took her hand for a moment and leaned against her and said in a loud whisper, "Guess what? I've got something to show you. But Maud says I'm to keep it a secret until later. Do you want to know now?"

She looked down into the liquid brown eyes and her heart sank—he had discovered how to use the toy cannon. "Later, darling, when everyone's gone. You can show me then."

He was disappointed, but nodded obediently and allowed her to lead him on to say hello to Mrs. Addington, with whom he was a favorite. Decernay stood nearby watching, and Sophia had a foolish desire for the man and the boy to turn to each other and rekindle the improbable friendship that seemed to be developing the day before. But they just greeted each other formally, and Harry passed on to talk to other people before he was taken upstairs again.

When it was time for the music, everyone was wild for her to play the harp, but her nervous tension was so great that she declined. Mrs. Addington did not believe she was genuine, and pressed her, but Colonel Coole helped her out by begging to be allowed to hear Miss Millicent on the pianoforte. When the piece was over he announced that the young lady's reputation as a pianist and singer had not been exaggerated, and there was suddenly a little group of practitioners all eager to entertain.

There was no doubt that Sebastian Coole had immense charm, due not just to his handsome face and figure, but to the ease with which he always seemed to find the intelligent, urbane thing to say and do. He had been a tremendous asset the whole afternoon, and she showed her gratitude. She could not help feeling his attraction, too, but it was not the strong, dangerous pull that took over whenever she met another's glance across the room. To her dismay, she knew she could dispense with Coole's company and that of the whole crowd for one second alone with the impulsive Vicomte de Cernay.

And eventually that moment was to come. The music ceased, the conversation over coffee reduced itself to a drowsy hum, the afternoon shadows across the avenue lengthened, and the guests began to drift away. At last there was only herself and Sebastian Coole in the vestibule, the open doorway framing the sight of the Addingtons' coach disappearing off between the lines of statues, gravel spurting under the hooves of the perfectly behaved team.

She could tell he did not want to leave. "Before I go, do please name the day when I can return a fraction of this magnificent hospitality, Lady Hamilton. Would you care to pay me a visit next Tuesday for dinner?"

She nodded and smiled. "You are very kind."

"I'm not sure I can assemble such company, but you'll forgive a poor bachelor in that regard. By the way, do bring the lad if you wish."

"Thank you," she said more warmly.

"Not at all." His gray hunter was now standing before

the door, but still he lingered. "Where is Monsieur Decernay? I didn't see him leave."

"I have no idea." It was true. She had desperately wanted Decernay to stay after the others were gone—and she was so intent on concealing this desire from every one of the departing guests that she had avoided speaking to him. Which meant that somehow in the last quarter of an hour she had lost sight of him completely. Standing with Sebastian Coole at the top of the steps, she scarcely attended to anything he said. She was haunted by the idea that Decernay might have somehow slipped off in his unpredictable way, misinterpreting her anxiety and tension as neglect. She was not only obsessed with the idea that he was pursuing her—she actually wanted him to. What if, by supreme irony, he had chosen just this moment to call off the hunt?

At last Colonel Coole said farewell and was gone. She stood on the threshold watching him disappear, his figure dark against the white of the horse's coat. Then the avenue and the gravel before the steps were empty. She steeled herself for returning inside and finding the house empty too. Still, there were two things to give her hope that Decernay had not left: he had not said a formal good-bye, and she had not seen his carriage brought round.

His caressing voice spoke behind her. "Lady Hamilton, my apologies. I was detained by your son." Knowing she could not hide the commotion inside, she looked at him over her shoulder. "I invited myself to see his room and look out the window at the sea. Then I was captured in the castle." He came to stand beside her. "I have seen a great deal of your beautiful house. May I be permitted to view the grounds?" She hesitated and he took one step down, then twisted to take her hand. "Come. We can enjoy the last of the sun."

She pretended to concentrate on the steps as he led her down, but she was aware of nothing but the sensation of her hand in his. At the bottom he released her and she stood looking up into his face, scarcely able to believe that this moment had finally come—or to work out what she should do next.

She found her voice. "The formal gardens are mainly roses . . . they are not even in bud yet. The shrubbery is . . . well, just shrubbery. Perhaps you would prefer to see the herb garden and the kitchen garden? Some of the trees in the orchard are in blossom."

"I should like that."

They walked side by side, his boots crunching on the gravel. When they reached the shaded corner of the house she shivered and he stopped at once. "You are cold! Let me go back for a shawl."

"No, no. Open that door, if you please; through there is the herb garden. You see how it traps the sun?"

It was hazy in the late-afternoon light, and the heat that had been stored all day in the high brick walls radiated into the center, coaxing into the air the mingled scents of mint and thyme, laced with sun-warmed rosemary. They walked around the carefully laid-out beds and she named some of the plants for him. When it came to the savory she did not know the French name, so he bent down and picked some to see if he recognized the flavor. Then she plucked a sprig of basil, but he would not let her put it in his fingers.

"Don't you know? Basil means hatred."

She dropped the leaves on the pebble path and gave a little laugh. "Are you superstitious, then?"

"Very."

At the door on the opposite side he paused with his hand on the latch and looked down into her eyes. From the lavender bushes on each side, splashed with sunlight and loud with bees, came the astringent scent of the leaves, overlaid with sweet nectar. His voice was so soft it scarcely disturbed the fragrant air between them. "Do you know the real significance of the word 'paradise'? It means 'a walled garden.' Why leave it?"

But he opened the door and let her out.

The kitchen garden, deserted at this hour, had been raided in the morning for some of the ingredients of the dinner. The rows of beans looked as though a whirlwind had coursed through them, and beyond them a host of other vegetables were flourishing in their neat, symmetrical beds. Beyond again was the home orchard, a crowd of bare branches, with a blush of deep pink on the plum trees.

"All this has looked the same for the last few hundred years. Nothing changes at Clifton."

"You are content here? You do not wish you could live at Birlingdean?"

She gazed at him in astonishment. "Harry will one day. Myself, no, never. This is home."

His expression was both troubled and amused. He put out a hand and lightly touched her sleeve, holding for an instant between forefinger and thumb the green sprig muslin she had worn in homage to the first warm day of spring. "You were born here. You grew up here, like a willow that anchors itself so deeply it cannot be transplanted." He dropped his hand. "But you are a mystery—you also traveled to the end of the earth without a second thought."

She smiled and crossed her arms over her chest, covering her elbows with her hands. "I was with my father."

He did not smile back.

She said lightly, "And now, monsieur, your tour is not complete without a view of the hothouse."

"By all means," he said. "It is getting chilly. I should not keep you in the open."

Clouds were creeping over as they spoke, and the warmth in the air was dissipating as she led him up a grassy slope through the orchard toward a line of cypresses that partially screened a glittering piece of architecture. It was an extravagance built by her great-grandfather, an elegant building made of broad, curving sheets of glass ribbed with steel.

Inside, at this time of the day, it was dim and hushed. She had expected to find the head gardener there, but a quick glance down each of the long aisles revealed no one.

She called out anyway. "Williams?" There was no answer.

She was alone with Decernay; the moment she had yearned for and dreaded. She needed to draw closer to him, to understand what drove him. Was this the moment of revelation, when she dared to discover the man he really was? She looked around, her heart beating strongly while she tried to keep her expression calm.

In the area where they stood, the racks on each side were lined with orchid plants. Most had finished flowering in midwinter, but here and there dendrobiums lifted their luminous faces.

"These are Williams' pride and joy," she heard herself say. "He is usually here at this time, seeing to the watering."

"It's beautiful," he said quietly.

She moved down the building at a slow walk, amongst burgeoning greenery that filtered the evening light, for the arched panes and slender frame of steel above let in a muted, pearly glow from the overcast sky.

She knew there was no one else about, yet she carried on as though Williams were going to materialize at any moment from behind some lush group of exotics. She went farther, past rows of seedbeds and rare bulbs and seedlings, toward the fernery. She knew what she was doing, but a tiny, detached part of her mind marveled that she was doing it.

They had ceased to speak. She was aware of every movement they made together through the moist air and she could sense him close behind her, guess the rhythm of his breathing, understand what his skin would feel like if it touched hers. It was almost as though they were one creature moving through the gloom, brushing past the hanging leaves of the ferns, coming gently, silently to a stop on the moss and leaf litter in the dark center of the hothouse garden.

She turned. He was inches away, quite still, his eyes probing hers, and in them she could detect uncertainty that was suddenly overwhelmed by longing. He put one hand gently at the nape of her neck, his thumb along the line of her jaw, tilting her face toward him. She said nothing; she lifted her hand and brushed her fingers through his hair, watching the eyes flicker and then open in wonder.

She had meant to speak, to ask questions, to demand answers. Instead, on a deep, wordless impulse, she slipped her arms around his neck, and felt his own close tight around her. Their lips met, she wound her hands into his hair, and as he brought his mouth down on hers she felt a hunger, a thirst that took over her whole body and made her cling to him fiercely.

He freed her mouth, strained her even closer and whispered, "I never dared to dream this."

She swayed in his arms, turned her head to read his face, her lips brushing his cheek, one hand buried in his hair, the other on his shoulder. "Yes you did."

The barriers had gone. In some profound, powerful sense, he and she already knew each other, for they had touched in imagination, in hidden longing, in the lonely hours of the night. There was no need now for pretense or restraint.

Holding her bound in his arms he began to kiss her again, with tender slowness. Then he explored her face, her neck and shoulders with kisses that were hard and lingering by turns. With delirious swiftness she began to adjust to his touch, to discover the exact texture of his skin, to hear his desire in his taut breathing, to see it in his eyes, which were darkened now like storm clouds gathering.

Then for an instant they held each other, breathing deeply, her temple against his, as though their thoughts were traveling on a pure current from mind to mind. His hands were spread across her spine, crushing the fine gown. So far he had touched only her shoulders and her back, his warm fingers sliding over the fabric, bringing slow fire to the skin beneath.

There was no need for explanations. For now she understood that his approaches to her, which from the very beginning had disturbed and even frightened her with their directness, came not from some sinister, foreign motive. His embrace held no hint of menace. He was here simply because his body belonged with hers.

There came a noise somewhere outside. She moved her head away from his and he began to release his grip.

It was the sound of metal on gravel, the stamp of heavy shoes. She pulled back farther, listening. They heard the big glass door through which they had entered creak open, and she turned to examine his face.

He smiled at her, the lopsided smile that she had seen more than once before. What it spelled this time she could not divine, for his eyes were full of desire, without a nuance of the humor or irony or protest that he might have felt at the intrusion. She brushed his mouth with her fingers, and he caught them and pressed them to his lips.

Then she slipped her hand free, stepped away from the magical space he inhabited, and led the way out of the fernery. She tried to make her voice work as she parted the fronds and emerged into view, and to her amazement it was perfectly steady.

"Yes, the tree ferns do grow well here. Mind you, they were planted when my grandfather was a boy. But the delicate plants— Ah, Williams, I was hoping you were hereabouts." She raised her voice and advanced, leaving Decernay in the rear. "I should like you to show Monsieur Decernay the best of the orchids, if you please."

The old gardener, a short, bulky figure in hat and smock, had just wheeled an empty barrow through the door. He shut it behind him. "Certainly, milady."

When they reached him, it was beyond her to pronounce anything more. She lingered by the door and pretended to look at the trees outside or the low plants at her elbow—anywhere but at Decernay, who stood listening, nodding in silence and avoiding her eye. She was bound up in him, with an intensity that gave something poignant and beautiful to the moment. She knew it would linger in her consciousness, the image of their figures trapped in the warm, still air, scarcely moving, while their hidden impulses surged within their bodies, like sap through the green limbs of the plants that surrounded them.

At last she said, in a gap between Williams' droning utterances, "I think it is time . . ."

Decernay moved at once, thanking the gardener and coming to her side. She bade Williams good evening, and the old man opened the door for them both and gave a stiff nod that had always been his version of a bow.

Outside, the cool of the evening hit her, and she shivered. He saw it, and was about to say something, but they had gone only two steps down the path toward the orchard when Ford, the majordomo, walked through a gap in the hedge on the other side. Sophia could see in the gathering dusk that he was carrying something over his arm.

He bowed, approached and held out one of Sophia's shawls. "Beg pardon, milady, but we thought you might be glad of this. I noticed it was some time since you stepped out of the house, and it does get cold about now, of an evening."

"That's good of you, Ford. Thank you."

Decernay stepped forward and took the shawl. As he put it around her, Ford said respectfully, "And I beg to let you know, sir, your carriage has been brought round to the front."

Decernay ignored him. His hands were on her shoulders, his mouth close to her ear. "Is there a side door to the house?" She nodded. "Then go inside directly; you should not stay in the cold. Allow me to take my leave."

She was about to protest, but he gave her shoulders the familiar squeeze she remembered from the ball in Brighton. Then, before the majordomo had a chance to read either her face or his, he stepped before her and made her a bow.

"Your ladyship, a thousand thanks. It has been an incomparable afternoon."

She pulled the shawl around her, wondering how she could bear to let him go. "I am so glad—" Her voice caught, and refused to say more.

He took a step back and gave her a last look, unseen

by the servant. Then he whispered, *"Bonne nuit, cher coeur,"* turned on his heel and walked away down the path.

She hugged the shawl across her chest and watched until the tall, somber figure disappeared into the orchard without looking back.

Good night, dear heart.

"Jacques says generals look for the high ground." Harry was draping a counterpane over cushions to create a hill in the rear of the British troops. "See, they're going to march up here."

"Tomorrow," Sophia said. "It's time for your supper. You mustn't call him Jacques." Just saying the name gave her a frisson. "It's 'sir' or 'monsieur.' "

"But he *said*." He giggled suddenly. "He calls me Aristide. Because ' 'Arry' is not a proper name."

"That's ridiculous!" He was not listening, he was concentrating on the soldiers. She glanced around the room, noting the neat battery of cannon trained on the "French" fortress, the scattered marbles, the piles of little figures lying beneath the battlements. She felt a pang of resentment against Colonel Coole for bringing the trappings of war into her son's life. And self-reproach, because she had not prevented either him or Jacques Decernay from encouraging Harry in his new interest.

She must repair the damage by tackling the question of the cannon. "What were you going to show me?"

"Oh!" Harry dropped the counterpane and ran to his desk. "Look, Mama, letters! I found them in the keep. I opened it with the special key!" He ran back to her and put them into her hands. "Maud says one is for you and one is for me."

She took them, turned them to the light, and saw the inscriptions. Next moment she found herself on the floor, sitting on the edge of the counterpane, her head swimming. Harry, surprised but pleased, settled himself alongside and looked up at her, wide-eyed.

"Are they really from my papa?"

With a tremendous effort she rallied enough to pick

up the little package that had fallen into her lap. *For my son.* She put her hand over the one that lay next to her on the floor. Dazed, she said, "*How* did you find them?"

"With the key." Harry took it out of his pocket. "You get the keep, and you lift up the roof and there's a little door underneath. Let me show you."

"Later, darling." She felt faint, but she must not let Harry realize; it was a matter of joy that against all odds he had received a last message from his father. With trembling fingers she broke the seal on Harry's letter.

It was a single sheet of paper folded around an object that revealed itself to be a solid gold pin, for a cravat or lapel. It was of a simple design—a bar with a horseshoe set into it, engraved with the letters A H.

She sat looking at it for a while, holding it in her palm, then turned to Harry with a smile. "Your father used to wear this when he was quite young; it was a favorite, because he loved horses, just like you." She leaned over Harry and carefully pinned it on his jacket. "Horseshoes are lucky. It goes this way, see? With the ends pointing up, so the luck can't run out."

Harry looked down at it with shining eyes, then said with a touch of awe, "What does the writing say?"

There were just a few lines. She read them out to him softly, feeling an ache in her throat but determined that she would not allow tears to tarnish the gift of this moment.

Harry, today the army calls me away from home again. I hope you never know what it means to leave behind the two most precious people in the world. You are just little, but I said a great deal to you as you lay asleep this morning. Now that you are older, let me tell you the most important things again. I love you and your mother more than my life. I pray that you grow strong and healthy by her side. When you are a man, do your duty without flinching, and courage will always come to you when you most need it. When you wear this pin, know that my thoughts and my hopes ride with you always. Farewell.

"Is that all?" Harry whispered.

"Here is his name." She traced Andrew's signature with her fingertip as Harry snuggled against her.

"Shall I keep this safe for you, darling?" He nodded and took the letter out of her hand to examine it.

As she picked up the other letter, she heard footsteps approaching. Maud appeared in the doorway, ready to fetch Harry downstairs for supper, and stopped short, surprised to see them sitting on the floor.

The letter began to unfold in Sophia's fingers and she looked down. "The seal is broken!" She gave Maud a quick glance. "Harry says you were here when he found this. Was it you who opened it?"

"Heavens, no!" Maud said at once. "What about you, Master Harry?"

Harry shook his head. "I put them on the desk, like you said."

Sophia looked more closely at the back of the letter. "Perhaps the seal cracked when it was taken out." It gave her a painful sensation to think of Andrew's letter in other hands.

"Was anyone else here?" She looked at Harry. "Cousin Sebastian?"

"No, milady. Master Harry found them some time after Colonel Coole went downstairs."

She said quietly to Harry, "Go with Maud now. I'll read my letter. And I'll tell you if there is anything in it that your papa would have wanted you to hear." She put her arms around him, careful not to crush the papers. "We are very lucky to have messages from Papa. He loved you very much."

Harry put his letter back in her lap and stood up. "Look, Maud," he said, thrusting out his chest. "I've got a horseshoe."

"So you have," Maud said in a subdued voice—she still felt accused.

Sophia managed to smile at her as the two went out

the door together. "Thank you for keeping the papers safe, Maud." Then she was alone.

She ran her fingers over the letter before opening it, tracing Andrew's handwriting on the outside. They had rarely written to each other; there had been no need, since they had virtually grown up together, and once they were married Andrew proved to be just as attached to home as she. He had penned so few words to her that this letter was a thousand times more important to her than the bright gold of Harry's pin.

In a vivid flash she remembered the last time she had seen her husband, in London, before his regiment sailed. She recalled her hopeless disarray, her resentment that he was leaving her and Harry, her fears for his life—all of which she had concealed, or believed she had concealed. In everything, they had been so considerate of each other, so restrained, so self-sacrificing. But Andrew was dead and she was living. He had paid the price. Would she feel less guilty about that if she had told him her thoughts and feelings more often, more freely? If she had offered him the gift of her candor?

Slowly, she spread out the sheets.

Dearest Sophia, if you have found this, it must be only after much perseverance. It must be because, knowing I am gone, you still have the urge to find out what took me from you and what led to my death. I have always admired your courage, which is far greater than mine. So I am giving you facts on which it was my duty to keep silent. By the time you read this, any danger to others will long be gone; I am telling you because I could not bear to leave this earth with such a secret between us.

Shortly after I joined the military I was offered an undercover posting in Spain, penetrating behind French lines and working with a network of Spanish spies to discover and pass on French campaign plans to Wellington's staff. I knew that by doing such work I denied myself the honest death of a soldier who falls with his face to the foe. I knew that whatever I might achieve for England could never be acknowledged, nor serve as a source of pride to you and Harry. But I accepted it, because we must do everything in our power to rid Europe of the horrors visited upon it by Bonaparte and his armies—the French atrocities committed against the Spanish people alone are unspeakable. Do you know that French plans smuggled to Wellington in this way made our victories at Salamanca and Vitoria possible? I cannot refuse to make my own contribution to such a cause.

I leave now on a mission that takes me even farther behind enemy lines, and far from the regiment with which you believe me to be fighting. I am dedicated to a dangerous project—after Bonaparte's Russian campaign, it is clear that the only way to stop his armies is to strike at their heart. This is what I have undertaken to do. I have two regrets—you and our son. And I have one misgiving, which I must confess to you, otherwise I am not telling you the whole truth.

Recently, some of our forays have been detected by the enemy, and I begin to think that this is happening just too often for coincidence. But I am not privy to secrets beyond my own small sphere—if information is leaking from London, better people than I have failed to stop it. As I leave on this mission, I cannot help wondering whether word has already gone out about where I am going and what I hope to accomplish. However, that risk is something every secret agent must come to terms with. If the blow is about to fall on me, dearest Sophia, I beg you not to let what I have told you add to your sorrow. I know the odds and, if I am betrayed or trapped, I have already chosen my course—to resist, and perish. Capture is not an option.

What more can I say, except to beg your forgiveness for undertaking work that forced me to lie to you? Yet I believe you understand why I did it. Do you remember our battle cry in childhood?—for Harry, England and St. George! I can only add that wherever

I go there is still another name locked in my heart.
Sophia. My dearest wife, I love you. Andrew

"No!" She crumpled the paper in her hands.

Simply being alive to read Andrew's letter seemed monstrous. And to do what she had just done with Decernay was the worst kind of betrayal.

"Andrew," she moaned. "How could you go? How could you go away?" Then she threw herself down and wept, her hands clutching her hair, bitter tears flooding the counterpane.

CHAPTER SIXTEEN

When Sebastian's carriage drew up before Clifton two days later, he was in a hopeful mood. Sophia Hamilton had sent him a message the afternoon before, declining his invitation to dinner because she was going to Brighton. He had replied at once, offering to convey her there himself, and she had accepted.

When he was shown into the vestibule, she emerged instantly from the breakfast room. "Good morning, Colonel. I promise not to keep you waiting long. I am all packed; let me just run upstairs to Harry."

He bowed and examined her. She looked tired, or perhaps upset about something, but was immaculately groomed as usual, and dressed for travel.

"My dear Lady Hamilton, take all the time you wish. I am at your disposal."

She stopped at the foot of the stairs and turned an anxious face to him. "I hope you are not going to Brighton for my convenience? That would be too selfish of me."

"Don't worry, I have business there myself."

While she was upstairs, he strolled out onto the steps as her luggage was fitted into the carriage. It had made sense for her to accept his offer, since the Birlingdean vehicle was more spacious than the one she had hired, so they would not be cramped up too close to his valet and her maid. The valet, in fact, preferred to sit on top with the coachman, and the maid would be well trained enough to keep quiet. Harry would no doubt be keen to chatter, but he would probably fall asleep at some stage.

She appeared wearing a soft russet pelisse with a high collar and her hair was concealed by a turban in the same color, trimmed with gold. She held a small travel bag, which he relieved her of as he gave her his hand down the steps.

She said, "That is full of tasty provisions from the kitchen, for the journey. I should have given mortal offense if I had refused it."

"It's for the child?" he said as he handed her in.

She paused at the door and looked at him in surprise. "Why no. Harry does not come."

As she got in, he carefully controlled his reaction. He had steeled himself for a troublesome few hours with the infant, a sacrifice he had been prepared to make for a very important cause, only to find it was not required. No matter what he did, he never seemed to get near enough to the deeply troublesome Harry. But he must be patient; the time would come.

He settled himself opposite Lady Hamilton, and the maid followed, ducking her head at them both and squeezing herself into the far corner.

Lady Hamilton turned her head, rather majestic in the decorated turban. "I trust you will be comfortable there, Lucy. Do please say if you are troubled on the journey."

"I shall be all right and tight, your ladyship. To say truth, it is quite a treat for me to go to Brighton."

Lady Hamilton turned to Sebastian. "Our last trip was uneventful, I'm glad to say. But not as smooth as this will be. Thank you for conveying me."

"Not at all. But I thought I would have the pleasure of taking Master Harry as well?"

She shook her head. "It is a short stay, and we should not have had time to do all the things he likes in Brighton. He is very happy to be home—Mitchell is teaching him to ride. We have a piebald pony, a placid little thing that suits Harry to perfection."

He saw the fond look in her eyes. "You are not going to coach him yourself?"

She shook her head. "I don't think a boy really wants to learn that sort of thing from his mama." Her look changed, she gave a mournful smile, and fell silent.

Sebastian observed her as the carriage began to move. She was gazing up at the facade, searching for faces at the windows. Suddenly the drooping corners of her mouth lifted and she gave a rapid wave as the horses swung them around and set off down the avenue. Farewell to the adored son.

There was a sadness in her that for once she could not hide. Not for the first time, he was struck by a strong idea of what her widowhood might mean to her. She was fulfilled as a mother, but there was no father in the idyllic family picture. If she had longings under that serene exterior, how had she borne the more than two years during which she spent every night alone? The thought stirred him, but he tried to put it aside and keep his mind clear. This journey gave him a unique opportunity to encourage her trust in him. He must not waste it.

What stirred *her*? What were her desires? At the dinner two days before, he had seen more than one hint of an attraction between her and Decernay. Subtle enough for no one else to notice except himself, but there all the same. The thing was unconscionable, and for her sake must not be allowed to develop—but it was possible he was overreacting. As far as he knew there had been no contact whatsoever the next day, and now she was rushing off to Brighton without a word to anyone in the neighborhood except himself. He had made inquiries and learned that Decernay was remaining at Joliffe, so the two were not about to meet in town.

"What takes you to Brighton?"

"An invitation." She stopped and looked at him almost apologetically. He had the usual feeling in such circumstances, a niggling sense of rejection. Last time they had spoken about Brighton, he had mentioned a party that she had not deigned to attend. This time, there was clearly an event coming up to which she did not expect him to be invited.

She went on with a little hesitation. "The note arrived yesterday morning. I did not feel I should refuse." A look of painful confusion crossed her face. "It came from His Highness, the Prince Regent."

If only she could be told of his own connection with Prinny! His mood improved. "A supper, a ball?"

"I am invited after supper, and not to a ball, but a phantasmagoria."

"A *what*?"

"Well may you ask. They are highly spectacular, I believe, a sort of magic lantern show writ large. He delights to surprise his guests with them."

He smiled at her knowingly. "Do I detect a lack of enthusiasm?"

She looked down at her gloved hands, clasped together in her lap. "It is more the manner of the invitation that disturbs me." She looked up, and a rosy blush spread along her cheekbones. "I wonder if I might discuss it with you?"

"I should be honored." By God, what had the fat satyr written to her?

"You were in London, I think, when the Corn Bill was going through the House. You'll remember the riots. I was at a ball one night and my father and I were anxious to get home to Bedford Square. Because of the danger in the streets the Prince Regent very kindly lent us his carriage."

"More likely to have drawn fire, I would have thought."

"No, his crest was not displayed. But there were two armed equerries."

The experience had gone deep; she had a haunted look. He said with quick concern, "What happened? You came to no harm, I hope?"

She shook her head. "We reached the house safely, but there was a wild crowd in the square and we had to make a dash for the door. I kicked off my shoes in the carriage so I could run more easily." She stopped. "If it is silly of me to be concerned, it seems even sillier to tell you."

"My dear cousin—I may call you that?" He took her silence for consent and forged on. "Tell me. You know it will go no farther."

All of a sudden he was aware of the maid, who was so still he had quite forgotten her. Had Sophia Hamilton overlooked her too? No, if she was prepared to speak frankly, she must have complete trust in the girl's discretion. He looked at her with sympathy.

She took a rather shaky breath. "Very well. Yesterday, as you know, I received the prince's note, nothing more than a gracious invitation for tomorrow evening. But there was a package with it. When I opened that, I found he had returned me my shoes." She paused here, for so long he felt obliged to react.

"Was there . . . ah . . . a personal note?"

"No. But here is my concern. He included another pair, modeled on the first as to size and fit, but made and finished in exquisite taste. They are covered with cloth of gold embroidered in glittering thread. A queen might wear them—if they were not fashioned for me I might have thought they were an order for Princess Caroline."

He gazed at her in astonishment. The old fox!

She caught his expression, and the blush reappeared, making her look almost angry. "You see."

He said slowly, "He has been over generous. That's not unknown, of course, with friends he particularly favors. I can imagine your concerns, though." He paused. If the prince had given offense, he must be quite sure his own words did not make it worse. "There are at least two things it would be convenient to know. The first is whether anyone else is privy to the gift."

She said with spirit, "No one shall hear it from me!"

"Second," and he felt almost as embarrassed as she, "whether he fancies you will be wearing them when you appear before him tomorrow night." He caught a flash of indignation and said, "About which you have already made your decision."

"I certainly have!"

"There remains a third. What will you say if he mentions the subject?"

She gave him what he thought of as "the Metcalfe look," which meant, "The matter is beyond discussion and my behavior is always beyond reproach." Mother of God, why bring it up, then? But he was supposed to be helping her. "How did you reply to his invitation?"

"I said I would be honored to attend tomorrow, and my next words were, 'I must thank Your Highness for the very thoughtful gift you bestowed on me.' That was all."

He considered for a moment, then said soothingly, "Whatever we may think of the prince's behavior, you have acted right. You have not made an issue of this by refusing his invitation, and you have conveyed your thanks, so there can be no reason for the subject to be mentioned tomorrow."

She said rapidly, "I *have been* grateful to him, I cannot deny that. If he had not come to my aid on that dreadful night . . ."

He watched the conflict of emotions in her face: gratitude for a friendly gesture; anger at that friend's presumption. He said, "He does have a generous streak. And it is wise to avoid too savage a quarrel with one's future sovereign."

His ironic tone made her give him a sharp glance under her lashes.

He went on ingenuously, "When *shall* you wear them?"

"Next time I am in London. Some suitable occasion will arise." Her thoughts ran on in silence for a while. Then she said in a serious tone, "Thank you for listening to me. Since my—" She paused, then went on. "Since my father left for Portugal, I have had no one to turn to for an opinion on anything. My closest friends are in London, and there are things that simply cannot be discussed in letters."

"I should be delighted if you would count me as a friend," he said. "As long as I am at Birlingdean, I am but a step away from you."

"Thank you," she said in a muffled voice.

Did she realize the effect she created, with that shift of mood in the midst of a conversation? From one word to another she could move from calm confidence to a touching air of dependence, so that the tone of her low, seductive voice, and even the colors about her, seemed to change. It was like watching a portrait spring into animation, like seeing a queen seated on a lofty throne suddenly cast herself on her knees, destroying the majesty of her own image. Everything he had thought or imagined about her had been altering too, ever since the first shocking moment when he carried her pliant body out of the stream.

Despite his hard-won pride in himself, he had always considered her as beyond his sphere; but, like a splendid tree, shaken by storms yet still erect, she was beginning to bend his way. He realized suddenly that he could reshape the future if he wished—it was not too late.

They continued on in silence, she with her back to the horses while he looked out on the rolling downland. They were traveling on the road nearest the coast, which avoided the more precipitous valleys like the Chute, and wound its way through verdant sheep country defined by the long, curved ridges that led to the clifftop eminences known as the Seven Sisters. He had an urge to tell her everything about his mission for prince and country, to confide at least that much, in the hope of tempting her closer still.

He curbed himself with difficulty, and was relieved when at last she spoke again, about matters that could cause neither embarrassment nor discord. The time passed pleasantly and they were beyond the Cuckmere, driving along a smooth, dry road in welcome sunshine, before she chose to ask his advice again.

"Tell me," she said, apropos of nothing, "when you were in India, did you ever have anything to do with army intelligence?"

He was taken aback, and she saw it. His mind racing, he really considered for a moment that some connection of hers knew about his secret mission to Brighton. But at his start of alarm she seemed surprised too.

He said, unsmiling, "If I had, I should certainly not be canvassing it!"

"No, of course not. I'm sorry. I put that badly. What I mean is, do you know very much about the way the military collects information? I understand so little of these things."

He allowed her a smile after all. "Quite right too." She was still looking at him expectantly, and after a moment's careful thought he gave in to the temptation to enlighten her a little. Just before he began, however, an unpleasant idea darted into his mind. Did she ask for herself, or another? Was there a man in the case, someone who had encouraged her to coax him into revealing something? The image of Decernay hovered at the back of his brain. Damnation, it was imperative that he find out what was going on there.

"Shall I start with what every army and navy officer knows?"

She nodded with a faint answering smile.

He threw a glance at the maid, who was fast asleep, then proceeded, looking sometimes out the window, but more often into his companion's dark, attentive eyes.

"England's network of intelligence is the best in the world, because we control the oceans. Gatherers of information can be sent to any corner of the globe and there are few hindrances to the return of dispatches."

"Do commanders always know what they carry?" she said, obviously thinking of her father.

He shook his head. "Only if they are an active part of the network themselves. Far better otherwise that they don't."

"I see."

"The chosen men within the services operate more or less alone and routinely send material back to London, coded if necessary. Others may manage agents in the field, locals or others." He was watching her expression;

curious but calm. What was she after, exactly? He was hoping for a clue from her reactions.

He went on. "Of course, there is a third source of information that has always been most important to the Foreign Office. Our diplomatic delegations."

She raised her eyebrows.

"It is common practice to send a man with each mission whose sole job is to gather intelligence within the country concerned. He usually poses as a trade official of some kind. It's standard in all our major embassies, where there may be more than one agent. And in complicated situations it is often useful to plant someone as a check on the principal man—spying on our own spy, so to speak."

"Really? For what reasons?"

"They vary. Changes of policy at home, conflicting interests abroad, outbreaks of hostility, readiness to invade . . ."

And there he saw it, the flicker in her gaze, the instant when his words came close to the personal.

She replied at once. "You've said nothing about spies in wartime. Those who go behind enemy lines."

"That is the most dangerous game of all." Whom did she have in mind? Decernay? "Experts of that kind are rare. In the field, of course, the army relies on scouts."

"But if a spy could pass on the enemy's battle plans to his own commander, that would be the most vital information of all, surely."

"Indeed." It had gone too far; he had to ask. "My dear cousin, I can't help suspecting something particular in all this. Have you heard something in town, or in our neighborhood, that worries you? Are you afraid that someone is picking up information about our forces or dispositions and passing it on?" She gazed at him with what looked like genuine astonishment. Cursing himself, he went on nonetheless. "If you have any such apprehension, do let me know. I may no longer be in uniform, but I have very close contacts with the army in Brighton."

"Good heavens, no. I was not thinking about *England*.

I . . . I was dwelling on the past. My thoughts were in Spain. The Peninsula War."

Light dawned at last. She was talking about her husband!

She said with a troubled frown, "What you say appalls me. About our agents conspiring against each other, perhaps betraying each other. Who could hope to keep a situation like that in hand, with people so far from home? Not the Foreign Office, certainly. It's frightening. How can you ever know whom to trust?"

The husband. Metcalfe had said that she already had doubts about the way Hamilton died. She could have asked all these questions before; why now? His mind became very clear. Yes, she had somehow found out for sure, at Clifton, that Hamilton was a spy. From one of the retainers in the know? Or from a document, lately uncovered, that had been hidden, left in a drawer for her eyes only.

He looked at her with caution. If he probed, she would close up. She hated betrayal—and that's what it would seem like to her if she named her husband's secrets to anyone else. He would spare her. And meanwhile turn the conversation in the second most interesting direction.

"But you do not question the need for such vigilance, I am sure." When she looked over at him he could detect a kind of horror in the depths of her eyes, and she seemed hardly to be listening to him. He continued. "Think of Sydney Town, for instance. While you were there, perhaps you were able to analyze for yourself the very mixture of intent that I was talking about. Nominally, its main purpose is as a penal colony. Strategically, however, Port Jackson is England's base for strikes into the Pacific and India. Our agents there must monitor the strength of our hold on it, and keep an eye on anyone threatening to weaken our position."

She was very attentive now.

He said it for her. "The French, for instance."

She colored slightly, but said with a half smile, "You

are suggesting there have been Napoleonic spies in New South Wales?"

"We know there have been. Quite enough French voyagers have passed through Port Jackson and Botany Bay to furnish accurate reports to the maritime ministry in Paris. The means for reconnaissance exist—and one must assume that the will does."

She shrugged, with the appearance of nonchalance. "I hardly think Bonaparte is planning to send a fleet to the ends of the earth at this juncture."

"No," he said softly. "He is much more likely to be studying the British army's state of preparedness at home."

She stared at him. "You are saying there are French spies in England at this moment?"

"Of course. In all the vital locations. Including, of course, the South Coast."

She was half incredulous and half alarmed. He went on. "I do not mean anything melodramatic by that— masked men prowling the countryside with drawn daggers. Perhaps a few Frenchmen may slip past the revenue men along with the smugglers. Who knows. But I am talking about French people who reside here, royalist refugees who have a place in society, whom we are so used to that the question of what messages they might send back to France never occurs." He shifted in his seat, setting one shoulder against the cushioned panel and looking out at the sunlit countryside. "In times of peace, the activities of such people cannot pose any serious problem. Most of them are harmless, even ludicrous. On the brink of war, however, they may give us pause."

He brought his gaze back to her slowly, to give her time to adjust. And with a small shock he saw, in the instant her eyes met his, just how enormous an adjustment it was. *She had not allowed herself to think about any of this in connection with Decernay.* It gave him a painful twist of the vitals to see what her instinctive allegiance to the man had been—strong enough to blot out any doubts that might otherwise have occurred to her acute mind.

The hound had tried to desert at Port Jackson, but

she persisted in a belief that he was innocent, and had
even written a letter to the court-martial to prove it.
Neither letter nor writer had been made public, but if
Sebastian knew of it—admittedly through the secret service—he could only guess there might be others in the
know as well. Imagine this woman, Lady Sophia Hamilton, risking such scandalous exposure! In a way he could
see why, having braved that risk, she would pledge this
foolish fidelity to the man whose life she had saved. If
Decernay's own loyalties turned out to be on the side
of France, then she would have committed not only a
futile act but, unwittingly, a treasonous one.

A stab of jealousy made him go on. "In wartime, it is
natural to delve a little closer into the motives of people
whom we take for granted during the peace. Purely for
the sake of example, consider a gentleman like Jacques
Decernay. One might ask, 'Why has this man, just at this
point, chosen to live at Joliffe Court, conduct his business
with a bank at Newhaven and pay regular visits to the
army encampment at Brighton?' We must admit, a satisfac-
tory answer does not immediately spring to mind."

He caught a defensive look from her and hastened on.

"To take the simplest question first—why is he living
in Sussex?"

He was looking closely, so he saw how her own inner
being responded. As did her face, with another telltale
blush. Mother of God, she thought Decernay was hanging about because of her!

For a moment, it was beyond him to speak, and it was
clearly beyond her. She avoided his gaze and looked
out the window, biting her lip. He had never seen her
more vulnerable.

The carriage rattled over a hard patch of flint in the
road and the maid stirred and awoke. The opportune
moment had passed, but he had sown the bitter seed.

He leaned back again, watching her averted face. He
would leave such topics alone now, and steer the conversation into more pleasurable pastures, for over the rest of
the journey he intended her to be lulled, grateful, even
diverted. He owed her that much. He owed it to himself.

CHAPTER SEVENTEEN

Paris

At last I know how to act, thanks to Fouché, jackal of all jackals. He and I are agreed that the Champ de Mai must not be allowed to take place. Bonaparte has set the date, 26 May, but preparations of every other kind are falling behind so badly that it's not impossible the grand review will be put off a few days. Whatever, I am ready.

The night before, I'm to present myself in the emperor's study to take down the last of his dispositions for the great occasion. Bonaparte runs through secretaries as no other commander ever—he seems not to sleep above two hours a night, and he can't think why anyone else does. There is no danger of discovery or arrest: Fouché volunteered my services, and the guards inside and outside the study door will be of his posting. Fouché recommended me, with that sly smile of his, as "the most wide-awake man in Paris." For that night, he can count on it.

It's simple. I ascend the stairs, a stiletto concealed in a sheaf of papers. I am admitted without question. I advance toward the emperor, who will have his head down, writing as usual. All I hope is that I have the courage to act when he raises it.

I shan't send the note to the tenth man yet; I'll wait

until the date is fixed. Besides, the last man will have
nothing to do. This cannot fail.

The afternoon following her arrival in Brighton, Sophia was walking along the Steine with Sir Walter
and Lady Beatrice Montague. It was a lovely warm day,
still and sunny, with clear skies that promised well for
the night, when people would gather in the street to
watch the fireworks over the Marine Pavilion that were
rumored to be a public feature of the phantasmagoria.
She had been trying all day to feel some interest in her
friends, their daughters and the coming events, but all
she had achieved was the appearance of it. Inside, she
was wretched.

She was in Brighton only because she had been desperate to get out of Clifton, the scene of her betrayal.
Andrew's letter had prostrated her; she hoped never
again to suffer the torrent of self-reproach that had
flowed over her after she read it. Andrew had died at
French hands, and only minutes before reading his last,
fond words she had been in the arms of a French soldier.
Her husband had probably been killed because of an
informer—and Jacques Decernay might well be just such
an informer, working for the French in England. What
did she know of the man whose life she had saved,
whom she had allowed to enter unchallenged into her
little society, whom she had been dreaming about from
the day she met him? Nothing.

And she had no excuses for such ignorance. She had
been deliberately, dangerously blind, for there had been
warnings. Her father had told her to keep her distance
from Decernay. Mary Ellwood had chided her for receiving him at Bedford Square, and had said that whatever
his pretensions to nobility, his sentence by court-martial
put him outside polite society. The Montagues, Sophia
knew, would not be receiving him again, and felt imposed upon by his attendance at the ball once they heard
the full story from Mary. And finally, there had been the
humiliation of receiving the gentle, tactful advice from

Sebastian Coole—advice that he would never have dreamed of uttering if it had not been for her own behavior. How many other people had seen and been shocked by her penchant for Decernay?

And here it was, the crux of it, the worst mortification of all: the truth of her own feelings. She was attracted to Jacques Decernay in a way she had never known before. She was in thrall to him physically, hence her past blindness and her present shame. She wanted him, with a longing that had overridden all her habitual reserve, all her sense of duty as a wife and mother. This was a passion no one had ever been able to warn her against, because no one could have imagined her succumbing to it, let alone herself.

Her first impulse had been to escape, to make sure she was nowhere within reach if he decided to press his advantage with her. Next morning she had received the prince's invitation—a godsend, in the circumstances— and she had used the next twenty-four hours to make arrangements for the trip and decide whether or not to take Harry. Leaving him at home had been the best solution, for she needed time to herself. She had not minded the idea of traveling with Sebastian Coole, since they had grown very easy with each other of late.

She had seen nothing of Decernay, and there had been no note of thanks from him for the dinner, nor any news from Joliffe Court. She should be thankful for those small mercies, yet every thought of him was torture. At one moment she yearned to see him, so that she could confront him with a changed aspect and a cold, forbidding end to all communication. He would think her affronted by the liberties he had taken in the hothouse; so be it—no right-thinking lady would have allowed them! Then she remembered his voice, his hands, his kisses as they stood clasped together in the warm darkness, and desolation swept over her. Never again to feel his skin against hers, his arms tight around her waist, his lips in the hollow of her shoulder. *Cher coeur.* Never again.

He would take her abrupt departure as a signal. She

could count on that, surely. He had sensed Sebastian
Coole's antagonism toward him—would that and her
own behavior be enough to fend him off? As for his
activities, she could rely on Cousin Sebastian to investi-
gate, if investigation was necessary. She had not realized
quite how close he was to the prince's regiment; in fact,
during these days in Brighton he was staying with the
commander. She was fortunate to have someone to turn
to, a friend who respected and watched over her with a
sensitivity that she had not known he possessed. She had
underestimated Sebastian Coole. And she had made of
Private Jacques Decernay a potent idol that bore no re-
semblance to reality.

While they walked the length of the Steine, with a
view of the facade of the Marine Pavilion on their left
and the passing crowd on their right, Sir Walter and
Lady Beatrice were busy nodding to their acquaintances
and chatting to each other, for they had given up trying
to get a word out of her. Sophia herself saw few people
she recognized, but all at once she noticed Sebastian
Coole walking toward them on his own. He saw her,
smiled, and tipped his hat as he approached.

When they had last been in Brighton at the same time,
they had not come across each other, and she had not
felt obliged to introduce him to the Montagues, much
less secure him an invitation to Honoria's ball. But this
time she had reasons for benevolence, and she was
rather glad to bring Sir Walter and Lady Beatrice to a
halt and make the presentations. She even felt, as he
turned back and strolled along at her side, that he was
the very type of gentleman that her friends must rejoice
to see her with—rather than a renegade so-called viscount from Normandy. They had hardly gone twenty
paces before Lady Beatrice began to fall under his spell.
He had a consideration for women that went perfectly
with his smooth good looks; he did not quite have Andrew's gentleness and good humor, for Sophia could always sense that he had hidden impulses that he kept
carefully in check, but it was precisely this control that
she admired. It was tempting to depend on him more;

to seek in his warm glance, his suave voice, a haven
from the deep trouble and guilt that overwhelmed her
every time she thought of Decernay.

Then, a little later, another quite different meeting
occurred. She was unaware of what was happening until
Sebastian stopped in the middle of a sentence and faltered in his stride. She looked up and noticed that
amazement had turned his face quite pale. She followed
his fixed gaze and saw a couple approaching: the man
was middle-aged, tall and in uniform, while the young
woman was small but with a perfect figure and an appealing face surrounded by abundant brown curls within
a poke bonnet. She was in mourning.

The lady saw Sebastian a second after he saw her; her
hazel eyes widened and one hand flew up to her bonnet,
as though it were about to blow away. Then she came
forward with dignity, her arm through that of the officer.

Sebastian said swiftly, but without his usual confidence, "Excuse me, Lady Hamilton. I shall rejoin you
in a moment. An old acquaintance . . ."

She was surprised, then pleased that he was so punctilious; he had known the Montagues only ten minutes and
was wary of forcing new people on them. She nodded,
and they all walked slowly on. As it happened, she was
privy to the whole encounter, for a press in the crowd
kept her within seeing and hearing distance.

"Mrs. Goulding," he said, in a voice that Sophia
scarcely recognized. "This is extraordinary. I had no
idea. It is amazing to see you here. Rumbold—"

The other man bowed and said, "Well met, Colonel.
We have been in Brighton only a day, but Mrs. Goulding
insisted that we take a few turns along the Steine. She
assured me there would be old friends at every point—
and so it has proved. Delighted to see you again."

Sebastian Coole kept his eye on the lady, who eventually said, in a rather breathy voice, "You are speechless,
Colonel." Her hazel eyes locked with his and then
flicked away so that Sophia felt their quick glance. "I
suppose you imagined me half the world away. But I
have come back to England, as you see. Lieutenant-

Colonel and Mrs. Rumbold were returning also, so they kindly accompanied me."

"And your husband?"

She dropped her eyes and did not answer.

Rumbold coughed and said, "You have not heard, Colonel? Soon after you left, the regiment was involved in a skirmish in the Bombay hills and there were a number of casualties. Tragically, General Goulding was the first to fall, at the head of his troops."

"Good Lord," Sebastian Coole said, then collected himself and tried to catch her eye again. "You have my deepest sympathy, Mrs. Goulding." He looked as though he would have liked to say more, but the situation was awkward. Sophia, held up by the people in front of her, and finding that the Montagues had fallen into conversation with a couple on the other side, could not move, and she was forced to eavesdrop. Lieutenant-Colonel Rumbold, however, experienced no such embarrassment; he stood very close to Mrs. Goulding and gazed at Sebastian inquisitively.

"Thank you." The lady looked up, and Sophia thought she showed a spark of what seemed like resentment, in reply to which a deep flush suddenly appeared over Sebastian Coole's cheeks. Then she took pity on him and murmured, "Since that dreadful day I have been most grateful to many good friends. I do not know what I should have done without them."

At these words, Sophia saw a gratified smile on Rumbold's face—and she could have sworn there was something much more than protective in his expression as he looked down at Mrs. Goulding. Sophia wondered whether Mrs. Rumbold had enjoyed the voyage back from India, watching her husband lavish tender care on the pretty widow.

Sebastian said, "I assure you that your friends in Brighton will be eager to do everything in their power . . . May I know where you are staying?"

"I have taken rooms at Gracechurch Buildings in Jerrold Street."

Rumbold had looked ready to move on from the moment they met, and the lady was obviously going to let him lead her away. Sebastian Coole bowed over her hand, in its black lace glove. When she walked off, she did not look back.

The crowd parted and the Montagues' party was able to move on together. Sebastian Coole walked at Sophia's side without a word, so preoccupied he looked almost downcast. Sophia wondered whether he had lost a friend in General Goulding, and pitied him, but she could not express that pity unless he chose to speak about the meeting that had just taken place. There had been a different tone in his voice as he spoke to the widow, one that Sophia had never heard before. Did he have an affection for her? There was the faintest sense of jealousy at the thought. She was becoming used to having Sebastian Coole to herself; it might be unpleasant to share him.

At the end of their walk, as they turned back the other way, he roused himself and gave Sophia a smile. "This is far enough. We must not tire you before evening comes—who knows how much energy it takes to enjoy a phantasmagoria? Would you care to take my arm?"

She did so, and they continued on in silence. At last she said tentatively, "I gather your old acquaintances were from India?"

He nodded. "Somehow, it was an odd sort of shock to meet them. I have been home for such a short period, but I am amazed at how much has changed, without and within. When I look back at my time in India it is almost like seeing another man." He glanced at her. "Am I talking nonsense? I wonder if you feel a little the same about yourself in New South Wales . . ."

At another time, this question would have seemed too personal; now, she felt she was responding to a friend. She gave a melancholy smile. "How very perceptive. Yes, Cousin, I often think the past is like a dream. It goes on touching our lives, it gives us an illusion of continuity, but we must accept that we can never return there."

"True," he said, "it's another country. And meanwhile, whether we like it or not, we live in this one." He took a few more steps, then gave himself a little shake and, lifting his head, gazed down the Steine, bright with the fashionable crowd, at the sunlit vista of elegant surroundings under a spring sky, and chuckled. "If I pronounce an end to philosophizing at this point, shall you object?"

She murmured, "Not on my own account."

"Excellent. This place and present company strike me as having the unmistakable hallmarks of perfection."

She gave a little laugh, and the Montagues looked back over their shoulders at them both and smiled.

A few paces farther on, she ventured, "As a matter of fact, I should be quite happy to dispense with the prince's entertainments tonight. My only reason for going is to extract a name from him." She looked at him. "A name you would not give me, even if you knew it. But I have hopes of prizing it out of Prinny."

Under the light tone he seemed to have caught something serious, for he gave her a very alert glance, then waited in suspense for her to go on.

But she thought better of it. He might disagree with her idea, and she was not in an argumentative mood. She was going to do what Decernay, for reasons that she had never been able to guess, had specifically advised her against. She was going to beg—or if necessary demand—that the prince give her an introduction to someone in the secret service who could tell her the truth about Andrew's death.

The Montagues' carriage conveyed Sophia to the Marine Pavilion at ten. She had dressed with excessive care, to make sure her apparel did *not* call for gold shoes. She had on a white gown trimmed with silver, with white satin footwear, and wore a chain of tiny pale flowers threaded through her hair. The girls were in raptures with her appearance and Sir Walter said she put him in mind of a moon goddess, which made her feel she had overdone things; but Lady Beatrice reassured her with one long, silent, approving look.

As the carriage bowled past the front of the Marine Pavilion she studied the illuminated exterior with a surprising tremor of anticipation. It was perhaps rather too monumental, but it had clear, symmetrical lines, with its semicircular portico in the center and the two-storied facades with bow windows on each side. These windows were all brightly lit, while those of the north and south wings at each end were less obvious, the shapes of the buildings melting away into the night. She quite liked it as it was, but the prince, having long ago orientalized the interior, was about to have the outside completely altered as well. She must remember to take a polite interest; it would keep him off the subject of shoes.

She was uncertain how many people he might have invited to appear after supper—if she were a solitary newcomer, entering the drawing room would be like running the gauntlet, especially since she was arriving without an escort. The carriage entered the grounds and she was driven around the building to the porte cochere. She was glad to see a number of carriages drawn up, and her nervousness dissipated as she was ushered in with a group of about a dozen people, two of whom she knew as friends of Lady Montague.

She was curious about the interior, which she had never seen. The guests were taken forward in slow procession, through an octagonal hall serving as a vestibule and then into a spacious, square entrance hall that had glass clerestory panels painted with dragons.

They then passed across a long gallery that appeared to reach the whole length of the building. It was lit with tasseled Chinese lanterns and fitted with low sofas along the sides, but it seemed a place of mystery and a strange kind of menace, perhaps because of enormous China vases and the life-size Mandarin statues that brooded in the niches to right and left. Sophia heard one of the women whisper to another, "He must be in the saloon."

The saloon itself was extraordinary: huge, circular and capped by a smooth dome from which hung a gargantuan chandelier. The patterned walls were a light blue set off by gilded decorations and floor-to-ceiling dark blue hangings. Here the rest of the party awaited them, standing in groups on the magnificent carpet or sitting against the blazing gold cushions of the ottomans around the walls.

Sophia scarcely had time for a glance at the room before the prince's welcome burst upon them. He was in an expansive mood, his cheeks as rosy as his uniform, his eyes sparkling with expectation. He actually came forward rather than waiting for the group to advance, singling out each guest in turn and beaming at them while all the formal greetings were exchanged.

"Lady Hamilton. A vision," he said, as she curtsied low. She rose and he held out his arms toward her as though inviting the bystanders to look at an exquisite portrait. Then his gaze dropped, and his voice took on a tragic tone as he repeated "Lady Hamilton!" in deep reproach.

Sophia prayed that he would not reveal his reasons for this crushing disappointment. After a moment's thought, he let his gaze run slowly up her body and take in her appearance all over again.

"But no!" he exclaimed. "The effect will not be ruined. In fact, I believe it will be enhanced!"

By now everyone was looking baffled, and with a glance around him he gave a rich laugh and said, "No, no explanations until the phantasmagoria begins."

This did not sound very reassuring to Sophia, but as her group merged with the other guests and they were served coffee, she was able to fade into the crowd and talk to Lady Montague's friends. They were an elderly couple, Lord and Lady Gorley, who had come down to Brighton from London with the sole purpose, it seemed, of giving the prince advice on the reconstruction of the Pavilion.

"We were invited to stay here," Lady Gorley said, "which was infinitely kind, but I have a horror of renovations."

Lord Gorley, silver haired and very much taller than his diminutive, quick-witted wife, said, "We recently overhauled the castle in Northumberland. Made the drastic error of taking up residence while it all went forward. Reason number one for attending on His Highness here—we've learned enough about timber, masonry and plasterwork in the last year to last several lifetimes."

"Gorley has," his lady remarked. "All I'm acquainted with is dust."

Sophia said, "The journals say the architect is John Nash. What does he plan for the exterior?"

"You haven't heard? The theme," Lady Gorley said in a neutral tone belied by the satirical gleam in her light blue eyes, "is Hindoo."

"*Hindoo?*"

Lady Gorley lifted her hands in an amusing gesture of helplessness. "Any questions are best addressed to His Highness. From what I observe, he will be quite thrilled to enlighten you."

Half an hour later, the guests were invited to move out of the saloon toward the evening's entertainment.

The prince took Sophia on his arm as they paraded across the long gallery, and she realized they were retracing their steps toward the entrance. Knowing that she was new to these glorious interiors, the prince showed her something to admire in every area: the lacquered cabinets in the gallery, the colored windows in the entrance hall.

The party was approaching the porte cochere again when she ventured, "What a pleasure to see the rooms, Your Highness. I have always liked the outside of the pavilion too. But your alterations are already underway?"

"They began in March. This is the first day I could snatch to see what is going forward. And the last for some time—I speed back to London tomorrow. The nation calls."

To the surprise of all the guests, the attendants now threw open the doors to the gardens, which were marked by glittering lights at ground level, provided by candles in small dishes that created a vaguely Oriental look. The spring night was cool, and faces betrayed some doubt as

to how diverting it would be to stand about on the lawns
for the next hour or two in semidarkness.

Relief and perplexity were shared when their host informed them that their destination was the royal stables,
diagonally across the gardens. A covey of footmen appeared with capes for the walk, the gentlemen's of fine
spun wool that reached to their feet, the ladies' of shot
silk. When they were all attired, it was obvious that the
colors had been carefully worked out—the men were in
russet, fawn or chestnut, while the women were in lighter
woodland hues, from dove gray to olive green.

Sophia's cape was brought out last, draped over the
arms of a footman who came up to her at a slow march.
It was cloth of gold.

Sophia stood there appalled, the center of everyone's
gaze, the prince watching intently as the garment was
placed around her shoulders. There was no clasp at the
front, so it flowed from each side of her neck like a
stole, putting emphasis on the gown that was revealed
beneath, snow white and trimmed with silver filigree.
The effect, even without the addition of the new gold
shoes, was exactly what Sophia had avoided all her
life: dazzling.

She tried to speak loud enough for most to hear, but
her voice would scarcely obey her. "What does Your
Highness mean by this? Are we taking part in a cha-
rade? Or a tableau?"

"Allow me to prolong the mystery a little further,
Lady Hamilton." He turned to the rest with an expansive gesture. "Now, let us all make our way to the
stables."

There was nothing else for it. She sensed the speculation frothing up behind her as the line of guests trailed
out into the night. Walking on the prince's arm in the
gloom, she had felt the need of a friend, a companion,
a man, to stay at her side and deflect the unwelcome
attention. The prince's favoritism could not have been
more marked if she were one of his London dalliances—
Mary had told her that there were several women known

to enjoy his patronage at the moment, one of whom, ironically, was a Mrs. Hamilton.

Then she chided herself; she was exaggerating. He was intent on theatricals and had no thought of setting his sights at her. She might be a widow, but she was not defenseless.

"I did think," he remarked, "that we could have taken the tunnel to the stables—did you know it leads over from the residence? It would have added something to the suspense."

Sophia, who was in quite enough suspense as it was, felt a chill that had nothing to do with the fresh night air. What a proposal, to go creeping about underground! It also reminded her of the rumor that there was at least one other tunnel under the pavilion, connected to the apartments of Mrs. Fitzherbert, an Irish widow with whom the prince had fallen in love in his youth, and who still lived nearby, though she was forbidden to visit the place that for many years had been her second home.

Terrified that he would use this tête-à-tête to mention the gold shoes, she asked him about the new work on the pavilion. Listening to his exuberant answers, she noticed that he never seemed to consider consequences: everything he mentioned sounded riotously expensive. He was not known for paying his debts promptly, if at all, and the newspapers at present were full of his wrangles with Parliament over his spending. She could only hope that Nash would not suffer the fate of Edward Saunders, the engineer of the Stables and Riding House, who was driven into bankruptcy, illness and an early death by the prince's refusal to honor his debts.

She thought of Saunders only while they were approaching the buildings, where the mighty dome of the stables loomed up black against the stars. Then they were inside and she forgot him. It was a place that took thoughts and sent them flying upward. The hemisphere of glass, lit from below by a circle of lights, glittered like an ice palace. Stuccoed arches between the soaring panes met at an astonishing height in the center, where a massive rosette of ventilators allowed warm air to escape—as though the stables were a kind of vast conservatory, in which the prince's purebred horses were cared for like tender plants.

There was a collective gasp as the group took in the scene. Sophia ran her eye around the great circle, looking for the horses, those of the racing stud that the prince was used to keeping at Brighton. The stalls were arched openings set at intervals in the circular wall, decorated tonight with woven greenery, but there were no horses to be seen either inside or out on the exercise floor, which was thickly strewn with sand and sawdust.

Instead there were figures drifting about, dressed in long white robes and busying themselves at various focal points. Opposite was a narrow platform strewn with fresh leaves, where a group of musicians with woodwind instruments were playing a plaintive tune. Nearby, against the wall, was a cairn of rocks surrounded by larger, upright stones within which a small fire burned. A slender woman threw herbs on the flames, and hot scents rose into the air, along with the perfume of incense from torches fixed all around the wall between the entrances to the stalls.

"Welcome, good people," the prince said solemnly, "to the Britain of the Druids."

"Dashed adventurous architects they had," Lord Gorley murmured as the group moved again, across the floor to a viewing platform in the center. The base was formed by the octagonal pool that watered the princes' horses, but it had been capped for this evening by a timber floor, a parapet and columns modeled on those of a Chinese outdoor theater, and finished with a pagoda roof that had lanterns hung from the upturned rafters. It was the perfect size to accommodate them, and the moment they ascended the ladderlike steps and took up their positions facing out into the concourse, the phantasmagoria began.

Almost in silence, with no accompaniment except from the reed instruments, people began to emerge from the dark alcoves. They were led by warriors in earth-colored cloaks, with leather helmets and round shields, holding clubs and spears. Rougher characters followed, clad in bearskins with long, tangled black hair, their faces painted in a lurid shade of blue that drew a whisper from Lady Gorley: "Hindoos?"

"My oath no, it's the Pictish horde," Lord Gorley remarked as the last of the ragged crowd emerged from their dens, their russet hair braided, stout shields and axes in their hands. "Let's hope someone in Drury Lane will take the wigs as a job lot."

Despite the ripples of amusement amongst the guests, the eerie atmosphere began to have its impact. The woodland music died away. Oblivious to their observers, the crowd, which now included women and children, shuffled in groups across the shadowy floor. They muttered amongst themselves and often looked toward the broad entrance, covered by an enormous curtain, which led into the Riding Room. Some menace was building up behind its undulating folds.

Then the drums began, and a shiver ran through both crowds. Slowly the curtain drew back, and a sinister light invaded the arena as rank upon rank of Roman soldiers advanced, their sandaled feet tramping forward, their rectangular shields, polished like mirrors, throwing before them the reflected brightness of the torches. In a phalanx bristling with spears, their plumed helmets gleaming, they marched toward the cowering Britons, wheeling them across the disc of the exercise yard like the gigantic hand of a clock marking the hour of destruction.

Halfway around, the Romans halted and struck their spears three times against their shields. Some of the ladies screamed. The prince, highly excited, drew his saber and waved it above his head, calling out "Rally, Britons, rally!" More screams.

Then the two sides fell upon each other. The native English, uttering howls and battle cries, flung themselves against the wall of iron, and the centurions responded with terrifying discipline to the shouts of their commanders. One by one, then in swathes, the Britons were beaten to the ground, and the shrieks of the dying echoed and reechoed in the dome far above their heads.

Sophia rested one hand on a column and the other on the parapet and watched the turmoil below with an anguish that took her by surprise. A young gentleman next to her said to himself sotto voce, "Invasion! Hell's teeth, why does he show us *this*?"

Then came the answer, to the sound of trumpets that blared from each side of the gaping entrance to the Riding Room. It was far too much for one of the prince's guests, who succumbed to hysterics. The din that followed was deafening: a rumble of wheels, a grating and jingling of harness, a pounding of hooves, as war chariots exploded into the arena. The horses might have been wild-eyed and unused to this kind of thing, the vehicles themselves might have been somewhat light as to structure and heavy as to decoration, but the sight had a splendor that raised a shout from the overstrained audience. There were five chariots, a risky number to cram into the prince's improvised circus, but the drivers handled their matched pairs of horses with skill. Behind each stood a warrior with a shining mantle across his shoulders, a circlet of gold on his head and a lance in his hand. In the front chariot rode the warrior queen, Boadicea, a slender youth cleverly made up and clad in a silver robe, a golden helmet and a flowing cape made from cloth of gold. Sophia's heart sank to her lily-white shoes at the sight.

The British chiefs bore down on the rear ranks of centurions at a hard trot, sand puffing up from the horses' hooves while the gilded two-wheeled vehicles swung and clattered. The horses were quite well behaved, except for the powerful gray geldings hitched to Boadicea's chariot. As they leaped into the arena, the point of its axle grated against that of another and the charioteer had to fight to pull them away and prevent the wheels from locking. The lad had a struggle with them, and through the noise Sophia detected that he could only keep them under control by lashing them with his high, carrying voice as he let loose a string of good Sussex oaths.

Once, then once again at greater speed, the glittering chariots with their riders circled the arena and cut the Romans to pieces. They fell in piles on the perimeter, dead and dying, the shields they left on the sand creating hazards for the horses while the lowly Britons took possession of their dwellings once more and cheered the victors on from their doorways, waving branches of greenery.

At last, with another fanfare, the teams wheeled and disappeared once more into the Riding Room. The guests, hysterical with relief, burst into a storm of clapping.

The prince, transported, cried out, "Victory! And now comes the celebration."

"We should thank the Almighty no one met their end in all that," Lord Gorley said. "A near thing, what?"

The prince did not hear him; he was bustling about giving instructions. The scheme was simple but alarming: five of the guests would take the places of the Britannic warriors and ride behind the charioteers in a victory parade while the prince remained with the rest to take the salute as they passed.

Three of the chosen gentlemen were willing, but Lord Gorley flinched when he received his invitation, and Sophia already had her mind made up. When the prince stopped before her, beaming, she said, "Your Highness, I am deeply honored. But I am sure you noticed the difficulties with Boadicea's team. As a judge of horses, you will not wish me to step into that vehicle."

"Quite right. Quite right," he said soothingly. "I confess they were an *aesthetic* choice. For you, dear Lady Hamilton, another pair has been arranged. They are gentle as mice and the procession does not go above a walk."

It would have been feeble and churlish to refuse. And the ride would rescue her from the prince, who in his excitement was looking at her with a franker appetite than he had ever permitted himself to show.

She did not like it, though. The little crowd of well-bred people about her looked disapproving, while in the ring there was a stir of noisy movement as the teams were led out. The musicians began a more jaunty tune, the English horde reemerged from their dens, while the Romans picked up their fallen weapons and marched around the other side to file through the gateway the chariots had just left. In the melee, Sophia could tell the horses were nervous and jittery.

Lord Gorley, giving her his arm across the trampled sand, said, "Fear not; I'll have a sharp word with your coachman. Leave it to me."

Boadicea's chariot was led out in front of the others as they approached, one lad holding the horses' heads and the former driver standing behind with the reins gathered. Sophia held her skirt out in front of her with her free hand and concentrated on picking her way across the littered floor.

"You," Lord Gorley said to the first handler as they passed, "stay where you are throughout. You," he said to the driver as he handed Sophia up, "are in charge of this lady's safety. Go beyond a walk and you'll have me to deal with, never mind about His Royal Highness."

She had not realized, until she took her place in it, how flimsy the chariot was. When she braced herself against the rear guardrail and reached out with each hand to grip it, the unsanded, prickly wood, bright with gold paint, felt like boxwood under her palms. She tried to reassure herself by studying the driver, a short, neatly built young man who was probably one of the prince's sixty or so grooms who lived above the stalls and would know the horses like his own children.

The horses. She looked at them properly at the very second that the trumpets sounded again and a great cheer burst up into the reverberating cavern of the Dome. They were the same pair as before.

There was no chance to protest, because that was when the fireworks started, with a crash that threatened to shatter the glass dome and shower a thousand fragments down on their heads. This final display was meant to burst upon them when everything else was over, but some impatient servant perched outside on the roof must have gotten the timing wrong. Suddenly the glass panes became a magnificent lens, focused on what looked like a constellation tearing itself apart. The noise electrified the horses and they reared, jostled the handler to one side as he fought to control them, then plunged forward, tossing their heads, each trying to pull a different way.

Several things happened at once. Sophia edged toward the side of the chariot, looking for a space so she could leap out, the charioteer lost two of the reins and bent to his right over the front bar to retrieve them, and a terrified pair of horses in the rear bolted forward and shouldered into the vehicle from the left, neatly tipping Sophia's charioteer out into the arena.

Then the grays were off, with a frenzied thrust of their powerful haunches, taking the equipage into the head of the mad procession. It was impossible for Sophia to jump. As the chariot bucked she grabbed hold of the front bar and her hand closed over a single rein just before it slithered away. She was trapped, fighting to stay upright, with the heaving backs of the horses before her, flame above and thundering hooves below. She had no hope of controlling the horses; in their panic they would trample anyone in front of them and run on until they tangled themselves with another team or dashed her against the walls of the prince's stables.

CHAPTER EIGHTEEN

Sophia was paralyzed with horror, her sight blurred and her throat dry. Then there was a mighty jolt as a chariot wheel bounced over some obstruction in the sand and everything snapped back into focus. It was like being trapped on a gigantic carousel. The fireworks roared and flashed above the dome and shards of light darting down into the arena turned it into a nightmare scene, illuminating all the dangers into which the runaway horses might fling themselves: the yawning archways; the fleeing participants, desperate to get out of the stables altogether, stumbling over their costumes as they ran toward the Riding Room; the makeshift pagoda in the center, filled with shrieking observers.

Fighting to stay upright, she waited until the chariot was running free for an instant and then hauled with both hands on the single rein. The near horse veered to the left, forcing the other with him, then tossed his head and jerked the rein fiercely, breaking his stride so that the equipage lurched to one side. Sophia was flung onto one knee, her cloak tangled about her, one hand on the rough boards, the other still gripping the rail and the rein. Both horses faltered again, then took off at speed. From her slanting perspective she could see a giant monolith approaching; next second there was a sickening concussion, sparks flew from the wheel beside her and the great stone toppled and smashed into the wall—they had collided with the miniature Stonehenge.

She tore away the cloak with her free hand, got one foot on the floor. Then it was the turn of the musicians' dais that exploded around her in a hail of splinters and twigs. She ducked her head until it was over, then laid both hands on the rail so she could look forward, between the plunging horses. Her heart failed. There was a child ahead, standing in the concourse, a wisp of greenery in his little fist, the other held up to his mouth. He was looking over to the side; someone was calling him, but he had no idea which way to move.

Sophia lurched to her feet, put her full weight on the rein again and gave a wordless scream that was obliterated by a last thunderous crash from the fireworks above. The near horse responded, swung inward, headed for the pagoda in the center. The explosions stopped. In the eerie lull, sulfurous air whipped by Sophia's face, sucking the breath from her lungs. Meanwhile everything seemed to happen very slowly. They missed the child by a foot. Another aeon passed in her helpless career and they missed the pagoda by an inch.

Then they were in the clear, running smoothly, and she could see what was ahead—the other chariots, which had been forced to a halt and were turning across her track as the drivers tried to wheel them around into the Riding Room. If this were a race, she would be about to overtake them. Except that there was no room to do it: they made an impassable line. In seconds she would be upon them, hurtling into the barrier of wood, flesh and bone like a flail.

Using the rein a third time was a gamble—if the horse reacted violently the chariot could turn over, but at least it would do so before it hit the others. Then she remembered the pair's obedience to their former driver. The young groom's control had been exercised not with the reins, but with his high-pitched, carrying voice. His commands, though effective enough, had been half lost in the din of the procession, whereas if she shouted now the pair could not fail to hear her.

She gripped the rein and the rail with both hands, leaned out and howled at the horses, willing the fluent message straight into their startled ears and down to their unquiet hearts.

"Whoa, you pair of sheep-faced, maggot-assed nags! Pull up, damn and blast your bot-ridden hides. Pull up!"

They listened, and their ears flicked back. They understood, and they began to slow. They heard—and so did every other creature in the stables. The grooms who were running out toward the other teams stopped in their tracks. The straggling parties of Romans and Ancient Britons shrank back against the walls. In the crooked line of vehicles up ahead, heads turned, aghast, as the round Sussex oaths rolled around the mighty dome.

She cried out again, the stable yard accent corroding her voice and waking the echoes. "The devil tak' you— pull up, you *worthless bloody mules*!"

And they stopped, so abruptly she nearly pitched over the guard rail and under their plunging hooves. Necks taut, sides heaving, they came to a halt just a few feet away from the chariot in her path, which had a pair of black horses and a tall occupant. Speechless now, she found herself looking into the bulging eyes of Lord Gorley.

There was a howl of voices behind her, from the direction of the pagoda. The nearest groom sprang to the head of the quivering grays. From her right came the figure of her own charioteer, limping between the equipages, one side of his face masked with blood. Lord Gorley was on the ground in an instant, apoplectic with rage. "Out of my sight!" he yelled, and rushed at him with a nimbleness that belied his age. The injured groom hesitated only a moment before backing off and escaping into the melee.

Lord Gorley turned to approach Sophia's chariot, but the Prince Regent made it there before him. His face was white and he was panting so that his high collar cut into his jowls, swelling his full cheeks. Panic had turned him into a grotesque.

"My dear lady." He was almost sobbing. "My dear lady. How could I *possibly* have let this happen to you?" He held out his hands in supplication, to help her down.

Somehow she was able to move, to pull herself upright, to pause above him, looking down with an expression that, despite the headlong plunge and her own loss of control, still held something of the queenly appearance he admired in her.

"Tell me you are unhurt," he begged. "The shock. I can scarcely speak. Let me make amends. Ask me anything, anything."

Through the shattering relief, in that weird moment of calm, one idea slipped straight into her mind. She had come to this appalling event with a purpose, and now if ever, when the prince was within her power, was the time to fulfill it.

She held his gaze. "I demand to know the name of England's head of espionage."

He stopped breathing and a grimace of disbelief contorted his features. Then, vanquished, he said with a kind of groan, "Colonel Sir Henry Hardinge. Why in heaven—?"

"And where is he to be found?"

He looked at her with wild eyes and gasped, "Brussels." Then, "Lady Hamilton, I *entreat* you to step down."

So she did, steeling herself to put up with his contrite ministrations, to cope with the reactions of Lord and Lady Gorley, and to confront the stunned and avid faces of all those who had just witnessed the most scandalous and catastrophic phantasmagoria ever staged.

Sebastian had decided he must make a call on Mrs. Goulding, for despite her coolness when they met, she would be expecting it. The problem was that he had arranged to quit Brighton early next morning with Sophia Hamilton, so in theory he would be out of town before the hour for paying visits. He could have his card taken around to her lodgings the next day, but not turning up himself would be received as a slight. The best stratagem was to pay an evening call. He could not be received unless she had company—the Rumbolds, for instance—but he could at least leave a message explaining his departure the next day.

He spent the better part of the evening at supper with his host, and waited until everyone else had gone to bed before slipping out to pay his call. When he arrived at Gracechurch Buildings, he found it impossible to settle in his own mind whether he wanted to be welcomed by Delia or not. A few weeks before, he would have had no doubts, which showed how much influence Sophia Hamilton was now exerting upon him. He waited in suspense below while his card was taken up; then a message came straight back down the stairs: Mrs. Goulding was at home and would receive him.

As he was led through the building, which was respectable if a trifle shabby, he imagined that friends must be with her, but when he was ushered into her little drawing room he found her alone. She came toward him with a quick step, then halted and made him a graceful curtsy from a yard away, keeping her eyes on him all the while in the direct way that he remembered. She was the least shy woman he had ever met, and whether she was annoyed or pleased she tended to show it.

Tonight it was the former. "Colonel Coole. What a surprise to see you here."

"I must apologize for the timing, but I leave Brighton early tomorrow morning. I could not go without inquiring after you."

"Inquire? There is nothing that a *friend* cannot guess directly. My husband is dead, and I have come back to shift for myself in England." She paused, then said with less vehemence, "You really did not know Goulding had been killed?"

He shook his head. "You have my sympathy."

Her smile was enigmatic. "Do I?"

He gave her a sharp glance. Could she expect him to rejoice at the death of a brave man? She caught the look, pressed her lips together and turned her face to one side. Her profile was pale.

"I meant it when I said your friends would do all they can for you. If there is anything in my power, you must tell me."

It was perhaps a dangerous thing to say, for he had no idea what plans had brought her to Brighton; the husband's family were from Lincolnshire and the duke resided in London. On the other hand, there had always been a rather heady frankness between them. Her sentiments might make him uncomfortable, but he could usually rely on hearing them.

She looked him in the face and lifted her chin. "Rest assured, I expect no such offers from you, sir."

"I am here, nonetheless. Come," he said, "did you imagine I would fail you?"

"Why not? You did before." She turned and walked farther away from him, pausing with one hand on the back of a chair. She was not going to ask him to sit down. Her straight eyebrows twitched inward across her perfect nose. "You abandoned me."

He felt a wave of admiration for her candor, which deserved a like answer. "Is that how it seemed to you? But think of the situation. You must have realized what was going through my mind. You were married, secure, respected. If you left Goulding and came away with me—or worse, if we were discovered—what could I offer you? Nothing but the ruin of your reputation, a house in the hills where you'd scarcely see me or another living soul—no family, no society, no life. I couldn't have kept you in anywhere near the right style; I never had the funds. You knew that."

She was pale still. "You could have spoken to me about it."

"If I had, I should never have summoned the courage to go."

The hazel eyes probed his, questing. "That's easy for you to say now."

"No. It's not." He sat down anyway, leaned forward and looked up at her; a slender, erect figure, in no way diminished since he last saw her, for she had a kind of defiant self-sufficiency that neither marriage nor widow-hood could alter.

"How did Goulding leave you?"

"Poor. There was nothing but debts. The family paid them and managed my passage home, but now that I'm in England their duty's done and they've made it quite clear I can't depend on them. If there had been children it might be different, but it frightened me, the idea of having a baby in such a place. As you know."

He felt a jolt, and she noticed it, her expression hard and tragic at the same time. She had always taken certain measures with him, but he had never guessed she did so with her husband as well. He said involuntarily, "Poor Delia."

She came and sat on the same sofa, not too close, and turned toward him with an ironic smile. "All I seek is a modest establishment. There's nothing for me in Brighton, so I shall go up to London soon."

Husband hunting—her only recourse. He felt more revulsion at this than he had ever felt about her being yoked to Goulding.

At once she changed the subject and the mood. "But you, now, you've fallen on your feet. I've heard about you all over town."

"I can't complain, I suppose."

"Complain!" She said it in almost her old, friendly, playful way. Then she changed the subject again. She would not dwell on the fact that they were both now free; she had too much pride. She made a kind inquiry instead. "Have you been home to see your family?"

"No."

"Do they know you're back from India?"

"Yes, I informed them. I've had no reply."

"Strange people," she said, and touched his wrist. It seemed a warm, natural action. "If I were your mother, I couldn't wait to see you. What about your sisters?"

Without thinking, he closed his fingers over hers. If anyone else had dared talk to him like this he would have given her short shrift, but Delia was the one woman he could confide in without increasing the bitterness inside. Like him, she came from a background of impoverished gentility and neglectful parents; like him, she had long ago cut herself adrift so she could make the most of what life had to offer, which at first was nothing except a good name.

"My sisters are all married to Irish gentry with land in the north country. Their estates are large, they enjoy a fine style of living and their husbands are grander, wealthier and less given to the drink than my parents ever were, even in their beautiful youth. So, in the natural course of things, my toplofty sisters never speak to my parents. And, truth to tell, my parents never speak to me."

Her reaction to his mocking tone was to clasp his arm tightly. "What set them against you?"

He looked into her eyes; he had always felt he could tell Delia anything. She was a thrilling mixture, for she had the cleverness of a woman with a sweet, girlish side to her that invited confidences.

He confessed a little more now, from the sheer pleasure of having her there at his side as a listener, not a judge. And it kept them off the subject of the immediate future. She liked stories: he would tell her one he'd never confided before.

"They deplored everything I did and everything I cost—my studies, my military training, my friends. Or perhaps they just guessed that that was the time, when I was in Dublin, that I really came to despise them. Mind you, I'd always been able to see how pathetic they were. As parents, as landowners, as guardians of a heritage. But it was in Dublin, when I got into the politics of it, that I could really understand their slackness and shame. They claimed to support the Act of Union of 1800, but as for any profit they might have made out of it, they hadn't the backbone or the energy. They might as well have joined the opposite cause—as I did." He saw Delia's movement of surprise, but he did not pause; suddenly the relief of voicing this was too great. "They thought—if they thought at all—that the Union was supposed to enrich Ireland, but what I could see coming from it, clear as day, was ruin and slavery, for as long as England dictated to the Irish."

She took her hand away and sat back a little, half-fascinated, half-alarmed. "You became a rebel, then?"

"I was a student. And I was in love."

Her eyes probed his and her face fell.

He said flatly, "She's dead."

She flinched, then said in a muffled voice, "You became a rebel because of her?"

"No." That was not quite true; he had followed Maureen O'Shea around like a puppy, and even now, looking back, he did not see how he could have done otherwise. She had been older than him, beautiful and bright as a flame, and when she turned to him and brought him into her life, everything she offered him had been irresistible. "No, they were my beliefs, at the time. But I did join the true church because of her."

Delia's expression changed at once. She took his hand. "You're a Roman Catholic?" When he nodded, she held the hand in both hers. "You're a Catholic, like me. And you never said! What a sin, to conceal it so!"

He smiled at the transformation. "I never saw the general's wife at confession either."

She shook her head. "Of course I had to renounce, for my husband's sake. Goulding wouldn't have married me otherwise. But you—you were free." The word hung in the air between them, then she looked at him with her head on one side and said, "Dear Lord, no wonder your parents turned against you! Did they cut you out of the will?"

"There's little to leave," he said. "As well you know."

Her eyes probed his again, and he saw both pity and jealousy in them. "Did you marry her?"

He shook his head, then brought her hand onto his knee and played with her fingers as he spoke. "I'm not even sure if she would have accepted me. I hadn't proved myself. She wanted me to sign up with one of the Irish regiments abroad and fight for Napoleon Bonaparte, for the sake of a free Ireland." Delia looked at him wide-eyed. He held her hand fast. "But she was arrested. It was the time when Charles Lennox was Lord Lieutenant—Duke of Richmond he is now, damn him to hell—and there was a new roundup of conspirators. Her whole family were arraigned. She died in prison, before the trial."

Delia gave a soft exclamation, slipped to the floor and leaned against his knee, her cheek on the back of his hand. They were silent for a long time, and he wondered if she thought him too moved to speak further. In fact, he felt liberated.

At last she said solemnly, looking at the floor, "So you might just as easily have joined the French army?"

He let her hear the scorn in his voice. "Mother of God, I said I despised my family, not that I hated them. No, there was never any question of that. Friends did though, I admit." Macready had been one of them. Decernay had challenged him with that name, after the duel at the encampment, but none of the bystanders could have guessed that the Irishman in question was an officer in the French cavalry. "I was desperate to put the whole thing behind me—get into the army and away. My having such dangerous connections put the fear of the devil into my parents, so I was able to force the price of a commission out of them, which they probably borrowed from one of my brothers-in-law. I've never set foot in Ireland since."

She turned her supple body and rested one hand on the floor. "No need, now that you've found your place in England. I've heard all about Birlingdean—what a fortune and what an estate!"

She sounded genuinely pleased for him, rather than envious. Or ambitious. He held her chin with his fingers and tilted her face toward him. "Only until the boy reaches his majority."

"But meantime you've the property, and an income."

"As trustee, yes. Enough to live on."

She said playfully, "Indeed, sir, but don't you long for more?" She pulled free and moved back to sit on her heels, just out of his reach. "If anything happened to the heir, you would have Birlingdean for yourself, is that right? There are no other males in line?"

"No. That is, yes, I should have Birlingdean and the baronetcy."

She went on in the same light tone. "What if you took Lady Hamilton to wife—should you obtain Clifton as well?"

"No, it descends in the female line."

"Oh good," she said, giving a little bounce on her heels, then rising gracefully. "I do like to have these things clear. Next time I include you in my devotions, I shall know what to pray for on your account."

He shuddered. "That's enough, Delia!"

She stood looking at him sorrowfully. "Bas, I was *teasing*." She smiled again. "You've forgotten how I like to tease?"

"No, I haven't." She was within his reach now and he put both hands on her elbows.

Before coming closer she said, "When do I get invited to Birlingdean?"

He thought quickly. She would never harm him if he remained her ally. "Next week. I'm having a house party and we're all going to the races at Epsom Downs."

"Shall I be seeing Lady Hamilton again?"

He rose. It was time he made his escape. "Only if you are very good."

She gave a little laugh. "Oh, but I am. I feel she and I are destined to be friends."

Jacques was furious. The first time he rode over to Clifton he was told that Lady Hamilton had gone to Brighton with Colonel Coole. He knew what it meant— she had fled. No one in the household could tell him when she was returning, but he knew they knew, because they told him Master Harry was in the house. She would never leave the Aristide in that kind of uncertainty. But she would leave *him* without a word.

He did not insist, the first time. He rode away on Mezrour as though he were astride a thunder cloud, his stomach knotted, his eyes narrowed as he raced through a landscape that suddenly he hated—barren, unrelieved, a featureless green mass plunging into the blue well of the sea.

The second day, he came without hope of her having returned, but with a determination to see Aristide somehow. She was not back, and the bruise on the new wound was worse than he had willed it to be. But finding the child turned out to be easy. When the majordomo shut the door on him, there was no one in the formal garden or at the windows, and he took Mezrour's reins and strolled along to the stables. There would be someone there to talk to.

Mitchell, the trainer and horse master, came out into the cobbled yard and took Mezrour's bridle as soon as he appeared, but the place seemed quiet.

"Where is everyone?"

"Up at the exercise yard, monsieur, with Scheherazade and a couple of the thoroughbreds. Care to take a look?" Mitchell had a slow, measured voice and eyes that were used to assessing horses and men—not always in favor of the men.

"No. I wondered if Master 'Arry is about." *Jésu,* what a name! Mitchell's lips were twitching over his effort to pronounce it.

"Matter of fact he is, monsieur. He's gotten it in his head the pony needs company when the others are out training. You'll find him in there," and he gestured toward the larger building on his left. "I'll be in the tack room." Meaning, well within sight and sound.

Jacques nodded and turned away, and behind him Mezrour gave a huff of impatience at being left.

Inside, the stables were dark and cool, surrounding him with the odors of dung and straw and the wonderful smell of the horses' sleek hair. Those still in the loose boxes swung their heads his way, hay drifting from their motionless lips as they ceased feeding to stare at him, ears pricked.

A nearby horse whickered curiously at him and Jacques saw a movement at the end of the row as the child's small, sturdy figure stepped into view. His face looked pale in the gloom—he was less confident without his mother, even nervous. But Jacques strode forward at his usual pace.

"Aristide! I hear you have a new pony."

There was a shy smile; then the brown eyes lit up. "Jacques."

"Is this the fellow?"

The boy turned a worshiping gaze on the creature in the stall. "He's called Prince."

Jacques gave his attention to the pony, which was a pretty pinto with a neat, dished face that showed a touch of Arab, and slim legs that revealed strength and resilience when he ran his hands down them. The lad's solemn gaze told him that nothing less than a full survey was required, so he made a thorough job of it. Prince rolled his eyes in protest when his teeth were being inspected, which caused giggles.

Jacques was impressed with the pony, and said so, then sat on his heels in front of Aristide and said, "Now, let's take a look at you. What have you been up to while your maman is away?"

"I drew a drawing. A soldier with a musket. But Maud said Mama likes flowers better. I did some flowers underneath."

"When is Maman coming home?"

A big smile. "Might be today." Then he gave Jacques a considering look that somehow seemed to probe all his secrets and said gently, "Don't worry. She doesn't go through the water."

Jacques frowned, wondering what he was talking about, then remembered the accident: it had happened at the ford below Birlingdean.

Aristide said, "Horses shouldn't go in the water, should they? They can't swim."

Jacques rose to his feet, picked the child up and propped him on a stack of hay. He knew the details of the accident: the capsize of the carriage, the mother and son being flung into the stream, two horses drowning. Surely someone had talked such horrors over with the child?

"Aristide, horses *can* swim. They just need to keep their noses well above the water. Do you know why?"

Aristide shook his head.

"You know what happens if *you* go under? You can shut your mouth and you can close the back of your nose, so no water goes down into your lungs. But horses can't do that. They can close their mouths, but their nostrils are open all the time. If they go under, the water runs straight down inside and they drown, very rapidly. No one ever told you that?"

Aristide shook his head again. "Don't tell Mama. She'd be sad."

She had not discussed it with the child. She had tried to protect him from the deaths; but he had seen the horses die, and he had kept it hidden, kept it inside his worried little head, to spare her.

"Horses don't mind water," Jacques went on. "Some of them love it. I had a cavalry horse once who liked to bathe in the river that runs by our farm. Even when he was too old to be ridden, he used to make me take him down for a swim."

"Have you still got him? What's his name?"

Jacques shook his head. "He died. Of age," he added quickly. Then he put out a hand and flicked the hair back off Aristide's brow, which was pale and fine skinned, like his mother's. "My parents sent me a letter; I got it today. They told me what happened to him. His name was Paragon." Idiotically, saying it brought tears to his eyes. He lifted Aristide down again, sniffed and said cheerfully, "Now. Are you going to introduce me to the others?"

They did the rounds of the stalls, but Aristide was thoughtful. After a while he said, "Come and see Jock and Sam." He took Jacques by the hand and led him through an arched doorway, one timber door of which was closed, into the farthest room in the stables. Out of the corner of his eye, Jacques saw Mitchell put his head out of the tack room and watch them disappear. He smiled cynically to himself.

Jock and Sam were Shires, who shared a stall at one

side of the enormous space that also stored their yokes and harness, brasses and leather, bags of feed and man-high stacks of hay, over which they reigned like kings with so much treasure.

"Jock belongs to Mama," Aristide said, pointing to the white-browed giant with a long, shaggy mane and a girth with the dimensions of a winepress, who regarded Jacques with mild interest.

"Mama says Sam belongs to me." Sam was leaner through the middle but with great bulging shoulders and haunches. He was magnificent, stolid, and feigned complete indifference to the boy and man behind him.

Aristide walked out in front of Jacques and looked earnestly up into his face. "Would you like Sam? He can be your horse. To keep."

It was such a surprise, such a generous act for a small child, that Jacques was speechless for a moment.

Aristide, sensing doubt, pressed his point. "You need a big horse. Mitchell says cavalry horses are big."

Jacques found his voice. "Thank you. No one ever offered me anything so marvelous. But this is where Sam belongs. Why don't I just come and visit him sometimes, with you?"

Aristide said uncertainly, "Isn't he right for cavalry?"

Jacques thought for a moment, then said, "Let's see. You grab that piece of wood over there. It's about the right length for a sword. And I'll have this." He took a rake handle that was leaning against the wall. "Now, just let me explain this to Sam."

Sam was turning in his stall, his massive feathered hooves scraping and thudding on the floor, his huge liquid eyes fixed on Jacques. Jacques talked to him for a moment, sliding his hand down the white blaze on the nose, letting the horse sniff his palm, making his own gaze speak the right reassurances.

Then he hoisted Aristide up onto the smooth expanse of Sam's back, sword and all, and hitched himself up behind him. Sam twitched his shoulders, then pretended they were a couple of sandflies, not worth bothering about.

"First the lance. There are three positions. At rest, which is upright. Put your hand here, under mine. Second, the charge. Cock your elbow, that's the way, and it sits here, along your forearm. Lean forward. Imagine how fast we're going, and you're keeping the lance in line the whole way."

Aristide began to bounce up and down. "Go, Sam, *charge!*" To his credit, Sam failed to oblige, but Aristide was excited now, feeling the thrill of speed and the challenge, and Jacques, chuckling behind him, was not sure he wouldn't slide right off the charger's slippery back.

Then they reached the enemy ranks, and with a roar Jacques lowered the lance for the thrust, and Aristide raised his sword above his head and gave a piercing cry.

At that precise instant, Lady Sophia Hamilton walked in, her face white with fury. The sounds died on their lips.

CHAPTER NINETEEN

Sophia fixed her gaze on Harry first, determined not to look into Decernay's face. Harry dropped the wooden sword as though it had burned his hand, then gazed at her with pleading eyes.

She had never been so angry in her life; she had to struggle to bring the words out. "Harry! Get down at once!"

Decernay let the makeshift lance fall into the straw, then slid to the floor and lifted Harry down. Her son took two steps toward her then stopped, numb and perplexed.

"Back to the house. Now. Go with Mitchell." She pointed to Mitchell at the doorway.

Decernay said, "*Le petit—*"

"Hold your tongue!" she cried. "Don't you speak to me! Harry, go."

Harry's lips began to tremble. He went to Mitchell, not looking at either her or Decernay, and when Mitchell put a hand behind his shoulders to guide him away, Sophia could see he was shaking.

She did not relent.

She said nothing more. She felt as though if she opened her mouth again she would scream.

Decernay waited, quite still, until Harry was out of earshot. His gray eyes were as hard as stones. "If you forbid him these things, it is the surest method to drive him straight to them."

She said angrily, "He needs no driving with someone like you around."

"You are missing the point. Keep his eyes closed, and one day he will walk away from you, to see for himself."

"Do you think I give a damn what *you* think?"

Either her indignation or the unexpected oath got through, for he started; then the beginnings of anger flared in his eyes. He said in the same uncompromising voice, "You depend on him."

She gasped. "How *dare* you say that to me!"

"You shelter yourself with your memories, your home and your father. Maybe I was wrong to hope otherwise— maybe that is the only way for you to be happy." His mouth twisted, as though the words were bitter to him, and the look he gave her was hostile, the embers in his eyes smoldering under the thatch of hair. "But do not lay that burden on the child. It is too much for him to bear. And one day, it will drive him from you."

"This is *outrageous*! Get out!"

"Why? Because I tell you the truth?" He was standing beside the great draft horse, his arm along the glossy neck, his fingers knotted into the mane. In their grace and strength the two figures belonged together, as though fashioned for a statue, monumental and enduring.

She took a quick breath. "The truth? That's not what I get from you. How can I believe a word you say? Fool that I am, I know nothing whatsoever about you."

He moved with such speed it was like a picture shattering before her eyes. She stepped back with a gasp, but he strode past her and closed the open half of the door, with a thud that echoed around the room and made the horses start.

Her way was barred. He stood with his arms across his chest, feet planted astride, and she saw in him now all the lineaments of the time when he rode with Napoleon's lite, in the omnipotent Grande Armée. Except that here that ruthless power was directed toward her alone.

Fear began to worm its way up her spine, slow and cold. "What are you doing?"

"It's time you heard about me. Since that's what you want."

"I want to leave. Kindly let me pass."

"No. You'll listen to this now."

If she called out, someone would come. But she could see that he would not let them through.

If he had been angry, she might have been able to summon the fury that seized her when she first entered. But he stood looking at her with brooding menace. She did not know this man.

He gestured with his chin toward a big oak chest just behind her. "Sit down, and pay attention."

She obeyed, because it put a fraction more distance between them. She sat with her back straight, her hands clasped in her lap. Her turban and the pelisse over her traveling gown weighed her down, and she felt tired and cramped from the journey, which was why she had bade Cousin Sebastian good-bye on arrival and let him drive away. In this confrontation, she had nothing to call on but her own inner strength.

He began in cold tones, his arms still across his chest, but after a while his hands drifted to his sides. When he glanced at her during the narrative he did so dispassionately, as though she were a stranger who had been promised certain information, at a price.

"My family is of the old Normandy aristocracy. We grew up with my parents in a château on the Vire: my brother René, my two sisters and I. René went to study law in Paris. I followed two years later. René was passionately interested in constitutional law, and also we both made a study of the Napoleonic Code. Bonaparte's genius fascinated us—his gift for administration, the way he drew the most talented leaders to him, the extraordinary scope of his mind, his dedication to keeping France independent, to transforming her laws.

"Our father supported us liberally and approved of our studies—my parents were very proud of René, who achieved brilliant success and seemed destined for a po-

sition in government. It will not surprise you"—he threw
her a sarcastic look—"that I was of a different tempera-
ment. I was happier in the saddle than at a desk. Restless, impatient, always tempted by what might be over
the horizon. My upbringing had already given me the
training for the military life: all I needed was a cause. I
thought I had found one with Bonaparte."

He began to move, pacing up and down in front of
the door, his boots whispering through the scattered
straw. His words were directed at his feet yet they were
quite audible, and driven by a range of expression that
Sophia found extraordinary, considering the softness of
his voice.

"But my parents and René were totally opposed. For
my parents, honor lies in family affection, social justice,
order and tranquility. They imagined my sisters would
marry and live near home—and so they have. They
thought René would take his place in the government."
He paused a fraction, then went on. "And I would finish
my studies and return to the château. My ambitions horrified them. But I was determined on my own course,
and in the end I used the funds they had given me to
purchase a commission. I left Paris to join the army without a word to anyone."

She shifted position; he glanced at her and said mock-
ingly, "The first of my mistakes. Hear them all before
you judge which is the worst."

He continued, without any self-satisfaction. "I proved
to be good at what I did and was admitted to the cuirassiers early. Men trusted me and followed me. Once I
knew I was making a success of it, I wrote home to
explain. My parents were devastated. They turned to
René, who had already guessed what I was doing. He
told them he would go after me and persuade me out
of the army. But he knew from the beginning that was
not possible, so when he caught up with me in Wagram
he joined up himself. We fought side by side for the
next three years."

He saw her consternation. "Yes. He did it to protect
me. He was the eldest. He promised my parents he

would look after me; that was the only way he could do it."

And you let him. She imagined him years ago, without that look of bitterness in his face, full of careless courage, riding to glory.

"Then the Grande Armée invaded Russia. Need I describe it to you? The world knows what happened to us there. Yet it failed to open my eyes. I stood in the streets of Moscow and watched it burn to the ground, I starved like everyone else as we struggled back across those endless, icy plains, and if my soul grew bitter it was because we had been defeated, not because we had brought devastation everywhere we went. Then came the crossing of the Berezina River."

He fell silent. He moved away from the door, in an arc around her, and stopped near the draft horses, his gaze on his boots. He did not retrace his steps; the door was unbarred and she could leave if she moved quickly. She stayed quite still.

"You have heard. It is one of Bonaparte's most famous and brilliant retreats. But he left thirty-six thousand men to the Russians on the other side. The Cossacks caught up with us at the river. Ney and Oudinot commanded the rearguard action. Men were cut down at the burning bridges, lying with dead and injured horses that bled into the water. René and I got over the river—but then he fell." He moved blindly, fetching up by Sam's shoulder and reaching out with one hand. "It happened behind me. Someone told me and I went back. I found him beside the road, in the ditch. The Russians had fired our artillery at us, over the river. There was snow on the banks, with black ice at the bottom. Everything around us was gray and red and black."

He was not looking at her, but staring ahead, his hand rhythmically stroking Sam's neck.

"I lifted him onto the side of the road. I let his head and shoulders rest on me, and he tried to speak."

Tears burst into his eyes and coursed over his cheeks, but he seemed unaware of them. His voice dropped further. "He died. I closed his eyes. When I looked up, I saw my comrades shuffling past. I saw the teams that struggled along with the last of the big guns, the chaos of retreat. I couldn't move. *I couldn't do anything.* Then Bonaparte rode by."

He looked at her then, and she saw all the naked horror of that moment pass across his face. "He rode by, as close as you are to me now, on his white horse. He was looking straight ahead. Maybe I cried out, I don't know, but he glanced at me. His eyes opened on mine and he sent me a message, sharp like a sword in the gut. Contempt and hatred. That is what he thrust out to me. He hated both of us—René because he was dead, me because I looked like death. He didn't want to see us; he wanted us gone, wiped off the face of the earth, out of his mind. He hated"—his mouth twisted— "my dead brother."

With a sound that he stifled in the back of his throat, he turned his head and put his forehead against the back of his fist, which was gripping the horse's mane.

Sophia felt tears prickle in her eyes, and she had an impulse to go to him, but this was too terrible for her to say or do anything to help. Perhaps he heard her sudden movement, for he lifted his head and continued, his cheeks wet and his eyes haggard.

"I was ordered forward, but I stayed to bury René. It was hard because I was wounded, but someone helped me, a man in rags, with no coat and no boots. We never spoke, so I don't know to this day if he was a comrade or a Russian peasant.

"At last we got out of Russia. I didn't know where to go or what to do. I could not go home. I got myself transferred to Spain, away from Bonaparte, out of the cuirassiers, out of his sight. All I wanted was death. I nearly managed it. I took a bullet at Vitoria, but the British hauled me off the field and made me prisoner and patched me up."

He pushed himself upright, rubbed both hands rapidly over his face and began to pace again. "I couldn't bear prison; it was worse than death. That was when I decided I had to do something to oppose Bonaparte. Join a campaign to drive his armies back across our borders. He had to be forced onto his heels, we had to smash his empire, confine him to France where he belonged. Then when he fell, he would fall at the hands of the French whom he had oppressed and cheated and slaughtered in hundreds of thousands."

He looked at her sardonically. "Mistake number two: I joined the Chasseurs Britanniques. You know their reputation—the Chasseurs were given the worst tasks; they were held in contempt, and no one trusted them. I had thought long and hard, but I had not realized what that would be like, being asked to kill my fellow countrymen. I did my duty but with iron in my soul. I always refused promotion and I was persecuted for it, but I had to draw the line at leading other men against my own. I was glad when they sent me to New South Wales, but once I was there, I was being slowly destroyed. What was I doing, acting as jailer to convicts in chains? I had joined the free French—but how could I fight Bonaparte from the other side of the world?"

He continued. "Mistake number three: I decided to come back to Europe." His gaze was on her and he saw her start. He gave her a mocking grin. "Yes, the scheme was mine. I wrote to my parents for funds—I never stopped corresponding; I just couldn't face them again. The money arrived, and I planned the escape with three other Chasseurs. I paid the Norwegian captain in advance and stole the boat. It all went like clockwork. On the day, I led the others down toward the beach, then stood sentry to make sure we got away safe. I told them, give me half an hour, and if I don't turn up, leave without me."

"My God," she burst out. "Then everything they accused you of was true."

He went on as though she had not spoken. "Mistake number four: I let them sail away."

"Why?"

"You. I had to prevent you from going down that track. If you had discovered them in the act, you would have tried to give them away, and you would have put yourself in danger. They were all devils; take my word, I was one of them."

She was almost breathless. "You were about to desert. I stopped you."

He made her a mocking bow.

She said with revulsion, "So when I wrote that letter to the court-martial, I lied for you."

"I'm afraid so."

She felt sick. She said dully, "You've been a liar all along."

He shook his head and walked up to her. The door was still closed on the silent stables beyond, and he stood very near. Her chance of escape was gone.

"I never lied to you." He dropped to the floor so that he was kneeling in front of her.

"You were going to desert. And you kept on trying, didn't you—looking for another opportunity? But they caught up with you first, in Greenwich."

He shook his head. "Mistake number five: I decided to stay in New South Wales. And when the order came to sail to England, I obeyed. And you know why. You *must* know why."

She looked at him, her hand to her mouth.

"You," he said. "Until I met you, I was a dead man. Then you rode up to me, one summer day, and I saw you and came alive again. I stayed with the Chasseurs for you; I came to England for you. I am here now for you."

She lowered her hand. "This is all lies too. *What are you doing in Sussex*?"

"Watching over you, whether you wish it or not. You saved my life twice. In return I dedicate mine to you."

"What about your personal vendetta against Napoleon? You've let that fall by the wayside?"

He flinched as though she had struck him, and she realized the shocking cruelty of that question.

But he answered her. "I must accept that other men, far better men than I, will accomplish what I long for. He will meet his end; if mine is not the hand, so be it."

She was looking at his hands as he knelt there before

her. Suddenly he put one out to take hers. She tried to pull away, but he crushed it with his fingers and bent so that his forehead rested against her knuckles.

He said with slow emphasis, between his teeth, "You must never . . . be . . . afraid of me."

She looked down at his bent head, and tears flooded her eyes. She could not resist touching his hair lightly with her free hand. She could not prevent herself from saying, "I believe you, about your brother. I am desperately sorry." She took a breath. "But how can I trust you?"

He raised his head. "I love you."

She did not shrink away. Caught by his gaze, she felt her heart lift, but fear swamped her again. Fear of joy.

He did not wait for her answer. He spoke again, in his soft, beautiful voice, as though he were pronouncing a spell. "I have loved you from the first second. I will never stop loving you. You don't realize how extraordinary you are, because no one has ever told you. No one has ever said what perfection there is in this noble mind, this exquisite face, this marvelous body." His fingers brushed her cheeks, drifted over her shoulders and arms; then his arms slid around her waist. He pulled her to him so that he was between her thighs, his hands in the small of her back. He whispered, "No one has said to you, *'Mon cher coeur, je t'aime, je t'aime pour toujours, au delà de la mort.'*"

He kissed her, molding his body to hers. She arched toward him and her hands gripped his rough jacket as she abandoned herself to his embrace.

The kiss was like a draft of heady wine. There was no mistaking now the truth she had been denying to herself for so long; her body belonged with his. The response coursed through her, all the stronger because of the miracle that was within her grasp—he was here in her arms, his lips and tongue speaking a silent language of which she recognized every nuance, every demand.

In her mind, she said it back to him. *My dear heart, I love you, I love you forever, beyond death.*

She hooked her arms up onto his shoulders, drawing

him even closer, and he released her mouth and bent to kiss the hollow of her neck. She hung her head back and he pressed his lips to her exposed throat. The turban came loose and her hair cascaded down her back, over his hands. He slipped lower and buried his face in the hollow between her breasts.

She refused to think. She could only feel.

Then, in one fluid movement, they were on the floor, in the sweet-smelling hay. His fingers rapidly undid the buttons down the front of her pelisse, then slid inside to find her breasts. She made a wordless sound and put up her hands toward his face. She saw a change as his gray eyes went as dark as gathering rain clouds and realized that he thought she was protesting against his touch. But she put her hands on each side of his face and smiled at him, letting him see her desire.

She was panting now, but he caressed her with tantalizing slowness. He brushed her breasts with his mouth, let his lips follow his hands along her midriff and across her waist. Then his palms smoothed the gown over her stomach, the silk clinging to her skin. It was as though nothing else existed but his touch and her body; the redolent new hay beneath her, the dark timber beams above, the great, patient animals, all her surroundings drifted away and dissolved into the warm, dusty air.

She closed her eyes, knotted her fingers behind his strong neck. Her own breathing punctuated his whispered words, expressing a new kind of pleasure so acute it was almost pain. Then all at once, when she thought she could bear it no more, he put his arms beneath her, cupped her with his hands and lifted her so that his mouth descended on the point of her greatest torment. It was a fleeting touch that made her gasp and tremble; then he released her and bent over her face, searching her gaze. She lay looking at him, wide-eyed, with her breath fluttering in her chest. She began to think that there was some deep magic being wrought upon her, taking her into realms where she yearned and feared to go.

"*Mon amour.*" He scooped her up and held her fiercely,

his cheek hard against hers, his whisper in her ear. "*Mon amour,* whenever I am away from you, I tell myself I must treat you with the utmost care. But whenever I see you, all I want to do is make love to you."

She clung to him, her arms wrapped around his head. Her chest was crushed against his, her skin on fire, her eyes closed.

After a long moment she opened her eyes and saw over his shoulder the vast, shadowed room, the shapes of the horses, the tall timber doors. The light that penetrated under the eaves had dimmed as the afternoon drew on, and the forms beneath were growing indistinct. But they represented the real world—the stables, the house and the people who surrounded her, any one of whom might be about to open the doors and step into the space that had been his and hers alone.

She sighed and stroked his hair. His arms slackened, he drew back and read the look in her eyes.

Without a word he raised her so that she was sitting on the oak chest. Then he knelt as before and tidied her pelisse, dusting the back of it and the hem of her gown with deft touches of his fingers. His face was grave and concealed his thoughts. Motionless, she watched him as though she would never see his features again, as though she must say farewell to him in her mind.

At last she coiled up her hair, and when she put the turban back on he tucked the ends up into it, his fingertips brushing her bare neck. She turned her mouth into his palm.

When he took his hand away, she said, "I think you should go."

He said, "I shall be back tomorrow, *mon amour.*" He bent and kissed her forehead, then turned on his heel and went out the door.

She sat there for a long time. At the other end of the stables she heard his voice, and Mitchell's, and then Mezrour's hooves clattering on the cobbles of the yard.

Later, she looked up to see Mitchell standing in the doorway, gazing into the gloom.

She raised her head. "How did Scheherazade go today?"

"Champion, milady."

"I've been giving it a lot of thought. I think we should try out that youngster from Joliffe Court. Arrange to have him here tomorrow, if you please."

CHAPTER TWENTY

Paris

I've sent the note to the tenth man by courier. The date of the grand review is fixed: the first of June. When he decided that, Bonaparte dictated the hour of his own death: midnight, when he summons me to his office.

I see little of Fouché lately, which makes the conspiracy all the more secure. He paid me the best of tributes, however, the last time we met, when we exchanged a few swift words out of the hearing of old Cambacérès.

"The world will be your debtor, Robert."

I whispered, "And yours, Minister."

He shook his head. "I work in the wings. It requires another kind of courage to take the stage."

Sophia woke next morning stunned. It was almost impossible to believe what had happened the day before. She had sought Harry out and comforted him, then allowed him the rare treat of sleeping in her bed for the night, in an attempt to prevent herself from thinking about Jacques Decernay. In fact she had thought about him for hours. It was like being drugged, lying motionless while Harry slept, her consciousness filled with a warmth and light that showed her for what she was—shameless, bound to a man's body so strongly that it was

as though he inhabited her and she him. She could imagine him lying awake dreaming of her too, his gray eyes
wide open, the thought of her like champagne coursing
through his body. She knew that if she could step from
her bed, go to Joliffe Court and walk into his chamber,
she would find him awake and waiting for her, abandoned to the idea of her, lost in a realm she had never
known to exist. She had no idea how long that wonderful
obsession held her in thrall, for all of a sudden a deep
dreamless sleep descended on her, and when she awoke
it was late. She rose and went down to breakfast to find
Harry fully dressed and fed, hanging about the breakfast
room to keep her company.

There were letters by her plate, one of which startled
her. "Darling! A letter from Grandpa."

It had come with one of the Portuguese packets that
regularly arrived in Newhaven. She scanned it rapidly.
"He'll be here soon. If all goes well, if they have fair
sailing, he arrives next week." She reached the second
page and her voice fell a little. "After that, they have
put him in charge of a transport to Ostend."

"Is he going to stay with us?"

She smiled. "Yes, for a few days. We must make the
most of him."

"Has he got a new ship? Can we see it?"

"I expect we can. We'll take you down to Newhaven
and go onboard."

There was not much of the morning left after that,
and during it she had to prepare for the trials of Scheherazade and the two other thoroughbreds entered at
Epsom Downs in a few days' time. Harry was coming,
on his pony, which meant someone had to lead Prince,
for she would not let him take the reins alone.

So she walked it herself, the half mile between the
house and the smooth stretch of greensward that had
always been the chosen ground for the Clifton trials.

She felt intensely alive, with a tingling alertness that
made her aware of every shift in the colors, movements
and scents around her. A week ago, the news that her
father was returning would have filled her thoughts, yet

this time, though she responded in the same fond way, her senses overrode her usual reactions.

Meanwhile Jacques Decernay was due to attend the trials, and she was completely unprepared for him. Her own behavior of the day before was so foreign that she could not measure it. Looking back was like peering at herself in a distorted mirror.

What *he* thought of her she could not begin to guess. Only a few days before, she had rushed off to Brighton because she had panicked about one stolen kiss. Now it was as though she had never been cautious or timid in her life, for she was going out to meet him without a trace of embarrassment about what had happened during the shadowy afternoon on the stable floor.

The boy Philip from Joliffe Court was already there and had informed Mitchell that Mr. Decernay was coming later, on foot. The news caused Sophia a secret shock of pleasure, for instinct told her it was no coincidence that he was walking; like her, today he found even riding too inactive.

Philip was as light as a whippet, with sensitive hands, and he turned in an inspired ride. Harry, watching from Prince's saddle, pronounced that Scheherazade liked him.

Then Decernay appeared, walking up the gorse-studded slope from the east with his determined, energetic stride, his hair drifting and glinting in the sunlight.

She tried to compose herself, and failed. By the time he got to her she was unable to pronounce a word, and he seemed little better. The others, too busy to notice, got back to the business of the trials and Sophia was left with him on the sidelines. Normally she would have cooperated with Mitchell much more closely, but Harry and his pony gave her the excuse to withdraw.

She had one hand around Prince's reins, just below the soft mouth, and she yearned for Decernay on the other side to reach out and touch her, however dangerous that might have been. When he stroked Prince's neck, or smiled at Harry, she was jealous.

She was bereft, as though everything they had said

and done the day before were thrown into question. Then, while everyone including Harry was cheering on Scheherazade and looking another way, he slid his hand down the pony's nose and his fingers glided over the back of her hand. She quivered, looked up as he drew away, and managed to speak at last.

She had to choose subjects that would not puzzle or disturb Harry, which ruled out just about everything she burned to say. But she tried.

"I received a letter from my father this morning. He comes home next week." Then she remembered his accusation: *You shelter yourself behind your father.*

He gave her a quick glance, but said in a neutral tone, "You must be very pleased." After a moment: "To stay?"

"No, he is posted to Belgium."

She could not tell if this seemed good news or bad to him, for he kept his eyes on the flying figures of the horses, now pitted against each other in a match.

She said, "How often do you hear from your parents?"

He grimaced but answered, "Every month or two."

She pursued it gently, "And how do they write to you?"

He turned. "What do you mean?" It was almost aggressive.

"With love, with understanding?"

He withdrew his gaze, his face bleak, but kept one hand on Prince's neck, caressing him behind the ears. "As ever. Their affection for their children does not alter."

"Then . . ." She hesitated, but it was clear he would give her no encouragement, "Why did you not go back? Once Bonaparte fell, once France was no longer at war, wasn't that the time?"

He shook his head. "I told you. If it were not for me, René would be alive, enjoying a high position in Paris, maybe with a wife and children. I cannot face my parents with that standing between us."

"But so many choices led up to that one tragic event.

You may try to blame one person, but it is too complex to be understood. It makes just as much sense to blame fate."

"No," he said. "Not fate."

Then your parents have lost two sons. She did not say it, however.

Sebastian Coole had tried to make her suspicious of Decernay. He had gone as close as he could to calling him a spy. Yet how could he be? He was a man of strong emotions, and these set him bitterly against France. He had a murderous hatred for Bonaparte, and he had cut himself off from his family and his birthplace. The English army had spurned him, so now he stood alone. A person of no country, he had chosen to live in her own corner of England, and follow the only allegiance left to him—the one that bound him to her. The heady thrill of that idea was enough to sweep Sebastian Coole's warning from her heart.

For a long time Decernay stood unmoving and unseeing. Then he swung around and looked back at Clifton, at the roofs of the home farm half-hidden in a fold of downland to the west, at the horses and men milling about on the green pasture before them. He was avoiding her gaze. He seemed about to say something, but Harry spoke first.

"Are you going to watch Scheherazade at the races?"

He turned to Harry and smiled. "Of course. Are you?"

"Of *course.*"

Suddenly Decernay said in a different tone, but without glancing at her, "Promise to come riding with me, the day after tomorrow."

She looked at him, startled. It was almost an order.

He said quickly, "I'll come and fetch you in the morning. Say yes."

"Yes," she said. It was impossible not to.

He was looking over Harry's shoulder. "Don't bring a groom—I'm sure you know the way perfectly. You can show me Friston Forest."

She heard hoofbeats behind them and turned. Sebastian Coole was riding up on his gray hunter, from the direction of Clifton.

Seeing Coole had made Decernay decide to leave— so this puzzling, unsatisfactory encounter with him would be the last for two days. Unable to help herself, she said, "Why not tomorrow?"

He turned his back on the approaching rider. "Tomorrow I go to Newhaven. A ship has come in."

She was new to this kind of disappointment, and to her mortification she felt tears in her eyes.

He said in a swift, compelling murmur, "*Mon ange, je t'aime.*"

Sebastian had the impression that he had arrived none too soon. The two had been speaking in low voices, ignoring both the boy and the business with the racehorses beyond. He had not caught a word of what they said, but if it was to do with thoroughbreds, or Epsom Downs, or anything other than themselves, he would eat his own very expensive hat.

As he got nearer he could see she looked agitated and Decernay was glowering, and some of the sunshine came back into his day.

He brought his hunter to a halt, not too close to the pony, and bowed low from the saddle, sweeping off the hat. "My dear cousin." He straightened and nodded. "Good day, Master Harry. Monsieur." His eyes traveled back to her. "What a delight to see you so well. But do you never rest? After the exertions of yesterday, the horrors of the evening before . . ."

"What do you mean?" He was a brusque devil, Decernay.

Sebastian addressed only her. "You remember when you told me, in the carriage, I begged for the story all over again? I could not credit it then, and I scarcely can now. Though I have been forced to retell it myself, several times."

Her cheeks were pink with embarrassment and her eyes looked moist. "To all our neighbors, I conclude?"

"Everyone has been making the kindest of inquiries,"

he said with sympathetic irony, hoping she would be grateful for the warning.

"About what?"

He finally let his gaze rest on Decernay again. "You have not been told? You do not get about enough in our little society, monsieur. Lady Hamilton suffered an accident at the Pavilion the night before last."

She interrupted him. "I *nearly* did." She flicked a swift, meaningful glance at Harry, who was all ears. "This is not the time or place . . ."

Decernay's eyes widened and he gave her a blazing look. "What happened?"

Before she could reply, Harry said loudly, "Mama?"

She reached out and put a hand on his wrist. "Sweetheart, the prince put on some fireworks for us at the stables. But they went off too soon and frightened the horses."

Harry looked at her openmouthed, then said, "What a *silly* little man."

She smiled; Decernay did not. "His Highness was extremely sorry, and no one was badly hurt. Nor," she said, anticipating him, "were any of the horses."

"Next time, I'm going to Brighton too," the child said. Then he looked solemnly from Decernay to Sebastian. "Grampa told me I'm the man of the house."

"And you've looked after me magnificently," she said. "I shall tell him that on Monday."

As the realization hit Sebastian, he could see Decernay's look grow a shade darker too. He had at least that in common with the Frenchman—neither of them wished the admiral anywhere but on the high seas. Decernay was hardly the kind of fellow Admiral Metcalfe would want to see hanging about his daughter. As for Sebastian, he preferred Sophia Hamilton to be as unprotected and available as possible to his own attentions. And the hedges around young Harry were quite thick enough as it was, without having the admiral's vigilance to counter as well. But he tried to look enthusiastic: "You expect your father home?"

"Yes, with the Portuguese packet. He is only here a few days, though."

His heart lifted. "How unfortunate. I looked forward to spending more time in his company. We saw so little of each other in London." He gave the three people in front of him his lazy consideration, noticed that only Harry looked at ease, and smiled at Sophia. "Meanwhile I come with an invitation. I have guests at Birlingdean on Saturday and Sunday—people from London and Brighton, and Addington *fils* has consented to stay a night. Nothing formal. I just felt Birlingdean could do with"—he shrugged—"a little friendly warmth. May I hope you will honor us with your presence?"

He could see it was quite unexpected, though she must have been aware of the preparations at Birlingdean because of the close connections between the servants of both houses.

She stammered a little as she replied. "That is very, very kind of you, Cousin. I—of course I should like to say yes."

"And do please bring Harry," he said smoothly, at which the boy gave him a polite smile.

"But I'm afraid I shall not be at liberty. There is so much going forward at Clifton just now. I'm sure you understand."

He ground his teeth. It was pleasant to be ignoring Decernay during this dialogue, but he wondered how much the Frenchman's silent influence counted in this refusal. "You will perhaps come over and pay us a morning visit?"

"You are very kind."

While Sebastian was trying to work out whether this meant yes or no, Decernay said abruptly to her, "I will have a word with Philip; then I must go. But you do not forget our rendezvous."

It had not really been a question, but she said at once, flustered, "No, of course not."

Decernay bowed over her hand and kissed it with a fervor that made Sebastian's hackles rise. Then he ran his hand quickly over Harry's hair, in just the same way that he would have caressed the pony, nodded to Sebastian and strode off like the barbarian he was.

Sebastian raised an eyebrow at Lady Hamilton, but she was gazing after the Frenchman and he could not read her features. Somewhat to his surprise, he had been left in possession of the field. That must satisfy him for today.

Jacques was continually astonished by the beauty of the English countryside. He had grown up on a river plain, where bright water meandered through pastureland under the high dome of the sky. His Normandy was a country of limpid air and wide spaces, inviting to the rider and the traveler. Here, on his way to Friston Forest, the landscape was intimate, constantly altering its contours to fold itself around him. Hawthorn hedges thick with heady flowers fringed the spurs of land that curved seaward from the rising ground ahead. The rampart of a hill would suddenly fall away beside him to reveal a lush valley backed by a repeating pattern of similar hills that receded into the west, clothed in distant blue woods. Now and then there were glimpses of farmhouses or villages in the hollows, disguised by trees and with only a church spire or a few chimney stacks to betray their presence. And farther up, where the earth swelled toward the high Downs, there were man-made mounds, the barrows that housed the bones and treasure of ancient Saxon lords lying in their green, neglected tombs.

Sophia Hamilton at his side rode a bay hunter almost as tall as Mezrour that knew the way as she seemed to, by instinct. Where the track was narrow he let her press ahead, so that he could watch her from behind and relish the perfection of her supple body and the grace with which she rode.

On the way he had made her tell him about the accident at the Pavilion. Thinking it over, along with the capsize at the ford, it had seemed to him to be one disaster too many with horses, but when he expressed his concern she laughed.

"I live like a dormouse," she said. "Horses are my only adventure."

"Then don't court it. You mustn't try to train Scheherazade, for instance."

She had shaken her head. "Don't worry; Cousin Sebastian has already warned me about that."

He winced inwardly, then forgot Coole and concentrated on her as she rode ahead. From the full, dark blue skirts of the riding habit that cascaded over the hunter's glossy back, her waist and upper body rose smooth and pliant as the stem of a flower. Her jacket was close-fitted across straight, steady shoulders, and her hair, caught up in a fine net under the brim of a black hat, lay coiled against the nape of her neck. He yearned for the moment when that well-groomed arrangement would yield to his fingers and he would feel her tresses tumbling over his wrists like silk.

He had no way to measure what had happened between them, or what was about to happen. He could only go on, his blood humming with the passion that drew him after her and had impelled him to England, so that he became the pursuer and she the prey. The impression was even stronger when they entered the woods and she moved farther ahead. In places, the dappled sunlight through trees confused her image to the point where she seemed to dissolve into the background of leaves; in others, where branches grew low and dense, the dim light washed around her as though in a mysterious pool where he would lose her altogether.

Once he could not help calling out, "Where are you going?"

She turned her head and shoulders, her face pale under the curled hat brim. "Not far. It's just below the brow of Friston Hill."

The ground grew steeper, and Mezrour's front hooves pounded heavily as he hauled his weight up the leaf-strewn path.

Jacques was closer behind her now. "Tell me, why are the hills called the Downs? It's crazy. Why not the Ups?"

She laughed. "I really don't know." The path swung across the slope and there was room for them to go side by side. "Perhaps they were named by people coming here from the higher ground in the north—the Weald. When you leave the Weald and pass through a gap in the hills to come south, you are traveling down."

"Where are we going?"

"To a beautiful place that I've only ridden through. It's a lovely spot to admire the view."

"I am enchanted with the view at this very moment."

He reached over and placed his fingers over her gloved hand. It felt lost in his big paw, and he squeezed it gently, as though it were a delicate creature that could be crushed by too much force. She did not take it away, but a second later the movement of the horses parted them, and she gave him a look under her lashes that told him she had sensed the same shock as himself when they touched. Nothing they said aloud could match the unspoken dialogue between her body and his. It dominated everything, even his breathing.

He felt a thrill that she had kept her word and come with him, for today was Saturday, when she might have chosen to accept the invitation to Birlingdean instead. Privately, it gave him a fierce edge over Sebastian Coole; publicly, it sent a sign to the rural circle over which she presided: Lady Hamilton of Clifton was being courted by the Vicomte de Cernay, and by agreeing to ride out with him alone, she accepted the first step in that courtship.

In the eyes of society, he was committed. But to what? He looked at her, and his heart contracted. He had told her he would not go back to France, but did she realize what he meant with regard to the château and the legacy of Cernay-le-Gaillard? In his mind he reviewed what he could offer her, compared it with what she already had, and found it all wanting. He could not even be generous with the truth, for whatever he might confess to her in this new, intoxicating stage of their relations, there was one subject he must never speak about: the husband, Andrew Hamilton, whose death haunted him, whose ghost stood closer to him than she could ever guess.

CHAPTER TWENTY-ONE

The terrace on the side of the hill might almost have been cleared by man, and perhaps it had been once, by timber cutters seeking the ancient beech and ash that grew in Friston Forest from the days before written history. If so, the stumps had long ago rotted away and weather had scoured and then smoothed the ground, for now it was a wide patch of wavy grass studded by wild-flowers and loud with bumblebees. From here, on horse-back or on foot, one looked southwest through a gap in the trees toward the silver thread of the Cuckmere River unraveling toward the sea. The other view was due west, across the hunched shoulders of the Downs, beneath which the land was divided into orderly stretches of browns and greens, where ploughed fields alternated with fields of new wheat or pasture that had hedgerows and shaws running between.

There was no one else about. In summer this was a favored spot for excursions, despite there being no access by carriage, but on this warm spring day the clearing was deserted, and in the mile-long ride up Friston Hill they had not come across another person.

As they stood looking south he turned and kissed her, sliding his arm around her waist, tilting his face in under the brim of her hat and blocking the sun from her eyes. His mouth was warm and her lips parted under the firm pressure. On the fringe of her vision was the sparkle of his sunlit hair, until she closed her eyes and swayed into him. She was aroused at once, but not with the frantic desire that had impelled her before; today they had the luxury of being alone and uninterrupted. Even while the long kiss claimed her, she felt a frisson of apprehension at so much liberty.

He released her, and smiled, and she wondered whether he guessed. In silence, he took her hand and led her across the grass into the shade.

The two horses were tethered side by side farther under the trees, where grass grew high around the slender trunks of a few young maples. The spot they had chosen for themselves was a gentle hollow at the edge of a hazel grove, where spreading branches created a pool of shade. Sophia stood and watched as he unhitched the big baggage roll from behind Mezrour's saddle, came over and dumped it on the grass, then knelt to untie it.

As he spread everything out, she said, amused, "How did you pack everything in? You'll never be able to put it all back again!"

"Then you'll have to help me consume some of it. The wine." He propped a long-necked bottle against the hazel trunk. "You'll like this—it's from Anjou."

"Not from Normandy?" She wondered if the wine had been sent to him on the ship he had met the day before. What cargo or person had been so important that he must hurry to Newhaven the day the vessel arrived?

He gave her a mock frown. "There we grow apples, not grapes. Sit down, *mon amour*." He smoothed one side of the baggage roll covering, which he had spread out to make a ground sheet and tablecloth in one. There were wineglasses and cutlery wrapped in table napkins, little pies, a wedge of cheese folded in a damp cloth, dried fruit and a loaf of bread that he produced from a starched napkin.

He chuckled at her amazed look. "This is nothing. Do you know what foot soldiers carry on the march?"

She shook her head.

He was arranging the picnic as he talked. "The rations they gave us were biscuits for seven days, meat for five, wine for two. We carried one blanket, one watch coat, two shirts, two pairs of stockings and two of boots, plus one pair of spare soles and heels. Rifle and sword bayonet. Powder horn. A canteen of water. And in the pouch, sixty pounds of ball cartridges."

She reclined on her elbow and eyed the loaf of bread, which he was about to attack with a large knife. "It would take a platoon to eat that."

"This," he said, "is a marvel. Mrs. Lillywhite tells me, Mr. Joliffe always takes such a thing when he travels on horseback. The cook roasts a whole fillet of beef, but not for too long; it must be pink and moist. Then he hollows out a loaf, places the fillet inside and puts it under a weight so the *jus* goes into the bread. Then when one does this"—he sliced it rapidly across—"there is the most wonderful cold beef one could ever taste. Ah!" He rummaged under the packets of fruit. "I nearly forgot, we have plates."

The meat with its crusty ring of bread was delicious. The wine had been stored in the icehouse in his cellar and had stayed fresh in the center of the pack roll, so that when he poured it the crystal glass went cool against her fingertips. Before she took a sip he raised his glass and set it gently against hers, holding her gaze as the delicate fragrance of the rosé wafted into the warm air between them.

"I drink to you, *mon amour*."

"My love."

She saw the spark in his eyes as she said it. The wine flowed down her throat and she felt instantly, ecstatically drunk.

They ate and sipped a little more. Then he reached over and took the glass from her hand and propped it with his own in a little niche in the grass. He moved the debris of the picnic to the edge of the coverlet and then stretched out and turned to face her, leaning on one forearm, and she was reminded of their first encounter in the woods of Sydney, when she saw that glint in his wide-open gray eyes, the half smile that touched his full lips, and the confident tilt of his head.

Whatever doubts, fears and mysteries had arisen between them since, none existed at this moment. He was waiting for her to make the first move and she did so without hesitation, slipping her fingers behind his neck and seeking his mouth, which tasted of apricots and wine. She slid beneath him and drew him down with her, sliding both hands across his chest and down to his waist, so that she could pull his shirt up and place her palms on the bare skin beneath. As she caressed him he made a sound deep in his throat and she answered on a sigh.

In the cushioned hollow, sheltered amongst the grasses and flowers, they lay in a tangle of limbs and clothing, dissolving in the sweet intimacies of desire. She rediscovered him; the sun-warmed smell of his linen shirt, his staccato whispers in her ear, the touch of his fingers gliding along her thigh, the poise of his body as at last she guided him to where she wanted him to be. They learned from each other: new ways to breathe, rhythms and cadences only they could share. Her eyes were open, and above his shoulder she saw the canopy of leaves dip and sway, pierced by darts of sunlight. Then his head dropped so that his cheek was against hers and she heard her name wrenched from him as if in pain, and the bliss that coursed through her seemed to shake and then shatter him too, taking them beyond words and beyond thought.

For an instant he collapsed onto her, crushing her with his weight. Then he rolled to one side and scooped her against him so that her cheek was on his chest and his chin on the top of her head. They lay entwined for a long time, breathing in unison. He ran his fingers through her hair, drawing it over her shoulder like a fan, letting it drift over one breast. She covered his hand with her palm and pressed it to her, feeling his warmth steal through her skin, toward her heart.

She was lying on his other arm, and he tightened it around her. He whispered, "I would do anything for you."

She slid her hands under his shirt, across the hard muscles of his waist. "Promise me you won't go to France." She felt his surprise and lifted her head so that her hair fell away from her face and she could see his. "I'm afraid."

"Don't be."

"How can I help it? I've lived my whole life in wartime. I know what it's like to watch men leave for war. I know what it's like when they don't return. Sometimes we have warning; sometimes the decision is made and they are gone in a week or a day. It's cruel, and endless, and wrong."

His eyes clouded.

She went on. "It's happening now. The peace was a phantom; the war never went away. Men are doing the same thing all over again, deciding to leave, enlisting. Men who have already served—Mitchell, perhaps. Cousin Sebastian. Or untrained boys, like Philip. Tell me you won't do it."

He smoothed her hair off her brow. "Shhh," he said. "Didn't I say, let France take care of Bonaparte?"

She shook her head. "It's not as simple as that. You know as well as I do, England and Prussia are about to invade."

"True. They'll try to trap him in Paris before he can move. He'll have a siege on his hands. Serve him right."

"No." She twisted in his arms and half sat up. She looked sorrowfully down at him. "That is the thinking that perpetuates war. Aggression, violation of territory, bring the same in revenge. It's a never-ending cycle— the powerful nations carry conflict to the farthest corners of Europe and the small ones are crushed or swallowed whole. Jacques—" She stopped at the sound of his name on her lips for the first time. Then she said gently, her fingers caressing his cheek, "England has no business crossing the border into your country. *Right* will not be served by our besieging Paris."

His voice was mild in return. "Not even to finish Bonaparte?"

She shook her head.

He went on in the same even tone. "Imagine a mad dog loose in your stables, mutilating your horses, putting their lives in danger. Imagine you have no one there to help you, no one to prevent it from savaging your defenseless animals. I, at Joliffe Court, have the means to rid Clifton of this terror. Wouldn't you wish me to pick up my rifle and walk into your domain and shoot the cur dead?"

"Only if I asked you. Anyway, it isn't valid. You know it's not. That is merely a hollow excuse for invasion. Bonaparte is not a mad dog."

He gave her the lopsided smile and leaned back. "*Non?* Just wait."

He was lying with his hands beneath his head, gazing up through the hazel branches, and she looked at him as though this were the last time she would ever see him. His shirt was open at the neck and the soft, filtered light caught his exposed throat, showing the smooth tan that he never seemed to lose, and the chin that was strong and aggressive even in repose. He was breathing softly, his chest scarcely moving, and the air was still so there was no breeze to stir his thick, tousled hair.

Somewhere beyond the maple grove, piercing the spring song of the other woodland birds, came the call of a cuckoo. A fritillary butterfly danced past, searching for its flower amongst the tangled grasses and the primrose, harebell and wild thyme. The green hollow hugged them lightly, enveloping them in the scents of clover and invisible violets.

He said lazily, "Aren't you forgetting? The army would not take me anyway."

She saw the expression under his half-closed lids, and caught her breath. "But you want to go."

There was a silence filled with the thumping of her own blood in her ears. She knew that look—she had seen it only too often before. It had been in Andrew's eyes. For the first time, she allowed herself to recall something about those miserable weeks before her husband went away. *Andrew had wanted to go.* He simply could not bear to stay behind. She could no longer hide the truth from herself—it had not been duty alone that called him to war. Somehow he had succumbed to a reckless urge she only half understood, a frenzy that seized young men on the brink of adventure, that made them risk everything to face horrors that only the most experienced commanders, only the old men in government who sent others forth into hell, could ever predict.

She drew her knees up under the crumpled skirt and lowered her forehead onto them. "If that is the way you feel, war will never end."

He reached out and pulled her to him gently until her body lay on his and he was looking up into her eyes, his hands plunged in her hair on either side of her face. "*Mon ange,* I'm not going anywhere. All I want in life is here. Now."

With one finger she drew a line from the top of his forehead, between the dark brows, over the bridge of his nose, down to his mouth. He caught her fingertip in his teeth and smiled. "Sophia."

It had a strange, lisping sound; she tugged her finger away. His smile widened. "I can't get used to the way the English say your name. *So-fire.* In French it is *Sophie.*"

He slid his hands to the tips of her shoulders, under the unbuttoned bodice of her riding habit, and smoothed the sleeves off her arms. She brought her knees to the coverlet on each side of his waist and shook her hair down her back.

He whispered, "Sophie." He pulled the front panels of her skirt out from under her and gave a quick sigh as she settled onto him, supporting herself with her hands on his chest so that she felt the quiver of his breathing.

The whisper pierced her. "So." Her neck bent and her hair cascaded forward, enclosing them. His hands cupped her breasts and she shut her eyes, plunged toward him. "Fire."

Riding. They had gone riding on Saturday. That was all Sebastian knew about the rendezvous between Lady

Hamilton and the so-called Vicomte de Cernay, and it was all he wanted to know, for the present. Meanwhile his own endeavors were in excellent train. He had finished his investigation of the prince's regiment and fixed a date to present his report in London. The party at Birlingdean had been so entertaining that some of the guests were still there and were staying on to go to the races with him at Epsom Downs.

On Sunday Lady Hamilton had gone down with the child to stay the night in Newhaven and await Admiral Metcalfe's arrival. On Monday they had all returned, to quiet rejoicing—the household was very fond of the admiral and deplored the fact that he was being posted away again so soon. Today, Tuesday, Sebastian felt bound to pay a courtesy call at Clifton.

He took his remaining guests, Delia and the Rumbolds, in the carriage. It was a pity they could not ride there, since Delia looked a picture on horseback and he was not above the idea of seeing whether he could make Lady Hamilton a fraction jealous.

He had had a private conversation with Delia before they left for the drive across the valley.

"You'll like the admiral. He's an excellent sort of man. In addition, you run every risk of making the acquaintance of the child Harry."

"A little terror?"

"No, quite the opposite. The neighborhood is in raptures over him. If you are too, I'm sure you'll be allowed an inspection of the toy room, guided by the infant himself."

She had looked at him quizzically. "Are you sure I shall *want* this privilege?"

"Only if you are very sweetly inclined to do me a small favor."

She pursed her lips in a way she knew he liked. "In return for what?"

"Let me explain." They were sitting alone in the morning room, and a slender arrow of sunlight shone through the window over the courtyard, lighting up one of her red satin slippers. "He has something of mine.

He and his mother stayed here one night, after the accident I told you of, and the child went exploring in one
of the attics and picked up a key. I was indulgent at the
time and let him pocket it, but since then I've found
there are a number of pigeonholes in desks and so forth
here that I can't open, and for all I know the key fits
one of them."

"Why not ask Lady Hamilton for it?"

He shook his head. "Young Harry can do no wrong.
Even mentioning it would make an unpleasant issue of
the thing."

"You want me to ask him for it?"

He shook his head again. "No, he seems attached to
the trinket for some reason. I should just like you to
borrow it. Ask him for a demonstration of what he can
do with it, if anything, and then at an opportune moment
hide it in your little hand and give it to me later. Is that
too much to ask?"

She threw him a tolerant smile. He had no doubt she
would consent, because since Brighton she was in his
debt—he had treated her with overt respect and covert
devotion during her stay, and given her every assistance
in discouraging the attentions of Lieutenant-Colonel
Rumbold.

She said lightly, "Not if you promise me something in
return." She waited for him to nod, and went on.
"Would you put some money on a race for me at
Epsom? I leave the choice of horse up to you. I have
every confidence in your judgment."

"And the sum?"

She smiled again. "My dear sir, let it be as handsome
as you please. The higher the bet, the easier it will be
for me to repay you when I collect."

Relieved, he had agreed at once, and now she was
looking speculatively at him as the carriage rolled down
the gravel approach at Clifton. They always behaved
with caution in front of the Rumbolds, so he could give
her only a quick lift of the eyebrow in return. Mrs. Rumbold, fair, stout and as neatly turned out as usual, was
looking out the window at the statues and rose gardens

lining the avenue. She had a kind of natural self-importance that even her vague doubts about Rumbold had been insufficient to shake, but Sebastian was glad to see that the grounds and fine buildings of the Metcalfes' seventeenth-century mansion inspired the lady with a certain awe.

They were more than pleasantly received. The admiral was gratified that Sebastian had visited so soon, very affable to Delia and the Rumbolds, and so delighted to be home again that every moment seemed a joy to him. Sophia Hamilton meanwhile was transformed by her father's return; Sebastian had never seen her so easy and expressive. As they took refreshments she sat talking to the guests with interest, and when Delia mentioned the walk on the Steine and a secret wish she had formed of meeting Lady Hamilton, she gave her a lovely smile.

"And when I heard about the phantasmagoria," Delia went on, "whatever anyone might say about *that,* I always replied, I could not conceive how you managed to keep such presence of mind. It is a wonder to me. It only made me all the more eager to know you."

Sophia Hamilton gave a slight start and the admiral turned toward her; Sebastian could see that the subject had not yet been mentioned between them. He wondered how much of the scandal she would share with her father when it came to the point.

Delia meanwhile was talking innocently of something else and the admiral was forced to give her his attention. Sebastian could predict what a rude awakening it would be for him when he realized how Brighton society was speaking of his daughter, following the disaster at the Pavilion.

Sebastian had been informed of it almost the second he rose the morning afterwards, and thus well before Sophia Hamilton mentioned it on the way home, though he had been convincingly taken aback and solicitous when she did so. The whole event had been told and retold about town and subjected to scrutiny from every angle. Everyone knew about the pointed invitation and the outrageous gift of the shoes—someone had been indiscreet there. Then came the account of His Highness's extravagant favoritism and Lady Hamilton's sly elevation to queenly status by way of the golden robe. The walk across the gardens in the dark. All the heavy-handed symbolism of the phantasmagoria itself, including her being placed at the head of the procession. And then the climax! He could scarcely credit her behavior himself, even though it sprang from a resourcefulness in her that he had recognized long ago and that few other people seemed to be aware of.

There could be only one good outcome from her point of view; she was certain to have scared off the Prince Regent. But everything else was an evil. There were well-respected people in Brighton who were already pronouncing Lady Hamilton persona non grata. Even the Montagues, fond parents of three impressionable young ladies, had been heard to use the word "deplorable" about her conduct, though only after she left their house. No one had visited Clifton since she returned, and he speculated whether she had had time to notice. She might well have been cut by acquaintances in Newhaven on Monday, but of course she had had other matters to occupy her there. Whether she knew it or not, her circle was temporarily reduced to himself, his own friends and that damned mongrel, Decernay.

During the conversation she threw him a questioning look, and he smiled. Later on, when the Rumbolds were strolling in the shrubbery with the admiral and Delia had begged to be taken upstairs to meet Harry, Sophia Hamilton found a moment to talk to him alone.

"I am so glad you brought your friends with you today. Mrs. Goulding is delightful. She is so natural and unaffected." He thought he detected an extra meaning in her glance as she spoke; she wondered just how he would take the praise. He felt a tremor of encouragement at this curiosity about his feelings.

He smiled. "She is not so relaxed with everyone—you put her at her ease."

"I should have liked to ask her what she meant about the phantasmagoria, but I didn't want to in front of my father. I would not have him disturbed for any consideration. But I know I can count on you to tell me."

He was flattered by her trusting look—and surprised by her composure. Only a few days ago, such a subject would have raised a painful blush, but today she looked radiant, in tune with herself and the world. He had thought he was growing used to her remarkable beauty, but as they stood together by the window he felt her power in a way that almost robbed him of speech. She was waiting expectantly, however.

He made an effort to control his voice. "My dear cousin, I can refuse you nothing." There was an answering flicker in her eyes, of knowledge and instant confusion, but she did not step away. "Otherwise I would rather be spared from telling you this. Brighton has made free with a great deal of gossip concerning the night at the Pavilion."

The confusion was still there, and she hid it by looking out the window to where the admiral and the Rumbolds were walking up from the shrubbery. She said very low, "Thank you. Don't tell me the details. I can guess them for myself. What would you advise me to do?"

There was a pause as he studied her averted face. Then he said gently, "Time and your character cannot fail to set things right. You need do nothing—except depend upon the devotion of your friends."

She turned, caught the look and felt the touch of his hand on her wrist without drawing away. "Thank you," she said again, and this time she did blush. But she said no more, for at that moment Delia returned to the room and the others came in through the front door.

CHAPTER TWENTY-TWO

Delia Goulding, who was always avid for the new, had never been to the races in her life, so she was fascinated by the prospect of seeing the Oaks run at Epsom Downs, and her sense of expectation was heightened by her first sight of the course as the Birlingdean carriage bowled across the open plain toward it.

What struck her most was the crowd—a vast concourse of people of every degree, gathered in busy groups, milling about or seated on the grass, some picnicking in their barouches, others perched in traveling carriages with the tops down and parasols up, vying to find the best view of the track. The town corporation, which ran the course, had put up no fences or hedges to mark the perimeter, so in time-honored tradition the villagers and country people who had walked miles for the spectacle were as free to roam about and seize their places as the wealthier visitors who could be expected to have more at stake. There were only two restricted areas: the stable buildings, open only to the owners, their teams and the officials, and the enclosure around the stands at the finish line, where spectators paid a fee to enter.

Sebastian, never one to rub shoulders with the hoi polloi, revealed himself to be a member of the Jockey Club and took his three guests in without charge. Delia enjoyed walking in on his arm and choosing the best spot in the tiers of seating. She was conscious of looking well, in a round gown that was the soft blue of the spring sky, set off by pearls and an ivory-colored parasol. The Rumbolds, a handsome enough couple when dressed as tastefully as they were today, were on their best behavior and did no discredit to the party. Bas of course looked a dream. He was in shades of gray, and around his neck was an elaborate cravat as pristine as a new fall of snow.

They found a position near the middle of the largest stand, and as he handed her to her place he gave her one of his special smiles, which told her she was beautiful and adorable and he was proud to be with her. She smiled back, knowing it to be true, and not knowing how long it would last; the usual mixture of pleasure and uncertainty gripped her as he sat down beside her. He took a swift look around, nodded to a couple of acquaintances and adjusted his hat to keep the sun out of his eyes.

"You are to ask me questions if anything puzzles you."

She swept the animated scene with her gaze. "It all explains itself rather deliciously from here. The men under the tall posts, with all the gentlemen crowding around—they are the bookmakers, I collect?"

"Yes."

She looked at the colorful knots of fashionably dressed people below them on the grass. "Who presides?"

"Sir Charles Bunbury, the chief steward of the Jockey Club, otherwise known as the Director of the Turf." He nodded toward the right of the crowd. "The gentleman in the maroon coat, with the cane."

"He wears a wig!"

"He's something of a relic, yes."

She was about to ask where Lady Hamilton was to be found—the stables, the enclosure?—then bit her tongue. She was not fond of hearing about Lady Hamilton, because Sebastian said very little about her. Which was a bad sign. *How* bad, she had not yet been able to divine.

Mrs. Rumbold brought up the subject for her. "I do not see Admiral Metcalfe."

"He will be attending on his daughter," Sebastian said. "Either in the stables or in the tent."

"Over there?" said Rumbold, squinting against the sun as he looked toward a little encampment on their side of the track.

"Yes, the big one with the scalloped fringe. The Metcalfes always put a marquee up for their own use at Epsom. They prefer that to the stands—easier access and so on. I said we'd stroll over and see them after the race."

"The whole thing must take days of preparation," Rumbold said, as though this was the first time running a racing stud had struck him as much of an enterprise.

"Yes, they have to walk the animals over and put the team up in the district for a few days. Keep the horses in tip-top shape and the jockeys out of the local taverns."

"And lodge the entry fee?" Delia said.

He shook his head. "All paid up and calculated months ago. The prize today is the sum of the owners' fees."

"How much?" Rumbold asked.

"Some thousands of guineas." He turned to Delia and said softly, "Now, are you quite comfortable? I'm about to place your wager."

She felt a thrill as his green eyes locked with hers. "How much? And which horse?"

"Sixty pounds on Scheherazade."

Her heart leaped and she whispered, "*Bas.* Are you sure?"

He grinned. "Have no fear. I've seen her move. Now, you stay put, I'm having the refreshments sent up to you. Then I'm going to fight my way over to Simmons. He's the only one I deal with—look, at the farthest stand." He pointed, and about fifty yards away she could see a mass of men on foot and on horseback, jostling around a big man with his back to a painted post, on a platform that kept him head and shoulders above the motley crowd.

The horses were led out while Sebastian was gone, a long string of them in their jewel-like colors, the slim riders perched high on their shoulders. She knew next to nothing about racing, but Rumbold was in his element, explaining weights and form and handicaps. Scheherazade had a chestnut coat burnished by the sunshine and a fine, floating tail. She looked unreal, far too fragile, like an idea of a horse that had stepped out of some picture. There was no sign of Lady Hamilton and her father, or Harry.

While the stewards were taking the horses to the far side of the course, she thought about the visit to Clifton, which she had found amusing. Harry was a trusting little boy, and he had been very ready to show her his treasures in the magnificent toy room upstairs. He demonstrated all the points of the model castle for her, including the lockable keep, for which she had coaxed him into producing the key. When she told Sebastian later that there had been letters in the keep when Harry first opened it, he looked disagreeable, then asked her questions. But Harry had given her no clues about who they were for or what was in them.

It was easy to palm the key after Harry put it back on the desktop. Then, while going downstairs again, she slipped it onto the fine gold chain she was wearing and let it hang down between her breasts, out of sight. If Sebastian had not been fondling Sophia Hamilton's hand when she stepped into the drawing room, she would have found a way to slip him the key the moment they got back to Birlingdean. As it was, she preferred to keep him in suspense, and pretended to ignore his inquiring looks. He must have been annoyed with himself for having been caught playing the affectionate friend with her ladyship, for he did not dare to press her.

When he suggested a stroll in Birlingdean Park late in the afternoon, she declined and left him stuck with the Rumbolds, which did not please him. And when they were all well away from the house she fished out the key and did a little tour of her own, choosing likely rooms that were empty of servants, and conducting a search that had a nostalgic piquancy to it, for it was a long time since she had been able to penetrate into the intimate corners of his life.

She tried every locked drawer and compartment. The key opened a number—it was in fact a little master key, made for the family perhaps a century before, if the age of some of the furniture was anything to go by. The containers that it opened, however, all proved to be empty. Except one. She found it in the chamber three doors along from her own in the main wing, which had clearly belonged to the lady of the house. It was lit by tall, mullioned windows overlooking the park, where Delia spied three figures walking by the ornamental lake below the terraces, and it was lined in blue damask, set off by great looped curtains with silver tassels. The dressing table, crowned by triple mirrors, was in the French style, with gilded trims and slender, sculpted legs. In the center of its painted top, flanked by silver-backed brushes, was a gilt box overpainted with crimson moss roses.

Although it had no keyhole, it looked like a jewel box. There was surely no jewelry in it now, however; Lady Sophia wore the Hamilton heirlooms and would do so until Harry took a wife. Delia wondered if Lady Sophia had ever slept in this room, or whether Sir Andrew had moved to Clifton immediately upon his marriage; Sebastian had not made that clear. Would Lady Sophia ever have made use of this casket; would she even recognize it? The doubts made it easier for Delia to lift the lid. The rosewood interior, lined with red silk, was empty. It was a pretty thing, though, and she took it to the bed to examine it, sitting on the edge of the satin counterpane. It had a central tray, which she removed. Then she lifted a second silk-covered panel from the bottom. Which revealed another shallow compartment in the base, fitted with a keyhole.

It was a perfect hiding place if you were going to leave something secret for the lady of Birlingdean. She had no idea just what Bas had been expecting to find in the house, but if anyone else were to come across this particular casket, it was far better, surely, that another woman should see it first.

Instinct told her, before she turned the key, that there would be something inside.

It was a single piece of folded paper, with one name scrawled on the outside. Delia unfolded it and read the message, then sat staring at the sky through the tall windows for a while and bent her head and read it again.

She locked the compartment, replaced the partitions and put the casket back on the tabletop.

Much later she gave Sebastian the key and received in return one of his special smiles. Let him look.

Jacques arrived almost too late for the Oaks. He went to the stables first, with the idea that she was likely to be there until the last minute, but he found just Mitchell and the Clifton grooms, and then only after threatening and bribing an official to gain entry. The stables were crowded and noisy, and in the boxes and stalls around him he could sense the horses' discomfort. Some were afraid, and he felt for them; he detested racing.

From there he walked over past the enclosure, toward the marquee Mitchell had pointed out. His stomach felt hollow; his brain was buzzing. With each step his resolution wavered between two poles: he was right to come; he shouldn't be here. In terms of the plan that his deepest desires had formed for Sophia, his presence here was inevitable. But in the light of this morning—at one point he faltered in midstride and nearly stopped. His was a harsh road to which he was entirely committed, no matter how terrible the outcome. Coming to her now, looking into her beautiful face and lying to her yet again, was a bitter mockery. But he had to see her once more.

He might have guessed it would be abominable. When he was ushered into the marquee he saw at once how pale she was. She was nervous, extenuated, and even the quiver of joy he detected in her face did not lead to a smile. He knew why: the race occupied all her energy. But there was worse to come, for when he had greeted her and winked at Aristide he turned to face the admiral and met with a frosty glare. His bow was barely returned. The man who had written the letter that saved his life was unwilling to exchange more than a few cold words with him now.

In the past, this reaction from "dear Papa" would have received no opposition from her. Today he saw, with a painful tug at his heartstrings, how practiced and steadfast she had been made by love. She smiled at her father, asked him if he would explain something to Aristide, and then moved with Jacques to the open side of the big, empty marquee, beyond the refreshment table and a crowd of chairs, to the vantage point that looked out onto the track not far from the finishing post.

He let her speak first.

"Thank you for coming to see us." She gave him a fleeting smile then looked straight ahead. "We have had no such friendly treatment from the rest of our acquaintances."

"What do you mean?"

"I was too preoccupied to notice at first, but we spent a little time in the enclosure just now, and that was quite long enough. My father is mortified. Forgive his reception of you—he is not himself today."

His stomach grew even colder. "Am I the problem?"

She gave him a troubled look. "I honestly don't know. I suspect it has more to do with what happened at Brighton."

He would have pressed her, but at that moment the bugle sounded, with a lonely, piercing call from far away, and a great shout rose from thousands of throats.

Beside him, she began to tremble. At once he pulled forward a chair and made her sit down.

Harry came skipping up. "Mama! It's started!"

She looked up at Jacques, her eyes huge with unspoken fear.

He grinned at her and said, "Come. Sherazade is fit and well, *non*?"

Her lips were white. "We've done everything we can. But she's so delicate. If anything happens, I'll never forgive myself."

"I can see them!" Harry leaped onto a chair, jumping up and down and making it wobble.

Jacques gripped his shoulder to keep him still. "What colors is she wearing?"

"Red and white. See? In the middle. You see, Mama? Grampa, Sherazade is *racing*."

Sophia said, "Yes, darling." Her father came to her side and she made to get up.

"No," Jacques said. He beckoned over a waiter and pressed a glass of wine into her hand. "Stay there and listen to Aristide."

The flying horses had disappeared from sight, blocked now by the dense crowd. Jacques ordered Harry down off the chair, took him to a point just outside the marquee, and hoisted him onto his shoulders. He could see the race himself now, the horses stringing out, going like the wind down the first long leg of the U-shaped course. But he let Aristide tell her what was going on, while he ignored the admiral and watched her instead.

She was dressed in white, like a lily. Normally the play of emotion on her face would lend her contrasting color, but today she was almost as pale as her gown. If only he could kneel before her as he had in the stable at Clifton and take her in his arms. Never again.

Aristide said, "They're in two bunches. Who's got purple, Mama?"

"Persephone."

"Well, she's in front. By a length."

Jacques smiled at Aristide's exactitude, but Sophia did not smile back. She looked down at her hands, twisted in her lap.

Persephone was the favorite at two-to-one, descendant of the Godolphin Arab and owned by Lord Gorley. Jacques hoped that Lord and Lady Gorley were not amongst the people who had given the Metcalfes the cold shoulder in the enclosure. Second favorite, Mitchell had told him, was Miss Chance. Jacques knew she was another descendant of the Godolphin, run by a London syndicate that was rumored to be placing an enormous bet on her. Jacques might loathe racing, but he had de-

tailed information on every filly tipped to win, his
sources being the self-styled experts amongst the regiments at the Brighton encampment.

The horses charged into the beginning of the turn.
Aristide called out that the whole field was still close up
to the leaders, and Jacques saw a little animation come
back into Sophia's face. Most of these three-year-olds,
like Scheherazade, had never raced before, so much
more was known about their bloodlines and training
than anyone could possibly know about their potential.
Scheherazade, purely on the Metcalfe reputation, was
running at five-to-one, but in reality there was nothing
to choose between her and the rankest outsider.

It was hard to decipher what was going on in the turn,
which made Aristide bounce on Jacques' shoulders with
anxiety. Then there was sudden confusion at the back
of the field, a horse tumbled and another ran wide, off
into the countryside, with jockey up around its ears,
fighting to stay on.

"A fall! They're running *away*!"

"Oh heaven." She leaped to her feet.

Jacques kept his gaze on the melee of horses. "It's all
right. The filly's up; so is the boy. Yellow silks. The one
that went wide is Persephone. She's out of the race."

"Scheherazade?" She clutched his arm.

"I can't see her."

"*I can!*" Aristide shouted. "Look!"

The three of them hastened forward, leaving the admiral standing rigid in the shade of the marquee. They
could all see the course now, beyond the swirling groups
of people. The din around them was deafening, but none
of them heard it; they were riveted by one of the most
glorious sights in English racing, as the fillies thundered
around the turn and into the Epsom straight.

Scheherazade was in front.

"*Jésu!*" Jacques felt Aristide go still, then looked
swiftly down at Sophia. "Is it too soon?"

"I don't know. But I believe she has stamina—otherwise I wouldn't have sent her out there."

"*Eh bien, courage.*'

It was agonizing. From this angle, Scheherazade's lead on the bunch behind her looked no more than half a length. On the outside, farther back, biding her time, was Miss Chance. He played with the ridiculous name in his head: Miss Chance out of *Mésalliance* and *Malédiction*. Then the drumming of hooves took over.

Scheherazade was still ahead. Aristide was going wild, nearly wrenching Jacques' head off.

Sophia went to put her hands over her face. "I can't look."

"You must. This is your race." He put his hand on the back of her neck, then took it away, his heart breaking.

He could see the filly clearly now, read her whole body as she pounded toward them, nostrils wide in panic and exhilaration, her eyes almost blind with effort, the fine legs flashing as they sliced the air. The lad Philip was stretched out over her neck, the mane flicking into his face. He had not used the whip yet. Jacques prayed the boy would not glance back, would not see Miss Chance gaining on the outside as the others lost ground, would not decide to lash Scheherazade over the last hundred yards. For her heart was in it, and her soul, to the last second of her endeavor; and to cut her flanks with the whip would be an insult past forgiveness.

Then, with shattering speed, it was over. The frenzy of the crowd surged to a crescendo, the two fillies rocketed by, neck and neck, and over the heads of the great mass of people packed around the enclosure, Jacques saw them hurtle past the post and beyond.

"Sherazade! Sherazade!" Aristide was pulling Jacques' hair out by the roots. He lifted him down to the ground, and the boy stood looking from one to the other, his brown eyes wide in disbelief and joy.

Sophia bent and clutched him as Harry threw his arms around her. "She's safe." When she lifted her face to Jacques, it was covered in tears. "She did it."

The admiral came over; he had had enough of being ignored. Determined to put an end to Jacques' intrusion, he addressed him dismissively as he took Sophia's arm.

"I deduce you had a wager on the winner, monsieur?"

"No. I never bet on horse races."

Sophia looked at him in surprise, but the admiral ignored him, saying to her, "Come, my dear. We have a victory to claim."

He had to let her go. He had to watch her walk away with Aristide, each of them giving him a quick glance in turn—Aristide's full of exultation, hers apologetic and tremulous with hope that he would stay and wait until the celebrations and the formalities were over.

He should have left then and there. But he lingered about in the crowd, observing the horses, listening to the spectators. Over by the stables he found a group of soldiers he knew from Brighton, who had been given the day off duty to attend the meeting and were eager to celebrate, however the races turned out. They discussed the Oaks, the winner and her owner, but he never said he knew Lady Sophia Hamilton; his heart was too full. He drank some ale with them, then strolled over to the stables to talk to Mitchell. Aristide was there, and his grandfather, and he had a chat with him for a while until the old man turned distantly and beckoned the boy back to his side.

And then, against his own planning and judgment and the dark prompting of his own fate, he went in search of Sophia again.

CHAPTER TWENTY-THREE

Sebastian was pretty content and Delia was rapturously happy, so much so that the Rumbolds seemed to have settled down to enjoy themselves too. Sebastian could see that the lieutenant-colonel had finally concluded he had no chance with Delia, and the wife was much better disposed as a result. After the ceremonies and congratulations were over, they all accompanied the Metcalfes to the stables, where the filly was handed over to the trainer and her good points were discussed all over again. The triumph brought the whole party together and Sebastian found himself swapping opinions with a groom, not something he made habit of normally. The excitement communicated itself to the horses in the building and one or two kicked up a fuss, particularly a massive stallion that had won an earlier race in spectacular fashion.

"A right brute," the groom remarked. "His stud fees will go up as of today, but I don't envy them as has the handling of him."

Delia, radiant over her winnings, which he had extracted from Simmons in cash, had insisted on paying him back his sixty pounds at once. She was a wonderful little thing in so many ways. It was a pity. He watched her talking to young Harry and regretted having to join in himself. She made such a fetching picture, inclined

toward the boy, both gloved hands on the handle of her
folded parasol with the tip balanced in the straw.

They all went back to the marquee for a final libation
while the carriages were being brought up, leaving Harry
behind because he wanted to join his grandfather, who
was talking to Lord Gorley at the other end of the
stables.

Sophia Hamilton looked tired, in an overwrought way
that Sebastian could not quite figure out. He wondered
if it was because of the circumspect manner with which
she was being treated—in any other year he was sure
the marquee would have been packed with friends and
well-wishers, but today the visitors were thin on the
ground. There were enough to keep Delia occupied,
however, and meanwhile he conducted a tête-à-tête with
the hostess at one end of the table.

"And what have you decided to do with the filly—
race her again?"

"Oh no," she said. "She will have remarkable foals; I
think today has convinced everyone of that."

"You know what struck *me* today? The number of
gentlemen from the army and navy, people like your
father, come to see English horses race on English turf
for . . . I was going to say, for the last time. How morbid
of me. I meant, before duty calls them away. It has been
an extraordinary day. Let us hope we live to see it
repeated."

She looked at him with all the alarm he had foreseen.
"Cousin," she said. "What are trying to tell me?"

He smiled into her eyes. "Forgive me for bringing up
the subject at such a time. I could not prevent myself."
There was actually a catch in his voice as he went on.
"I go up to London soon, and I do not expect to be back
for some time. I have requested a posting to Belgium."

"*No,*" she said.

"Forgive me," he repeated. "You are the first to hear.
No one else knows."

There was a movement nearby, and before he could
really gauge her reaction to the news she turned her

head. Her expression changed completely—she looked both trapped and ravished at the same time.

The man on the other side of the table was Decernay.

For Sebastian, it was a very full moment. He had just told the woman of his dreams that he was about to fight for king and country. Two paces away, staring at them both with a kind of stifled ferocity, was a social pariah who had forced his way into an exclusive gathering of that woman's friends and family.

Sebastian put into his gaze all the cold steel he had summoned up at their first meeting in Brighton camp, and the Frenchman lifted his chin.

But there was an interruption. Mitchell came rushing into the marquee, stopped when he saw Lady Hamilton and gasped, "Beg pardon, milady, but for heaven's sake come quick. It's Master Harry. He's slipped into the stall with that devil of a stallion and we're at our wits' end to get him out!"

Sophia exclaimed and ran around the table toward him, and Sebastian followed. Mitchell looked from him to Decernay.

"He's that fearless. He thinks every horse is his friend."

Sophia was already halfway across the tent when Sebastian turned and said in clear, damning tones to Decernay, "This is your doing, sir. You put notions into that child's head that—"

He never finished. He had a split second to see rage flash like lightning in the Frenchman's gray eyes and hear Delia scream, and the next instant a fist slammed into his face, snapping his head back and toppling him straight off his heels toward the table. Then there was a sharp rap on the back of his head and the world went black.

There was never another day like it. No lady's horse had ever won the Oaks before, that we knew of. True, the filly was registered as Admiral Metcalfe's, but any head groom or stable boy who knew me, Mitchell, knew the hand that trained her. Maybe that was what put things out of kilter, the way Lady Sophia Hamilton walked through all the public fuss and frolic at the admiral's side, like the queen she is, taking it all in her stride. The crowd buzzed and growled like no one had heard before, and they didn't seem to want to leave. There was a welter of curiosity about her and the filly that made everyone restive; you couldn't get away from idle chatterers, and in the stables there was a fearful crush, most of the intruders being quality, with gentlewomen amongst them too. The lads who'd gotten their horses out and away after the earlier races were lucky—the rest of us had Lucifer's own job to keep our own quiet, and we all muttered curses and prayers for the crowd to get sick of jawing and take themselves off home.

Some of the mounts were already making capital nuisances of themselves: a big bay gelding belonging to one of the stewards that was well used to such botheration and should have known better, cut up rough when they were putting him into his box and let fly at the partition and stove in a couple of planks with his heels.

Lord Gorley's stallion, Jupiter, should have been kept out on the turf right from the start, if you want my frank opinion, where he could do no one any mischief, tethered to a stake with a tolerable radius around him. They had no business keeping him in a stall, but what can you do when his lordship is a bosom familiar of Sir Charles Bunbury and his trainer swaggers about like a Bashaw with three tails?

No one saw Master Harry strike up his own bit of private banter with Jupiter—they say that's how it began. He was all for making friends with him. The trainer was nowhere near; he'd long sidled away to join the service of the jolly god. Our lad Harry must have slipped under the rail into the stall, and I wager what happened next would have frightened him out of a year's growth if he'd been of a different pedigree. First we knew there was a squeal from Jupiter that sounded halfway between fury and panic. Someone cursed the devil of a trainer and took a wary look at the stall, and lo and behold there's Master Harry bailed up in the far corner with the stallion tossing his head and starting at him. Now the boy is only knee high to a grasshopper, take him all in all, and the stallion had the wind up, like he would if there were a a rat under his nose.

My heart stopped the second I saw what was what. I called out, "Master Harry, don't move. Stay where you are, now; we'll get you out of there."

Easier said than done—Jupiter rolled an eye at me and let us know what he thought of anyone coming near by smashing his hind hooves into the rail with a crack that echoed around the building. I never saw a racing crowd so quick to retreat from the action; everyone shot back a good number of paces. Meanwhile I was in agonies, I don't deny it.

It was a hell of a fix. Little Master Harry looked frozen, but it was only a matter of time before he lost his nerve and moved. If he did, the stallion would fling out at him, and he had the nice choice of coming down sharp and quick with his front hooves or swinging round to deliver a bone crusher with his iron heels. It was a big stall; he had the room to do it.

Lord Gorley and Admiral Metcalfe came over, as close as they could get without sending Jupiter into a frenzy, and the admiral looked as though someone had shot half the stuffing out of him. Everyone, including me, had thought the lad was with him, a common mistake in such a crowd. He put on a brave front to the boy and gave him a stern order not to budge, but you could see his lips quiver as he said it.

It would not be long before young Harry panicked. And meanwhile Jupiter was making angry noises in his throat and pawing at the floor and snaking his neck around in a gothic fashion that reminded me he had a diabolical bite on him too, fit to take your head off.

I yelled to Harry to keep still, then I ran—to find Lady Hamilton. Not the stallion's trainer: a lot of good that would do, so late in the afternoon, the trainer being a devil of a boy for a drop of the creature.

No matter what happened in the Hamilton marquee,

I shall always be glad that when I got back to the stables the big Frenchman was with me, elbowing his way through the press of people with her ladyship right behind him. Decernay had been in and out of the stables all afternoon, talking to the little lad, and myself, amongst others. A brusque kind of fellow, with something on his mind other than racing, I judged, but damn me if there's anyone else in Sussex who knows horses as he does.

He told everyone to stand back, and they all obeyed. No wonder—word got around the building fast that there'd been an unheard-of bit of violence down at the track, a mill between him and Colonel Coole, and the colonel was stretched cold on the turf. How's that for an elegant day at Epsom with the *ton*? People looked at me when they heard and I just shrugged.

Decernay wasted no time. He said in the low, firm voice you'd use to a dependable hound, "Stay still, Aristide." Aristide is his pet name for Harry, don't ask me why.

Next thing he shifted into Jupiter's line of sight and stood there, concentrating on the stallion without moving a muscle. Jupiter's ears went back, then pricked, and he swung his head to take a good look. Then Decernay started talking, all in his own damned lingo. It was a slow advance, but steady. The stallion was curious, then held in place as though the man was saying something the big brute actually wanted to hear. You could swear he was answering too, signaling something with his eyes and his uneven breath. He didn't jib when the Frenchy sank down under the bar and then stood, no more than two feet from the stallion's long nose and flaring nostrils.

Jupiter flung his head up and rolled his eyes down to keep the man in view, and you could see the quiver on his neck and withers that said he was about to rear. But Decernay stood his ground, still talking, and though he went no nearer he held out his hand. Jupiter tossed his head again and suddenly lowered it, his forelock bobbing, and all at once he stretched out and touched the man's fingers with his lips, blowing like a grampus. They stood there like that, in that hairsbreadth contact with each other, and then Decernay stepped forward and began to smooth his hand over the horse's neck.

All this while Harry had his back pressed against the wall, like a little figure carved in wood, though there were tears in his eyes—not of fright, but cruel disappointment, as though the stallion had wounded him. As Decernay stepped forward and put one hand up behind the stallion's ears, he gestured behind his back with the other. Harry moved, hidden from the horse by the bulk of the man's body, until he was almost out of the stall. Then he slipped under the rail and ran to his mother.

There was a sigh from the crowd like a gust of wind, but it was a tribute to man and boy that no one lost their heads and made a rumpus. The Frenchy stayed with the horse, still soothing it with the soft nonsense he talks. Lady Hamilton flung herself on her knees, white gown and all, in the mess and debris on the floor, and took Harry in her arms.

You could hear the words as he sobbed them out. "Mama! Jupiter doesn't like me!"

She grappled him close as though she'd squeeze the breath out of him.

He cried, "I wanted to be friends. Jacques says you can explain. But Jupiter won't *let* me."

She looked up then, over her son's head, as Decernay gave the stallion a last pat and left the stall. He straightened and stared down at her, and behind and around us the stables came to life again, everyone murmuring at once and beginning to turn to each other and shift about.

The noise and movement came back with a vengeance. But there were two who stayed quite still—Lady Hamilton on the floor, and the Frenchman.

I'll never forget her face or his. She was ashy pale, and the anguish made her huge dark eyes look as though they were hollowed in marble, like a living statue. His brows were snapped down so low they put his eyes in shadow, but you could still see the terrible glance he threw at her, and how his lips drew back from his teeth—he looked like that before he struck down Colo-

nel Coole, and no wonder no gentleman cared to stand
in his way.

I saw him take in a quick, deep breath, the way a man
does when he's had enough, when he's about to let rip
with a curse or a sob—and devil take me if I know which
it was with him. Next thing he turned his shoulder on
her and walked away.

He disappeared through the crowd as swiftly as he'd
come, and as he strode toward them they parted like
grass before a scythe. And that was the last we saw of
him.

It was half an hour before Sebastian could take any
action at all. Whenever he tried to stand he felt sick and
dizzy; there was no chance of his putting one foot in
front of the other, let alone leaving the scene where his
dignity had been flung in the dirt.

Finally Delia and the Rumbolds got him into the carriage and despite his protests found a physician to examine him. He was concussed, of course, but not so badly
he didn't know it; the confusion was more in his vision,
which periodically blurred. All he wanted was to get
back to Birlingdean, and he told the fellow that in no
uncertain terms.

The trip was a nightmare. The Rumbolds were appalled
and said very little, though he and the lieutenant-colonel
exchanged a look that told Sebastian that Rumbold knew
exactly what was required of him before he and his wife
returned to Brighton the next day.

Delia was solicitous and frightened. Each time he
flicked out of consciousness, which happened rather too
often, he would come to with his aching head in her lap.

When they arrived at Birlingdean, he had lamps lit in
the library and by a supreme effort of will managed to
sit there and write the challenge that Rumbold would
take to Joliffe Court at first light.

He still had the taste of blood in the back of his
throat. He wanted it there when he woke in the morning.

*   *   *

The Tuileries

The study is the perfect place for the deed, when you consider it. There Bonaparte sits bent over his vast desk, working hour after hour, surrounded by the grand, polished paneling, the heavy furniture clasped and decorated in brass. As I mount the stairs, I can see it in my cold mind's eye, the magnificent parquetry, the luxurious drapes all providing a fitting backdrop for an assassination equal to that of Caesar. As I walk quietly up here with my papers, the efficient secretary prompt and eager for my midnight duty, I swell and grow, altering to fit a monumental scene. I am about to glide out of the wings and into history.

He will exit in glory. He should be grateful.

The door. Massive, gleaming, about to open on the event that will shake Europe. On either side, familiar guards. We do not even exchange glances—they know me and, thanks to Fouché, they also know my purpose.

Two raps. It opens. Inside, another guard steps back to let me in, deferential and silent. The door closes behind me.

He is on this side of his desk, leaning on it, studying a map. I am staring at the back of his bent head. The atmosphere in the room is thick with concentration; I can scarcely breathe; I can feel sweat on my forehead, on my upper lip. The sense of brooding authority is so strong that for an instant I believe I should wait, like the dutiful servant that I am, until he notices me, tells me my tasks.

But I already have my task.

I step forward.

He begins to twist around. Now is the moment. Now.

The guard is close behind me, at the ready. And just as I am about to take the last step the man turns to face me.

He is smiling. His eyes glisten with silent, mocking laughter.

He has been waiting for me, sly as a jackal.

Fouché.

CHAPTER TWENTY-FOUR

Sophia expected to have to put up with a long, wretched discussion with her father on the way home from Epsom, yet to her surprise she managed to avoid it. He waited until Harry was fast asleep on the seat beside her and then tried to tell her what he thought and ask her questions, but she cut him off.

"I don't wish to discuss it."

He went pale around the eyes and shrank back. She felt instantly guilty: she had never used that tone with him in her life; he only made such inquiries for her own welfare, and he would be parting from her again in two days, for how long he did not know.

After a tense silence, she spoke of the race, and only the race, but the brutal moment when Jacques smashed Sebastian down kept flashing back into her mind. They had inquired about Sebastian before leaving Epsom. Sophia had wanted to do so personally, but her father had discouraged her—they should not distress Harry any further, and the issue was now between the two men alone, a statement that was creating a field of ice around her heart that made it hard to converse on any subject.

She could see her father found the whole drive painful, not because he couldn't dictate to her but because she was shutting him out.

As they turned up the avenue of Clifton, toward the

lights of the mansion gleaming through the darkness, he said wistfully, "I did wonder whether you might like to join me on the voyage. I'm going on to Brussels, and you would be surprised how many of your London friends are there at the moment."

It was transparent: he wanted her away from Jacques and absent while the terrifying business between Jacques and Sebastian was played out.

She raised her eyebrows. "Is Brussels safe?"

"Good Lord yes, otherwise why would I mention it? It is Wellington's headquarters, after all. Fully protected by the Allies."

It was after midnight, and they all went straight to bed. Harry said sleepily that he would run down next morning and tell Prince about Scheherazade. Her father kissed her fondly, with a lost, worried smile, and Sophia hugged him back, full of remorse.

She knew she would not sleep, so she sat up in bed determinedly reading her correspondence, putting off the horrors of thought.

There was a message from Newhaven; repairs to the Clifton carriage were complete and it would be delivered to her the next morning.

And there was a letter from Mary Ellwood, the first for a fortnight. It began with a flurry of London gossip, mainly political, then moved to the personal.

. . . Do you recall when we were very young you sometimes took the wasted trouble of trying to rein in my more reckless tendencies? If so you must pardon the following, as a late return of favors, however surprising the reversal of roles.

Be not alarmed, but accept a friendly warning: if you were thinking of coming up to London before the summer, don't. You would hate it, and despise everyone for their stupidity. I'll give it to you *sans ambages*: your name is being linked with Prinny's. No one believes it, but at least half of society insists on talking about it. Five times a day someone asks me what happened at the Pavilion and I say with perfect sincerity

that I've had no word from you. Then I get a full
description plus innuendos. What rather chills me is
that the story receives no embellishments as it goes
the rounds, *for it needs none.* Prinny smiles mysteriously whenever your name comes up, or so I hear.
Private Decernay is also mentioned as a *contender.*
One is given the impression that a prince of the realm
has found it necessary to drive off a foreigner with
fireworks. Forgive me for this last, but someone was
heard to wonder yesterday how soon the prince would
go down to Brighton again to rusticate.

You can imagine the treatment I give people in public. In private, I had a word with your friend Lady
Gorley the other day, before she went down to
Epsom. She is categorical about the response you
should make.

"Frontal assault, the only remedy. You remember
some yokel pitched burning straw into Gorley's carriage during the riots in March? She should do as I
did—threw it straight back. All it cost me was a good
pair of kid gloves."

Brave, but not quite what I would recommend. Stay
home and let London mull for a while. Then everyone
will depart for the summer and come back with their
heads full of other froths and fancies.

Better still, join us in Brussels for a month or two.
Ellwood goes there on a mission, and I am to accompany him with the little ones. In fact, and you are the
first to know, there is another little one on the way. I
know you will share my joy. Ellwood wants me near
him and my physician says Brussels is very healthy,
with a far superior air to London.

There, have I said enough to tempt you into our
company: a work-harried minister with a pregnant
wife? Let me recommend Brussels to you, however,
as a social restorative. Our dear friend Charlotte Lennox is the arbiter of taste there in all things English.
You are assured of a loyal and sparkling welcome.

Do come: it is so long since we saw each other and
I have no opportunity to visit you in Clifton as you

so kindly proposed—we sail tomorrow. At least *write*
soon; our address is below.

With love from your staid, matronly and ever affectionate friend.

Next morning the message came back to Sebastian
from Joliffe within the hour: the Vicomte de Cernay
would meet Colonel Coole wherever the latter proposed,
as soon as the latter was fully recovered and fit for the
engagement. Decernay named as his second Edmund
Paine, Lieutenant of Hussars. It irked Sebastian that despite all his own efforts Decernay still had a few friends
amongst the remnants of the army at Brighton. Never
mind, they would soon be consigned to Belgium. And
Decernay to the devil.

Sophia went about doing the usual things at Clifton
in a state of racking tension, but meanwhile life around
her seemed back to normal. Her father kindly rode over
to Birlingdean to inquire after Cousin Sebastian and
found him farewelling the lieutenant-colonel, Mrs. Rumbold and Mrs. Goulding, who were returning to Brighton
together. The admiral kept his visit short in order not
to tire Colonel Coole; apparently he looked bruised and
unwell, but was grateful for the call. She did not ask
her father what they had spoken about—the subject that
haunted her would not have been mentioned.

Harry was his usual ebullient self, obsessed with his
pony and eager for the arrival of Scheherazade and the
string of Clifton horses that would arrive home later in
the day. He also asked to go down to Newhaven and
see Grandpa off on his ship the next day. Sophia told
him she would think about it.

What she did think about made her so sick that at
moments she had to sit down and suppress a wave of
nausea. Inconceivable though it might seem, two men
were determined to kill each other over her. After yesterday's event there was no shadow of doubt that a challenge would be issued, and no prospect of averting the
duel. And it would be deadly: they were both trained to

kill and their courage and seriousness of purpose were unquestionable.

Looking back, she could scarcely credit that this had been allowed to happen, but she still knew whom to blame. A woman more knowledgeable about the arts of courtship would have seen from the first that both men were pursuing her and would equally have recognized under the suave, gentlemanly demeanor of Sebastian the same deep impulses that drove Jacques. A superior woman would have known how to manage the situation. But she had gone blindly on and broken every rule. Her intimacy with Jacques had exposed him, wounded Sebastian and brought them both to this confrontation.

She could not approach Sebastian; it would achieve nothing but his mortification and hers.

She could not reason with Jacques; his actions the day before had proved that.

She could not ask her father to exert influence, because she knew whose side he was on, which meant that he would deplore the duel but not prevent it. The honor of a gentleman was at stake; it was not another gentleman's place to interfere.

She loathed conflict, and she had brought it to her home ground. She detested the games of war that men played amongst themselves, yet she had allowed them to make her the cause of one.

She had betrayed everything she believed in. Except love.

And amongst the guilt was anger. She could not forgive them for using Harry as the excuse for altercation. There again, she had opened herself up to disaster by encouraging Jacques' friendship with her son—but for Harry to be made the issue was shameless, on both sides.

At times she let herself wonder whether Jacques could be persuaded to extend an apology to Sebastian, on that ground alone. Could he countenance a duel based on an argument over an innocent child? Then she plunged again into despair. The motive was deeper than that, too profound for her to comprehend or alter. And by the rules of dueling, no apology could be offered after a blow.

She ordered dinner early that day, for something to do, though when she sat down at the table she could hardly eat. Harry sat with them, en famille, a treat because Grandpa was going away.

Afterwards the coach maker arrived from Newhaven and they all inspected the carriage, which had been very creditably restored. It was driven around to the stables, and Harry went along to watch the team being unhitched, then harnessed to the hired coach, coaxing the admiral to go with him.

Before the coach maker went around to the kitchen for refreshments he halted Sophia on the steps with a quiet word.

"May I mention something further to your ladyship?"

She turned, disappointed. He was being well paid for the repairs and she disliked haggling. She could hardly hold herself together, let alone bandy words about his craftsmanship.

He caught the look. "I'm satisfied, your ladyship, and I'm confident we've done good work for you. But in all conscience I couldn't settle without letting you know about one thing." He was a solid, bluff man, a little like her own coachman, Combe. Planted four square on the gravel, he was a solemn figure. "It's about the axle, the one that snapped and caused the vehicle to overturn. If you recall, I mentioned to Combe at the time that I thought it was out of the common to see a break like that?" He raised his thick eyebrows at her, rather as he might when interrogating one of his apprentices, and she felt obliged to nod. "Well, we naturally removed it in the course of the repairs. I kept it, but had no opportunity to get a decent look at it until yesterday."

He paused, the gray brows drawing in. "It's a shocking thing to say, your ladyship but—" He paused a bit longer.

She fidgeted. He adopted this portentous air in order to criticize the workmanship of the original London

coach maker. She looked impatient, to encourage him
to get it over with.

"It's my belief the break was deliberately caused, your
ladyship. I examined it closely, and the axle had been
filed a quarter of the way through, near the right front
wheel." He saw her eyes widen. "I could show it, if
anyone cared to look—I've kept it in the workshop.
Now, only you would know where that might have been
done. My guess is, at your last halt before you went
down the Chute. Which would have been . . ."

Her mind had gone blank. She struggled to remember. "Alfriston."

He nodded. "With a smooth road from there on, even
allowing for a few potholes, the axle would hold out.
But a deep enough drop, one like the bad road at the
bottom of the Chute"—he shook his head—"was bound
to snap the metal like a carrot and overset you."

It was impossible. She said sharply, "Have you mentioned this to Combe?"

"Yes, milady. He and I were about to discuss it over
our bit of tea. But if you'd like me to fetch him now—"

"Please."

It was insane. She had been coming home from London—there was not a soul on earth who could have had
any wish to prevent her arriving. What motive was
there? Spite against her from someone in the neighborhood? But she had been away two years! It would be
an abnormal hatred that could survive that long or force
someone to make such elaborate plans, for they would
also have had to find out exactly when she was traveling.

As for *how* it had been achieved, she could not imagine. Only Combe could throw light on that.

When he arrived he looked deeply perturbed. All the
misery of the accident seemed to come back to him, and
he stood just as he had then, turning his hat round and
round in his hands.

She questioned him kindly. She was right; it had been
at Alfriston where they had last halted. She and Harry
had taken refreshment in the parlor and Combe had

seen the horses unharnessed and then had a bite to eat in the kitchen.

"How long were you out of sight of the coach?"

"Perhaps a quarter of an hour, milady."

"And where was it—in the yard or the coach house?"

"They backed it under cover; there were two more equipages in the yard."

"And when you came out, the fresh horses had been put to?"

"No, milady. I had to wait a little longer for that. I had a mind to give the ostlers the edge of my tongue, but they was busy, so I let it pass."

The coach maker cut in. "So there was time for someone to meddle with the coach before the new horses were put to?"

Combe rounded on him. "With a great tearing file? There'd need to be more than one rascal to manage that—one to do the mischief and the other to stand at the door and explain the racket!"

The coach maker shrugged. "Many a man will turn rascal if he's paid handsome enough."

Combe looked about to explode. Sophia said, "That will do. I trust you both, and I don't wish either of you to mention this until we have examined it properly." She looked at the coach maker. "Thank you for telling me. Please keep the axle on your premises until I decide what to do about it. And, Combe, thank you for being so helpful. We'll speak about this further." She turned to go up the steps.

"Good day, your ladyship." Dismissed, they both nodded and walked away.

She went inside, but not upstairs. Her legs were unsteady and she needed somewhere to sit. She chose the morning room, dim and deserted, where no one was likely to find her.

She sank into a seat by the window, next to a low table that held a bowl of sweet peas she had picked that morning. The scent penetrated her, sweet and sensuous.

Someone had tried to kill her and Harry and make it

look like an accident. Jacques' half-serious comment about the Pavilion disaster swam into her mind on a drift of perfume from the flowers. "That sounds like one too many accidents with horses." He was right; there had been others.

She went so cold she shivered.

She began to count them.

The capsize at the bottom of the Chute.

The terrifying pursuit in the fog, which she had evaded by dashing to Joliffe Court.

The phantasmagoria. Could that have been arranged? It was possible: if you could bribe an ostler at Alfriston you could suborn one of the prince's grooms at the Pavilion—and pay another servant to set off the fireworks at just the wrong moment.

Panic lanced through her and she stood up, her hands tightening into fists. She was the target. Then she shuddered and sat down again. No: Harry had been with her in the coach and on the ride in the fog. And the last terrible threat had been to Harry alone, when he nearly lost his life in the stables at Epsom.

She put her hands over her face. Someone was prepared to murder her child to wound her. Then she saw a connection—might she have been at risk there too? Someone had encouraged Harry to enter the stall with the enraged stallion. Wouldn't they have counted on her trying to save him? But instead, Jacques had been at hand.

She lowered her hands. Jacques had come to her aid twice; he had been forced into it by the unusual circumstances, but he had not hesitated either time. If yesterday had never happened, she could go to him now and confide in him, and together they could try to work out who wanted her dead and why. As it was, she must figure it out herself. Before something else happened.

The person who was carefully stage-managing these accidents had to be someone who knew both her and the district well, someone with ready access to the places she frequented. But she failed to see their motive. She had no money, power or influence that anyone could destroy or usurp by killing her. Clifton and her private fortune were at present willed to Harry, with the admiral as trustee. Birlingdean she had no claim on. She had no political influence in the region, and the only time she had ever clashed with her neighbors was when she forbade the local huntsmen to ride over her land. She could hardly imagine Viscount Gage mounting a vendetta against her because she hated fox hunting!

She took her recollection painfully back to the beginning. What if the first attempt had been made to prevent her returning home? But once that failed, and she was here in the house, the accidents had continued. Was it a scheme to prevent her doing something in the future, something that would logically follow from her being at Clifton? She thought quickly—entering Scheherazade at the races? But the attempt on Harry had been *after* the Oaks was run.

For a moment she thought of questioning Harry about who had spoken to him before he slipped into the stall with Jupiter, who might have subtly encouraged him to take such a risk. But she and the admiral had already talked it over with him, and the candidates were legion: most of the grooms and trainers listened indulgently to his chatter and exchanged opinions on horseflesh with him, as did Cousin Sebastian and Jacques, at different times, and even the admiral himself. Which had made Cousin Sebastian's accusation doubly unfair, and no doubt that was why Jacques reacted so quickly.

Once again she brought her mind back to the journey from London. Was there anything out of the ordinary that she had intended to do when she reached Clifton? She shook her head: there was just one thing, and it was insignificant to anyone except herself—she had planned to find out how and where Andrew had died and exactly how he had served the army in the months before his death. No one really knew of this plan. Her father had half guessed it and disapproved. The Prince Regent might have guessed. But she had never owned it to anyone else, not even to Cousin Sebastian during their discussions about espionage. Similarly, no one knew about

the key she had found at Birlingdean or the letters in
the keep, except Harry and Maud, who had been asked
to stay silent.

Then her heart began to beat unevenly. One person
did know of her plan: Jacques. He had even been about
to argue with her over it at the Montagues' ball. He had
known of it since before she left London, because on his
own admission the de Villiers had passed on to him her
conversation with the Prince.

She remembered how she and Jacques had spoken
together, alone in the corner of the coffee room at the
ball, when she had told him there was a Colonel Belton
stationed in Brighton, Andrew's commanding officer at
San Sebastian. She had said she wanted to question the
colonel and he had looked startled.

Then he'd snarled at her, "*Don't*—" and the Montagues interrupted them.

As it turned out, she had never been able to consult
Colonel Belton, for he had been transferred to Ireland
at a moment's notice. Because someone with dangerous,
covert influence *wanted* him transferred?

Her mind was on a horrifying course, but she could
not stop it. Jacques had arrived in the district at the
same time as she had. He said he was there only because
of her. What if that was true, in a sense that he could
not expect her to guess?

She put her hands to her cheeks. This was insane.
What motive could he have for not wishing her to discover Andrew's activities as a spy? Why would a former
private of the Chasseurs Britanniques fear such information coming out? She clasped her hands over her ribs,
and her heart beat too strongly again. He would fear it
if he were a spy himself, a double agent for France. He
would fear it if her path to Andrew led to him as well.

She remembered his bitter exclamation on the night
he came to Bedford Square. "*If you only knew. How I
pity you.*"

He had always known more about her than she had
about him. Which had made it so much easier for him
to lie.

She shook her head. The letters—could he possibly know that she had read those messages from Andrew? Then she remembered the afternoon on which the letters had been found, the day of her grand dinner. After Harry discovered them, Maud had left them on the desk. So when Jacques went up to the toy room, after the meal, they would have been in full view.

Jacques could have seen them. Alone there with Harry, he could even have seized a chance to pick them up and examine them. In fact, when she herself was given them, the seal of Andrew's letter to her was broken.

She took a deep breath, tried to reassemble in her mind the man she loved. The man who had knelt before her and told her he loved her on the very day that he confessed how he had lied at the court-martial, conspired to desert . . .

She remembered Jacques' face as he told the story of his brother's death. She believed him implicitly, because she knew grief too well; no one could feign that depth of emotion. But she had only his word that his brother had died in Russia. He might just as possibly have died after the Russian campaign, in Spain, fighting Wellington's armies. She imagined the scene, Jacques finding his dying brother, collapsing beside him, wounded himself. What if it was an English officer who had killed René, and it was against the English that Jacques had sworn vengeance? He might even have known the identity of the Englishman who fired the fatal shot. That was in fact a more plausible explanation for the way Jacques had turned coat and become a Chasseur—not to wage a quixotic one-man war against the distant Bonaparte, but to wreak his revenge on his brother's killer. *What if that man had been Andrew Hamilton?* What if Jacques' vendetta included Andrew's wife and son?

She struggled to think clearly of the other occasions. At Joliffe Court, she had hurtled toward him out of the fog, and he had come striding to her from the stables, a gun in his hand. To all appearances, he had been shocked by her story of the pursuit in the fog and the

anonymous horseman that his servants had failed to find.
Where had he been ten minutes before? Cleaning the
shotgun, he said.

But she remembered Harry noticing the click as the
gun was cocked. *I heard that, in the fog.*

The phantasmagoria. Anyone with sufficient funds
could have arranged that. Anyone with a fine knowledge
of horses, who had the common touch with men who
cared for them . . .

The incident with Harry at the races. Cousin Sebastian
had instantly seen where the blame for that might rest,
and he had not hesitated to say so. But Jacques had tried
to stop him, to shut his mouth before the accusation
was out. He had committed the unthinkable—striking a
gentleman in polite company—to silence Sebastian. But
just a fraction too late.

"No," she said out loud and sank to her knees on the
floor. "He loves Harry. He loves me."

It was too agonizing to think of what it was like when
she and Jacques were together. She thought instead of
how he treated Harry, like a little brother, gaining his
absolute trust and friendship. But to what end? She had
always known that he did it mainly to get close to her.
And in the course of that friendship he had placed Harry
at risk at least once, playing at war on horseback in the
stables. How easy it would have been for him to do so
a second time, at Epsom. Once Sebastian challenged
him, of course, he was put on the spot and forced to
undo the mischief he had made.

She pushed herself up from the floor and got to her
feet. It was unbearable; if she had to live with these
suspicions any longer, her heart would burst. There was
only one thing to do.

She went upstairs to her chamber and ordered her
riding habit laid out. As she changed with feverish haste,
she heard Harry and her father come back into the
house. She told the maid to let them know she had gone
for a ride. Then she went down the back stairs to the
stables.

CHAPTER TWENTY-FIVE

Sophia carried a pistol and ammunition tucked under one breast and buttoned in tight beneath the bodice of her riding habit. If Mitchell noticed the difference in her shape, he could hardly comment on it, and she did not tell him where she was headed.

The firearm was a Forsyth, which operated with a percussion lock so that no powder pan was required, a mechanism that made it safer and easier to carry and load. The admiral had made her learn to use it, and she had practiced at sea on the long voyage to New South Wales, her potshots over the side cheered by the officers of his ship. She had refused at first, but her father had asked her whether she was prepared to leave Harry an orphan if she ever needed protection and her companions could not provide it.

She thought about the painful irony of that as she rode to Joliffe Court. Jacques had used much the same argument when he spoke to her of the threat from Bonaparte. He could never have known that she possessed her own means to destroy any "mad dog" on the rampage. The unloaded pistol pressed cold against her, under her heart.

She had brought it, but she could not believe in its necessity. She could not accept that Jacques was her enemy. Even riding toward him now, driven by fearful uncertainty, her body longed for the warmth and strength of his. On the day she had first seen him at Joliffe Court, she had felt a crazy impulse to throw herself into his arms; today part of her felt the same, though the stakes had risen perilously since then.

It was a warm day, but cloudy, and as she approached Joliffe Court, the mansion and its environs, bathed in a soft light, looked ordered and well cared for. She paused at the gateway, at the top of the sloping avenue between the pleached limes. No one was working in the gardens at each side, and the house was quiet and peaceful.

She had meant to ride straight to the front steps and claim entry like a normal visitor, counting on the public call to ensure her safety, just as it had before. Instead, she dismounted and tethered her hunter in a little grove of trees outside the wall. She hesitated a moment, her hand against the stones, her head bowed. She felt weak and unsteady. She did not have the resources for a direct confrontation, but she must see and talk to him somehow.

Finally she plucked up the courage to enter the gateway and walk to the right through the limes, seeking a side path that would take her down through the shrubberies toward the stables. He had told her he often spent time at the stables or the farm. If he were there today, she might come upon him in a natural way, and the difficult questions she had to ask would come more readily.

Halfway to the stables, she had still not seen anyone about. She stopped at a garden seat under a yew hedge, drew the pistol out and tried to load it. Her hands trembled and she gave an involuntary, dry sob as she did so. It seemed like the ultimate betrayal.

Shakily she stood, laid the pistol and the little pouch of ammunition on the worn timber of the seat and walked on. She could not face him with a weapon in her hand. Her mind was numb, her limbs felt heavy; she went on automatically now, no longer sure what she would do when she reached him.

When she got to the stables they looked deserted.

There might well have been people in the buildings on the far side, but she could not hear them, and when she entered the main courtyard there was no one to be seen. Then she caught the faintest of sounds from the tack room, which opened directly onto the cobblestones where she stood. Today the doors were pulled to, only a crack showing between them.

She approached stealthily, held her breath and peered in.

It was dim inside, and it took a moment for her eyes to adjust. Then she felt gooseflesh down her arms: he was there, turned side on to her, sitting on an upturned box. She could see his profile outlined against the lime-washed wall beyond, so stark and intent that she expected him to be instantly aware of her, to swing around and see her, leap to his feet; but he was oblivious, totally preoccupied with what he was doing.

Beside him was another box, a large traveling chest with the lid back, with accoutrements propped against it and spread on the floor around his feet. He was getting the things ready, preparing to pack them into the chest.

Breathless, with the blood thumping in her ears so loudly she feared he could hear it too, she made herself identify what he was bending over with such concentration.

The arms of war.

There was a steel helmet, high crowned, with black horsehair tumbling from a copper crest; it alone was enough to make her heart plummet, for there was nothing like it in the English army. The tall plume was white, indicating a senior officer. Black knee-high boots lay beneath a long gleaming scabbard, and propped against the chest beside it was the straight sword that it housed, a heavy-cavalry weapon with a brass guard that shone in the half-light. Someone had just burnished it.

And now he was polishing another object: a broad steel breastplate that he held across his knees, the leather straps and copper buckles rustling in the straw at his feet as he rubbed a cloth back and forth across the mirrorlike surface in hard, savage strokes.

It was the breastplate of a cuirassier.

He was surrounded by the armor and the weapons of an officer in the French heavy cavalry, faithfully preserved and now fiercely reclaimed. Paralyzed by horror, she looked at his face: the lips drawn back from the teeth, the demonic frown, the bitter flame in the deep-set eyes. He had never belonged to her; his mind and his soul were already in France, with Napoleon Bonaparte, with the army he was going to rejoin. Her lover—her deadly enemy.

She had to put her hand over her mouth to stifle a cry. Then she retreated backward, her eyes on the crack in the doors the way an animal might view a snake about to strike. Every step increased her terror, for the soft scrape of her riding boots on the stones seemed impossibly loud. At the corner she turned, glanced out toward the gardens, then looked back over her shoulder. The courtyard was silent; nothing had moved.

Then she was around the corner and off. She could not prevent herself from running, but she kept to the grass at the side of the path to minimize the noise. In the shrubbery she zigzagged from one patch of cover to the next, snatching a glance back behind her when she could. She retrieved the pistol and pouch from under the yew tree, scooping them off the bench in desperate haste.

She was panting hoarsely when she reached the top of the slope, but no one challenged her from behind, no one leaped out from the gates to stop her leaving. Her hunter flung his head up when she darted toward him. She hoisted herself up and wriggled onto the saddle, leaving the gown bunched underneath her, pulling the horse's head around before she had even gotten a firm seat. Then she took off like an arrow and galloped through the copse of trees through which she and Harry had once fled on Scheherazade. It seemed so long ago, it might almost have happened to another person.

He had never loved her. He had toyed with her instead, like a tiger with its prey, reveling in his power to kill, lazily choosing the moment for the fatal blow.

She wept as she rode, the tears streaming across her cheeks, wetting the hair at her neck. She took deep, ragged breaths that made the hidden pistol grind against her ribs. The tearing sobs caused a pain in her side, and she slowed the hunter to a walk. She gave a groan, and the horse stopped in alarm. Then her stomach cramped and she leaned out of the saddle and heaved until she felt she would break in two.

When it was over her hands were shaking and her face was cold. She adjusted her clothes, sat upright, as hollow as a figurine, and let the hunter pick his own way to Clifton.

Later, when she was home and changed and able to face what had to be done, she went looking for the admiral.

She found him in the saloon, teaching Harry the rules of backgammon.

"Papa," she said, "we sail with you tomorrow, to Belgium."

Sebastian had intended to go over to Clifton and bid the admiral farewell, but he still felt infernally low and riding was not a tempting prospect. Nor was taking the carriage, now that he lacked the company of Delia and the Rumbolds. So he sent a note instead.

Sophia would be bereft, having to part with her father again so soon. He must think of something to entertain her.

The servant came back with the information that his note had gotten to Clifton too late—the family had risen very early to go down to Newhaven, for the ship sailed at midday on the rising tide. Sebastian went back to the accounts, which he preferred to do himself, since the steward whom Andrew Hamilton had relied on was too much the traditional old retainer to be trusted with some of the finer points.

At two o'clock, he was surprised to receive a note, folded and sealed and delivered by a special courier who announced that it was from Lady Hamilton. He frowned: why would she send him a message while she was on

the road home? Alone in the library again, it struck him
that she might be in trouble of some kind and need his
help. With a sense of foreboding, he tugged it open. He
was right.

My dear cousin,
   Forgive me for disturbing you whilst you are unwell—I send sincere wishes for your recovery from
myself and my father, though he does not know I am
sending this letter. But I *must* write—first, to apologize
for not taking leave of you. I am going to stay in
Brussels, and I left too suddenly to say farewell. Pray
do not see this as neglect—on the contrary, *I have the
greatest need of your friendship.*
   I also depend on your experience—you once said
your connections with the army are closer than they
appear. I take this to mean that what I say here will
lie within your field—if not, I am sure you will know
who should be told of it.
   I have reason to believe that our neighbor, the Vicomte de Cernay, has been operating as an agent for
Bonaparte. If he were arrested, sufficient evidence of
this would be found at his residence. Urgency and
speed are required, however. Beyond that I can offer
no more information, and I would serve no purpose
by staying in Sussex for the outcome, which I leave in
your hands.
   I shall not attempt to describe my feelings on giving
you this news. There is one thing, and one only, that
makes it palatable to me; I pray that *official* intervention into his affairs will preclude any *private* confrontation that he may have insolently provoked.
   My dear cousin, I write this in the greatest distress.
I can scarcely see the page. But I hope it is clear
enough to give you reason to act.
   With sincere esteem, Sophia Hamilton

She had gone. That was the first thought that overwhelmed him. Sitting slumped at his desk in the library,
he crushed the letter in his hand. She was gone without

warning, and it was impossible to snatch her back. Then
he spread the letter out on the desktop and pored over
it again. She must have written it in a frenzy, for it was
full of the most uncharacteristic features: dashes, un-
derlinings, muddled sentences. She must have penned it
onboard ship, just before sailing, moments before she
turned her back on the events she had set in train.

She depended on him to act, and swiftly. It gave him
a fierce satisfaction to know that he was her instrument
in the most terrible decision of her life.

He shouted for a servant and plucked a piece of note-
paper out of the shelf in front of him. He unstopped an
ink bottle and dipped in a pen, wiped the tip carefully
against the rim, then wrote with deliberation and signed
in a firm hand. It required only two lines, for Sophia's
letter would go with it to lend conviction. He had no
doubt about the response.

He felt like putting her paper to his lips before he
folded it into the other; he regretted parting with it even
for an hour.

He sealed it and handed it to the servant. "Take that
to the stables. They're to saddle my hunter and put the
best rider up, I don't care who. He's to take that to
Major Hooper at Exceat Barracks, wait for a reply, then
come straight back. And I want the carriage brought
round."

Then he forced himself to wait a while, which was
unpleasant because his mind kept going back to Sophia
Hamilton. Why choose now, months after she endorsed
that foolish letter to the court-martial, to turn against
her protégé? Whatever she had seen at Joliffe must be
damning indeed. How she had discovered it occupied
him even more unpleasantly; the thought of her being
inveigled into the Frenchman's confidence made his
blood boil. But now she had taken fright and fled, out-
raged and wounded, and left him the field of action.

The interval he had set himself dragged on while he
fidgeted with impatience. In all the weeks that Decernay
had been living in the district, Sebastian had never un-
earthed a shred of evidence as to what he was up to. At

last, Sophia Hamilton's letter provided the excuse for a raid, and the raid would uncover enough to condemn him.

When the time was up, he took what he needed out to the carriage and gave directions for Joliffe Court. On the way he thought through all the strategic possibilities and rehearsed his account to Hooper. It must be crisp and convincing and would also serve as a resounding finale to his London report.

First, he needed to vouchsafe a reason for not waiting for Major Hooper. It went like this: he had intended to time his arrival at Joliffe with that of Hooper and his squad, but on second thought he recalled the urgency of Lady Hamilton's letter and decided to get there himself before Decernay or the evidence could be spirited away.

To minimize the danger of tackling the French agent alone, he took in the carriage a cavalry sword, a brace of pistols and a carbine. On arrival he planned to stay in the carriage and send the servant in with the demand that Decernay leave the house and meet him at the bottom of the steps.

He and the Frenchman had a private affair of honor current between them; it was reasonable to assume Decernay would come to the parley as requested.

On being informed that Sebastian was there to place him under arrest, Decernay was likely to do one of three things. One: resist, supposing he carried arms, in which case Sebastian would have no choice but to defend himself and shoot the fellow dead. Two: walk back into the house, in which case Sebastian would follow and subdue him by force—shooting to wound, though bearing in mind the high risk of killing him in such a struggle. Third: Decernay might suggest that they decide the matter by bringing forward the duel. Sebastian would point out that this exposed them to a contest without witnesses, but in the end he would yield to the Frenchman's request. There were two outcomes here: Sebastian would get the upper hand early and kill him before Hooper arrived; if not, he would hold him off until Hooper intervened and made the arrest by force of numbers.

He knew which course of action he preferred. Dispatching Decernay would give him time to search the house and outbuildings before Hooper marched in and the military took over.

He reached the approach to Joliffe under a low, overcast sky that was in concert with his mood. The jolting of the carriage had made his head spin, and he fought to collect himself as the horses' hooves bit into the gravel of the avenue. Mother of God, what a rendezvous this would be if it came to a duel. He was damned if he would back out, however,

There was no one about when the carriage pulled up across the bottom of the steps. He motioned the coachman down and sent him to knock on the door, meanwhile taking the opportunity to load and prime one of the pistols. He had brought the carbine only in case there was trouble on the way, but nothing on the drive or in the grounds had aroused his suspicions. Besides, Decernay must have found as soon as he arrived in the district that Sussex folk were resistant to anything that might nudge them out of their age-old habits. Find them a fresh channel for smuggled goods and they'd listen to you; offer them money to double-cross their neighbors, and they'd turn you in before they could spit.

Time passed, the coachman knocked again, and Sebastian's instinct told him something he did not wish to believe. The door eventually opened and the housekeeper held a dialogue with the coachman on the threshold. Sebastian could not hear the words, but the language of the way they stood made him curse under his breath. He leaned his forearm on the top of the half door and took a quick look across the facade, behind him and before, then beckoned.

The housekeeper came down toward him, holding up the hem of her skirt as she negotiated the steps. She looked sedate and matronly, and her curtsy was dignified.

"Is Monsieur Decernay in?"

"I'm afraid not, sir."

"When did he leave? When does he get back?"

She was miffed at his brusqueness and took her time answering. "He left about two hours ago. We have not been informed when he will return."

He said between his teeth, "Where has he gone?"

"We have not been told. Our orders are to keep the place in order for a long absence."

"You must know where he was headed when he left!"

"Hastings, I believe."

His hand clenched on the sill. "What is his forwarding address?"

He could see her weighing up where her loyalties lay. Then she said, "The Château of Cernay-le-Gaillard. In Normandy."

The Prince Regent was in an excellent mood. A new coat with intricate raised gold embroidery on the breast, shoulders and collar had just been delivered to Carlton House, and he looked forward to wearing it on the warm June evening to come. The effect would even outshine his uniforms, which he wore more frequently of late.

The security investigation of his own regiment, the Tenth Hussars, had been completed, and in his report the Irish colonel who conducted it apparently gave the officers and men a clean bill of health. This, though nothing less than the prince had expected, was personally gratifying. It seemed the colonel had been commended for his thoroughness. But he had let fall some concluding remarks about a French viscount living in Sussex that sounded quite uncalled for, since the Frenchman's residence, searched on suspicion of espionage, had yielded nothing. The prince disapproved of the unaristocratic sport of French baiting, and doubly so in this case since it involved a close friend of the Marquis and Marquise de Villiers, who were perfectly well-known to be part of his own inner circle. The colonel had overstepped the mark. Since then, however, the fellow had removed himself by taking up a commission in the Tenth; he was now presumably in Belgium.

The news from Brussels was encouraging and full of interest—the Prince of Orange was constantly to be seen inspecting his troops, rattling around the city in full military regalia and getting under his allies' feet. It confirmed the Prince Regent's private idea that he himself could do most good where he was. As the wise, the beautiful and unattainable Lady Sophia Hamilton had once told him so gently, he was not a warrior. And he had his own ceremonies to plan, the most splendid being next week's baronial fete at Arundel Castle for the six hundredth anniversary of the signing of the Magna Carta, on Tuesday the thirteenth. Today's *London Gazette* detailed the lavish banquet over which he would preside on the twenty-first with his brothers York and Clarence, where all the Knights of the Garter would appear in the full costume of the Order. A new Gothic building had been erected for the occasion, and for three days there would be tournaments in the ancient style, succeeded by balls.

Bonaparte meanwhile seemed to be minding his own business. The same *Gazette* mentioned that over the last month he had been observed walking through the streets of Paris, frequently alone. At a review of nineteen thousand of the National Guard, he "entered the field on foot, attended by a small staff, and passed through the lines, examining and conversing with the men with great familiarity, and after the review returned to the Palace of the Thuilleries."

June, the prince rather thought, was to be a month of cavalcades; July the month of war.

CHAPTER TWENTY-SIX

For Mary Ellwood, the atmosphere of Brussels was like that of Brighton when the militia was in town on parade, magnified a hundred times. During the day there was an enormous bustle in the streets, and everyone spent a great deal of energy looking at everyone else so they could successfully plan the diversions of the evening. The streets were thronged with military traffic, and English carriages jostled those of the Brussels townspeople at every corner. British officers swept down the elegant thoroughfares turning the heads of the pretty Belgian women, while the young bloods of Brussels plotted the conquest of the astonishing number of London beauties who had chosen to spend the summer in their city. On the edge of town there were cricket matches, horse racing and valiant British attempts at foxhunting—these last a failure, however, due to a lack of cooperation from the foxes and the local landowners. Only a few regiments were in the city, the rest of the army being stationed in the surrounding villages, but enough officers were given leave after dark to make the Brussels parties memorable for their dash, verve and very late hours.

Mary could not have chosen a better place to enjoy Sophia Hamilton's company, for they saw a large circle of friends, the entertainments were nonstop and yet there were many hours when they could sit or walk, with their children or alone, and relish homely pleasures in a stimulating foreign environment.

All was not well with Sophia—but Mary had known that before enticing her to Brussels. On the first day she had pressed her unmercifully, and by the second she more or less had the story, with the strict proviso that she mention it to no one, and particularly not to Ellwood. She had so far kept her promise, but as time went by and they had no news of either of the gentlemen involved, she began to feel something of Sophia's anxiety.

The business with Decernay was much worse than she could ever have predicted. Brussels at present was seething with affairs, but nothing could outdo what her friend had been up to in the mild countryside of Sussex! True to form, Sophia had given no details, but one had only to look at her face when she spoke the man's name . . . The duel shocked Mary; it sounded brutal and unnecessary to start with, and she was worried that, though it was now the fourteenth of June, there had been no rumors of it and thus no news of the outcome. If Decernay was a spy, he could well have decided to assassinate Colonel Coole and then escape directly to France. When she mentioned this fear to Sophia, her friend explained that this had been her main reason for writing to the colonel from Newhaven. How much that letter had cost her, Mary could only guess. She looked thinner, she had less of her usual calm dignity, and for the first time in her life she seemed to want new company. There at least Mary could be of use.

Both women enjoyed walking, and in the fine weather they often chose to stroll in the fashionable part of town, stopping now and then to shop or talk to their acquaintances. In the early afternoon one day, they were emerging from a haberdasher's on the Rue de la Madeleine when a contingent of light cavalry came rattling down the street toward them. Mary would have taken no notice, but all at once Sophia gasped and grabbed her arm. Alarmed, Mary looked from her contorted face to the first rank of the hussars and caught sight of an officer on a gray horse, who in his turn was staring at Sophia. She had the impression of a strikingly handsome face and intent eyes; then she felt Sophia go limp at her side.

She turned to support her, and snapped at the haberdasher's servant by the door, *"Une chaise, tout de suite."*

"I'm all right," Sophia murmured, white to the lips.

"No, you're not. Hold on to me, for pity's sake."

By the time the chair was brought, the officer was at Mary's side. He had broken ranks and moved to the side of the thoroughfare, flung himself from his horse and impatiently motioned the hussars to proceed without him.

Sophia sank into the chair and looked up at him in speechless supplication. It was only then that Mary realized who he must be.

He took off his shako and stood looking at Sophia without a word of greeting, completely ignoring Mary and struggling to control his features. At last he spoke.

"It is obvious, madame, that I am the last person you wish to see. What amends can I make you for being alive? Only this, and it gives me no satisfaction, I assure you. At your specific request, a call was made on . . . a certain Frenchman, but he had already left the country. We are reliably informed that he is in France."

Sophia gave a sort of retching sob, bent her head and put one hand over her eyes. Then, after a second of aching silence, she lowered her hand and looked up at him again, while the bystanders gazed at her with fascination.

"Cousin Sebastian," she said in a low, intense voice. "Can you believe I do not rejoice to see you safe?"

"You are most generous." His lips hardly moved, and his green eyes were as pale as ice.

"Where have you been since—?"

"In London," he interrupted. "Then I came across to take command of a squadron of the Tenth Hussars. I have but just arrived, from the coast."

Sophia took a shaky breath and said in rush, "Cousin, you must allow me to introduce you to Lady Mary Ellwood. Mary, may I present Colonel the Honorable Sebastian Coole."

He bowed graciously but did not open his lips. Sophia got to her feet and supported herself with a hand on the chair back as Mary made an attempt at conversation. "Are you billeted in the city, sir?"

"No. We are about to be given our dispositions—we'll be at Grammont."

"Then you will not have the opportunity to attend on Lady Hamilton at Baroness Meilland's this evening?"

"I shall not be in town again for days. I have my squadron to attend to." There was the faintest contempt for frivolity in his voice, and considering the circumstances she could scarcely blame him.

"A pity," she said with a smile. "The Duchess of Richmond gives a ball tomorrow evening. We should have been happy to secure you an invitation."

His upper lip curled slightly, but he answered with a quiet, "Thank you."

The little audience was beginning to disperse, and Mary felt it was time for Sophia to rally and contribute something.

Finally she did: "Was all well at Birlingdean and Clifton when you left, Cousin?"

"Yes." He looked at Sophia again. "I trust your father and son are both in good health?"

"Yes, thank you."

"And you are staying where?"

"At the Hôtel d'Angleterre. You will find a number of your acquaintances in Brussels. Lieutenant-Colonel Rumbold is here, and Mrs. Rumbold. Mrs. Goulding stays with her, at the Hôtel de New York."

His face betrayed no reaction.

When he did not reply, Sophia's lips quivered and she said in a rapid murmur, "I beg you to believe, I shall be eternally grateful for the consideration you have always shown me. And in the days to come," she said more firmly, "my thoughts will be with you."

He said, "I must go." Then he took one of her hands

and bowed over it. "But I shall never forget those words."

He nodded to Mary without taking his eyes off Sophia, then turned on his heel and went to his horse, which had been patiently waiting with its reins trailing on the ground. He replaced his shako, swung into the saddle and took off down the thoroughfare without a backward glance.

Mary drew Sophia's arm through hers and they continued in the opposite direction in silence. All at once it came to Mary that she had seen him before, on a cool spring day in London when she and Sophia were riding in Hyde Park. He was the dark-haired rider who had been watching Sophia, motionless, from the shade of the trees.

She could contain herself no longer. She looked at Sophia's pale profile and burst out, "My friend, what have you done to that man? He is in love with you—and he hates you for it."

Sophia and Mary went back to the Hôtel d'Angleterre to fetch Harry, then drove to the town house on the Rue Neuve that the Ellwoods had leased for the summer.

Mary, all her curiosity aroused again, posed a hundred questions that Sophia tried to answer clearly, but all the while one refrain surged through her mind: *He is alive. I did not sign his death warrant.* It was a relief so close to joy that she felt drunk with it. And at the same time it brought back all the guilt and horror of her weakness over Jacques Decernay.

He was a spy, and he had tried to kill her before she found out what he was and the crimes he had perpetrated. When she denounced him to Sebastian Coole and demanded his arrest, she had done the right thing—for herself and Harry, for Andrew, for England. Yet when she signed Jacques' life away the pain was so great it was as though she drove a weapon into her own soul. The love that she had believed they held between them was more real to her than the bitter truth of his treachery. She still ached for his touch as deeply as she had in the green glade in Friston Forest. Her enemy was living. And despite all the wrongs he had done her, she could never again summon the strength to wish him dead.

She confessed only the facts, and Mary pressed for more, but she had to put a stop to the confidences when Mrs. Goulding came to call.

Delia Goulding was a frequent visitor, as she seemed to prefer their company to that of Mrs. Rumbold. She spoke of her hostess kindly, however, and said she felt closer to her now that the lieutenant-colonel was on active duty and Mrs. Rumbold craved companionship.

The three women sat in a sewing room at the rear of the house, which had French windows open onto a court-yard and a lawn where Harry was playing with Mary's two boys. Sunlight slanted in through thin, half-drawn white drapes that billowed now and then in a lazy breeze. Mary had on her lap a tambour of embroidery; she was not especially fond of needlework, but while they were sitting about it was the only way she could indulge her need for activity. Mrs. Goulding, perched on the edge of a sofa next to Mary's chaise longue, was idly sorting her silks for her.

Sophia sat where she could look out into the garden and keep an eye on the boys. She glanced toward Mrs. Goulding, wondering what it must be like to be in Brussels with no particular object in view and without close family or friends for support. Several times Sophia had been on the point of telling her that Sebastian Coole was now with the army, but she was worried that she would not sound natural when she said his name. From her observation of them together, she was almost sure that Mrs. Goulding felt much more than friendship for Sebastian, and she was equally positive that the feeling was not returned. To mention him might imply that she herself was claiming him in some way—and she could make no such claim. She sometimes suspected, like Mary, that Sebastian might genuinely be in love with her, but when she examined her own feelings she could find nothing like the dangerous attraction that drew her to the raw, painful memory of Jacques. To respond to

Sebastian Coole, she would need to resemble the serene, trusting young woman who had married Andrew Hamilton. But that woman no longer existed.

Sophia kept quiet about Sebastian. She would have hated to wound Mrs. Goulding, for she had come to like her; she was lively, engaging, and put herself out to please without being ingratiating. Her interest in the children was genuine, and she had an ease with them that soon made her a favorite. What was more, Mary liked her too, for her sense of humor.

Finally it was Mary who mentioned Colonel Coole, but Mrs. Goulding was bending over the sewing basket at that moment and Sophia could not see how she took the news.

"It was a brief meeting in the Rue de la Madeleine and he was going straight on to his post," Mary continued. "A pity we could not have seen more of him, at the ball tomorrow night perhaps." No one answered, so she said to Mrs. Goulding, "A fine figure of a man, and graceful. Does he dance well?"

"Yes. I'm sure Lady Hamilton will agree with me that he does most things well. There is a completeness about him that is very winning."

Mary brightened. "That was just my impression when I first saw him!" She gave a quick interrogatory glance at Sophia. "But it was a mere fleeting glimpse, in Hyde Park, months ago. He was not in uniform then. Sophia, give us your opinion—is he more becoming in uniform or in plain dress?"

She smiled. "You are asking the wrong person. I like no one the better for being in uniform."

"Oh, I must beg to differ," Mrs. Goulding said at once. "Haven't you noticed what regimentals do for a man? It gives him epaulettes if he has no shoulders and stiff boots if he has no calves—"

"And sense and resolution where those happen to be lacking also," Mary cut in.

"And if he is *already* a paragon," Mrs. Goulding laughed, "it gives him a new dignity with which to wear his perfection." She said playfully, "Goodness, why else am I in Brussels except to admire the finest and the best?"

Sophia looked at her with compassion. There was no doubt that she was here principally to search for a husband, and Sophia could not help admiring her frankness and strength of spirit. She said quietly, "You have spent many years with the military. There must be moments when Brussels just now seems very familiar?"

She received a nod and a smile in reply, and then Harry ran in and interrupted them. He stopped in front of his mother and said crossly, "Tony says my pin is on upside down. It isn't, is it, Mama?"

She looked at the gold horseshoe pin that Andrew had handed down him, which was attached to the lapel of his jacket. "I'm afraid Tony is quite right, darling. Here, I'll fix it for you."

"But it's the way it *ought* to be. Jacques said so. He said Papa would wear it this way."

It was a shock. Bent toward him, she felt her eyes go hot. "What nonsense. Why on earth would he—?" She controlled her voice. "He never knew your papa." She turned the pin around and fastened it again, with the curve downmost. "There. Remember I told you, it goes this way so the luck doesn't run out."

He stepped back and looked down at it with a little frown. "Jacques says a man makes his own luck." Then he turned and ran outdoors again.

Sophia sat and looked after him, dazed. She was nonplussed by what he had said; it sent shivers up her spine to think of Jacques talking of Andrew with Harry.

She remembered suddenly a pin that Jacques himself had worn in his cravat more than once, at the Montagues' ball and at her dinner at Clifton: an onyx horseshoe surrounded by diamonds, worn with the curve uppermost. What sense did it make for him to tell Harry to wear his the same way?

Neither Mrs. Goulding nor Mary said a word, but she felt their puzzlement. Mary would no doubt be disappointed to see how much a mere name disturbed her. Mrs. Goulding would be speculating that "Jacques" must be the man she had seen on just one occasion, in the marquee at Epsom, when he smashed his fist into Sebastian's face.

Eventually the other two struck up conversation again, still on the subject of uniforms, and Mary seemed determined to draw Sophia in.

"I remember once Andrew went with us to a party in London wearing his dress uniform and you were vexed with him. I thought he looked magnificent. What was your objection?"

"Mary, how would you feel if Augustus were to walk into this room now and announce that he has been made an aide-de-camp to Wellington?"

Mary was startled. "That's absurd. His duties—his value—lie elsewhere. I should not believe him."

"And if he insisted it were true? If he were about to leave you and go off to march on France?"

Mary stared at her. "I should be horrified. You're not suggesting—he hasn't said anything to—?"

"No!" Sophia rose, went to the doors and looked out into the garden. "I just want you to glimpse what it is like. To understand something that Mrs. Goulding and I already know."

There was a silence; then Mary said tentatively, "Sophia, there is no denying that war demands sacrifices. From both men and women. And I agree, the sacrifices differ."

Sophia turned to face her. "Yes. And ours is the most cruel—because we know war is wrong and yet we condone it. You will see tomorrow, the day after tomorrow, next week, how the women will embrace their men and let them go into battle, without protest, swallowing their tears, making their sacrifice in silence. It's a betrayal."

"I'm sorry," Mrs. Goulding said, "but I'm not with you. A betrayal?"

"Of love." She looked at Mary again. "The same love we have for our children." She went over and sat beside her friend. "You know how we feel when we hold our babies, when we touch their little soft limbs and their lovely skin. The thought of anyone hurting them is so monstrous, so cruel, it's impossible to contemplate. There is no more absolute love than that. Every mother on earth wishes the same for her child—a long and happy life. And it's a love that goes beyond." She smiled at Mrs. Goulding, who was looking lonely. "It goes out to everyone's children, wherever they are, whatever their country or race. It is the love that makes us all human."

Mary's reply was gentle. "Then they grow up, my dear, and life takes them from us."

"But *we* do not change. We know what love, peace and harmony are like, we know it absolutely. We have been given this knowledge, yet we betray it every day by not speaking out. Without a murmur, we allow the forces in society, the powers in international affairs, to turn our sons over to butchery."

Mary looked unhappy and unwilling to hazard another reply, but Mrs. Goulding said in an awed voice, "I see. I see now what you mean. Whenever I see the image of the Madonna, it speaks to me in that way."

Sophia smiled at her again. "Yes, you understand. And you will know it in your heart and soul when you hold your first baby in your arms."

To Sophia's consternation, Mrs. Goulding's eyes filled with tears. "If only . . . but I never could in India. I was so afraid."

Sophia was instantly beside her on the sofa. "Forgive me. How selfish of me."

"No, I love to hear you speak." She could say no more, and when Sophia put her arms around her she leaned into her, crying softly. Sophia, her eyes wet, looked across the top of her head at Mary.

Mary gazed at her with the oddest expression of despair and wry reproach, then went back to her embroidery.

In the afternoon before the Duchess of Richmond's ball, Delia Goulding tried to take a nap, but it was impossible. Lieutenant-Colonel Rumbold had found an excuse to come into town and managed to spend half an hour at the Hôtel de New York, during which Mrs.

Rumbold had been almost frozen with apprehension and Delia had had to keep the conversation going. Finally, when she left them on their own to say their good-byes, Mrs. Rumbold was so distressed she seemed reluctant for her to leave the room.

Delia was familiar with all of it—the agonies of uncertainty, the disbelief when the worst imaginings became reality. Much as she admired Lady Ellwood and Lady Hamilton, she knew neither could rival her knowledge of war, though it was a distinction she would sooner have been without.

Rumbold was a good commander and a clear-sighted strategist, and when she asked for accurate information, he was used to giving it. It was not pleasant. It appeared that Bonaparte had achieved another of his incredible forced marches, driving north from Paris more swiftly than anyone could have calculated, and he had actually been camped right on the French border the night before. His army might well be in Belgium by now, but whether he was advancing, or where, was not known.

Meanwhile Wellington, who had lately spent most of his time conferring with the Prussian General Blücher about a joint invasion of France, had his forces deployed on a very broad east–west front, with the Prussian army positioned in the east near Ligny, barely in contact with his own. The duke was as usual extremely careful about protecting his supply lines and the escape route to the coast, so significant numbers of troops were posted in that direction to prevent Brussels from being cut off. Rumbold reassured the women that there was no fear of Bonaparte aiming for Brussels itself, however, as the city was not his object. When the French army's movement was ascertained, Wellington and Blücher would carry the battle to Bonaparte.

Delia understood perfectly, which meant she also understood the dangers. The principal one was the distances between the corps of the allied forces; the Prussians, for instance, were thirty miles away from Wellington's center. Another was the difficulty of concentrating troops quickly in order to mount an offensive.

Or repel one. There was a tension in the city that she remembered from times of crisis in Bombay: suddenly there were more couriers flashing down the streets, more horses being forcibly requisitioned from the surrounding farms and brought into town . . . the army could never get enough horses. She thought of the tens of thousands of men, gathered in a hundred different places, sitting around waiting to find out where Bonaparte was coming from.

Mrs. Rumbold had a nephew in the Cameron Highlanders, camped on the outskirts of the city; some of them would entertain at the ball tonight, dancing over swords. Lady Hamilton's horse trainer, Mitchell, had joined up on the day she left England; he was with one of the regiments held in reserve to guard the town. Delia thought of the Prince of Orange's corps and the Dutch-Belgian forces under Wellington's command. They had once been under Napoleon's, and who could say whom they would prefer when the tide of battle came to the full? She thought of Sebastian, somewhere along the Dender River where most of the cavalry were stationed. Bas. What was he thinking and planning out there; why had he come? She knew much more about Sebastian than he guessed—but she could not know his mind.

CHAPTER TWENTY-SEVEN

Lieutenant-Colonel Colquhoun Grant had been in the saddle all day and was hot, tired and exhilarated. He had had a short conference with the duke and was snatching a respite at the town house where he was billeted before he pounded out on the road directly south, which instinct told him was now the shortest route to Bonaparte's army.

He had had a dramatic day trying to get information about the French into Brussels; one of his dispatches from the field had actually, through heart-stopping incompetence, been sent back to him, and he had had to ride in with the vital news himself. His scouts meanwhile had been hard at work keeping Sir Henry Hardinge abreast of events, which was exhausting since Hardinge was the duke's liaison with Blücher and was therefore half a day's ride away at Ligny. Obviously there was nothing quite as certain as doing the reconnaissance himself, and he had a young fresh horse champing at the bit in the yard right now. But he must fulfill Sir Henry's request first, so he walked down to the parlor, where he had agreed to receive a visitor alone.

Lady Sophia Hamilton was standing in the middle of the room, looking out the window into the crowded street, but she turned on hearing his step. He was struck at first by the beauty of her face against her black hair;

her skin was pale and she looked as cool as marble. But he observed her closely as they greeted each other and sat down, and saw then the contrasting redness of her lips, which looked soft and full, as though she had been biting them.

And, because he had trained himself to notice such things, he also saw how transparently her face betrayed her feelings. He could tell she was disappointed not to be seeing Sir Henry, but there was something about himself that made her hope for something nonetheless. He couldn't imagine why, unless she had a constitutional attraction toward sweating men in uniforms that looked as though they'd been trampled by cavalry.

He could at least apologize over the first issue. "Sir Henry conveys his regret at not being able to meet you, Lady Hamilton. He received a letter from His Highness the Prince Regent mentioning your concerns and he would have been only too pleased to see you. But his duty lies with Field Marshal von Blücher, as I'm sure you'll understand."

She nodded. "Of course. I have been told you are in charge of intelligence here."

It was a statement, not a question, so he did not reply. This meeting had been requested on her behalf by the Honorable Augustus Ellwood. He had been annoyed initially by the breach of security, but if the Prince Regent and Sir Henry wanted him to answer her questions, he had no choice but to comply.

She did not look demanding, however; on the contrary, she had a mournful expression. "You may not be able to help me. My questions are about the past, you see; they have nothing to do with what you are responsible for at the moment." She paused and clasped her hands in her lap, looking down at them. Then she raised her eyes. "But I have come so far, I must ask. Can you tell me where my husband died, and what he was doing for the army at the time?"

She must know Sir Henry had already briefed him. She had courage and perspicacity, therefore, and he had only to be direct in return.

"You are aware that he was involved in espionage, Lady Hamilton?"

She nodded.

"He led a number of operations in Spain, but his last mission was in France." He saw a spasm cross her face; she was preparing herself. He gave her what he hoped was a compassionate smile. "I must tell you, it was not an official mission. It was a personal one, which he proposed to Sir Henry and which Sir Henry was most reluctant to endorse. But not only was your husband very persuasive, Sir Henry also had a high regard for his abilities—he thought there was a strong chance he would succeed."

"What was he trying to do?"

"Assassinate Napoleon Bonaparte." She saw her eyes widen and said quickly, "Distasteful, I know. Not what you would wish to hear. And as the duke would say, frankly that is not how wars are won." He paused a little to let her recover, then said in kinder tones, "There is a story behind it—I don't know the fate your husband met with, but I can explain how his mission came about. Would you like me to tell you?"

She murmured, "If you please."

"This is based entirely on what he told Sir Henry. Some time in the early spring of 1813 a group of military officers met secretly in a loft in Paris. We do not know how many—perhaps a dozen. Sir Andrew, though he was one of them, did not even know most of their names. The group included Frenchmen, Englishmen, a Spaniard and a Prussian, united in one determination, that Bonaparte should be eliminated. They all knew the dire risks of making the attempt, but they agreed to it, one and all, and swore a solemn oath to carry it out."

He shifted in his chair and examined her. She was trying to reconcile her memory of her husband with the idea of him as an assassin. He could not help her with that; he could only go on. "They concluded that they could not fulfil the task as a group or recruit others; the danger of discovery was too great. These were desperate times and the plan they came up with was equally desperate. They concluded that each man must be prepared to act alone when his turn came.

"So they drew lots to decide the order. Each gave his name and an address to the person preceding him and memorized those of the man who would follow him. Beyond that, they sought no information before they parted, and they never saw each other again. The best way to protect secrets is to have none to keep.

"They chose a simple course. The first man was to make his own plan of attack, set up the assassination and select the date when it was to be accomplished. This might take weeks, months, depending on his access to Bonaparte and his ability to circumvent those around him. As soon as he was certain of the date, he would send a package to the next man, something ordinary like a book or a packet of snuff, with a slip of paper inside it, on which he would write the date and the mark that the men had chosen as their code sign.

"The next man had nothing to do then but wait. If the date passed, and he learned that Bonaparte still lived, then he would know the attempt had failed and his predecessor had been executed." He paused. Her face was frozen, as though the thoughts behind it were making her blood run cold. "That is what happened to Sir Andrew. He received a slip of paper and knew his time had come. It is to his honor as an Englishman that he did not leave on his mission without disclosing it to Sir Henry. To his eternal regret, Sir Henry accepted that your husband had sworn an oath and allowed him to fulfill it."

She looked betrayed. "And you don't know any more?"

He shook his head. It seemed cruel; she had come to him for reassurance, and all he had done was open old wounds. Then he rose, went to an escritoire near the door and found a pencil and paper. "There is one small thing I can show you—the code sign that each man writes beside the date." He looked over at her. "I say writes because we can assume that some of the secret company your husband belonged to are still alive. You see, they had an agreement that if Bonaparte were imprisoned or exiled they would not raise a weapon against him. So all the while he was on Elba they would have made no attempt on his life. Now that he is back in power, he is a target again."

He drew the sign and brought the paper over to her. "Here it is. Omega, the last letter of the Greek alphabet. The sign to mark Bonaparte's end."

She took it, her gaze fell on the paper, and all at once it trembled in her fingers. She said in a strangled voice, "A horseshoe."

"I beg your pardon?"

She got to her feet, the paper rustling in her hand. "Omega. It looks like a horseshoe with the curve uppermost."

Light dawned. "You mean you've seen it before? On a message to Sir Andrew?"

"No, no!" She shook her head. "But I *have* seen it, yes. Andrew left—he left a gold pin to my son. A horseshoe." She went very still, and the dark eyes fixed on his seemed to deepen, as smooth water does under the shelter of trees.

At last she said with deliberate calm, "Does the name of Jacques Decernay mean anything to you?"

If he had not been standing so close to her, if the atmosphere in the room had not been so extraordinary, she could not have taken him by surprise. But when she said it he felt the impact and it showed in his eyes.

"You do know him," she said, holding his gaze. "Is he one of the company? Is he one of *your* agents, like Andrew?"

He took a step back. "I regret, Lady Hamilton, that subject is not within the frame of our meeting."

"You don't understand. All this time I have been thinking the *opposite*. I have been thinking of him as the enemy. And all along, if he was waiting . . . If that was what took him away, a little slip of paper . . ."

Jacques Decernay? The temptation to ask *her* questions was so great he had to physically repress it by folding his arms over his chest. "If you have any more inquiries about Sir Andrew, Lady Hamilton, please do not hesitate to contact me again. And I'm sorry I could not be of greater service today."

She shook her head. He realized the wild expression in her eyes was hope. Then he watched her accept that the interview was over, control her features, even manage to smile at him. Her lips were quivering. "No, I'm grateful. You've been very good. Thank you for keeping faith with me when you must be so terribly occupied. I shan't press you; it's not fair."

She came forward and held out her hand, and he bent and kissed it in farewell, with the amazing sensation that somehow, for the last quarter of an hour, she had been doing him a favor instead of the other way around.

Sebastian came to the ball ready to enjoy himself. The day before, when Lady Ellwood mentioned it in the street, the notion of attending had been repugnant, but he had changed his mind since, and it had not been difficult to work some influence and make sure he got one of the hundred and seventy-five invitations that the Duchess of Richmond distributed to the cream of English society in Brussels.

He was compelled to come because of the frisson he would feel when he walked onto the duke's territory, looked Charles Lennox in the face and knew that the other man had not the slightest clue about him in return—Lennox, Duke of Richmond, the Lord Lieutenant who had murdered the ardent republicans of Sebastian's student days. What could serve hatred better than to exist at close quarters with the thing one loathed and remain unsuspected? English confidence, English manners, English pride used to intimidate Sebastian when he was younger; they created a kind of smooth, shining organism that was too seamless for him to penetrate. But he had long learned how to move unchallenged within that impeccable structure, and though it might still look whole and pure on the outside, he knew the inside was corruptible, and that it could be eaten away and destroyed.

He had always grasped for the very best England could offer and cordially despised it at the same time. This ambivalence had colored his career and his ambitions, and for most of his life had shaped not only his thoughts but his very sensations. He remembered how alien he had felt as a child, distanced both from his parents and from the world of school and relatives in England. Without any guidance from elsewhere he had had to painfully discover himself, push himself to see how far he could go, find the courage to measure what he was capable of. Those discoveries had been lonely, frightening and full of intense, shuddering excitement. He remembered Friston Forest and the fox in the trap— he had dared himself to mutilate it, just to see if he could. He had not wanted the brush as a trophy; he had thrown it away. The horror he felt half an hour later, when they all came across the dying animal together, had been equal to Andrew's and Sophia's. But different, because it was shot through with a darting sense of his own power.

The venue on the Rue des Centres that the Duchess of Richmond had reserved for the ball had apparently once been a coach display room. It certainly looked big enough when he saw it over the duchess's shoulder as she welcomed him. The duke stood nearby talking to a couple of hussars, and Sebastian glanced sidelong at the sharp, haughty profile. It surprised him how little animosity he felt, but then this was a night for larger issues. Lennox could wait.

He moved in and chose a position to one side for a while, to observe. The ballroom was a showcase of gleaming wood, lined with panels of wallpaper patterned like a rose-covered trellis. The brightest jewels within it were the officers in their glittering uniforms, while the women glowed like flowers in soft petal colors, cream or white. He could not see Sophia Hamilton, but she must be there; it was almost eleven o'clock.

The two hussars came up to him and made themselves known: Captains Verner and O'Grady from the Seventh British. He told them he had ridden in and was returning to his post after the ball. Their arrangements had been more leisurely; they had hired hotel rooms in town, brought their dress uniforms in from camp, and had dined regally before they turned up. It was obvious from all this that they were unaware of what was happening scarcely twenty miles away. He told them what he had just heard; in the afternoon Bonaparte had pushed north on the road to Brussels.

Captain Verner said, "My God, what's the duke going to do?"

"He thinks it might be a feint. There was a meeting at ten, but no orders have gone out yet."

O'Grady said, "We'll not see him here tonight, then. Should any of us be here at all?"

"He promised to attend. I gather he's going to keep the promise, so as not to alarm the ladies." Then Sebastian said with a smile, "Excuse me. I've just caught sight of my cousin, Lady Hamilton."

Her father was with her. Sebastian had not expected the admiral to be still in town and was irritated for a moment, but on second thought decided it was useful to have another ally. Lady Ellwood was very well disposed, and the admiral had been positively affectionate in the wake of the business at Epsom. Everyone around Sophia Hamilton was inclined to look fondly on his courtship—which was handy, if he intended to pursue it.

He had made up his original schemes for Harry while he was still in London at the very beginning, and though they had been frustrated so far they had never altered. He had sketched an outcome for Sophia Hamilton at the same date, but by contrast, ever since he had first touched her, on the day he lifted her out of the stream at Birlingdean, he had been wavering over the execution of his plan.

It was almost like being two men. The first, greeting her as he did now, caught her look of embarrassment before she lowered her eyes and saw the sympathetic blush on her cheek, and wished that he could put a hand under her chin and make her look into his face so she could see the undiminished worship in his gaze. The second man, bowing formally to the admiral and exchanging conversation about the ball, felt a flash of contempt for them both that seared like a flame at the back of his mind. Neither had done a single thing to deserve his mercy.

"Cousin," she said when she overcame her surprise, "I imagined you miles away. What will you do when the ball is over—do you stay in town?"

"No, I must go straight back to the cantonment. It's a long ride: I shall have to leave at midnight, like Cinderella."

There was a nervous answering smile. "Some say the officers will be called away even earlier than that. Rumors have been flying around the room all night. What have you heard on the way in?"

"Enough to make me eager to snatch a few dances while I can. Will you do me the honor of standing up with me in the next?"

She consented, and while they were on the floor he explained to her what he had told the hussars earlier. It was clearly no more than she had expected and she took it calmly. This was the woman who had swooned over the thought of Decernay dying, but would stand steadfast when the emperor came marching in to smash the allied army to pieces.

She said, "I have discussed it with my father, and we will remain in Brussels, no matter what. He advises me that a retreat is always chaos and we shall face fewer risks if we stay put."

"Quite right. Besides, rest assured, Bonaparte does not covet Brussels. And even if he did, his aim would be possession, not destruction."

"And you!" she exclaimed. "Why am I even thinking about what might happen to us? Do you know what tomorrow holds for you, where you will be deployed?"

"Not yet." It was true; he was committed to playing the game, which meant tamely awaiting orders from British command. All the information he had gathered had long since gone to the recipients, and whatever happened on the field must be theirs to manage as best they could. It gave him a certain sense of freedom now that battle was about to be joined, and an odd melancholy that befitted a soldier going to battle.

As he watched Sophia Hamilton circle gracefully around him with the movement of the dance, he felt a rare kinship with the other officers in the ballroom. For many, it was the last time they would enjoy the warm sparkle of a summer evening, the play of candlelight over the soft shoulders of pretty women, the waft of floral scents, the murmur of talk around a handsome room, the flash of apprehension and delight in a young lady's eyes as her partner whispered to her of danger and of love.

When the dance was over and they left the floor he kept her hand in his for a moment longer than necessary and she did not try to pull it away. They stood apart from the crowd in a little space of their own, surrounded by a host of curious faces, which he ignored. He was gazing into her eyes with the knowledge that his own showed for once an unequivocal desire—to possess, not to destroy.

"I would give anything to be able to ask you just one question. But I know too well this is not the time or the place." He paused.

She looked both sad and alarmed, but held his gaze.

"May I ask another instead? It is very humble. When this business is over, when I return, may I hope we can go back to our former good understanding?"

Her response was instantaneous. "You have no need even to ask. It is exactly what I wish myself."

At that moment, Delia Goulding walked by on the arm of a grenadier officer. She had heard at least the last exchange; he could tell it immediately from the way she avoided his gaze and by the set of her slender shoulders. He cursed himself. He should have looked for her from the second he stepped into the room and kept an eye on her since. Now his demonstration of proprietorship over Sophia Hamilton had been viewed by just the person from whom he would have preferred to conceal it.

He could not move off to tackle Delia, however, as the admiral came up and said in his fond, gentlemanly way how much he had enjoyed watching his daughter dance. They talked on for a while and then suddenly the bystanders went still and even the dancers seemed to falter—the Duke of Wellington had entered the ball-room. The hostess's daughter, Lady Georgiana, at once left the set and went up to him. Everyone saw her anxious face and knew what her inquiry was.

The duke bowed and gave her a calm smile. He was a man of few words, but he relished female company—his choice of companions in Brussels had already scandalized the English matrons—and he gave her a short but gracious reply. He did not look tired, and the fine skin over the aristocratic bones had a fresh bloom that belied the labor and anxiety of the previous few hours.

The dance resumed and the gaiety continued. Soon afterwards a messenger ran up the steps to the main entrance and asked to speak to Wellington. Sebastian, standing near the duke, overheard without trouble: the way to the coast was clear and there were no French to the west around Mons. Napoleon's drive must be straight toward Brussels.

The orders went out and the din of drums, bugles and pipes rolled through the city as reveille was sounded. Joining the Metcalfes on the sidelines, Sebastian could see the duke's aides circling the room and speaking softly to various commanders. Men began to slip away, to take off their dancing pumps in the vestibule, don their boots and hasten back to their regiments.

An officer of the Cameron Highlanders whom Sophia Hamilton knew came up to beg her hand for the next set. Before accepting she looked at Sebastian, and he chose the moment to excuse himself.

"I must go. I shall just say hello and farewell to Mrs. Goulding; then I shall be off."

He was pleased with his tone: light, but suggesting deep, hidden regrets.

She reacted in kind, her dark gaze full of sympathy. "May heaven preserve you, Cousin."

He bowed over her hand as the Admiral said gruffly, "We are proud of you, sir. Godspeed."

It took him a minute or two to find Delia, during which he tried to compose himself, for she would need careful handling. When he got to her a youthful officer was just about to lead her onto the floor, so he cut in, annoying Delia a little and the officer a great deal.

She looked at him with a challenge in her eyes as he swept her into the dance. It was a waltz, which she danced superbly, her pliant waist sinuous against his palm.

"That poor boy. You're lucky I didn't make a scene. You never could order me about, Bas, so don't start trying now."

"Is this the way to greet me, after all the time I've spent thinking only of you?"

"Of me? Don't you mean Lady Hamilton?"

"We are relatives. One doesn't think of one's relatives—one endures them."

"Oh," she said softly. "You've never been tempted to reorganize their little lives, then?"

He said idly, steering her through the eddies of dancers, "What do you mean?" She did not answer, so he looked down to examine her. She had a reluctant expression, as though she regretted having come out with the question. Quite right, too. It had always been beneath her dignity to show jealousy; it was one of the things he used to admire her for.

And there the conversation languished. Having denied his interest in Lady Hamilton, he had nothing more to say. Insisting on the subject would only make Delia suspicious all over again. The two women had obviously gotten closer since he last saw them together, but unless Delia was bursting with enmity against him he could not imagine her discussing the Bombay affair with Sophia Hamilton. She must know that she would instantly lose the lady's esteem if she did.

After several minutes of silence, it was a shock when she spoke. She was not looking at him but at the swirl of people around them, and he could not tell whether the sheen of moisture on her bright hazel eyes was caused by emotion or the energetic movement of the dance.

She said, "I loved you once."

He began to feel cold.

She had a puzzled tone that made her sound younger, less sophisticated, more like the vulnerable creature he had first met on the croquet lawn of the club in India. "I really did. The only way I can explain it is—you seemed different then."

He was lost, so he picked up the only available thread. "We all change, Delia."

That roused her and she gave him a mocking smile. "Or we stay just exactly the same. But it takes some people a long, long time to find us out."

"Are you trying to say I didn't love you? For better or for worse, madame, I did." It was surprising that the past tense hurt a little. But she had started it.

She said almost dreamily, "I thought you were beautiful, and brave, and clever and—complete." She was taunting him. "That was my feeling about you. The complete man."

He was totally cold now. He had heard enough. If she said another word he was going to tell her to shut up.

The music was ending, but it took an age, surging into a series of deceptive flourishes that set people laughing and tottering around them as they tried to keep up. They were the only couple who stayed in tempo, their bodies perfectly synchronized, their faces turned in opposite directions and their features frozen.

When the music finally stopped they halted abruptly, as though on the edge of a precipice. She let the hem of her white dress fall from her hand and took a little dipping step sideways so that his fingers left her waist. Her face looked sorrowful, with just a shadow of reproach, but her eyes were dry.

"Good-bye, Sebastian." And that was it.

He sneered, "No blessings on my sword arm, Delia? No fond farewells?"

All at once the tears rushed out and trembled on her

lower lids, ready to spill over. "If I could have you back, the way I thought you were . . ." She struggled for speech. "But you don't exist."

Then she spun on her heel and ran away into the crowd.

CHAPTER TWENTY-EIGHT

◁━━▷

Sophia both relished the ball and loathed it.
The frantic bustle of it answered to her inner mood, for she had felt a quickening of emotion ever since the encounter with Colquhoun Grant in the afternoon. If Jacques was one of the band dedicated to annihilating Bonaparte, at this very moment he must be either amongst the cuirassiers in the French lines, drawing ever nearer to his prey, or perhaps closer still to her, scouting for the British. What Grant had told her confirmed a premonition: Jacques was close by. At first it had seemed sheer self-preoccupation, for he had told her he could not bear to be apart from her, but she believed him intuitively, as though there were some strong bond between her body and his that could not be severed. She had tried to shake off the idea, but it persisted, sparkling in her consciousness like forbidden joy. The love that had been her shame pulsed through her veins, dominated every moment she spent alone. She was bound to him, her body yearned for his in a way that she now accepted, as naturally as breathing, as inevitably as death. She could deny this passion no longer, and instead of taking her strength away it renewed her, with every waking moment, with every recollection of his touch, his voice, his secret vows of love.

What frightened her about the ball, on the other hand,

was the accent of doom that she heard even in the most frivolous exchanges around her. She noticed the quick alterations of color on the women's faces, the nuances of feeling on those of the men. No one could conceal the undercurrent of tension that accounted for the punishing amount of wine that some of the officers went for at the select late supper, the way some of the ladies looked at the duke—awestruck and supplicating at the same time—the glazed expression on younger faces and the contained suffering on those of older people who had been through this before and must bring themselves to credit that it was about to happen all over again.

And through it came a chilling conviction that went straight to her heart: Bonaparte's object was Brussels. The moment Sebastian had said it she had known the emperor wanted possession. What was more logical, given his situation? If he could crush the allies, the next step must be to take Belgium and the Netherlands, which would give him not only a secure border to the north and a string of ports facing England, but two more armies to mold to his purposes. Now, when she looked around the ballroom, it was as though she could see his still, watchful figure poised on the outskirts, biding his time, choosing the moment when he would raise his arm and sweep all the ebullient crowd into a jumble of dislocated bodies, scattering them over the bare floor like broken dolls.

She danced to banish the image, accepting every invitation, responding openly to whatever each gentleman chose to speak about and finding that nothing was too trivial or too momentous to discuss in this weird atmosphere of dread and exhilaration. The only dance she did not take part in was the waltz, but when she explained to the officer who had asked her he immediately drew her aside and fetched her a glass of punch and they settled themselves on a sofa, where he sat talking to her as though he had known and adored her all his life. If the waltz had ended five minutes later, he would have proposed. When she accepted the next partner he was so bereft she put both hands on his shoulders and kissed his cheek, and they gave each other a look that stayed with her forever afterwards. It was like saying good-bye to a brother. He left the ballroom at once.

Then came the moment she had feared, when Wellington withdrew. At around one o'clock he was in conversation with a gentleman who announced that he was retiring.

The duke said unhurriedly, "I think it is time for me to go to bed likewise." He had a quick conversation with the Prince of Orange, then spoke a few words to his host, asking if there were any maps that he could consult, whereupon he slipped away toward a side room without drawing attention to his departure.

There were very few men in uniform about now, most of the remaining guests being Brussels residents or visitors like her. The admiral stood out on the other side of the room, where he was talking to Mary and Augustus Ellwood. Sophia was trying to catch his eye, and failing, when Delia Goulding came to her side.

"Are you leaving?" She sounded tense.

Sophia said, "Soon. Can we take you back to the New York?"

"Thank you, but I shall go with Mrs. Rumbold."

Sophia looked at her more closely. "You don't look well. Why not sit down for a while?"

"Yes. Will you join me? There is a room over there; it's empty now that so many people have left. There is something I *must* tell you."

"By all means."

It was a card room, lined with striped yellow wallpaper and furnished with just one table pushed against the wall. Sophia was surprised that Mrs. Goulding half closed the door behind her. She herself sat facing the doorway so that she could see out into the corridor, but the other chose a straight-backed seat beside her that was out of the line of view. Mrs. Goulding took some folded pieces of paper out of her reticule and held them on her lap, laying her little hands flat upon them, one on top of the other.

She needed no encouragement to begin. She looked tired, but her voice was firm and her gaze direct. "I have been speaking to people about you lately and observing you all night. You must forgive me, but from what I hear from your father and Lady Ellwood and Sebastian Coole himself there is just one conclusion—he intends to marry you."

Sophia started. Absurdly, she felt guilty as well as embarrassed. Something in this ghastly evening had destroyed Mrs. Goulding's usual self-control; she could be saying this only out of resentment and jealousy, which up until now she had kept hidden. Sophia could find no answer to what sounded like an accusation.

Mrs. Goulding read her expression and her cheeks went an angry red. "I say this for your sake, not mine. I loved him once—now he disgusts me."

Sophia could only look at her in horrified wonder.

"Lady Hamilton, he is a liar and a traitor. He is a spy for the Irish Republicans, he is in league with Bonaparte and he betrayed your husband to the French. I have the evidence to prove it."

Sophia stared at her. "How can you say this?"

"I didn't want to! I hate having to confess. But for your own safety you must be told." Delia Goulding's eyes glittered with defiance. "When I was staying with Sebastian Coole he asked me to do him a favor, to find a little key of Harry's. He said it might open something at Birlingdean."

Sophia said, "Good God." She was too astonished for anger.

The other woman went on. "Sebastian seemed very anxious, and I wondered what he expected to find. If it was documents, I thought they might be about the inheritance. He is wild to have Birlingdean, you know. He doesn't like Harry standing in the way. So I looked myself, in case I found something you ought to see." She held out the first piece of paper. "This was locked in a jewel box in the main bedchamber. It's for you. From your husband."

Sophia took it, her gaze fixed on the other woman's drawn face. The shock made her voice quiver. "This is incredible! How long have you had this?"

"Read it." Delia Goulding rose from her seat and walked away a few paces. "I promise to answer your questions. But save your contempt until you know everything."

Sophia bit back another protest and spread the paper out on her lap. The short message was hastily written, in Andrew's hand.

My darling,
  A last word before I leave. Months ago I met Sebastian Coole in London, before he went to India, and I told him what this mission would be if one day it fell to my lot. Why? Because he is Harry's trustee. But it was wrong of me—you are Harry's mother and my wife; you have *twice* the right to know. So I tell you here just what I told my cousin, no more, no less—I have sworn an oath to kill Bonaparte. I did not confess this before, because I was afraid my secret would lower me in your eyes. But I go now to fulfill that oath and you must be told. And if I do not return, you have at least one person in whom you can confide—my cousin is a fine man and you may put your trust in him. Forgive me. I love you. Andrew

After what seemed a long, blank time she raised her head. "Sebastian Coole has known about Andrew *for years*."

Delia Goulding gave a tight, bitter smile. "And he never let on to you."

Sophia shook her head.

"He didn't want you to find out. Because he betrayed your husband to the French. Sebastian has been an informer for Bonaparte ever since he was a student in Dublin, when he became a Republican. In one of his messages to Paris, he warned someone about the plot, to make sure your husband was intercepted."

"How can you know this?" Sophia cried.

"I didn't, until I found this letter." She held out the other piece of paper. "It is from one of the most powerful men in France. Sebastian is not named, but I know it was addressed to him because I found it amongst his things."

It was written in English in a clear hand adorned by careful flourishes.

My dear sir,
    Once again I take up my pen to express my appreciation of the copious information that you send us with such regularity and precision. I cannot overstate the importance that the supreme commander attaches to our alliance with the Republicans of Ireland nor the esteem in which he holds those allies who, like yourself, take an active part in the promotion of the cause. Today he more than once referred to you and your fellows as "brothers in arms."
    I wish I could adequately express the emotion with which he also received your warning of possible danger to his person. For you to advise him of this despicable scheme in advance and to give him so accurate a portrait of the pretended assassin shows a tenderness of his safety for which he can scarcely thank you enough. It is at his request that I pen this letter. For the sake of your security I do not superscribe your name, but since I send this by a trusted courier I have pleasure in subscribing my own, as a mark of deep respect and gratitude and of the distinguished sentiments with which I personally regard you, my dear sir, and the assurance of which I hope you will have the condescension to accept from your very sincere and devoted friend, Joseph Fouché, Duke of Otranto.

Sophia began to shiver. She looked up at Delia Goulding. "You know who this man is."

"Of course. At the time when your husband left England, Fouché was Bonaparte's minister of police and he ran the French secret service. And now Bonaparte has reappointed him."

Sophia looked at the two letters lying side by side on the lap of her dress. She felt a wave of grief and revulsion. "Sebastian betrayed my husband to Fouché long before Andrew went after Bonaparte." She lifted her head as the next thought sliced through her mind. "And he is still in league with him!"

"Yes. Why else would he keep the letter? It is a superb reference if ever he wants to slip over to France."

Sophia held up the letter. "And how long have you had *this*?"

"I found it during my last night at Birlingdean, after the races." She was avoiding Sophia's gaze. "It was so horrible, coming back in the carriage, thinking of what had happened. I was with Sebastian in the stables at Epsom. He spoke to Harry alone; he paid him much more attention than he ever had before. Then later he accused Monsieur Decernay, and for hours afterwards, all the time I was looking after Sebastian, all I could think was—*he could just as easily have done that mischief himself.*"

She began to pace about, looking at the floor. "I knew I had to have another look through Sebastian's papers. I'd given him the key, so I couldn't unlock any of the places I'd searched before, but after the Rumbolds retired I crept down to the library and checked his desk. It was open—he'd been writing there before he went to bed, but he was too done up to remember to lock it. That was when I found that letter from Fouché. And I knew exactly what it was about, because I already had your husband's."

"You didn't tackle Colonel Coole?"

"How could I? There's no knowing what he is capable of."

Sophia looked at her in outrage. "He caused my husband's death and you say he's a threat to my son! You had a duty to tell *me*!"

"I was going to. I went back to Brighton with the Rumbolds and I thought about it all the next day. Then I made inquiries—I was trying to decide whether to risk a letter or go to see you—and I was told you had left the country. And next thing, Sebastian had gone himself." She glanced at Sophia with blazing eyes. "Why do you think I am in Brussels?"

Sophia could not sit still. She rose too, and saw the other woman start. But she could feel no mercy for her. Not yet. "Really? You took your time."

Delia Goulding lifted her chin. "Have you never deceived yourself over a man? I kept hoping to be proved wrong. I kept trying to believe that Sebastian had only toyed with France. I hated to think that he would hurt your little boy." Her voice filled with pain. "I hoped he would leave you alone, leave you out of his plans. But tonight I could see it so plainly there was no doubt. He wants everything he ever schemed for—and you as well. I brought these papers with me, praying that I would not need to speak out. But when I saw him with you, I knew it was all over. Now you know. I have betrayed him, as he deserves."

"As he betrayed others." Sophia looked at Delia Goulding's tormented face and lowered her eyes. "I won't ask what this has cost you. But I am grateful."

"What will you do?" The question came out in a whisper.

When Sophia looked up she saw that Delia Goulding was very pale. "I don't know. But this is a matter for British intelligence. Are you prepared to swear that you found the letter from Joseph Fouché among my cousin's papers?"

"If you insist." The other woman's voice trembled. "But he is on our side at the moment, whether he likes it or not—he commands a squadron against the French. He may have been playing a double game over the last few years, but for *now* the only cards in his hand are English. He is out at Grammont, waiting to ride into battle. Is this the time to accuse him?"

"That is not for me to decide."

Mrs. Goulding paused by the empty doorway. "You despise me."

"How can I?" Sophia burst out. "Any mistakes you have made, I have made myself, twice over. We will talk of this again—if you can bear to."

Delia Goulding's eyes, glazed with anguish, hardly seemed focused on Sophia. She murmured, "Good night," and left the room.

CHAPTER TWENTY-NINE

Jacques, leaning against the wall of the building that faced onto the Rue des Centres, was looking down a side alley into the thoroughfare, which was thronged. Brussels had been roughly awakened; there were officers in their dancing pumps and dress uniforms calling for horses, troops moving in a column up the road, supply wagons being forced amongst the traffic while the drivers cursed and shouted. Artillery caissons drawn by big, heavy horses were being impeded by the peasants' carts coming in from the countryside for the early-morning markets, driven by men in the red nightcaps and blue smocks that marked them as Bruxellois citizens.

Jacques' head was still humming from the long ride he had just made, but he knew he would be offered no rest—there would be messages to carry, once the Duke of Wellington had taken in the news he had brought into town.

He watched the street as he waited, but all he could think of was Sophia. He had heard her name only to-night, when he came in after sunset with a dispatch for Colquhoun Grant. She was in the city and she had called on Grant himself, according to the lady of the house where the colonel was billeted. The woman had eyed Jacques askance at first, for he was dressed in the rough attire of a Belgian field-worker, but while he waited to speak to Grant he managed to get her into conversation. He dropped the strong rustic accent he used as part of his cover, and she had been too intrigued to dismiss him to the kitchen or the yard. They talked of the danger to Brussels, the dreadful rise in the price of foodstuffs, the householders' fear of looting, and the English visitors, many of whom were already in flight along the road to Antwerp. When the lady mentioned Sophia's name his heart almost stopped and he had difficulty making his careful inquiries. But she could tell him no more than he already knew—she, the admiral and Harry had come here from Ostend and were staying at the Hôtel d'Angleterre.

Was she at the ball? She might be dancing at this moment in brilliant candlelight, a few yards away from where he stood on the dark cobbles. He watched the carriages on the Rue des Centres, looking for the Hamilton crest, for he knew they had shipped the Clifton carriage when they sailed from Newhaven.

Suddenly the door beside him opened and one of Grant's men put his head out. "You're needed. The duke wants a word."

He said with a wry grin, "What—they don't believe me?"

"Devil a bit!" the other said. "Come on. Step lively."

They went through narrow servants' ways to the area behind the ballroom, leaving the racket from the kitchen and sculleries behind them and penetrating the brighter part of the building where there were strips of carpet on the polished floorboards and the sound of music and voices drifted into the paneled corridors.

Coming out of the lonely night into this festive atmosphere was like stepping into a hectic dream.

A door opened, he was shown in and then it shut behind him.

It was an anteroom that held a few tables and chairs and just two men—Grant, looking alert and solemn, and Wellington. The duke was in resplendent dress uniform and he had not long left the ballroom, but the pleasant part of his lordship's evening was evidently over. He examined Jacques with a direct stare, the nostrils of his fine nose pinched.

He said to Grant, "This is how your scouts are turned out these days, is it?"

"This one in particular, sir. He passes for a Belgian peasant."

"And that's how you got so near their lines?" The question was for Jacques this time, who saw no need to answer. The duke gave a peremptory nod at a map spread out on the table before him. "I want you to confirm what I've just been told. Show me Bonaparte's headquarters, for a start. You can read this, I suppose?"

Jacques stepped forward until he was standing beside the duke, stretched out his arm and put a finger on Charleroi. "He took it from the Prussians at noon."

"And you say Maréchal Ney is further advanced?" said the duke.

Jacques nodded and pointed to the village of Gosselies. "Here."

"With what forces?"

"More than fifteen hundred cavalry and just one battalion of infantry, *mon général*."

The duke gave Jacques a sharp glance, as though he wondered if he were being mocked. Then he said, "Not sufficient to attack Quatre Bras." He paused, looking hard at Jacques. "But that's where they're aimed, in your view?"

"Yes."

The duke banged the map with the edge of his fist and muttered, "Humbugged, by God."

Jacques could see by Grant's face that he had heard this refrain already. "Bonaparte's right wing went on pursuing the Prussians this afternoon, *mon général*. They were beaten back across the Ligne brook. I last saw them retreating to the northeast."

"General von Blücher will regroup. We'll hear from him before morning." The duke straightened, stepped away from the table and looked Jacques up and down with keener curiosity. Then he suddenly said in French, "You're no more Belgian than I am, are you?"

"No."

"How long have you served under English colors?"

"Since June 1813, after Vitoria. In the Chasseurs Britanniques."

"Ah!" the duke exclaimed; then a wry smile lit up his features. "By God, I never thought I'd be owing a thing like this to one of you fellows!"

"Am I to take that as gratitude, General?"

"Take it as you like," the duke said crisply. "You've performed a damned fine service today. And I can't think of anything more apt than leaving you at the disposal of Lieutenant-Colonel Grant."

Grant glanced at Jacques and said in English, "Thank you, Decernay. Dismissed. Report to me in an hour, Rue Royale."

Jacques brought himself to attention and looked the duke in the eye. An indefinable spark shot between them; then the duke's expression became distant and he nodded slightly, as he might to a gentleman who had just bade him good night.

Before Jacques could move, the duke said to Grant, "Come with me. There's work to be done," and strode out of the room.

Left alone, Jacques lingered to absently roll up the map. Then he dropped it on the table and went to the door. He looked up and down the empty passageway, wondering in which direction he should leave. There were fewer voices now and the music sounded melancholy. The ball was almost over.

Suddenly a lady stepped out of a doorway farther up, an apparition clad in white and silver, shimmering in the dim corridor.

She saw him and gasped. He looked at the pale, beautiful face suffused with amazement and ecstasy and opened his arms.

Sophia threw herself at him, colliding with his chest, and he caught her in a suffocating grasp. Her fingers dug into the coarse cloth of his jacket and her face pressed against his warm skin at the neck of the collarless shirt.

He encircled her with one arm and with the other hand pushed open the door as he scooped her through into the empty room. The door swung to behind them, slamming with their combined weight.

They kissed as though it was the first and last time they would be together, as though death was hunting them and they would perish if they could not somehow hide in each other, their bodies melting to become one.

Between kisses she caught a look from him that flashed at her from under the dark brows. She said in anguish, "I suspected you."

"I know. You spoke to Grant. What did he tell you?"

"Everything about Andrew. Nothing about you. But I guessed—you're after Napoleon. You could have explained!"

"Never. You would have been ashamed of your husband, and despised me."

"I still wish you had!"

He took her face between his hands. "You would have tried to talk me out of it. You would have given it a name. Murder. But I won't relinquish this—too many men have gone before me. I am the last and I shall carry it out." He gave her the bitter, lopsided smile. "I managed to keep it from you all that time, and then you come to Brussels and hear it from Grant! He's forbidden it too."

She went to speak again, but he kissed her violently, straining her body against his until she felt breathless and giddy.

When she could speak she put both hands on his chest and searched his gaze. "I love you. You should have told me everything. Everything." He did not answer and she went on. "How long have you been an agent for England?"

"It began in Spain, when I became a Chasseur. I offered myself as a scout and there was a major who trusted me and used me constantly. Then he was recalled to London and I was returned to the ranks. I was willing to serve, but I refused promotion, so the army became very cautious with me."

He took her hand and drew her down to sit beside him on a small sofa just inside the door. "The worst thing they did was to send me to New South Wales. I was in despair—if the message came about Bonaparte, think how long it would take me to return!"

"But how could you expect to get it?"

"I used my home address all along, and I kept in touch with my parents. They forwarded my mail—that's how I did get the message at last, on the morning of the races at Epsom. So I knew I had to go and leave you behind. When I went to the racetrack, I thought it was the last time I would see you. Forgive me for the way I behaved—I was insane. I hardly knew what I was doing."

She wound both her hands into one of his. "When you were transferred from New South Wales, once the war in the United States was over, why did you come to London?"

"For you."

She leaned forward and touched his lips with hers, then drew back before he could respond. "And?"

"I wanted to make contact with the major who employed me in Spain. Bonaparte was on Elba, so I was no longer waiting for the call. I had no purpose left, and I needed one. But I was arrested, and then after I was released I found the major was dead; he had been killed not long before in a London street, by footpads who were never caught. I wondered if it was counterespionage. I couldn't find anyone else who knew me; I had no allies left, no one in the army who trusted me. So I went down to Sussex, to be near you. And to wait for the signal."

She shivered, "Thank God Sebastian Coole never found out about you!"

He frowned at her. "What?"

She let go of his hand, opened the reticule around her wrist and took out Fouché's letter. "Coole betrayed Andrew to Bonaparte. If he had known about you he would have done the same again. Or worse." She put the letter in his hand.

He took it without looking at it. *"Coole is a spy?"*

"For the Irish Republicans. Read that and see."

He swore, then squeezed her wrist and said, "Forgive me. But I should have guessed. He had friends in Bonaparte's Irish regiments."

"How could you guess? His family never did and nor did we. It took a poor, jealous woman to find it out." She saw the change in his expression and said at once, "Delia Goulding. She found that letter amongst his papers. Read it."

He scanned it quickly, his mouth set in a hard line. When he had finished it he got to his feet and stood for a moment with his head bent, thinking. At last he said softly, "The Frenchman before me was in the government. Not quite as close as Fouché is to Bonaparte, but almost. He would have talked to that snake every other day. He never stood a chance."

"Nor do you. Don't try to get to Bonaparte now. Please don't, for my sake."

He stared at her, the gray eyes dark as storm clouds. "I'll tell you what—I'll deal with your bastard cousin first." He folded the letter and thrust it into the waist of his breeches.

"No! Just give that letter to Grant."

"I have unfinished business with Colonel Coole. Have you forgotten?"

She had been going to tell him about the threat to herself and Harry, about the attempts on both their lives that Sebastian Coole had carried out—the very acts that in her terror and doubt she had blamed on Jacques himself. But this was not the moment. Not while he stood there with murder in his eyes; not while he was bent on adding another personal vendetta to the first.

But as the very thoughts flashed into her mind he read her face and his own changed. He said in a heated rush, "The chase in the fog—that was Coole. Aristide at Epsom—that was him too. *Mon dieu.* And I was so obsessed, I let it all happen."

She shivered. "It's over. He's at the front and I know about him now."

"Where are you?"

"The Hôtel d'Angleterre."

"Not safe enough. Take Aristide and go."

She rose and went to him. "My love, my darling." She put her arms around him. "Did you come straight here from Hastings?"

He held her tightly, then said in a contained voice, "Yes. I knew in my guts what Bonaparte was going to do, and I wanted to offer my services to intelligence here. So I could be near him—and you." He smoothed her hair from her forehead. "I demanded to see Grant, and there were enough Peninsula veterans here to vouch for me. He was a spy there for Wellington in 1812, before the French army got hold of him. He escaped and rejoined the duke last year."

"When do you see him again?"

"Now, tonight. I know what he'll say—he wants me to find out where Bonaparte's right wing has gotten to."

She clung to him. "Give him that letter. Tell him Delia Goulding is prepared to swear she found it in Sebastian Coole's papers. Leave this to Grant. Follow his orders and be a Chasseur again. Not . . ." She could not say the word.

He said nothing, and his arms tightened.

She said, "Do your duty if you must and come home to me. It is enough that you are in this fight. I beg you not to carry it further."

He took her by the shoulders and held her so that he could see her face. "How is Aristide?"

"He's fine. He misses you."

"Tell him we'll be together when this is over, for the rest of our lives." He looked deep into her eyes. "I'll make any promise you wish for his welfare."

She clutched at him, her fingers tangling in his shirt. "Promise me this: don't go after them!"

He took her hands, crushing them against his chest. "It's too late." He saw the agony on her face and his mouth twisted. "*Bien*. There are two men on whom I swear vengeance, *mon amour*. Which of them would you wish me to spare?"

She whispered, "You know which one. Your honor as a soldier tells you which one."

"Je t'aime," he said, and kissed her until she reeled in his arms. *"Au delà de la mort."*

Then he released her, wrenched open the door and was gone.

CHAPTER THIRTY

For hours the soldiers poured into the streets to gather at mustering points around the city, as the bugles and pipes continued to shrill, batmen and valets raced about under orders from their officers, and householders lit candles in their windows to watch the stream of wagons and men flow by.

The regiments were rallied, issued with rations of bread and beef for three days, then told to fall out where they stood. They lay down and slept, if they could, on the cobblestones—then at half-past two, while Wellington was asleep at his headquarters, they began to march out of town on the way to the crossroads of Quatre Bras. The Ninety-fifth Rifles in their dark green uniforms with black accoutrements. Perponcher's Dutch-Belgians, sallying forth to defend their homes. The Seventy-ninth and Ninty-second Scottish regiments, surging out by the Porte de Namur to a skirl of the pipes . . . The duke's concentration of his forces had begun.

Jacques left a little before them but used the same direct route as far as the Prince of Orange's headquarters at Genappe, then struck east toward Ligny, to report to Hardinge and Blücher.

After days in the saddle, Jacques knew the environs almost as well as the duke, who had been riding about them for weeks. He found his way by the contours of the land, the familiar shapes and smells of scattered farm dwellings, the intermittent light of the moon, and his trust in Mezrour. The big stallion had been worked hard, but would never let him down. He was a superb night horse, stepping unconcerned through trackless crops of wheat and rye, gliding through the cool forests with all his senses alert to the creatures around them, stretching his long legs and going like the wind when the way ahead was clear enough for a gallop.

It was eerie, striking out into the darkness, not knowing how far the French had driven the Prussians, tensed for the challenge from an outpost, a cry from a sentry on picket duty, the sudden sight of a score of men bivouacked in a field or an orchard, the sound of the alert and a flurry of movement as they snatched their rifles from the pyramid stacks and leveled them at him, shocked into deadly wakefulness. He carried no weapon himself. He was supposed to be a farm worker, after all. And it would have been pointless—he was already outnumbered thousands to one.

When Sebastian woke he was looking at the moon, framed by timber. It was more than half full, bright and inimical, like an eye glaring at him around a black corner. It was mixed up with the dream he had just had, and he had to struggle to reassemble the images. He had been at one end of a long corridor, Sophia Hamilton and Delia Goulding at the other. They were walking away from him, looking back over their shoulders, their white, half-turned faces almost touching. Their arms were linked, drawing them together, and light from some kind of festivity beyond streamed through their fine dresses, delineating their shapely bodies.

He propped himself on one elbow and listened. The camp was dead quiet—the squadron was sleeping. With a bit of maneuvering he might have been commanding a brigade, but he had pretended to be overcome at the privilege of serving with the Prince of Wales's Own and eager for whatever posting he could get. As it was, with a smaller body of men he enjoyed more flexibility. He was better informed than they, knowing how soon the signal would come, how quickly they would have to shake off tiredness and get on the move. They were in the reserve, but Wellington would want them close.

His mind slipped back to the women again, and the cold menace of the dream sliced into his consciousness. He had said far too much to Delia when she first came to Brighton, and he had made the situation incalculably worse by bringing her into contact with Sophia Hamilton and then asking her to steal for him. He had let his guard down with both women. And now, being back on active duty again had disoriented him; he should have been sufficiently alarmed by Delia's behavior at the ball, but it had taken hours for the warning to sink in. He could not afford them to draw closer to each other. He had to know how much Delia had already said. He must deal with her.

Jacques was walking along a country track with a hen over his shoulder. It had tried to protest when he caught it on the blind side of a walled farmyard, but he had muffled it in his smock, and when he was a safe distance away he had taken it by the legs and soothed down its wings, talking companionably as he strode along. Now it was limp and comically resigned, its wings folded, the soft feathers warm against his bare neck.

When he had gotten to Sombreffe where Blücher was snoring the night away, they had roused Hardinge for him. Hardinge had listened to the messages and then ordered him to rest until the general awoke. Instead, Jacques left Mezrour safely tackling a big pile of feed, extracted the Prussian sentries' password from a friend who looked after the horses, then slipped out of the dark hamlet into the countryside.

He had crossed the Ligne brook where trees grew thick on both banks, then walked along farm tracks as faint light crept into the sky and men sallied out to begin the day's work in the fields. After catching the hen he stopped and chatted to people and asked what the French were paying for provisions. Everyone was amused by his having such a meager scrap of produce for sale, and thought him idiotic as well as poor; but they watched his hands as they talked, and took care not to mock him.

Just before the sun came up he judged it was time to head back to Sombreffe. He was on a little knoll at a crossroads, talking to a hefty man with red cheeks who had just told him which regiments were encamped in the wood over to his left. Here and there amongst the trees Jacques could see the flicker of breakfast fires starting up. He remembered what it was like, French camaraderie before a battle, so different from the last two years. He turned his back on the sight and found himself facing a village.

"Any point in going there?"

The other gave a sour grin. "Fleurus? I suppose, if you're after visiting the emperor."

Jacques' heart thumped. He stared at the jumbled line of rooftops and trees until his eyes watered. When he could command his breathing he said, "Then it looks like today's the day for the Prussians."

The other nodded, then turned and stretched out his arm. "He's not there yet, mind, but that'd be the spot for him. You see the old windmill? It gives a grand view of the district; if he took a spyglass up he could direct everything from there, like moving toy soldiers across a carpet."

"What makes you think he'll come this way?"

"My cousin has the best inn at Fleurus. The couriers left at five to tell Bonaparte that Ligny's seething with Prussians." He grimaced. "When the sun's well up, this bit of land will be no place for the likes of you or me."

"You're right. I'll take the other road."

Jacques bade the other farewell and set off to circle back the way he had come. His head buzzed with lack of sleep and a febrile, haunting excitement. He could not count on Bonaparte's arrival, nor be certain of snatching a chance to exploit it. But for the first time he felt the nearness of the prey.

At the farm he let the hen go. It gave him a manic

look as if it had never seen a man in its life before, then scuttled around the corner of the stone wall. As he waded into the Ligne, swallows darted in front of him, flicking the surface with their beaks; and later on the outskirts of Sombreffe a lark rose suddenly from the grass near his boots, spiraling up into the blue and uttering a bubbly greeting to the new day.

At one o'clock Jacques was woken by the sound of hooves and voices going by the stables. He peered out between the slabs of timber below the eaves of the hayloft and saw Wellington ride by with some aides. Hardinge was with them—he must have spied the duke coming in and gone out to meet him on the road. Jacques lay back in the straw, cursing himself for having slept so long. When he had given Hardinge his reconnaissance report, the colonel had written up a dispatch, handed it to another rider and ordered Jacques to take some rest: "Twenty-four hours on the hoof is sixteen hours too many. Get your head down."

He was in Bussy, a pretty little place not far from Ligny where Blücher had established his headquarters, ironically enough in a large windmill. The top of the edifice apparently furnished a magnificent view of the French forces drawn up beyond the brook that Jacques had crossed that morning. He had a mind to see it.

He scooted down the ladder, gave Mezrour a pat and went to the saddle hitched over a rail nearby. Tied to the back of it was a packroll, which he unfastened. Folded inside that were a spare pair of riding breeches, a fresh shirt and a jerkin of the same soft, worn leather as his boots. They were not a uniform, but they were clean, and after a wash at the pump in the yard he put them on, lacing up the shirt and cinching in the belt of the jerkin as drops of water splashed down on his fingers from his wet hair.

At the mill, they sent him up the ladder so Wellington could examine him about the morning's foray. The duke asked a few questions about Fleurus and then ignored him, while General Blücher surveyed the scene through his spyglass. Even with the naked eye it was possible to distinguish between the divisions, and it was with a ridiculous lift of the heart that Jacques made out in the distance a packed squadron of the Imperial Guard.

The old Prussian general was examining the nearest French infantry when suddenly his white head stopped moving. They all followed his gaze down to a small knot of men on horseback amongst the advance units. A staff officer standing a pace in front of Jacques, said involuntarily, "Bonaparte!"

They all held their breath. He was a small gray figure on a white horse, unmistakable because he remained the center of a little circle that eddied amongst the columns of men.

"He got there at eleven," the officer said. "We heard the cheers from here."

Napoleon was half a mile off, but Jacques felt as though he were staring him in the face. His fists clenched and his legs felt unsteady.

When the generals released him he went to the stable and stood there for a long time, unmoving. Then he leaned his head against Mezrour's neck to think. It was too late to infiltrate the emperor's troops, and the gear he needed for the purpose was with the rest of his baggage in the hamlet of Waterloo more than fifteen miles away. It was René's gear. He had asked his parents to ship it to Newhaven and had gone down to collect it and bring it to Joliffe Court on the day before he went riding with Sophia in Friston Forest. He had sworn to himself that when the moment came he would confront the emperor wearing his brother's cuirass and accomplish the deed with his brother's sword . . . but that was impossible here and now, for the French were about to attack. Once they advanced, he might try to get to Bonaparte through the flashing barrier of his own countrymen, but the idea revolted him.

He had meant to take care of Coole first. But he would not know where Coole was until he could get back on the Brussels road.

He banged his forehead against the hard muscles of

Mezrour's neck, startling him. He was ready for the fight—whom was he ready to kill?

Then he stepped away from Mezrour and made his decision. When the Prussians took on Bonaparte, he would stand with them. If a weapon fell to his hand during the charge, he would use it.

After Wellington departed, Hardinge had no immediate duties for Jacques, so he used the opportunity to move Mezrour back to a little farm on the road east and pay the farmer to keep the stallion hidden in the barn behind a wall of hay. As he trudged back he went over the reasons for this decision, wondering whether he was being overcautious. But a sentence of Wellington's stuck in his mind. During an hour's consultation between the two generals, the duke had reportedly said to Blücher, "Everybody knows their own army best; but if I were to fight with mine here, I should expect to be beat." Blücher had exploded, saying his men were there because they were burning to fight—and win—but Jacques understood the duke's reservations. The chief of staff believed in using reverse slopes and the shelter of walls and buildings, whereas most of the Prussian army was ranged along inclines within excellent view of the opposing French.

On the road to Ligny, Jacques fell in with an artillery crew hauling a twelve-pounder forward, and he put his weight into the effort. When they had maneuvered the big gun through the village to the battery he stayed on, sharing a pipe and speaking French with a youngster from Alsace who had joined the army only a year before.

The first deep booms came not from the guns at their side but from the direction of Quatre Bras, nine miles away. A murmur ran through the dense ranks of the Prussians, and at the same moment they saw a ripple in the crowds of French, like a breeze stirring through a field of multicolored grasses. From then on there was something unreal and absurd about everything. Jacques had never in his life had to coldly await a French charge.

The battles he had seen as a Chasseur—San Sebastian, Roncesvalles and Sorauren—had been British initiatives on very different terrain. When the drums began to roll on the other side of the Ligne, he watched the dazzling kaleidoscope of the French troops in a strange state of dislocation. They looked invincible.

It took him an hour or more to realize half the Prussian army secretly thought the same. It began as an artillery duel, which kept him busy; then a French infantry charge cut a giant swathe through the troops at the center of the Prussian lines. At this point a platoon of soldiers from Ligny rushed down the slope past the guns and Jacques joined them, by instinct, only to pause halfway, riveted by what was going on in the fields below. Not only were the front lines of Prussians being pushed back, some of them were turning. They actually tore into the reserves who were rushing toward them, like backwash meeting an incoming wave. So he advanced to rally them.

With some of the younger ones, he simply shouted in their faces. With older, more determined men he tackled them if they were within reach, and when they hit the ground, he ripped the rifle out of their hands and prodded them to their feet with the butt. Then when they stood there gasping, he rammed the weapon across them, into their arms, and gave them a push in the right direction. Some of them went back, some cursed and walked on past. Oddly enough, no one tried to shoot him.

Then he helped the wounded. It started when he saw two hale soldiers dragging an injured lad to the back of the line. He took the boy himself, hoisted him over his shoulder and left the other two to sheepishly rejoin their comrades. The boy had suffered a raking bullet wound to the thigh; he bled on Jacques and cried with the pain all the way. Jacques carried him to a church in the village where they were taking the wounded and propped him half-fainting in a corner. He tried to get the surgeon to look at him, but the man was too occupied, so he got a needle and thread from him and stitched the gash himself; the bullet had not lodged in the flesh, so it was best closed up and bandaged.

As it happened, the boy was braver while Jacques tended him and hardly made a sound. At the end of it he said, "Thank you. I'm sorry I cried."

Jacques touched his shoulder lightly and stood up. "If a man didn't cry over this, he wouldn't be human. Don't worry, you'll survive." At the time, he almost believed it.

But the whole day went to hell, under a blazing sun. The French artillery took its toll right along the Prussian lines, even amongst the reserves. Then the French infantry stormed the fortified farms and hamlets, destroying whole units in their path. Jacques directed a team of stretcher bearers and commandeered a mule to carry more wounded men back to the village. It was endless and exhausting, and they found fewer men alive, for hour by hour the fighting grew more savage and both sides had ceased to give quarter.

Fires broke out across the string of settlements as the French penetrated the yards and lofts and cellars where the defenders tried to take shelter. In the east, the French cavalry was hounding the Prussians across the open fields. On the outskirts of Ligny, soldiers fought hand-to-hand for the possession of every street. The church where Jacques had taken the first wounded lad became a target, then a bastion against the blue tide of French soldiers, then a raging inferno when it was hit by an incendiary.

Blücher himself led a counteroffensive in the west.

"Kinder, haltet euch brav! Now lads, hold fast! Don't let the *grande nation* rule you again! Forward, in God's name—forward!"

The troops cheered and obeyed, and Napoleon immediately sent reinforcements to deal with them. The flames in Ligny mounted higher.

By five o'clock Blücher had used all his reserves. At six the battle raged without cease all along the front, the sun was descending behind storm clouds and it began to rain heavily. At seven thirty, two hundred French guns opened up a barrage on the Prussian center and then the battalions took the onslaught of a punishing charge by the Imperial Guard.

Ligny fell, and the battle surged through it like surf over a crumbling castle. The pockets of resistance were divided from one another by acres of dead soldiers and horses. Jacques was now working again beside the big cannon he had helped to haul through the village. They took no direct hits, but at one point he was thrown to the ground when a shell burst nearby. When he got up, he saw the whole crew was dead, except for the youngster from Alsace, who had a piece of shrapnel in his chest. As they crouched by the gun, looking around at the carnage on the slopes and the close, bloody melee in the fields below, the rain stopped and the sun began to set in glorious gold beyond the smoke.

The Prussians were on the brink of disaster; they had to stem the French before nightfall. At his feet, the young artilleryman gave a groan and pointed. Jacques turned to look. Across the cluttered ground, bearing straight for the center of Blücher's line in a broad, terrifying phalanx, came the cuirassiers. The French infantrymen, seeing them stream through their ranks, gave a mighty cry, *"Vive l'empereur!"* and a volley of musket fire crashed harshly across the Prussian front. As Jacques went down, the smell of cordite filled his brain with blackness.

When the cannonades began in the middle of the afternoon, they were audible in Brussels and a considerable number of citizens and visitors went out to the ramparts to listen. Sophia, declining this entertainment, went to visit Mary with her father and Harry and stayed for tea.

Ellwood came home with a few snippets of news, gathered from a Colonel Canning; the firing they could hear was coming from Quatre Bras, where Wellington was holding out against the storm, though he had scarcely any artillery and no cavalry; they were still moving up. The Dutch-Belgians were taking a beating, partly because of the Prince of Orange's rudimentary knowledge of tactics. French heavy cavalry had overwhelmed the Sixty-ninth, which had lost two full companies. They must expect to see wounded straggling into town very soon. Meanwhile nobody could say where the Prussians were, or what might be happening to them.

Sophia, who had heard enough, went back to the hotel. Later, when it grew dark, she read to Harry in bed while the admiral went out to supper alone. She could not rest, yet talking exhausted her and she was not up to seeing friends. Nonetheless she received a short, breathless visit from Charlotte Lennox who had much more recent news, from a Colonel Hamilton.

"He is not a relative, by any chance?" The plume on Charlotte's turban drifted whimsically as she angled her head with the question.

"No."

"He is aide-de-camp to Major-General Barnes. He is full of praise for our troops and rather admires Bonaparte, considering the clever way he has got between both our armies. Bonaparte has thrown his right wing at the Prussians."

"What is happening there?" She said it too quickly, but Charlotte did not notice.

"We have no idea. But at Quatre Bras the losses have been appalling. Poor Lord Hay is gone. The Duke of Brunswick too—the Brunswickers are smashed to pieces. And Wellington himself was within an ace of being taken by a body of French lancers. He had to fly them at the gallop; he was racing toward a ditch occupied by some Gordon Highlanders, and he shouted at them to lie quiet and set his horse at the fence and sailed clear over the top of them!" She shook her head at Sophia, the plume fluttering like a startled guinea fowl. "There is more, but I shan't burden you with it. I know your expressions so well; inside, you are begging me to hold my tongue."

When Charlotte rose, Sophia did also. "Thank you for coming. And thank you for the ball last night. I think it gave the men heart; you should be proud of that."

Charlotte suddenly embraced her. "It seems unreal. So much has happened since."

For Sebastian, the forced march to Quatre Bras had been unamusing, and he had only four hours' sleep before being woken in the dark by the sound of firing along the British and French lines. It was a false alarm and eventually died down, but repose did not follow. Everyone else's batman seemed to be up and preparing breakfast, so he dug his own out of his slumber and sat watching the flicker of fires being lit amongst the bivouacs.

The sun rose on an unholy scene of dead men and horses scattered in stinking mounds across the fields before the lines, testimony to the army's fierce resistance against Maréchal Ney's forces. For something to do, Sebastian formed the privates into burial parties. Hundreds of the dead had been stripped by looters during the night, and some bodies were stark naked. The dead horses were already stiffening in the sun. He went around shooting the wounded ones himself.

No one knew what had happened to the Prussians, so later in the morning Wellington ordered the brigade commander, Major General Vivian, to pick out a reconnaissance party and send them out on the road toward Ligny. Vivian allocated the task to a troop from the Tenth.

Not long after they had gone, Sebastian repaired to the corner chosen for the latrines, well out of sight of most of his squadron, then strode back in haste.

"Saddle my horse," he said crisply to his batman. "I'm commanded to Ligny. Hurry, man. I want to catch the troop as quickly as may be."

He left the thing vague; his squadron was welcome to imagine the instruction had come from either Vivian or Wellington.

On the way out he rode up to his second in command and delivered his orders for the next few hours. Then he darted off to the east through the great, loud, sprawling camp.

He did not swing back toward Brussels until he was well out of sight of malicious observers. His horse felt energetic and nimble and he could easily have caught up with the party if that had been his intention. He contemplated the problem of justifying his actions without too much concern. For all he knew, the afternoon might bring death to everyone to whom he had spoken in the morning, and the reconnaissance party itself stood every chance of being welcomed by Napoleon's brigades the moment they showed their faces anywhere near Ligny. He hoped their reception was a hot one.

Meanwhile he would ride into Brussels armed with the excuse of a commission from Vivian. As he sped up the road toward Genappe, he realized Wellington was going to have to pull back, otherwise he risked being outflanked by Bonaparte and having to deal with him on one side and Ney on the other. The army would have to make a stand nearer Brussels, or it would be cut off from the city and the supply lines. A smile formed under Sebastian's new regulation mustache; the cavalry, some of whom had marched fifty miles to Quatre Bras, and the artillerymen who had busted their guts getting there the night before, were soon going to have to turn around and trundle back the way they had come, with Ney's lads nipping at their heels.

Jacques awoke when the sun came up. He thought he could remember coming to in the dead of night, then being too weak and exhausted to move. He must have sunk into sleep, despite lying oddly, one leg hooked over the waist of a dead gunner, the other under the caisson of the cannon with his shoulders propped across a linstock. It took him an age to roll to the side and then force his back to bend the other way so he could finally raise his head and work out where he was.

The bullet or shell fragment that had knocked him out had scored across the top of his head. The wound was tender and he had a crashing headache, but the blood had congealed.

The youngster from Alsace was only three paces away,

stretched out motionless in the shade of the big gun. Jacques crawled to his side and checked for a pulse, but there was none. The lad's face looked waxy and his eyes were half-open. Jacques closed them. There was a bloody knife in the soldier's hand. Jacques tugged it away, wiped it on his filthy breeches and tucked it in his belt. The lad must have used it against looters; the dead around them were all in uniform, but there was no doubt the boy had wounded someone in the blackness before dawn, before he died.

Still keeping low, Jacques looked out onto the fields below. The earth was strewn with dead—red and blue together, with here and there grotesque mounds of men piled on horses piled on men, where cavalry had broken full tilt into squares of infantry. French soldiers were moving across the battlefield, burial parties or soldiers gathering up rifles. He had to move. This was a captured gun and he was astonished there was not already a guard on it.

It was easy; he had only to pretend to be looting. He was covered in blood, but any dedicated looter probably ended up the same. If he kept shy of the village and made gradually toward the Ligne brook where there were a few trees for cover, he might go unchallenged.

He found he could walk, and the maneuver worked; every twenty yards or so he bent over a dead body and feigned taking something from it—gold from the pockets, a watch, a loose button. He remembered the midshipman on the man-of-war as they slipped in to Greenwich, when he handed him a pewter button off his coatee and said, "A souvenir, of a time never to be repeated, *Dieu merci*." Some of the dead looked no older than that boy.

Once he was over the brook it would be a long walk to where he had left Mezrour. The Prussians must have been chased to Sombreffe and beyond. Hardinge, if he was alive, would assume Jacques had fallen. If he could get to Mezrour, he could get to Waterloo. After that, it was time to go hunting.

CHAPTER THIRTY-ONE

Sophia had hardly slept the night before, for panic crashed through the streets as soon as the wounded began coming in. The Dutch-Belgians were most affecting, as they struggled back to their homes to fall into the arms of their distraught families. Half the residents of Brussels seemed to descend on the streets, getting in the way of the military going south and fighting with each other over transport that might take them to Antwerp or to Ghent, where Louis XVIII with his court was awaiting a victory to which he had so far made little contribution. Watching from her window while Harry and the admiral slept in the next room, Sophia had seen fisticuffs break out between gentlemen arguing over carriages and women standing in doorways with half-awake children clinging to their skirts, agonizing over whether to go or stay, and with no guarantee of a conveyance if they did go. Then the remnants of Belgian cavalry began to tangle with stray cattle—the army commissaries had decided to move the army's beef on the hoof as close to the lines as they could get before butchering it. The traffic jam was complete.

After daybreak, and as the morning drew on, the crush lessened. The sound everyone feared—cannon fire from the south—did not make itself heard, and at times a brief, ominous quiet settled over the city. By midday it was possible to go abroad, and to get some exercise the three of them walked to Mary's.

On the way the admiral said, "Ellwood may have news of the Tenth."

She caught his sympathetic look and cringed. She could not bring herself to mention Delia Goulding's extraordinary revelations. She had not told her father about Andrew's last message or about the man to whom she had given the damning letter from Fouché. In this time of crisis, she could only stay sane by protecting Harry and her father. The admiral's world would fall apart if he knew Sebastian Coole was a traitor. Somehow, amongst these extraordinary events, she had a wild hope that Coole's fate would be meted out—and even if it was to be by the British rather than the French, at least her father would learn of it only when it was accomplished.

She and Harry were not in danger while Coole was at the front. They had no idea whether the Tenth had arrived at Quatre Bras in time to take part in the battle the day before, but they knew they were there.

She could not be comfortable at Mary's. Sometimes she felt a temptation to confide in her about the encounter with Jacques, to pour out to her the turmoil inside; but telling anyone else seemed a sacrilege against the bond she and Jacques had forged in those few moments together. She said his name in her heart and kept it there like a talisman.

Later, when they were back at the hotel, she felt guilty for not making the visit longer, for Harry was weary of being cooped up.

The admiral said, "Well, young man, what if I were to take you for a turn about the Place Royale, so we can inspect the horses?"

Harry turned to Sophia eagerly. "May I?"

"You're to hold on to Grandpa's hand every step of the way. And bring me back a mille-feuille from the pâtissier on the corner. Promise?" She said to her father, "The clouds are gray, Papa. Harry can take the umbrella."

When she was alone, she sat in the window and looked out at the street. It was impossible to read or rest—she could only think of Jacques. She tried to remember every second they had spent together, with memories that burned like slow fire. She tried to believe they would both come through this worst of perils, but her brain could not conjure up images of peace.

The admiral and Harry had been gone only a short while when her reverie was interrupted by another visit from Charlotte Lennox. The duchess stayed only the minimum quarter of an hour, since there was a host of other friends waiting for news.

While they talked they heard a far-off growl like thunder or gunfire, and both strained to listen. At last Charlotte shook her head and sighed. "No. It's a storm coming."

She embraced Sophia again as she left and said, "What tales of woe I've brought you. I wish there were a merrier set of subjects to talk about. Oh no!" She drew back, her face falling. "Oh, dear me, how could I forget? There is something else. You are quite well acquainted with Mrs. Delia Goulding, I think?" When Sophia nodded she went on. "The most awful accident. Mrs. Rumbold is beside herself—no one can conceive how it happened. Sometime today, there is no saying when, Mrs. Goulding fell from her hotel window."

Sophia took a step back. *"My God!"*

"Her room is at the rear of the New York; she was found by a scullery maid in the courtyard below. She was quite senseless, and there must be frightful internal injuries. She cannot live." She looked at Sophia mournfully. "Why did I come? I leave my house determined to spread a little cheer, but everywhere the talk comes round to catastrophes. Forgive me. Come and see me tomorrow, if you can get through the streets, and I promise to make you smile at *something* if it kills me."

When Charlotte had gone, Sophia felt genuinely afraid, with the cold, paralyzing terror that only manifest evil could inspire. She stood rigid in the center of the room, her mind spinning. Her father and Harry—they would still be on their way to the Place Royale, but by what route? If only she had stayed at Mary's; Harry could not be touched at the Ellwoods', whereas in the open, in the city, with his grandfather, who knew nothing about Sebastian Coole . . . But she had little chance of finding them if she went after them. She could only wait and prepare for their return.

She managed to move, crossing the room to lock the door. She stood for a moment with her hand on the latch, remembering Delia Goulding, who had been asked to steal a tiny key from a small boy, never dreaming how strong a trap had been constructed around it by the man she loved. Now he had cast her away.

It was appalling to feel so sure about what had happened. Somehow Sebastian had been able to quit his post and come into Brussels. He had sought out Delia Goulding, and whatever she had said to him, whatever he had forced out of her, had been her sentence of death.

She calculated how long it would take her father to return with Harry. They must all leave then, at once, for other lodgings, and ask the hotel not to pass on their new address. She rang the bellpull to call a servant, and while she waited she took the Forsyth pistol out of a drawer, loaded it carefully, and put it under the cushion of a chair that faced the door. Her fingers did not tremble as they had when she tried to load it at Joliffe Court. This time she had no doubt who her enemy was.

An attendant quickly answered her call, and she unlocked the door and let him in. He stood openmouthed when she told him that the manager must make haste to find them another hotel. He raised protests, but she was insistent. They had no complaints about the service, she explained, but the noise disturbed her son. Surely, with so many people fleeing the city, there must be accommodation available in a quieter part of town that they could move to before nightfall?

The man disappeared in some dejection, and she returned to the window. It began to rain, thick curtains of water rippling down the street, driven before the coming

thunderstorm. Harry and her father would be soaked,
even with the umbrella. Her eyes searched for them in
the downpour. Sebastian Coole too could be somewhere
out there now, deciding on his next move. If Jacques
had denounced him to Colonel Grant, Delia Goulding
would still be alive. On the other hand, perhaps the
order had gone out for his arrest and he had evaded
capture, speeding into Brussels first to take his revenge.
If so, he would have left by now, to the coast—or
crossed the lines to take shelter with the French.

She was so intent on the street outside and deafened
by the rain pounding on the roof that she did not hear
the door open smoothly behind her, nor remember that
she had failed to lock it when the attendant left. She
was so preoccupied with thinking of how to keep Harry
safe that she had no inkling that there was another person in the room.

Then her scalp prickled as she sensed someone close
behind. She began to turn—and got no farther. Long,
steely fingers clamped around her throat, her whole body
jerked with the shock and a white flash shot through her
brain. She struggled and tried to cry out, but that second
of panic had been her undoing. Before she could gather
mind or body to fight her attacker, her sight blurred and
she knew no more.

Sebastian was furious, but it was an anger that gave him
a magisterial detachment, as though he were looking at
events through expensive crystal. Just as he had with Delia,
he released pressure at the second he felt Sophia go limp, so
that he caused no bruising to the neck. As with Delia, it must
look as though no one had laid a hand on her. It would
be insane to throw the woman out the window this time;
he would smother her instead. But later.

He lowered her into a straight-backed chair and tied
her hands together behind it with cord he had brought
for the purpose. He had not had long to concoct the
plan, but so far it had gone without a hitch, the admiral
having made things easy, of course, by removing the boy.

He had no idea where they had gone, and he might have only half an hour, but that would suffice.

She was coming round, so he gagged her with a kerchief and put another cord tight around her ankles.

He locked the door to the corridor, searched the drawing room quickly, then went into her chamber, pausing just a second in the doorway to look over at her. She was still groggy, and all her defenses were down. When he caught her eye, he could see sheer terror, which gave him a jolt of pleasure but increased his anger. The bitch; there was no need for any of this. It should not be happening. In order not to strike her, he strode into her room and began the search.

When he found nothing, the rage was harder to control. He went back to her and saw she was awake now, and desperate, though trying to hide it, trying to think. He leaned over so his mouth was an inch from her ear.

"Where is the letter? I know you have it—Delia told me. She told me everything; she was on her knees begging by the end of it. So don't lie to me. There's no point—I can see right into your duplicitous mind." He grabbed her chin, forcing her face toward him, and straightened. "It's here, isn't it?"

She shook her head. That was a start. But she didn't make a sound, which was cheek, any way you looked at it. Granted, the traffic and the deluge in the street outside would drown any kind of cry she might utter through the gag—but no sound at all was defiance. She was gathering her resources.

He went to the connecting door, opened it and looked in. The boy evidently shared the bedchamber with the grandfather. He went through it carefully; he wouldn't put it past her to secrete the letter amongst the son's toys; the family had a bizarre habit of doing that. Not finding it made him quake with an impatient ire that darted through his veins like sparks.

He went back to her. "Don't cry out or I'll kill you now." He yanked down the kerchief, untied it and put it in his pocket.

Her voice was like a thread, but her chin was up. "You'll get nothing from me unless you free me."

For answer, he snatched his saber out so swiftly it sang as it left the scabbard, and she flinched away from him. Then, before she could begin to collect herself or speak, he cut the cords off her wrists and her ankles with single, deft movements and swept up the pieces to put them in his pocket.

He stood before her, the saber glistening in the air between them, the tip poised motionless above her sternum.

Suddenly she said, *"Why?"*

Before he could stop himself, his left hand came back and he hit her on the side of the face with the flat of his hand, so hard she tumbled to the floor. Her hair came loose, and she looked at him through it as though she were gazing at an alien.

He backed away, unlocked the door, sheathed the saber and sat down at a table two paces away from her, his sword arm resting along it. He didn't want the door barred. If someone turned up, he preferred to give the impression he and she were just having a cousinly chat. If anyone came right in and she tried accusing him, he would deny everything and call her a crazy woman. Delia, the only person who could have sworn Fouché's letter was written to him, was taken care of. It was only this one's word against his.

She had noticed how quickly he could move, and she knew him now—the man she had never seen before, the stranger. It was nearly time.

"Where is the letter?"

She said slowly, as if drugged, "I don't have it."

"Who does? The admiral?"

"No!" she said violently. "He has no idea about you."

She was protecting her father. But she was also telling the truth; he was not boasting when he said he knew when she lied, because her every emotion always showed in her face.

He said with deliberation, "Who has the letter?"

"Colonel Grant."

He stood up, but she didn't flinch this time. It goaded him to fury again, but he kept it inside.

"You're lying. I spoke to Grant today—if he'd gotten it he'd be after my entrails."

He took one step closer. She raised herself to her knees, using both hands on the seat of the chair. She looked like a clown, one side of her face red and the other white. If she had not been so stupid he would not have had to kill her. After he got rid of the child he would have it all—Birlingdean, the baronetcy and the Hamilton fortune. He would have let her share it. But she had soiled herself with Decernay.

Then he thought of what Grant had said earlier, a chance reference to Decernay, as though he had expected Sebastian to know the man was in Belgium. It was just another piece of unwelcome news that had fueled the rage inside him. Suddenly the name exploded in his head and he said to her sharply, "What about Decernay?"

And he read the reaction at once as it bloomed beneath the transparent skin on her left cheek, rushed like a warm current through the deep, dark eyes.

"You gave it to him!"

She shook her head at once, the black hair flying, and he knew it was true, as surely as if she had screamed it in his face.

He said, "I'll find him. I'll cut him into a hundred pieces. If only you could be alive to see it."

It was time. He leaned forward, arms outstretched.

She rose onto her knees and her hands came up toward him.

She held a pistol. And just as his fingers touched her skin, the cold eye of the barrel stared him in the face and she pulled the trigger.

Harry always loved excursions with his grandfather. Grampa had a warm, enveloping hand that steadied him without tugging, and he never hastened, which meant short legs could get along just as well as long ones. The talk was unhurried too, studded with favorite phrases

Harry heard from no one else, round and satisfying to practice on his own or drop into dialogues later, like pebbles into a pool: "By Jove," and "make a rum fist of it," and things he couldn't say in front of Mama, like "as the Devil would have it." And he could ask Grampa questions, wherever and whenever, and be sure of an answer. He could pronounce a new term like "bollard" and before he knew it they would both be unmoored from it and drifting in a sea of words and explanations and reminiscences that might send them on an hour of voyaging before they got anywhere near homeport.

They took their time going round the Place Royale and sat down at the café on the corner so Grampa could smoke a pipe and Harry could sample the ginger beer. Then they bought Mama's pastry and walked back, playing a game to see who could spot the most sorts of regimentals as troops and horsemen clattered by. The admiral, who was irritated that everyone was not at the front, saw more than Harry, and had to be politely warned if he counted colors twice.

When it began to rain they put the umbrella up and then laughed when it turned out to be so pitiful against the torrent. Grampa said they'd just have to pick up their feet and make a run for it, and they were both fagged by the time they got back to the hotel. They were soaked and dripping and they scarcely had breath for the sea shanty that they sang while climbing the flights of stairs to their rooms.

Halfway up they were overtaken by a bustling servant. "Excuse me, Monsieur l'Amiral; would you tell her ladyship that we are still having difficulties with the accommodation?"

"What, pray, are you talking about?"

"Lady Hamilton's request. The manager is still trying, but rooms are not as easy to find in Brussels as you might think.

The admiral stopped and stared at him, baffled.

The man made a hopeless gesture with his hands. "Perhaps her ladyship would be content to stay one more night?"

The admiral gave him a doubtful look, then said, "I shall speak to her." He was frowning with puzzlement as they went up the next flight of stairs.

And then there was the loud crack like a thunderclap and the breath whistled out of their lungs. It was a gunshot, and the sound had come from behind Mama's door.

They tore up onto the landing, with the servant behind them. Harry stopped outside the door and looked up and saw that his grandfather's eyes were wide and pale. Then Grampa pushed Harry aside and flung open the door.

The servant hung back, but Harry looked in at once and saw his mother stretched on the floor. He dashed in under his grandfather's elbow, hardly noticing the man who stood beside her, and bent down to call her name, gazing fearfully at her white face. She looked the way Maud had done once, when she collapsed in the heat on a walk along the cliffs. Then he saw her eyelashes move and he knelt beside her. She opened her eyes. The next few things happened in a matter of seconds.

"Mama! You *fainted*."

Then he saw the pistol, right next to him on the floor, inches from her outstretched hand. And he looked up at the man and saw the blood.

The admiral roared, "Hell's teeth, what's going on here?"

The man was Cousin Sebastian, and the blood was flowing from a long gash that had been torn across his right cheek, staining his collar and glistening in the light from the window.

Mama stirred and tried to raise herself.

The admiral's voice trembled, but the blue eyes blazed like ice under a winter sun as he looked from one to the other. "For God's sake, what has happened?"

"What does it look like?" snarled Cousin Sebastian. "Your daughter, sir, is an hysteric!" And he strode out of the room.

"No!" Mama cried. "Stop him!"

Harry began to go after him, but she cried "No!" again and grabbed him by the back of his coat, dragging him toward her.

He was still holding the wrapper with the mille-feuille pastry, which was crushed against him in her tight hold.

The admiral let out another roar and darted to the doorway, where he collided with the servant. Then he stepped out onto the landing and yelled, "Stop, sir! Stop that man!"

But no one did; he had been far too quick for them. It was not long before the admiral came back into the room and crossed it and stood at the rainwashed window, cursing under his breath. Harry knew without looking that Cousin Sebastian must be riding away up the street, covered in blood, and very, very angry because Mama had shot him.

Then the admiral bent over and gently lifted Mama off the floor and set her on the chair. He stayed like that, leaning over her, with a terrified look on his face that Harry had never seen before.

"He's gone. Take your time, my dear. Slowly now; you're quite safe. Just try to tell me what happened."

She said, "I closed my eyes."

Sebastian flew southeast from the city on a fresh horse, his face stinging and his mind on fire. There could be hell to pay for leaving the brigade so long, but he'd had no choice; the danger from the letter outstripped all others. Decernay must be found, and he had a fair notion where, for Grant had told him the Frenchman had yesterday been detailed to reconnaissance duty with Hardinge.

The countryside was a sea of mud, and riding across the boggy fields was painfully slow. He kept to the lanes, which were fractionally more passable, and badgered everyone he came across about the Prussian position.

It was odd, picking his solitary way through farmland in the shifting light, dreading that darkness would descend before he located the Prussians, or that he would fall prey to a spearhead French party pushing up between the two armies. Hobnobbing with the French at this point was no part of the plan, whatever assumptions the idiot women might have formed. Mother of God, he'd as soon crawl back and live in a blessed bog in County Antrim.

Then luck swung to his side; at a bend in the road in the middle of a godforsaken hamlet he came face-to-face with a Prussian scouting party on horseback. It was a moot point who was the more startled, but fortunately there was still light enough for them to recognize his uniform before the first man hauled out his pistol.

The saints be praised, their army was at Wavre, a town not far off. The scouts didn't know Decernay, but a corporal had heard of him; he'd taken part in the debacle at Ligny the day before. Beyond that they knew nothing. Sebastian headed off in the direction they pointed out. Decernay was either dead or hanging about at Wavre currying favor with Blücher. Once that issue was taken care of, Sebastian promised himself a good supper, a bed in a comfortable inn and a whole night under shelter, out of the bloody rain.

It had taken Jacques until midday to reach the farm where he·had hidden Mezrour and most of the afternoon to reach Waterloo. Progress was pitiful due to the storm, the sodden terrain and his tendency to lose the feeling in his legs and begin to slide out of the saddle. Mezrour got to predict when each collapse was occurring and would hunch one shoulder in an attempt to jerk him upright again. It was thanks to the stallion that he did not finish facedown in a wheat field somewhere, smothered by the mud.

He found that his gear was at the little farm on the outskirts of Waterloo where he had left it. The peasant and his wife told him the village had been chosen as Wellington's headquarters and the army was moving back from Quatre Bras to take up position around nearby Mont Saint-Jean before nightfall. He stood swaying on his feet in their warm kitchen and tried to size up their enthusiasm for the allied occupation. They were already used to accommodating the Dutch-Belgians, who must have almost drunk the village dry by now. If he moved out and tried to struggle down the road and locate the Tenth Hussars as they came in, he had no guarantee of success before dark and there was every chance the billet would be snapped up by someone else in his absence.

In the end it was the good wife who made up his mind for him. She said, "Sit down here, why don't you, and let me look at that scalp of yours. And if you've a louis about you, my husband can get you in some capital white ale, and we'll single out a plump chicken, and our son will bring over some feed from the neighbor's for your horse."

So he sat, and allowed himself to think about food and rest and dry clothes, and of what he could do in the morning once Wellington had disposed his army in clean lines of battle. To find the Tenth, he would merely have to open his mouth and ask. So he shut it, and closed his eyes too, and let the darkness slowly fall.

When Sebastian woke at six the next morning it was still raining and he had a foul taste in his mouth from the evening before, during which he had combed Wavre and found not a sign of Decernay. He had ridden into town with the story that he carried dispatches for General Count Bülow von Dennewitz, so he had had to fraternize with the Prussian officers while adroitly sidestepping the general himself. He learned that Bülow was to command the advance guard who would march through Wavre first thing, to be followed eventually by the whole army, in fulfillment of Blücher's pledge to support Wellington in the coming battle.

Sebastian preferred to have the road free before him when he made his own swift return to the brigade. He breakfasted on an omelet and a buttery plate of sautéed potatoes and left the inn at a quarter to seven, just as the first of Bülow's troops were moving out of the village. With a little paid help he put into execution a simple but effective delaying tactic, and at seven o'clock a series of fires mysteriously sprang up in the streets of Wavre. Despite the damp they burned with frightening intensity.

As Sebastian darted out onto the open road in front of Bülow's column, he looked back; the conflagration had taken greedy hold on the village, turning the troops into desperate firefighters and trapping the rest of the army behind it. He grinned, then set his teeth as the wound on his cheek began to throb. He would carry the scar for life. It was time someone paid for it.

CHAPTER THIRTY-TWO

When dawn broke on Sunday the eighteenth of June, the German infantry at the farm of Papelotte woke to silence. Some of the men, opening heavy eyelids and peering through a curtain of thin mist and drizzle, were seeing the place for the first time, having taken up their positions in the pelting rain of the night before. It was a malodorous place, the smells curling up into the damp air from the rich, churned mud of the paddock where dairy cows usually grazed, from the pig troughs in the narrow run outside the byres and from the manure floating between the cobbles of the yard. Outside the great square of the main buildings, along the margins of the farm, the shelter was meager—low walls, ditches, hedges and a few stands of lime trees to protect the bivouacs—and there was a rank smell from sodden hay that soldiers had piled on the ground in a vain attempt to keep themselves off the flooded ground during the long, chilly night.

The beasts who would have animated the daybreak with their noise were all shut inside the thick-walled barns, and the peasants who had tended them the evening before had melted away, leaving the farm to the new occupants, who examined it in the uncertain light, wondering which bit of ground, which angle of wall, which gateway or roofline would frame for them the deciding moments of the battle to come.

The officers and men in the buildings clung to sleep a little longer, but the men in the open rose and stretched and rubbed their stiff necks, and pulled wet cloth off the small of their backs and their chests and then felt it suck back onto them again like a second skin. Before they turned to talk or breakfast, they moved about, glancing past the threadbare cover to where the French right wing must be stirring too.

It was a watercolor landscape, made up of umber wheat fields beneath slate-gray clouds, and on the horizon there was a long splash of olive green where woods washed over the enemy troops, concealing them from view. Two gun batteries were quite visible in front, however—dark, menacing shapes that looked as though someone had drawn them with a sharp pencil on the fluid background. The French were closer to Papelotte than to almost anywhere else in the whole of Wellington's battle lines. If a man wanted a naked look down the barrel of Bonaparte's intentions, this was the place to stand.

Then they broke the silence with the familiar bustle of a new day, lighting fires under eaves or in lean-tos, cooking up the last of the rations they had carried out of Brussels on Friday and digging into their packs for whatever drops of comfort they had managed to hoard against this long-awaited event.

They had hours. Neither army would move until the rain ceased and the ground began to dry out. Even then there was little chance that either side would be able to limber up and drag the big guns about at the gallop. They would have to stand and pound away from where they were. But both sides looked to their other weapons, cleaning rifles and discharging them to make sure they were dry, so that the sharp crackle of gunfire echoed across the valley.

The rain stopped at nine, visibility improved and they felt a more solid sense of the hosts that were gathered to support them. The nearest British troops, under the command of General Picton, were as close to them as Papelotte was to the French, and they knew that the reserve cavalry were strung out along the top of the ridge behind them and on the reverse slope beyond. The very tip of the left wing was secured by more of their own kind—Prince Bernhardt von Saxe-Weimar's Second Nassau Brigade. At some stage Bonaparte would try to turn them, to outflank the army before Blücher and his boys could arrive. They were ready for him. More or less.

The center was fronted by Dutch-Belgian regiments, with crack British infantry massed at their backs. There were two fortified properties in advance of these lines— the château and grounds of Hougoumont, and the big farm of La Haye Sainte. If the French were to charge the center they must pass by or between them. Like Papelotte, these well-guarded advance posts allowed riflemen to enfilade advancing infantry or cavalry, and offered temptations to a commander who might divert troops for their capture.

They expected the artillery to open first, but when the firing began it came from the direction of Hougoumont; French infantry were streaming across the open ground toward the woods where Nassau and Hanoverian troops had been placed to protect the approach to the farm. Just before midday Wellington's artillery found their range and began a fierce barrage, sweeping the front ranks off their feet. Then firing started up all along the line and the smoke drifted east toward Papelotte, obliterating the marshy smell of the mud and the lingering odor of cattle.

Half an hour later the French were reported to be swarming through the trees around Hougoumont, having crushed all resistance. Wellington might have sent a few reinforcements to hold the farm itself, no one could tell, but he had not been coaxed into diverting any troops from his packed center.

At that point Papelotte received a visitor, an Irish hussar from the Tenth, acting as an aide for the general.

He rode across the open ground and up to the gateway without a glance toward the French or a care for their artillery fire and was welcomed in gentlemanly fashion by the commander, in the main parlor of the farmhouse. It transpired that the hussar, Colonel Coole, had just ridden all the way from the tip of the right wing, miles off at Braine l'Alleud, weaving slowly through the battle lines with a sang froid that matched his name. He was looking for someone, a French-speaking private by the name of Decernay who was probably being employed as a courier—tall, fair-haired, last seen in Waterloo wearing buff breeches and a leather jerkin, unarmed but with a manner that suggested he'd as soon cut your throat as look at you.

No one had seen Decernay, and the hussar seemed to take that badly at first, his eyes glittering and his mouth clamped shut. He had a fresh wound across his cheek and a bloodstained collar that lent him a savage appearance, but the rest of his uniform and his accoutrements were in perfect condition, and when he took his scarlet shako off he revealed a fine head of black hair and handsome features.

He was plied with the last of the commander's brandy and prevailed on to give a report of the French attacks. He said Wellington had been darting about behind Hougoumont, keeping an eye on the hottest point.

Earlier on, Bonaparte had been viewed streaking along his front lines on a gray horse, raising *"Vive l'empereur"* from his massed thousands. Then he had retired in the direction of La Belle Alliance, where he would have a good if distant view of the field. Most of Wellington's troops were drawn back out of sight beyond the ridge of Mont Saint-Jean, so French assessment of their strength was difficult. Cannonballs from Bonaparte's closest batteries were sailing up and over onto the blind side, while the troops at the edge of the ridge were being ordered to lie flat and let them pass overhead. If the French tried a charge up the slope, the colonel assured them that the men at the top could rise and send them flying back down it again like cattle tumbling off a cliff.

Before he galloped back up the hill to rejoin his brigade, he asked them to keep a sharp eye out for Décernay, who apparently fancied his chances as an informer for Bonaparte. When asked what they should do if they found him, he replied, "Shoot him on sight."

Not long after he had gone, the real stuff began. It opened with a vicious artillery barrage from the cannon opposite and from Bonaparte's huge battery at La Belle Alliance. Most of it went over Papelotte, seeking the troops behind, and because of the wet ground it tended not to ricochet and plough at speed through the soldiers and defenses in the usual fashion. It was a filthy thing to face, nonetheless, and so was the sight it was preparing them for: the advance of the French right wing. Cavalry came first, undulating through the cornfields to the right of La Haye Sainte, with their swords and cuirasses glinting even in the dull gray light. The defenders of La Haye waited until they could sight them on the flank and then poured lead into them, turning the charge into a tangle of mauled horses and riders, though a few figures broke free and continued boldly on to be pulverized by the gunfire from Papelotte.

The infantry followed, a total of three divisions marching forward, rifles bristling, treading with such awesome discipline that the ground shuddered with the tramp of their feet and the rolling thunder of the drummers' *pas de charge*. Papelotte and the left wing were vulnerable, less solid than the right, because this was where Wellington was counting on the Prussians turning up. But there were no Prussians, just gigantic columns of French, two hundred abreast. The Allied artillery scoured the first ranks of the French with double shot but they rolled on and surged upon Papelotte like a blue tide breaking.

Then they became distinguishable as units, firing volleys across the scattered outposts where the men in green crouched behind thickets and shrank into the cover of the stone walls; and next thing they were individuals, as deft with the bayonets as hunters sticking wild pigs, their eyes glassy with determination, as though victory were stamped already across their brows and they had only to forge on until the emperor cried halt.

They took the outposts, the hedges, the ditches and the huts. Then they took the farm. No one ran; they were pushed back. No one gave up; they died, on the slippery, manure-washed cobbles of the courtyard or in the narrow races where the cows walked to milking. No one turned from the fight; they were forced back, striving to regather below the hill behind.

Still no Prussians came to stem the slaughter—but at the last minute Wellington sent Picton's infantry rushing down the slope. They poured through, carrying the survivors with them. Picton, his black eyes flashing with inner fire, was killed at the head of his troops, who battled on for a while and then wavered. Next, when it seemed that the French would stand their ground forever, cavalry came charging down from the center, fresh and full of fight, dodging the obstacles and the piles of dead. These were Uxbridge's men, and they swept the French relentlessly back, beyond the farm buildings and into the wheat fields, trampling the soldiers down like stalks of grain as they went, losing almost half their number but scattering the French at last toward their own lines.

La Haye Sainte was now French and Papelotte had been retaken by Saxe-Weimar. Wellington's center had held. And there followed a hellish kind of lull. Except for the persistent skirmishing around Hougoumont and the regular pounding of the cannon, a dull, aching stillness settled over the two armies.

After the attack at the Hôtel d'Angleterre, it took Sophia all afternoon to reorganize her family and her friends around her. By instinct she turned to them all for help, but she realized it was ultimately up to her to decide what should be done, for only she could provide the revelations and the reassurances they needed to hear.

The first stratagem was to get out of the hotel and find a residence that could be guarded day and night. The solution was simple—they moved to Mary's. Harry himself suggested who should guard them, because ever since arriving in Brussels he had been clamoring to visit Mitchell, who was garrisoned in the city. The admiral used his influence, and Mitchell came to bivouac in the garden at the rear, surrounded thenceforth by a little unit of boys, amongst whom Harry seemed to forget the terrible instant when he had rushed into the hotel room and seen his mother stretched out on the floor.

The following hours were not so easy to get through. At last Sophia must tell the truth about Sebastian Coole and his long campaign against her, but she recounted it to three very different listeners and all had their own anxious and incredulous moments. There was no one else to supply information—inquiries revealed that Delia Goulding was still alive but had not regained consciousness, and Sophia would not let them interrogate Harry about the Epsom incident.

For the admiral, it was a cruel shock to believe such infamy of a gentleman whom he had come to favor. Nonetheless, the first breach had been made when he saw Coole standing beside his prostrate daughter, and he could never forgive the way the man had practically run from the room when he was confronted. Once the admiral was convinced, he was all for action: he wanted Grant to be informed and an arrest to be made.

Ellwood reckoned this almost impossible in the present state of affairs. During their intense discussions in the saloon of the Ellwoods' house, it was Mary who reacted first, coming to sit beside Sophia and putting her arm around her waist, while Augustus had taken a while to consider all the evidence. In the end, however, he proved the most clearheaded of the four. He also managed to mention Jacques Decernay without the confusion that overspread the admiral's face whenever he said his name.

"I could wish Decernay had seen fit to give that letter to Grant yesterday evening. He must be determined to finish the business himself."

"High-handed!" the admiral could not help muttering.

Ellwood smiled slightly. "For all we know, he is thinking of your family and your sensibilities, sir. Imagine yourself returning to Sussex with the news that the master of Birlingdean has been killed in battle. Compare that to going home with the story of a traitor's execution. Which is the lesser evil?"

Mary said, "But if Coole is not arrested, no one can ever be sure what mischief he did in London and Brighton."

Ellwood nodded. "True, but we can make some guesses." He looked at Sophia. "You said Decernay's only contact in London was murdered before he arrived?" When she nodded, he said, "Unless I am mistaken, that was barely a week after Coole came home. He had never operated in England before—he began his intelligence work in India. It took a while for his credentials to be accepted in London; perhaps the major was an obstacle? At any rate, Coole was given the task of investigating the prince's own regiment, the Tenth Hussars. There were concerns about one or two officers, but of course Coole cleared them in his report. As soon as this affair is over the whole issue must come up for review." The sly smile appeared again. "I shouldn't like to be the one explaining that to His Highness."

Sophia went to bed that night exhausted but with the knowledge that Harry was safe and that Ellwood would pass on to the secret service everything they needed to know about Sebastian Coole. She woke in the morning still tired, but full of determination. It was beyond her now to sit around and wait; she needed action. No protests could prevail, and she spent the morning helping with the wounded in the neighborhood church. Before midday, about the time when cannonades began in the south, Mary arrived to join her, wearing a maid's apron and with her hair scraped back in a comical tuft at the back of her head.

"I saw a lady I know in the street just now and she didn't recognize me! Then we got talking. Do you know she'd been to the Grand Café on the Rue des Eperonniers expecting it to be open? Can you imagine? Of course, the whole staff has decamped, the cooks and the footmen and the maître d'hôtel. The place is like a tomb."

"Will you come with me soon and see Delia Goulding?"

"No, I shan't. I promised Ellwood. And you should come home for dinner. Why are you in riding dress? There are no horses to be had; the mayor has gotten them all for the military."

"They haven't laid hands on our carriage horses yet. I had one brought round. He's a big fellow, but he'll be easier to ride than the Shires at Clifton."

They worked side by side for an hour, bringing water, cleaning wounds, bandaging, talking to the men of comfort and shelter and home, and avoiding the subject that hung about them like the smell of blood and gunpowder in their clothes—the three-day battle that was still raging to the south.

When Mary had gone, Sophia mounted and made her way through the crowded streets to the Hôtel de New York. Rumbold was there, having come into town to escort the last of the ammunition trains back down the road to the army. He gave her the news in his succinct, measured way before she went into the sickroom: Wellington was sticking it out and waiting for the Prussians. The French had not yet mounted a full offensive. The pandemonium in Brussels was as foolish as it had ever been—time enough to panic if Wellington's center went to pieces.

In the sickroom the quiet was shattering after the busy noise outside. Mrs. Rumbold rose from her chair by the bedside and came forward, tears in her eyes, then recoiled when she saw bloodstains on the cuffs of Sophia's habit.

"It's nothing, I have been tending the wounded. How is she?"

Mrs. Rumbold shook her head and drew her toward the figure in the bed. "She wakes for just a few seconds now and then, but she cannot speak."

Sophia looked down at the white face of Delia Goulding and shivered. "What does the physician say?"

"Four ribs are broken, but in his opinion her stomach and lungs have escaped. If her spleen had been crushed—" She shook her head. "He says she must have been unconscious when she fell, so the relaxation of her limbs saved her from worse damage. She connected with a canvas awning on the way down. It collapsed, of course, but it prevented the severest injury—to the head." She gazed at Sophia in perplexity. "How can she have been *unconscious*?"

Sophia took her away from the bed and sat down to tell her in a low voice everything about Sebastian Coole. Somehow Mrs. Rumbold's horror was the more intense because she had to suppress it in the hushed room. But in one sense it was not a surprise; she had guessed Delia's passion for him and suspected him of exploiting it, though she had never known how far he was prepared to go.

Before she left, Sophia sat in the chair by the bed and held Delia's small hand, spread on the coverlet. "When you wake, my dear, do not be afraid. He cannot touch you again. You are safe. I promise. Wake and get well, and come back to your friends."

She had asked Rumbold to wait for her, and after a quick farewell to his wife he rejoined her in the court-yard of the hotel. She was mounted and ready at the porte cochere, through which could be seen the three wagons of ammunition and the cavalry unit that would escort it to the front.

As soon as he appeared she said to him, "I shall accompany you." She indicated the baggage roll that was resting behind her on the horse's crupper. "The soldiers tell me there is hardly any medical aid or equipment at Waterloo, even though that is where most of the wounded are taken. I intend to help."

He gaped at her. "Your ladyship! What about your family?"

"Mrs. Rumbold has kindly agreed to send them a message."

"But the road is just about impassable. And the danger—"

"If you can make your way through, Lieutenant-Colonel, so can I."

He looked up at her in admiration and dismay. Then he made up his mind. "I'll take you to Waterloo. Not a step farther. Though I'd feel better if you were armed, at least." He added with a shrewd look, "I hear you're a dread hand with a pistol."

She gave him a sardonic smile. "Not at all. I have a tendency to shut my eyes."

CHAPTER THIRTY-THREE

The few remaining men who had first occupied Papelotte recognized the Irishman when he appeared
again that afternoon, not long after three o'clock. Some
said he had joined in the charge with Uxbridge's cavalry
and they had seen him at work with his saber amongst
the retreating infantry. Others swore he had ridden up
alone afterwards in the same devil-may-care fashion,
looking keenly about him like a glossy eagle after prey,
ready to pounce if he thought it worth his while.

A different group of Saxe-Weimar's officers accepted
him into the courtyard this time, and there was no liquor
to share until he took out a flask of gin, whereupon the
faces around him brightened. While the officers passed
the flask he climbed quickly up the makeshift ladder that
had been constructed of tables, chests and chairs, and
took a peek over the top of the courtyard wall. He stood
there a while, leaning on the coping stones, and then he
leaped down and proceeded to make himself agreeable
to his companions, saying he would take a pipe with
them before he left.

A sergeant and two privates kept sentry above, though
there was nothing new to see. Bodies lay strewn from
the very foot of the wall into the distance, most of them
dead, since the wounded had crawled· or been carried
behind the farm. Not all the fallen horses had died yet,

but by this time they were silent in their agony. One charger had had both forelegs blown off, but nonetheless it had steadily grazed a semicircle around itself at the far end of the cow paddock, until a corporal who could take the sight no more exposed himself to fire by running over and shooting it through the forehead.

The spots of cover in the middle distance were still performing good service, and the lads had dug in farther behind a low wall near the biggest group of lime trees. These details were not always visible, however, as the scene changed from moment to moment because of the smoke that rolled across the valley. It formed a dirty screen, created by the two-hour bombardment from the cannon of both sides, the discharge of tens of thousands of rifles, and rockets that had ignited rogue fires in Hougoumont and La Haye Sainte and come blazing down amongst the British infantry at the top of the ridge.

The smoke grew thicker, a massive cloud that hugged the ground and obscured everything beyond twenty yards. It made the sentries uneasy and one of the privates bent to his rifle, his cheek glued to the butt with the barrel resting secure on the coping stones.

All at once they saw something waver within the brown-gray veil; a narrow shape, impossibly tall, like a giant on stilts. There had been no challenge from the outposts, but perhaps none of the other sentries had seen this thing in the murk. The sergeant too crouched low and took a sight along his rifle.

The figure began to define itself, emerging from the swirling background with wisps of gray coiled around its shoulders and head. It was a tall man on a great black horse, moving at a walk, the beast's body dipping toward the ground with each step as it carried the double weight smoothly forward in ponderous, majestic rhythm. For a long, confusing interval the figure was painted only in the colors of smoke—the dark knee boots pressed to the charger's dusky sides, the gray breastplate and the helmet with its black floating horsetail, the pale face with gray staring eyes like those of a ghost, fixed on nothing.

The sergeant fired, the single shot echoing around the courtyard and bringing the officers' heads up fast.

The bullet lost itself in the dim distance. The vast, undulating form kept advancing.

On the second shot, from one of the privates, the smoke eddied back and pearly light from the overcast sky limned the figure, making a silver mirror of the breastplate and pointing up the dark blue of the officer's coat and the scarlet epaulettes and facings.

"A cuirassier," breathed the sergeant, who had never seen one close before.

"What?" said his commanding officer. "What in God's name is he at?"

The rider came to a halt, facing them across no more than fifteen yards of ground. There was not a flicker in the deep gray eyes that surveyed them, and they could plainly see the grim set of his full lips, since he did not wear the regulation mustache.

The second private gazed back at him as though he were an apparition. "Do I fire, sir?" he whispered. "Can bullets go through that steel?"

The other muttered, "Why aren't our cavalry fitted out like that?"

"They will be after this," the sergeant said. "And so will the British."

There was a tense pause as they strained to see what was going on beyond the rider. They could not hear the tread of horses and there were no other shapes billowing behind. The horseman was alone, as though he had been molded within the secret cloud by some miraculous hand and set there to confound them.

All at once a voice boomed out, accented but clearly understandable to the startled men behind the wall. "Colonel Sebastian Coole!"

None of the officers could suppress a movement of surprise, and they all looked at Coole. For a second he remained absolutely still, his head raised and his face expressionless. Next moment a grimace crossed his features, so swiftly no one could tell whether it spelled shock or a strange kind of excitement.

The sergeant, having no idea how to react, took the pointless course of shouting "Halt!"

The cuirassier gave him a long, baleful look, then repeated just as clearly, "I am looking for Colonel Sebastian Coole. Where is he?"

Three heads turned from the wall toward the officers below. There was a pause of a few seconds, during which Coole looked down at the cobbles and put one hand on the hilt of his saber.

Then he lifted his head and said in frigid tones to the sergeant, "Tell him I'm here. Ask what he wants."

The sergeant cleared his throat, then took aim with his rifle before shouting, "Colonel Coole is here! State your business and come no closer."

The cuirassier gave a bark of triumphant laughter that made his horse start and then thump its heavy hooves one by one on the ground. "He knows my business. He knows me, Jacques Decernay. Let him meet me. The day has come."

Inside the still courtyard, the commander stared wide-eyed at Coole. "What does he mean?"

The colonel's green eyes flickered with savage amusement. "A duel, gentlemen. If you will be so good as to officiate."

The duel at Papelotte was presided over by the military commander, a tall, dark-haired gentleman with a dignified air, who walked out onto the littered ground with a measured tread. He summoned two officers to act as seconds, flanked by the sergeant and four privates who were ordered to clear the area and hold the Frenchman's horse. At his side was Colonel Coole.

The Frenchman dismounted, took off his helmet and held it against him as he brought his heels together and gave a quick bow. So far he had not acknowledged Colonel Coole, but once he and the commander exchanged names he switched his gaze to the Irishman. The look that passed between the opponents was electric, but neither spoke, and after a moment the commander began the formalities.

"Gentlemen, I charge you to tell me who is the offended party in this dispute."

"I am," the Irishman said in a firm, carrying voice.

"Monsieur," the commander said to the Frenchman, "by the rules of combat, there is no compromise of honor if the offender admits to being in the wrong. Are you prepared to apologize?"

"I struck him," the offender said with a lopsided grimace, "but not hard enough. He issued the challenge; I am here. Let us proceed."

"About time," the other said contemptuously. "You've been dodging me since last month!"

The Frenchman growled, "If I had known then that you fight only with women, I would have settled your account at once."

The commander summoned his English and said sharply, "The time for insults is past. You have chosen to decide this by the sword. Gentlemen, we provide you a clear ground to fight and these two officers as your seconds. Do you accept them?"

The officers, each armed with a bayonet sword, were standing beside the combatants, who glanced at them briefly and then nodded. Within a few moments the arrangements were complete. All obstacles were removed from a wide area below the whitewashed wall, which was now topped by a row of avid faces. The combatants were réquested to take off their coats. The Frenchman's second helped to undo the copper fastenings of the cuirass and laid the breast- and backplate reverently on the ground at the feet of the charger. The Frenchman took off his sword belt and the blue and scarlet coatee, then he stooped over the pile of accoutrements, grasped his scabbard with his left hand and with the right smoothly slid his sword out and stood erect.

It was a French heavy-cavalry weapon, the blade long and straight with a tip ground to razor sharpness and an elegant hilt fashioned into triple curves of gleaming brass that locked over the whole hand. The watchers along the wall studied it in fascination. Cuirassiers seldom carried other arms in a charge—they depended entirely on this classic, daunting weapon, which had the sharpness of a lance and the weight of a saber.

The Irishman disrobed without haste, doffing his scarlet bell-topped shako, folding the fur pelisse and the lavishly braided dark blue dolman and handing them to his second. He removed his crimson sash so that he stood there in simple gray overalls, striped with yellow down the sides of the legs and worn over fine black boots. He drew his saber with a flourish, before letting the second unfasten his belt and sabretache and put them aside.

The weapons were unequal in length and employment. The saber had a slightly shorter reach than the sword because of the curved blade with which hussars slashed at the enemy as they rode them down, while the cuirassiers favored one clean thrust straight from the shoulder. Which meant that in battle the French suffered more hideous wounds and the British a quicker death.

The commander called on the seconds to check and compare the weapons, then said, "The swords differ, gentlemen. You have a choice: We can search amongst our own for an equal pair, or you may"—he struggled for the correct phrase—"you may submit to chance."

The Frenchman said at once, "Give me whatever you want and I'll fight with it. But his hand will never touch this sword."

The commander turned to the Irishman. "You are the offended party, sir, therefore you have the choice. Will you accept matched swords from us?"

The Irishman gave this a moment's thought. The German weapons would be unfamiliar to both men, so he might well demand that it be put to the toss, in which case he would at least get a fifty-fifty chance of drawing the longer sword. But did he want it? Practice was everything, and if his expertise was with the saber he might prefer to retain it.

He said, "Devil take the difference. Let's get on with it."

The commander nodded to the seconds, who instructed the opponents to extend their swords and position them so that there was the stipulated one foot between the tips. The duelists were both right-handed.

There was a lull in the cannon fire at this point, but the shield of smoke still lay between Papelotte and the French. The commander took a glance around the scene, as if to convince himself it was real, then spoke.

"I charge all here to bear witness. These gentlemen have agreed to submit their argument to the sword. They have approved the ground and the weapons. They do not wear any defense or cuirass. There are no notches in the blades. Here is the protocol." He took a breath, then said solemnly, "The use of the left hand is forbidden. If a party claims he is wounded, or if a second sees blood, the combat is stopped. It can go on only if the wounded man consents."

The Irishman smiled here, with a sarcasm visible to all observers. There was no mistaking his meaning; if it was his saber that inflicted the wound, no one would be asking the wounded man a thing.

"The grounds of Papelotte are under the command of His Highness the Prince of Saxe-Weimar. If there is a threat from the enemy, I have the power to stop this duel at any time. At the word '*Allez*' you will advance on each other. If you break any rule, the second of your opponent will raise his sword and yours will say *Halte!* If you are stopped you must step back one pace and remain on guard."

The opponents were looking at each other as the commander spoke, and their intensity was such that they were scarcely listening; they were speaking with their eyes instead. There could be no doubt that this was the final phase of a long quarrel. What was the cause—a woman, a wrong done in battle, a death? The only clue came at the end of the commander's speech, when the Irishman said suddenly, "Where is the letter?"

The other brought his sword up across his body and touched the hilt to his broad chest, where his braces pressed against the blue linen shirt. "It's here. Come and get it."

When he lowered the sword, the seconds, standing opposite each other, depressed each weapon with the tips of theirs and looked expectantly at the commander.

"*Allez!*"

The seconds sprang back.

It was as well for the man to the right that he did so, for the Irishman leaped into the space the officer had occupied, whirled the saber out from his body at lightning speed and brought the blade slicing toward the Frenchman's bare neck. Another split second and it would have taken his head clean off.

But the Frenchman pivoted, swinging his heavy blade up and twisting his body and legs to position himself for the shock. He smashed the flat of his sword against the saber with a clang like a hammer on an anvil from which the watchers, gasping, could almost taste the sparks. Then with a downward sweep he disengaged and stepped back, his eyes wide, searching the other's gaze for his next move.

To see the Irishman press the attack was a lesson in speed. His attempt at surprise had failed, but the first concussion of the blades demonstrated the strength of his wrist and his resilience; the steel had no sooner parted than it rang again as he aimed a backhanded sweep at the Frenchman's jaw. This was parried; then with an instant twist of the saber he prevented a follow-through directed at his own midriff.

Watching them, men forgot to breathe; the opening moves were so fast that the blades whirled in the silver light like the spokes of a great metal wheel. The combatants were oddly matched, yet there were similarities—the light, instinctive footwork, the sureness of balance. The Irishman's supple footwear slid and scuffed over the uneven ground, while the Frenchman in his heavy knee boots moved with magical fluidity, the only sound being the thump of his hobnailed soles as he planted himself swiftly for a parry or a counterthrust.

There was no blood yet, except the dried stain at Coole's throat, but there were near misses. The swordsmen watching concluded the two men had not fought each other before, for they did not always predict the opponent's maneuvers and there were occasional miscalculations—quickly remedied, for these were masters at combat.

Then all at once Coole was bringing his saber down in a near vertical swing to the other's head when the Frenchman sidestepped, deflected it and while the other was fractionally off-balance propelled a darting thrust into the shoulder.

The second's sword came up, the other yelled *"Halte!"* and next second the two were standing with three paces between them, their weapons raised.

The Frenchman, his chest heaving, examined his opponent in silence. Then those nearest heard him mutter to himself, *"Sacré bleu."* The Irishman had twisted away at the last moment and the keen edge of the sword had cut a diagonal slash that went deep into the tip of the shoulder and extended across the left pectoral.

Then a second called out, "Mein Kapitan, they are both bleeding!"

Coole, momentarily losing color as he examined the gash in his shoulder and chest, looked up. It was true; a trickle of blood was descending from the Frenchman's hairline onto his cheek.

The big man put his left hand to his face and then flicked his fingers, irritated. "He hasn't touched me. I got this at Ligny."

"That thumping great helmet must have crucified him since," one of the men on the wall remarked.

"Do you wish to resume?" the commander said to the Irishman.

"Mother of God, let's to it."

Startled, the commander paused a moment, then cried, *"Allez!"*

The result was an explosion. The big man sprang to the attack, and it was only then that the bystanders realized what he had been holding in reserve. His moves were devastating; the sword arced and spiraled, smashing the Irishman's guard down again and again with punishing power. He gave him no room for anything but defense, and despite the Irishman's dogged resistance and the unfailing strength of his wrist, he was driven back toward the watchers, so fast that he nearly crashed into the wall below them, while the Frenchman's blade chipped away a whitewashed segment that spun into the dirt like a snowflake.

Then somehow the Irishman rallied. His shirtsleeve was soaked and blood dripped from his left hand, but the injury had not slowed him down. He managed an astonishing variety of athletic moves, half crouching to take a swing at the Frenchman's legs that would have crippled him if he had not bounced above it, and several times coming within an ace of splitting his shoulder.

Suddenly, to the disbelief of the watchers, the big man smiled. It was a fleeting, unpleasant grin, but it marked a decision. A second later they saw what it was, for he pulled off a lightning thrust to the body, the Irishman staggered back, the seconds cried out in unison, and everyone could see, on the Irishman's half-bared chest, a neatly incised diagonal cross—the second cut, unevenly bisecting the first, had sliced through the fabric and strap of the overalls and sketched a bright red, oozing line across shirt and flesh.

For a moment the Irishman bent over, supporting himself with his sword hand on one knee, his breath whistling through his teeth. The Frenchman too was panting, sweat and blood streaking his skin, the wide gray stare never leaving his enemy's face.

Then the Irishman stood up and his mouth contorted with fury. "The game's over. Now you die."

The commander tried to catch his eye, perplexed. "You mean . . . you want to continue?"

The green eyes snapped and the reply was a snarl. "Try stopping me again and I'll finish you off as well."

If the commander spoke then, no one heard him against the din of the blades. The combat had been fierce and protracted, and the men still fought like demons, but neither had anything left to draw on now but their training and skill and ingenuity—and the hatred that stood in their faces for all to see, naked and consuming.

At one point the Frenchman spoke on a sharp rush of air as he parried a massive swing of the saber: "She asked me to spare you."

"Tell her to get—" but the last word was lost as the Irishman dealt with a brutal lunge to the throat.

"But I said no."

The other did not seem to hear. He fought like a dervish, and the saber whirled with a rhythm that suggested some kind of eastern dance, exquisitely, murderously refined. And it was in the midst of his own glittering display that he died.

No one caught the infinitesimal hiatus in timing nor saw the minuscule space between the blades that made way for the swift, fell progress of the Frenchman's sword. What they saw was the impact, the stupefying instant when the long shaft of steel accomplished its work, transfixing the heart and exiting through the spine. The Irishman's black head tipped back, and for a second the open green eyes seemed to be challenging the sky. The Frenchman stood totally still in the lunge position, his arm outstretched, his eyes fixed on the point where his sword had penetrated. Then the saber dropped from the victim's nerveless hand and the limp body arched back over the end of the sword. The Frenchman straightened, put his broad left hand against the other's chest, and with a growl that masked the sound of the blade leaving flesh and bone, he drew the sword out and let the Irishman fall.

He collapsed, his legs bent under him, the red left hand dropped back into the dirt and the right opened, as though ready to seize again the saber hilt that lay inches from his fingers.

The Frenchman stood for a moment looking at the dead man at his feet. Then he tossed his head and flicked the hair off his forehead with his left hand. He strode over to the pile of accoutrements, stooped to pick up the hussar's crimson sash and carefully wiped the blade of his sword. He dropped the sash on the ground and went across to his horse.

The commander gestured to the sergeant and two privates to lift the body and carry it into the courtyard, and stared at the Frenchman with consternation.

It was over; there was nothing more to be said or done. But it struck them all that the enemy who had ridden into their midst and brought this enormity to pass was about to turn his back on them and depart scatheless. In the absence of any orders from the commander, the Frenchman's second was helping him on with his gear.

It was impossible to tell what the stranger was thinking. The strong, distinctive features had congealed into a blank mask under the smeared blood and sweat. His chest rose and fell unevenly as the cuirass was buckled on, and his fingers were less than steady as he rammed the sword back into the scabbard and fastened the belt. When he took the steel helmet and held it as before to make his farewell, the eyes that met the commander's were as fathomless as the ocean at nightfall.

His soft voice was quite uninflected as he said, "Thank you. It is finished. You will never see me again."

"Wenn Gott also will," said the commander.

The cuirassier mounted heavily and replaced his headgear, cinching the gold chinstrap with such firmness that the watchers on the wall could not help wincing. He saluted them all with a hand to the peak of the helmet. Then the charger pivoted neatly and stepped away, its long tail drifting with a fluid motion that was mirrored by the black horsehair swinging across the rider's back. The great beast moved off with slow dignity, the tall figure receded, and in less than a minute it regained the region of smoke, melting into its folds to be swallowed up forever.

CHAPTER THIRTY-FOUR

At Ligny it was the wounded men that claimed me. Today it was the horses. When the assault began, Ney led it—Ney, the bravest of the brave. I went toward La Belle Alliance, thinking to meet the emperor, but I found Michel Ney. I watched him snatch up his men in that unbelievable frenzy, that fiery commitment that sends a man forward like a rocket, the air burning up with his passing, the very memory of him turning to stardust and flying into nothing as he goes. When that gigantic horde of cavalry thundered up between Hougoumont and La Haye Sainte, they created a vacuum behind them and I followed into it, impelled by a puissant gravity that I will never feel again.

They got to the top. The cavalry crested the ridge; they took the British guns. They hovered there in their hundreds, mutilated but triumphant, blazing like comets across the only sky that the British troops could see. I knew the infantry beyond would form squares and the gunners would retreat within them, relying on the riflemen to hold our horsemen off. It was then, gazing up at the glorious melee, that I realized Ney had not ordered our foot soldiers to follow. The cavalry were completely unsupported. If they could not break the squares, they would have to withdraw when their strength gave out.

And they did, pouring back down the hill, the horses stumbling, men and animals dazed and bloodied, riderless mounts crashing about, witless and bereft. The horsemen plummeted toward me, some erect and staring, some dying but riveted to their saddles, some sliding forward over the manes of the horses like men drowning in a rough tide, some so hacked about that their blood flowed as dark as that of their mangled steeds. And there was Ney, having lost his mount and seized another, rallying his cuirassiers and lancers, gathering more men for another charge.

I knew that when it happened most of the horses without riders would turn and run back up with their fellows to the crest; I had seen that tragic behavior time and again in battle. So I put Mezrour to the gallop and captured as many as I could, grabbing the flying reins and leading the horses to a grove of trees not far from the infantry lines, tethering them there and racing back for more. Many were wounded—shot during the advance, or slashed and stabbed by bayonets as their riders forced them at the squares—but if they could move freely I saved them.

It went on and on. The cavalry charged four times, without support and never carrying anything with them to spike the murderous guns. Bonaparte cannot have meant this. Maybe even Ney had gone beyond knowing what he did.

Word had come that the Prussian advance force was marching in from the east, ready to engage our right flank. Bonaparte sent the Young Guard to intercept them—babies, from the regiment he created for his baby son. Once they were gutted, the Prussians plunged on, engulfing farms and villages, driving ever closer to Bonaparte's headquarters. The crisis peaked; Ney rode back to ask the emperor for more cavalry. I should have gone after Bonaparte then, shadowed Ney, tracked him down behind the lines. Yet I could not leave; I was trapped in the smoking valley, between the two mighty armies, caught up in the frenzy of the struggle.

Ney returned alone. The slaughter went on in the gathering dusk. Hougoumont had fallen at last, burning to cinders around its captors. Then Bonaparte released the

*Imperial Guard, the greatest, the final resort. Here they
came, towering like titans in their tall busbies, tramping
in impeccable formation, the most splendid body of soldiers on that field of battle, the most loyal, the most coura-
geous. And he who owed everything to these
extraordinary men, the general who had relied on them
for victory after victory across Europe, sent them forth
on a lie. He had spied the rest of the Prussian army in
the distance and out of his desperation, he sent out word
that reinforcements had arrived.*

*All around me, the soldiers bellowed in relief and ado-
ration. "Vive l'empereur!" I knew at once, in my bones,
that it could not possibly be true. The Imperial
Guardsmen were sacrificed for nothing. They marched up
Mont Saint-Jean and into hell for a liar.*

*Why does that matter so much? Why can't I bear it?
All I know is that when the Guard broke, something
broke inside me too. When the English hussars came
surging over the crest and down the slope with those shattered heroes running before them, part of me died.*

*This retreat is like nothing I have ever seen, more horri-
ble even than Berezina. The whole army has fallen apart.
Artillerymen unhitch the draft horses from the cannon
and flee. Soldiers take to their heels and bayonet anyone
who gets in their way—officers, friends, no matter whom.
There can be no surrender; anyone trying to give themselves up will be killed, for the Prussians have joined
the pursuit, shrieking revenge. Tonight mercy is not even
a word.*

*The horses that I rescued fly away like whirlwinds,
bearing terrified men. I offer one to Ney; he is stumbling
along, leaning on a corporal's shoulder. I pretend not to
recognize him; he is weeping. When he rides off, I take
a different course, skirting west of La Belle Alliance on
a farm track I reconnoitered long ago . . . last week. I
must link up with the road farther south, for Bonaparte
will be on it, his driver desperately lashing the horses, the
handsome, well-sprung vehicle bouncing on the paved
surface.*

I have the corporal's rifle slung over my shoulder.

Bonaparte will be protected by the last of the Imperial Guard, but I will not touch a hair of their heads. This is between him and me; all I concentrate on now is getting within range.

Mezrour is suffering as I reach the road. He will burst his lungs to get me there, but he cannot carry me back. No need, once it's over.

Genappe is before me, the buildings intact, no Prussians streaking in from the flanks—the pursuers are not here yet. But something is seething through the village, I can see darting figures in French uniforms, hear a bugle call, shouting, the clatter of feet and hooves.

Out into the trampled fields, hugging the outskirts, I circle around until I reach a stand of trees near where the road leaves the village. I am sure now of what I shall find, from the quality of the noises that come from just beyond that building, on the other side of that wall. I dismount. Leave Mezrour with his head hanging as though he will never lift it again. Load the rifle. Walk forward. Sophia begged me to spare him. Peace and justice mean more to her than the oath I swore in Paris a lifetime ago.

Napoleon is there. The door of his coach is open, he is getting out. He pauses on the step, looking hastily about him. He is surrounded; there are aides on horseback and a tight circle of guardsmen, and in the center an officer holding the reins of a gray horse. Its eyes are rolling, its whole body quivers with nervous excitement.

No one has seen me. I rest the rifle barrel on the plastered wall in front of me, lay my cheek to the stock. Even when he steps down he is in my sights. They pull the horse toward him, urge him to mount, and panic speaks in their every gesture. But he freezes. He is quite still, looking my way.

It is as if he knows I am here. He knows the trial is over, judgment has been passed. He feels the weight of it already on that lofty brow; it settles behind those dark, fixed eyes, presses into his brain.

He stands before me, the condemned man.

He moves; he takes the horse's reins. I do not pull the trigger.

I gaze at him—one last look at the general who drove an army into this Gehenna and now flies from it without a backward glance.

He is mounted now, a small, tense figure with the eyes of a hunted animal.

René did not die for this man. René died for a France that is no more, a France that may one day be again. If I murder this murderer, I lose all honor worth the name.

With all Sophia's imaginings of what war must be like, she could never have predicted that Waterloo would be full of women. She had left Brussels with a mental picture that belonged to childhood and found herself scratching it out and redrawing it as she and Rumbold forced their way along the road. Somehow, when she had allowed herself to think of a military campaign, the figures in the action had lined themselves up like Andrew's toy soldiers around the wooden castle, with not a female in evidence. Yet in reality women were everywhere, and the closer Sophia came to the sound of the guns, the more there seemed to be.

They were from all walks of life. She saw farmers and villagers who were prepared to offer water or sell food to the people who tramped by in both directions. She noticed servants pausing in the street on errands to watch the wounded pass, or call out to a messenger who was hurrying to the front, all avid for news but cast into confusion the moment it was tossed to them: Wellington had been blown to pieces; the Prussians were trapped in a ring of fire; the Prince of Orange had lost a leg; Wellington was about to fall back on Brussels; there were hundreds of deserters from both sides skulking in the forest of Soignies. When she and Rumbold stopped outside an inn and sent in for drinks, she saw girls working in the dim interior who for days had been serving Dutch-Belgians, Scots, English, Nassauers and Hanoverians, and in their resigned and knowing faces she could read the perception that they might be serving Frenchmen by the end of the day.

On the highway there were horsewomen like herself, some with a groom, often alone. She saw their strained faces and did not interrupt them as they hastened by. They were searching for husbands, lovers and brothers, perhaps for sons. No, please, not sons. Once she saw a pretty woman in a beautiful, flimsy gown with a blanket over her shoulders, standing at a crossroads looking into the distance. Her shoes were torn to pieces: it was shockingly obvious that she had walked out of Brussels on the night of the Duchess of Richmond's ball. Sophia leaned over to say something, but she was forestalled; the young woman glanced up with the distracted, dismissive half smile she would have bestowed on an acquaintance at a party to whom she had no intention of speaking. Sophia rode on.

At Waterloo itself were the campaigners—the consorts and families who traveled with the baggage trains of the armies and maintained the closest commerce between camp and field. Most were Germans who had followed the allies into the environs of Brussels and moved in behind them when they were deployed to Quatre Bras over Thursday night and Friday morning.

These women had become part of the village, and there was not an aspect of the occupation that did not come under their rough and ready influence, including the traffic in the choked streets. If anything needed to be done, and done quickly, one of them was the most likely to bring it about, whether it was finding meat for the evening stew or forcibly making room on someone's floor for yet another injured man.

Rumbold left her at a large inn at the side of the main road where he knew and trusted the owners. When he had gone, she did the rounds of the village, asking after Jacques Decernay, a tall Belgian with tawny hair, probably a scout, who might have ridden through the day before. No one knew the name, but one woman on the outskirts of the town said a man of that description had stabled a horse with her for a night and then gone off in the morning with an immense baggage roll strapped to the saddle, heading toward the English lines.

Sophia said, "Does he have dark gray eyes, the kind that force you to talk to him the moment he looks at you?"

The woman chuckled. "I could give you thirty years, madame—you expect me to notice that sort of thing?" Then she saw Sophia's expression and relented. "I'd say he *did* seem capable of a vast deal of cheek, but it's been knocked out of him for a while. We fed him, though, before he left. God grant you find him—you could do a lot worse than that man."

Sophia went slowly back to the inn. If it had not been for the pushy, practical and apparently callous attitude of the army women, she would never have been able to cope with the sight of the casualties there, let alone assist them. The soldiers she had tended in Brussels after the first assaults had at least been mobile enough to make their way into the city, though many had since died, from loss of blood, exhaustion, fever or brutal surgery. Vast numbers of the men at Waterloo, however, were so mauled they would never move again. The injuries were horrific and the stories terrible. She learned there of the clashes at the top of the crest when cavalry and infantry fell upon one another—Englishmen spitted to their horses by lances; a cuirassier who charged a cannon single-handed and was blown to fragments; French guardsmen so mutilated by hussars' sabers that they took their own lives.

She worked in the main saloon of a large inn at the side of the main road, partly under the eye of an exhausted surgeon, partly supervised by three efficient German women who accepted her unsmilingly and gave her directions mainly by gesture. She preferred this lack of communication; she wanted to concentrate on the men and give them what they needed; a friendly touch, a kind smile.

Inside her, it was otherwise. Inside, the terror built.

Back in Brussels, she used to yearn for the cannon to stop firing. Now she knew what it meant if they did—

another charge, another massive concussion as men died face-to-face with the foe. And the thump and roar of the guns spelled out specific horrors, the shells, cannon-balls and canister shot that scythed through the ranks of waiting infantry. One of the soldiers told her that amongst the flying missiles and the rifle fire you heard the strangest sound, like the humming of bees around your head.

The sun had come out just once that day, but she had not noticed it. One of the men said to her, "I kept a sharp eye on the lancers, I tell you, but when the first devil got close I was stood so the sun shone straight in me eyes. They're ten feet long, those lances. I tell you, it feels like twenty."

When dusk fell, the innkeeper lit a few tallow candles. The cannon fire became sporadic and someone said only the guns closest to Waterloo were operating, not those of the French. No one dared to believe it.

Half an hour after the ordnance stopped, there were cries in the street. There had been traffic and shouting all evening, but the tone of this was different. "Boney's beat!" were the first articulate words she heard amongst the din. The clatter of hooves and the sound of running feet grew louder and faster. "Depend upon it! They went down like birds!"

The soldier she was tending shut his eyes. "Thank Christ."

She felt sick suddenly and had to sit down. When he opened his eyes he turned his head. "You're knocking yourself out, ma'am. Take a breather, do." After a pause he said, "There's someone you're waiting for, I surmise?"

She nodded.

"Then you must keep trusting he's been spared. Bear up, ma'am, and go into the street and ask. I know the sound of victory; I can hear it clear. We've come through, bless us all."

She got unsteadily to her feet. "I think I shall just go and take the air."

His gave her a wistful smile of farewell.

Outside it was pitch-dark, but light streamed from open doorways onto the thronged streets, and people set lanterns in the windows to guide the riders in. The cavalry came first, crowding through the village in groups or in pairs. One horseman made his way in alone with a standard that bore gilt eagles with their wings outstretched. He was cheered as he went.

Sophia leaned against the rough wall of the inn, breathless. She believed it now. Victory. The French had fallen. Bonaparte was crushed. The weight on her heart doubled.

There was just one question she wanted to shout into the dark street. But no one could answer it.

Eventually the foot soldiers and gun crews began to come in, and a pair of infantrymen stopped at the inn door to peer inside. She said to one of them, "Excuse me. Do you know of a scout named Jacques Decernay?"

"Can't say I do." He saw her face and said, "I'm sorry, ma'am."

She heard herself say, "Does Wellington live?"

"My word, ma'am, indeed he does. If you'd seen him when he called the Guards to rise up and smite them, you'd have said he's immortal."

"Where is he?

"Gone to meet up with Blücher, in the direction of Belle Alliance."

"And Bonaparte?"

The second soldier said, "If Blücher lays hands on him, he's dead. The general, now, might judge otherwise."

"So Bonaparte has not been captured?"

"No, ma'am."

She looked for Rumbold or other familiar faces amongst the officers still streaming in, but there was no one she recognized. At one point the crowd got jammed to a standstill and she caught sight of a hussar in the uniform she knew best. When she drew alongside him her heart was pounding so hard in her throat she could hardly speak.

"I beg your pardon. Have you heard of a scout called Jacques Decernay?"

He looked down at her—a young man with sandy hair and a bushy red mustache and a somewhat dazed expression. His voice was abrupt, but his manner was obliging. "Afraid not. One of ours, the Tenth Hussars?"

She shook her head, then managed to say, "Perhaps you have news of Colonel Sebastian Coole? He took command of a squadron of the Tenth on Thursday."

He shook his head. "I regret, I've not heard of him."

"Were you . . . how did you fare?"

"We were in reserve all day, on the left flank. At the last the general summoned us to the center, and we stood still and took punishment from the Imperial Guard for nearly an hour before we got the order to advance. Then we had the honor of being in the first rank of the charge, and thank the Almighty we carried all before us. We took sixteen guns and a great parcel of prisoners, but we were called off the pursuit when it got dark."

The horses in front of him began to move. Sophia said, "So Bonaparte has gotten away."

"Not if the Prussians can help it. They'll be chasing him to the gates of Paris."

She thanked him, turned and began walking against the flow of people. With the tramp of hooves and feet around her, she could not hear her own riding boots on the uneven cobbles. Officers on horseback leaned back from the saddle to watch her as she went, and the soldiers looked startled to see her amongst them, but no one put themselves in her way. She scanned their faces but did not speak, moving amongst them like a ghost.

At last she reached the outskirts of the village. Far out in the countryside, in every direction, she could see flickering campfires where units had been ordered to bivouac for the night. There were fewer men now approaching the village, and no light to see them by. It was hard to walk this rough road in the dark, but it would be harder still to return to the village with its lights and human voices, having to act like a real person while she felt this vast, cold emptiness inside.

She had no hope; the sound of the guns had pounded it away. But she kept walking. Then the moon sailed out from behind ragged clouds and she stopped to look around her.

The moon was almost full. She was standing in a black-and-gray landscape bordered by the dark velvet band of night pinpricked by fires. In the middle distance she could make out clumps of trees, their contours softened by their own shadows, and low walls sketched beneath in strong charcoal lines. Beyond those were fields of trampled crops, swept flat as though by a giant hand.

A finger of cloud advanced across the moon, and just before the light disappeared she caught a glimpse of two figures far off on the road, a man leading a horse. She stayed still in the dark, waiting.

She breathed in the night smells: faint wisps of smoke, thin and acrid; the summer scent of cornstalks beside the road, broken by passing hooves; horse dung on the paving stones; the peppery tang of geraniums growing at the foot of a wall.

She waited, not daring to think. She was a pulse, beating. She was an intake of air.

The clouds slipped from the moon and light poured down, painting the road silver, giving an ashen sheen to the man's hair, lavishly sculpting his tall form and the shape of the black horse.

She began to run. She stumbled, picked up her skirt and ran again. The pair ahead of her broke apart, the horse flinging back its head and giving a high whinny of protest. The man rushed forward, a dark blue figure racing toward her with long strides, his heavy boots ringing on the flagstones.

She reached him first, which was ridiculous, illogical, but exactly how it felt. When they met it was as though he was at a standstill and she threw herself upon him, her arms strangling him, her lips crushing his, her body flung against his like a wave against a rock.

They kissed, panting, and as they said each other's names over and over the light faded around them. They stood clinging to each other in darkness, though their heads were full of stars.

She said, "Tell me you've taken no hurt."

"None. Not this time."

"Where have you been?"

"Everywhere. What are you doing here? Where is Aristide?"

"He's safe in Brussels. Safe. We are all safe." She wound her fingers in his hair and drew his face down to her shoulder. "I can't believe it."

He pressed his temple to hers and then raised his head. "I killed him."

His horse came toward them with purposeful steps, and Jacques turned his head to glance behind. In the dim, wavering light she examined his profile, which was taut and fearful, and she caught her breath. He meant Sebastian.

"Was it swift?"

"Yes. I'll tell you some time. Not now."

She could not let him see her face, so she hid it against his chest. He smelled of smoke. She pushed her mind forward to think of the other man, the one she had begged him to spare. She felt his hands on her back, holding and claiming her; she had to ask what else those hands had done today.

The horse's nose nudged her and she looked up. "Mezrour!"

"He's jealous of you. He always will be. But he's fond of Aristide."

She put her hands on each side of his face and saw for the first time the dirt and blood and tracks of sweat down his cheeks. "Where did you go? What did you do?"

"I got as far as Genappe, in the retreat. I had on my brother's uniform—if anyone was going to stop me it would have had to be a Prussian. I found Bonaparte. I had a rifle, but I threw it away and let him go. On the way back, I laid René's sword on the battlefield. That's where it belongs." He took her hands and lowered them, then bent to kiss her fingers, concealing his face.

She saw that the top of his head was black with blood, and shuddered, but when their eyes met again she said, "*Mon amour*, now we can live."

He gazed at her in anguish. "In three days I have been with the English, the Prussians, the Germans and the French. I don't know where I stand."

She put her hands behind his neck, leaned back and looked up at him, with the gentle moonlight streaming around them. "You stand with me."

HISTORICAL NOTE

I first read a biography of Napoleon Bonaparte when I was eleven years old, and I have to confess that for a long time he fired my imagination more than any other leader of men. The daredevil heroes of our youth never fade, however our judgment of them may alter later on! This book sprang from a special interest in the Hundred Days. I realized that Napoleon's surprise landing in the south of France, and the simultaneous riots and terror in London, were so dramatic that the opening scenes of the book needed only to reflect what really happened in that first week of March 1815.

I wanted to place the English–French conflict at the core of the story, and thus my three central characters had to wrestle with divided loyalties—especially the Frenchman Jacques Decernay, who first appears in British uniform. Chasseurs Britanniques played their part in the Peninsular War and the War of 1812, yet they have been little studied by historians and were barely touched on by contemporaries, one of whom, Colonel Harry Smith, left us the famous comment, "that mongrel regiment." I have stayed true to the facts about the Chasseurs' formation, disgrace and disbandment, but there is one detail—a punishment duty to the penal colony of New South Wales—that I found in just one source. So

I may have stretched a point with regard to Jacques Decernay's service in Sydney, though Lachlan Macquarie's Seventy-third Foot did indeed sail away on the *Wyndham* on the date specified. Incidentally a British reenactment group, the Artillerie Légère, includes Chasseurs Britanniques in its forces.

As for Sophia Hamilton's Sussex life, Clifton and Birlingdean are fictions, but of course Firle Place and Viscount Gage are not. The barracks at Exceat, against which Sir Henry expressed many vain objections, continued to supply troops to the Martello towers along the south coast throughout the threat of invasion, and remained in use until 1822. Brighton, which constantly saw British tourists and noble refugees arriving from France—often complete with carriages, gold and the family porcelain—was as lively as I have described it, though I cannot confirm that the Prince Regent was able to make his lightning visit just then to inspect the renovations at the Pavilion.

English racing history includes some illustrious women owners and trainers, which gave me the excuse to send Sophia Hamilton and Scheherazade to Espom Downs in June 1815. In fact, the filly that won The Oaks at odds of three to one that year (with Mouse and Nadjda in second and third place) was named Minuet, and she raced under the colours of the Third Duke of Grafton.

The time that the Hamilton family spent in Brussels before the battle of Waterloo must be amongst the most liberally documented few days in history. The elegant streets and hotels, the social amusements and pastimes, culminating in the Lennoxes' ball, provided an authentic backdrop, while I found that Grant and Hardinge, Blücher, and of course Wellington himself, proved necessary figures in a story where individual destiny was tightly bound up with the military—despite Sophia's struggle to shape her life along different lines. Where to place her in the city was easy to decide, while making sense of the battles through the eyes of Jacques Decernay and Sebastian Coole was more of a challenge. I moved the men over the battlefields in faithful step with the record, but tried to tread different ground from that already covered by many fine writers.

No one has ever quite worked out who started the fire at Wavre on the final day of battle, so I took the liberty of having Sebastian Coole strike the spark. Equally, one of the many real plans to assassinate Napoleon Bonaparte could well have been in action at the time. Jacques Decernay's decision when faced with the opportunity bears comparison with that of the Duke of Wellington when the emperor came within range of British marksmen during the battle: "That is not how wars are won."

ACKNOWLEDGMENTS

I am tremendously indebted to Ted Power, whose on-the-spot research and unfailing interest contributed many vital touches to the picture of Brighton in March–June 1815.

I am very grateful to my cousin Neil McKernan for kindly extending my knowledge of the East Sussex countryside, and to Peter and Penny Woolgar of Firle House, who gave me particulars of Sir Henry, Fourth Viscount Gage.

It was historian Rosemary Broomham who sparked my interest in South Head Road and early horse racing in Sydney. My thanks also to Delamere Usher for information about the running of The Oaks at Epsom in June 1815.

To Isolde Martyn and May Wong, sisters in arms: thank you for your wise and friendly encouragement.

Many thanks to Anne Bohner and New American Library for believing in this book, and once again I pay special tribute to my talented agent, Kristin Nelson.

In her first years, New Zealander **Cheryl Sawyer** lived just a few steps from the sea, and her favorite places are still within sight and sound of an ocean, whether they be Caribbean islands or coastal towns on the Pacific rim. She has two master's degrees with honors in French and English literature, and her early years of teaching included a university tutorship in French. After living and working in England, France, Italy and Switzerland, she returned to the South Pacific to pursue a career in publishing and writing. She has had three previous historical novels published, *La Créole*, *Rebel*, and *Siren*, and is the author of a children's book and an academic translation of the journals of explorer Jean-François-Marie de Surville. She currently lives in Costa Rica. Her Web site is at www.cherylsawyer.com.

He was a pirate and plunderer—
but she was a treasure not easily taken...

Siren
by **Cheryl Sawyer**

**From the coral beaches of the Caribbean islands
to the colorful streets of New Orleans, Siren—an
epic of high seas adventure, passion, intrigue,
and war—will leave you breathless in its wake.**

"Gloriously textured [and] seductive."
—Bertrice Small

"Captivating, lush and romantic."
—Madeline Hunter

"A powerful love story."
—Isolde Martyn

0-451-21377-7

**Available wherever books are sold or at
www.penguin.com**

All your favorite romance writers are
coming together.

SIGNET ECLIPSE

COMING JULY 2005:
Much Ado About Magic
by Patricia Rice
Love Underground: Persephone's Tale
by Alicia Fields
Private Pleasures by Bertrice Small
Lost in Temptation by Lauren Royal

COMING AUGUST 2005:
Home at Last by Jerri Corgiat
Bachelorette #1 by Jennifer O'Connell
Dangerous Passions by Lynn Kerstan

New York Times bestselling author

Lisa Jackson

Impostress

Owing her sister a favor, Kiera of Lawenydd
promises to pose as Elyn on her wedding day.
The ruse is to last just one night, but the
following morning, Elyn is nowhere to be
found! Surely Kiera won't have to spend the
rest of her life wedded to a man to whom she
could never admit the depths of her
deception—even as her desire for him
grows impossible to resist.

0-451-20829-3

S006

The steamy novels of
Sasha Lord

Under a Wild Sky
0-451-21028-X

Ronin, a battered warrior, seeks refuge from his
enemies in a secluded wood, only to be attacked by
forest men. But when Ronin takes the men's leader
captive, he soon learns that this young man he's
holding prisoner is actually a beautiful woman whose
passion for life and love matches his own.

In a Wild Wood
0-451-21029-8

When Matalia seizes Brogan trespassing in her
family's forest, they begin an adventure that will
endanger their lives—and they discover a passion
that will challenge their hearts.

Across a Wild Sea
0-451-21387-4

When a violent storm casts Xanthier ashore, Alannah
gives in to an untamed desire. And a promise made in
the heat of passion transforms their lives forever.

**Available wherever books are sold or at
www.penguin.com**